D0041692
DISCARDED
Library
Western Wyoming Community College

SEVEN SERPENTS & SEVEN MOONS

The Texas Pan American Series

SEVEN SERPENTS & SEVEN MOONS

DEMETRIO AGUILERA-MALTA

TRANSLATED FROM THE SPANISH

BY GREGORY RABASSA

UNIVERSITY OF TEXAS PRESS

AUSTIN & LONDON

The Texas Pan American Series is published
with the assistance of a revolving publication fund established
by the Pan American Sulphur Company.

Publication of this book was assisted by a grant
from the Center for Inter-American Relations as well as a grant from
the Rockefeller Foundation through the Latin American translation program
of the Association of American University Presses.

Originally published as *Siete lunas y siete serpientes*
(Mexico City: Fondo de Cultura Económica, 1970).

A section of chapter 3 was previously published in
Mundus Artium 9, no. 1 (1976): 140–145.

Library of Congress Cataloging in Publication Data
Aguilera-Malta, Demetrio, 1909–
Seven serpents and seven moons.
(Texas Pan American series)
Translation of Siete lunas y siete serpientes.
I. Title.
PZ3.A2835Se [PQ8219.A36]   863   79-10516
ISBN 0-292-77552-0

Printed in the United States of America

To Benjamín Carrión

This sort of saga is mine only in part.
In the way that a voice belonging to a
CHORUS sings—in transitory form—
a SOLO whose melody might also have been
sung as well by other fraternal voices:
those of José de la Cuadra and Joaquín
Gallegos Lara—now travelers on the
endless journey; and those of Alfredo
Pareja-Díez Canseco, Enrique Gil Gilbert,
Angel F. Rojas, and Adalberto Ortiz, who
still send theirs off to the horizon.

SEVEN SERPENTS &
SEVEN MOONS

ONE

The Wizard Bulu-Bulu—up in the house—split the darkness with his fatigued arpeggio.

"The same thing, Minga?"

From down below, Dominga. Not stopping. Not turning.

"Yes, Papa."

"How long is it going to go on?"

"Who knows, Papa!"

"Don't you think it's been a lot already?"

"A lot, Papa."

Ña Crisanta, the Wizard's wife, joined in with anger she had trouble holding back.

"Don't be so hard on her."

"It's been seven nights now."

"She's got the Moon."

"Too much Moon."

A brief silence. The Old Woman spoke again. This time as if to herself.

"The Moon stretches and curls up inside of us women."

"The Moon doesn't blindfold us. Look at Minga!"

Dominga, going off with the serpent hanging. Her soft skin taunting the darkness. Her wavy hair in tongues of black flame. Her jaw tense. Her eyes closed? Her breasts tense too. The serpent hanging. Her hips in the bulky rhythm of a rocking canoe. The wind's thousand machetes wounding her sex. The serpent hanging. The tremulous steps inscribing it on the jungle. Rocking it on the green trapeze. Supporting it on the nerves of leaves and branches. The serpent hanging. Hanging from her right arm. Her right hand. Clutched in her clenched fist. Her five fingers tight around the neck. Hanging. Dead. Hanging. Another night. Hanging. Dead.

"Do you see her?"

"Yes. What about it?"

"The Serpent and the Moon are in her."

They were in her. The Serpent. The Serpent hanging from her fist. The Other hanging inside. The Moon. Not the Moon with silver horns. The Other One. The one which jabbed the confines of the senses like a cancer with fingers of anguish.

The first of those seven nights—lying on her mat under the netting—she became aware of the arrival of the Tin-Tins. (The duty of the Tin-Tins is to make women pregnant.) With their enormous heads—birds' nests, maybe? With their tiny papaya-seed eyes. Their open sucker-fish lips. Their compact bodies. Their muscular arms and legs. Two Tin-Tins. Made only of nerves, muscles, and sex. Sex. Two Tin-Tins. Always naked. Sexes like the trunk of an ax-shaft tree. A living mast growing from between their legs. Two Tin-Tins. They went along leaping like kangaroos. They spoke a language with roots in the jungle. They drew near. They stopped. They lifted up their flat noses. They sniffed. Then eyes yellow with light penetrated the darkness. They drew nearer. They were at the bottom of the house. They seemed to pass through the bamboo fences. They were about to come through the door. They stopped again. They looked at each other. They came forward again. They stopped again. They looked at each other again. Their eyes were aflame. They raised their voices. The tone became angry. The gestures wrathful. Almost immediately they began to hit each other. Strange, they didn't hit with their hands. Their feet. Or their heads. Nor did they attack with fingernails or teeth. No. They beat each other with their members. A strange duel, first they crossed them. In an unlikely salute. For a brief moment they studied each other. One the other. Then those absurd weapons drew apart. Quick as a flash they began to use them. As if each member had taken on the solid thickness of a truncheon. In the absorbed silence of the night, on impact, the hardened flesh gave off a sound that was the squeak of cured leather. Or elastic wood.

Dominga, almost without realizing it, tightened her legs. In a premature defense. She crossed her hands over her sex. She was trembling with fear and anguish. What was going to happen? She tried to cry out in alarm. She couldn't. A sudden paralysis had come over her body. She was only able to place her hands where she had them. She had the feeling that a hundred powerful bonds had lashed her to the ground. What was going to happen? One of the Tin-Tins had to win. She was certain of that. Perhaps he would kill the other one. He would leave him on the ground. Then he would come in. Or he would jump through the window. He would come leaping in. Little leaps. Over to the corner where she had laid her mat. There, with his sex. Nothing but his sex. Not using his hands. Or his arms. Or his mouth. Only with his sex would he lift or tear the net. Would he stand looking at her? Would he run his scratchy hands over her body? Would he use his sucker's mouth to cover her whole body inch by inch? Or would he not waste his time in preparatory maneuvers and leap on top of her, unable to hold back? Maybe she wouldn't be able to establish a clear chronology of the swift actions. It would be something simultaneous. Feeling him covering her. Having to open her thighs against her will. Feeling—like a hot machete—the thrust of the fleshy dagger inside of her. The pain. The panic. The desperation of feeling her intimate parts tear. The little monster's dizzy rubbing...He, in a kind of diabolic dance, would creep inside her like a vine. Almost to the middle of her body. And there the sticky rain of human sap, bathing her in a small flood. Without caressing her. Without succeeding at any moment in getting her to vibrate in unison. Or would she vibrate at some point? Or, in spite of her will, would she respond, flesh to flesh, sex to sex, in one ineffable instant, to the savage copulation?

Everything was happening as she had thought. One of the Tin-Tins had hit the other on the head with his glans. The second one had staggered for a few seconds. He had fallen. The victorious Tin-Tin landed on the loser with one leap. He began to beat him about the face. Still with his sex. The one beaten tried to avoid the blows at first. With his hands. His arms. His elbows. As best he could. Little by little, his resistance weakened. His blows had less strength and precision. Finally he was motionless, as if dead. The victorious Tin-Tin let out a strange guttural grunt. One of triumph and challenge. He looked toward the house. Right at Dominga, who was on her mat. Under the netting. Without turning to the defeated Tin-Tin, he advanced. He advanced. She closed her eyes. She tightened her eyelids. In a vain attempt, she tried to join her thighs even tighter together. She couldn't. Then, defeated, she gave herself over to the unexpected.

A hiss arose. A long hiss. Chilling. It broke the night into a thousand pieces. She opened her eyes. Inside the cobweb of shadows she saw—in turn—two startling eyes. They seemed to glimmer at ground level. She tried to see better. Was it a single pair of eyes? Or were there many pairs? They surrounded the victorious Tin-Tin. Drawing close to him. There were two eyes. Only two eyes. The two eyes of a snake. She saw them close in—a carrousel of lights—around the small satyr. The latter leaped back. She could see the snake clearly. An X-Bonetail! Instant death in its fangs. Little by little, it stood out more clearly against the shadows. A live lasso twirled steadily by an invisible hand. It moved rapidly around the Tin-Tin. He began to dodge it. Trying to bend it with blows from his member. Of no use. It was as if the X-Bonetail had wings. It coiled about the unlikely penis. The impregnator made extraordinary efforts to defend himself against the constant feints. The rattlesnake coiled. It stretched out its symmetrical body. It lifted its head to the level of the little man's eyes. It threatened him with its aggressive fangs, which seemed to multiply. At other times the multicolored rings—regular springs with scales—vibrated. They changed position without rhythm. The Tin-Tin fenced with his sex. His best instrument of defense. For a moment it looked as if he were going to win. Using the glans—he held it like a broadsword, with both hands—he gave a blow to the serpent's head. He knocked it to the ground. The rattler stretched out in its death throes, tiny electric lumps along its body. The Tin-Tin leaned over to finish it off. He raised his member to loose the final blow. The X-Bonetail—lightning made scales—rose up again. Before its adversary could retreat or defend himself. It sank its fangs in him. With a shriek, the Tin-Tin, still holding his member, with long leaps went twisting into the jungle—to die after a short time.

Astonished, holding her breath, Dominga watched the scene. She began to recover. Her muscles relaxed. She took her hands away from her sex. It might have been said that she was heavier. Like bathing in a freshwater pool after coming out of the salty sea. She tried to rise. She couldn't. She made an attempt to get dressed. Not that either. There was still an injection of lead in her arteries. She decided to wait for daybreak to get up. She made herself comfortable. She made ready to sleep. She closed her eyes. She didn't stay that way for long. She felt another presence. Strange. She opened her eyes again. She was paralyzed again. The X-Bonetail was there. It had raised its head. Through the fine mesh of the netting she saw its bulging eyes. Its tense little tongue. Its reeling body. It was rocking from side to side. As if trying to make her seasick. She closed her eyes again. She opened them. It was her last movement. The viper was slipping in under the netting. First it put in its head. Then, inch by inch, its whole body. Because of her rigidity, she couldn't tell the instant when the serpent slowly came in. Slowly. Until it reached her. And established the first contact with its scaly, icy skin. A chill ran through her. From head to toe. The snake kept on advancing. How could she stop it? If only she were capable of making some movement! Impossible. She had the feeling that she was turning into a statue. Cold. Motionless. While the X-Bonetail kept on crawling over her. Wrapping her up. Climbing—with unrestrained coiling—up to her neck. There it rose up again. The triangular head confronted her. It stared at her. Was it hypnotizing her? The little tongue vibrated. The fangs seemed to grow longer. If only she could hum a tune. It was what Bulu-Bulu did in cases like that. She couldn't. Where was the courage? She couldn't do anything. Simply turn herself over to fate. Determined at that moment by the rattler's decision. Suddenly it became motionless. Was it surprised that she wasn't defending herself? That she didn't show the least sign of life? Who could say? In the meantime, Dominga's breast was throbbing. Her heart was a hollow wooden drum. That dying drop by drop lasted only a few seconds. The reptile began to withdraw. It sank its head between her breasts. It took hold of one of them. At the same time it rattled—with its bony tail—between her legs.

Dominga made a supreme effort. She tried to move. She couldn't. She tried again. In some obscure way she convinced herself that if she let herself be conquered it would be all over for her. If she stayed that way a few seconds more it would soon be too late. She had to act. Right away. She tried again. She concentrated all her strength in her right hand. She managed to move it slightly. That gave her courage. She could! She kept on fighting the paralysis. She raised her hand. Slowly. Incessantly. She was bringing it close to the viper. It seemed not to notice her movement. Suddenly she grasped it. The neck. She squeezed with all her might. She could! The serpent trembled. It didn't defend itself. Its coils were loosening. Loosening. For a few brief moments it wriggled. It gave a few last quivers. Finally, in turn, it was motionless. Dominga got up. Without letting go of it. It was like carrying a plumb line. She left the house. With her left hand she took one of Bulu-Bulu's machetes. She pulled it out of the trunk where it had been stuck. Without letting go of the viper, she took several steps into the woods. After a hundred yards, she laid it on the ground. With the machete she dug a trench, narrow but deep. There she buried it. When she put an end to the job, she went back to the house. She went up the steps. Absentminded. She lay down on her mat. And she fell asleep. With great peace.

That was the first of the seven nights.

On the second night the X-Bonetail appeared again.—Was it the same one or another?—With less fear now, when the serpent wrapped her in its scaly hoops, she had complete control of herself. She strangled it again. Digging another trench. Burying it. The third night the exasperating visit again. Another strangling and another burial. And the same thing happened on successive nights: the fourth, the fifth, the sixth, the seventh. Would it go on the same indefinitely for all the nights to come? Would she have to go through life strangling and burying vipers for all the rest of her days?

Up above—in the oven darkness—the eyes of the Wizard Bulu-Bulu sparkled.

"I'm going to set fire to the jungle."

His wife looked at him with surprise.

"Why?"

"That way I'll put an end to all the serpents."

She understood.

"What about the moons?"

"I'll erase all the moons in her eyes."

"The serpents and the moons are in her."

"Or I'll keep her inside the earth. In the vessels of the dead Bulu-Bulus."

"Better yet, help me find a man for her."

"A man?"

"Yes. A man. Only a man can take the serpents and the moons away from her."

Dominga—as on previous nights—came back to the house. She

came in slowly. She didn't seem to notice them. Nor did it bother her that they saw her naked. She neither looked at them nor said anything. She went into her room. She went to sleep, given back over to her innocence. At that moment, approaching Balumba—the island of the Wizard Bulu-Bulu—was Colonel Candelario Mariscal. As always, in his canoe pulled by turtles.

TWO

Old Crisanta—an erect bunch of shriveled plantains—muttered.

"I wonder what that son of a mule is up to, coming here at this hour?"

"Be quiet!"

"Isn't he the son of a mule?"

"He might hear you. He's got a thousand ears."

"Why shouldn't he? He's the son of The Evil One too."

"You're making that up. The Evil One doesn't have children with Christians."

"Not with Christians. With mules. He's the only one who can make mules give birth."

"Nothing but gossip."

"It's not gossip. Father Cándido..."

Father Cándido hadn't said so. How could he have said such a thing? A saintly mouth. But he must have known all about it. Hadn't he taken him in when they left him at the door of the church?—He still had a church then.— It was Candlemas. That's why he gave the newborn child the name he has. Along with his last name: Mariscal. Candelario Mariscal. Evil tongues claimed that the Colonel was the son of the Priest. He had him on one of his canoe trips. When he went to help some Christian have a proper death. Maybe he got worked up over one of the women taking care of the Person. And right there he had his fun with her. After all, flesh calls for flesh. And priests, no matter what they say, are made of flesh. From such pleasure there came what had to come. Maybe Cándido himself brought the child in his canoe at midnight. He left him by the church door. So that on the following day, when the Sexton opened that door, he found the baby. It was naked. The Priest appeared almost at once. He said that God had sent him.

"God? Old Longtail himself."

"That's what evil tongues say."

"Is the truth something else?"

"Of course it is."

The truth—what they accepted for truth in those parts—was that Old Longtail had been prowling around Santorontón. For several months before that famous Candlemas Day. Maybe those were his first strolls through the town. Not only had he been seen in person—can you say "person" when talking about Mandinga?—but many had even had dealings with him. He would usually appear late at night. He never took his hat off. A black hat. Hairy. Maybe it was to hide his horns. Still, he fitted right in. Like all Christians—of course, he wasn't any Christian! Rather, he leaned toward the left. Maybe because of his tail. It must have bothered him. He arrived all at once. Without knocking on any doors or windows. He went to the waterfront. To the bars. He searched out the tables where people were drinking the most. He treated everybody. He told dirty jokes. He laughed with a flapping jaw. He pulled out great wads of money. He wouldn't let anybody pay. He made them drink rivers. Until long after midnight. When the alcohol changed people's perspectives. Then he helped instigate fights. Sometimes he took part himself. They started with insults. Then came the blows. First with fists. With feet. With heads. Finally, as is natural, with the weapons closest at hand. Knives. Machetes. Even harpoons. They went out into the dark streets. Along the sea. There the steel brightened the night with lashes of light. White light at first. Then it turned red, pitahaya juice. Most of the times the leftovers were a dead man. On the damp and sandy earth. From time to time the dead men were two. And there were nights when Old Longtail's harvest was even greater. Three. Four. Or more dead men. Something curious would happen the next day. The bodies had disappeared. It was said that they had gone into the jungle on their own two feet. Or, also on their own two feet, they had jumped into the sea. Since there were no tracks, opinions differed. Some even swore that things were upside down. It was the sharks who came in on the high tide. They came up onto the beach. And they gobbled them up. "Just imagine, beached sharks!" Others asserted that it was the buzzards. They came in flocks. They lifted them up with their talons. And they carried them far off in peaceful flight. To have their banquets. A bunch of nonsense! The bodies had been carried off by The Evil One. Who was going to deny him his prey since he himself had set it up? It was not until a year after Father Cándido had taken in Candelario that Old Longtail stopped visiting them for a while. This was because the Priest could no longer bear the gossiping. He brought the Burned Christ—he hadn't been burned yet—out of the church. And he walked him all through the town. It was easy. Santorontón had less than fifty houses in those days. Counting all the houses, even those with no walls, just four poles and a roof of bijao branches. As was to be expected, The Cursed One was frightened off. He didn't come back for a long time, even to take a look at his own son.

Ña Crisanta reaffirmed:

"Nobody can deny that. The Colonel is the son of Himself."

"You're stubborn, like a donkey in a mud puddle."

"Because until just a little while ago he had the smell of brimstone on him."

The Wizard put in after her final word:

"What about the Mule?"

"Pancha the Mule smelled of brimstone ever since he appeared."

Pancha the Mule had been the cause of talk in Santorontón for years. All of a sudden—during the days when Old Longtail was up to his tricks—her belly puffed up and she began to have vomiting spells and fits. She became more insolent then ever. She refused to let herself be harnessed, much less ridden. Nor would she let anyone get near her. When that happened she would froth at the mouth. She kicked at the four winds. And she would break out into a run. During the day she almost never went through town. She only appeared at dusk. Half-wrapped in a blanket of shadows. She gave off sparks from her eyes and her hoofs. She went right through. She reached the dock. She looked at the sea. She shook her scraggly mane. Then she went back and sank into the darkness. Where could she have gone? Into the forest? Into the limitless waters? Was she made of shadows? Only Old Longtail who went with her would know!

Bulu-Bulu put on a hypocritical smile.

"And God. God knows everything."

The Old Woman paid as much attention to him as a crocodile to a horsefly.

"When the Colonel was born, Pancha the Mule disappeared into thin air. She was never seen again anywhere. Not even her gallop was heard in the distance. Besides, why was the newborn baby left naked? What Christian woman would abandon her child without some kind of rag? Only a beast. Who doesn't know about such things."

The Wizard twisted about, the segments of a hairy caterpillar.

"I can see that you're all mixed up, Crisanta."

The Old Woman was about to answer when nearby, at the foot of the steps, Candelario Mariscal's gruff voice was heard.

"Good evening, Bulu-Bulu."

"A good evening to you, Colonel."

"Can you put me up for the night?"

"Of course, Colonel! Come in!"

In two strides Candelario climbed the bamboo stairs with mangrove steps. He hunched over a little so that his broad-brimmed straw hat would not hit the top of the doorway. There he stopped to look at the Wizard. Bulu-Bulu's cigar, as it was lighted up, illuminated his face from time to time. He looked like a monkey with dysentery. A spark of doubt crossed his mind for a moment. Would the thing he was doing be favorable? Would it be just the opposite? Why, instead, not say good-by to the master of Balumba and tell him that he couldn't stay in his house that night? Maybe he would come back another time when the north wind was favorable. He recovered. After all, what could he lose? Since he was already there, why not try it? Having decided, he turned to the Old Woman. She was not much more than the shadow of her husband. A forced smile arched her upper lip.

"Good evening, Ña Crisanta."

The skeletal lady answered with a sour voice.
"Evening."
The Wizard brought over a stool.
"Have a seat."
While the officer was sitting down, to Crisanta, with authority:
"Fix the Colonel a mat."
The latter clarified things:
"Thank you very much, Bulu-Bulu. It won't be necessary."
"Aren't you going to sleep?"
Candelario frowned.
"I can't sleep. That's why..."
He held back in spite of himself. Suddenly rage seemed to dominate him. That interested the Wizard exceedingly. Was he going to turn into a crocodile? When would his eyes start growing smaller? Was his skin getting hard? Was he beginning to turn green and yellow in color? Was his noisy tail already growing? Anxious, he asked:
"What?"
The voice of the one addressed became hoarse. Angry.
"That's why... I came to see you."
Bulu-Bulu went over to him. He studied him rapidly. Puzzled at seeing him still Man—not even Man-Crocodile—he asked him again:
"Are you sick?"
"I don't know."
"What is it, then?"
The eyes flashed in a strange way. He repeated:
"I already told you. That's why I came to see you."
Ña Crisanta crossed herself.
"It must be the doing of The Other One."
The Colonel had calmed down again. He fastened his coffee-brown eyes on her. In that bony, pale-dark face those eyes seemed only to be a prolongation of his skin. His voice was calm again.
"What did you say?"
"Nothing."
The hypocritical smile wrinkled Bulu-Bulu's toothless mouth once more. He looked at the Colonel. Then at his wife. With a certain complicity.
"Crisanta, why don't you wake up Minga?"
"What for?"
"So she can make us some coffee."

She tried to protest.
"But she just went to bed."
"All the same."
"I can make the coffee for you."
The Wizard tightened his face.
"Didn't you hear me? Do what I tell you."
"All right. All right."
And she went to the other room, muttering.

When he was alone with the Wizard, Candelario was on the point of letting out a laugh. So, was he going to put himself in the hands of that cadaverous midget? He, Colonel Candelario Mariscal, whose mere presence brought trembling to women's snatch-crabs and men's jawbones? How could he have come so low? He deserved having his balls fried in dogfish fat. When the news got around his enemies would have their bellies all swollen from laughing. He was about to say his friends too. The fact was that he had never had any friends. The few who followed him always did so unwillingly. They shat with fear at the mere thought of leaving him. They knew that one curse from him brought on the stamp of blood in most cases. Poor bastards! What about him? Him? The way he strutted around and when it came right down to it, here he was looking for a cure from a witch doctor! And what a witch doctor! He looked again at the hat of unraveled straw that covered only a part of his fried-porkrind hair. His bulging cheekbones. His thick lips. His uncovered chest. His patched pants. Rolled up above the knees. His bare feet. Was this the man who was going to cure him? He felt as bad as on that afternoon—so many years ago!—when his godfather—because Father Cándido was his godfather—had furiously thrown him out of the church. Out of what remained of the church, that is. He drove him out with kicks. Throwing insults at him that he had never heard from him before. That he didn't even think he knew. He vainly denied that he was the one who had done that. And if he had done it he hadn't realized it. Maybe some other hand had pushed his. It was all in vain. The Priest—his eyes flaming, his shouts thundering—accompanied every phrase with a solid kick from his heavy boot. "Cursed was the day I took you in! Lowborn wretch! I hope you die soon! I never want to see you again for all the days of my life! I could kill you! Go away!" It was an occasion when he thought his godfather had gone out of his mind. "Go away! Don't ever come back to these parts again!"

"Tell me what it is, Colonel."

Now, maybe even his own godfather would laugh. The years certainly must have calmed him down. Maybe he'd forgiven him—don't they say that it's a priest's duty to forgive? Or maybe not. In any case, even if he still hated him, it would have to make him laugh. Or maybe it wouldn't make him laugh, him or anyone else. One and another, they all came to Bulu-Bulu one day. It was recounted that he always said: "My house is the house of a soapmaker; if you don't fall in here, then you slip in." On the other hand, extraordinary things were said about him. To his hospital—for he did have his outdoor hospital—came a multitude of the hopelessly sick from all four horizons. They came in hammocks carried on a bamboo pole. On stretchers improvised from mangrove braces and crossed vines. In wheelchairs. Or dragging along, rotting gastropods, until they came under the roof of his hospital without walls. There they were lined up—men and women, old people and children, rich and poor, friends and enemies—one beside the other, waiting for the mysterious treatments. And there were only two solutions there according to the master of Balumba: "Three feet under the ground. Or walking away on their own two feet." What was certain was that a great number of them walked away.

"What's wrong, Colonel? What can I do for you?"

In addition to his qualities of a Healer—based on infusions of herbs, jungle creatures, or denizens of the sea—Bulu-Bulu had, according to what he had been told, a good store of magic words. And that wasn't all. He also possessed certain occult powers. For example, in the jungle he rode jaguars. In the sea, hammerhead sharks. Sometimes he also took their shape. He could disappear at will. And—perhaps the greatest of all—he was capable of dividing his body into pieces which still maintained their own independent life. So? So? Maybe he was only doing what he could. What he had to do. On the other hand, what doctor, what other person would be capable of getting rid of his illness? It wasn't worth the bother consulting other witch doctors. Besides, they were far away. To the north.

He made his decision:

"Well, you see, Bulu-Bulu. I don't know if you still remember the Quindales."

The Wizard's left eye trembled with emotion.

"No one will ever forget them, Colonel."

"As you know, I..."

In the night of shadows they were interrupted by shouts. They seemed to come from everywhere.

"Candelario Mariscal! Candelario Mariscal!"

He shuddered.

"My godfather!"

The Healer's left eye quivered even more rapidly.

"Father Cándido!"

The Priest kept on thundering:

"Wherever you go you bring trouble. Why did you come? Go away!"

The last word seemed to become entangled with things. The small fireplace of fitted stones. The bunch of bananas hanging in a corner. The hammock tied with thongs of uncured bull hide. The bamboo walls. The bijao roof. The nearby trees.

"Go away! Go away! Go away!"

THREE

At the mouth of the inlet. Across from Bulu-Bulu's house. In the stern of his dugout canoe made of pechiche wood. He was still thundering:

"Go away, damn you! Go away!"

His gray hair made the shadows sway. His six feet seemed taller. His cassock was pulled by the fingers of the wind. He brandished his paddle like a weapon. In his trembling right arm.

"If you don't... I'll kill you!"

From the bow came the voice of the Burned Christ. Dream? Reality?

"A padlock on the mouth is the quickest way to heaven."

He was half-lying on the bottom of the boat. To one side was the Crown of Thorns. At his feet, lying on its side, was the Cross. The Priest tried to guess what he meant. To scrutinize his expression.

"That's all I needed. For you to row against me!"

"I'm rowing with you. It's for the salvation of your soul."

"What do you mean, salvation of my soul! You're only doing it to annoy me!"

"You're wrong."

"I'm sick of all your sermons. I'm the one who preaches sermons. Have you forgotten that?"

He didn't answer the question. His voice took on the tone of a reproach.

"Cándido!"

The latter paid no attention. He was blind with rage.

"One of these days I'm going to throw you overboard. Cross. Crown. Loincloth. Everything."

Jesus—in a quick transition—laughed heartily.

"What will you live off, then? Begging for alms? Now at least you can say mass. Baptize. Help people die properly. Apply Holy Oils. And all that simply by taking me along."

"You think you're the All-Time Champion, right?"

"You know perfectly well that I'm beyond victory and defeat."

"That's why you take advantage."

Serious once more. Peaceful, Christ reasoned:

"A priest should be more careful of what he says. Besides..."

"What?"

"You shouldn't let yourself be carried away by anger."

"Oh, no? What about you? Didn't you get all worked up when you drove the money-changers from the Temple? Or were you dancing happily there with a whip in your hand?"

His Interlocutor explained things simply:

"The Temple is the House of God. And I..."

He interrupted him.

"You have the right to do whatever you please, is that it?"
The voice of the Nazarene became strangely soft.
"Cándido: now you're the one who's taking advantage of the trust I've placed in you."
The Priest swallowed hard. He made an effort as best he could. Finally he got control of himself.
"That's right. Please forgive me! You know the way I am! Gunpowder on my tongue."
"Forget about him. And now that you've let yourself go, let's be on our way! We have to get to Daura. To see Clotilde Quindales."
"Do you think we ought to go?"
"Why not?"
"You know she's a woman who..."
"No matter. Clotilde Quindales needs us. Urgently. That's why she sent José Isabel Lindajón to get us. She wouldn't tell him what it was all about. Even though he thinks it has something to do with Dr. Juvencio Balda. Did you forget?"
"Yes, you're right! Let's go, then!"
Then, after a moment of silence, he added:
"Can I borrow the Cross?"
"What for?"
"You know very well what for. Stop playing absentminded on me!"
"Show some respect!"
"And it won't be the first time. Besides, it's just for a little while. I'm so tired!"
"All right, then. Take it!"
"Do me the full favor. Help me!"
The Son of Mary got up. He went over to the Wood. Cándido did the same. Between the two of them they placed it on the middle seat of the canoe. As almost always when they went through these maneuvers—in spite of the protests of Jesus—there was an ample mast hole. They placed the longer beam there. Then they hitched it to a brace on the bottom. Once the Cross was standing straight, like a mast, the Priest took off his cassock. He put the sleeves on the horizontal arms. With two pieces of rope he tied the bottom end down. That was how a kind of black sail took shape. With that done, they both went back to their original places. For an instant the Priest turned his face toward Bulu-Bulu's house, lighted by the weak light of a lamp.
"You'll pay me back. Damn you!"

As if repenting his words, he crossed himself. He looked into the night. Toward the darkness. Using his paddle, as a rudder, not rowing, he held the course. They were getting farther and farther away from Balumba. At the same time a serenity was growing inside of him.

"Blow, ye winds! Blow!"

Once more the voice of Christ came from the bow:

"If this southeaster keeps up we'll be at the Quindales place pretty soon. On the other side of Santorontón."

Santorontón! He had come to Santorontón—how many, many years ago?—when the fingers on his hands were more than enough to count the houses there. He built the church with his own efforts. —Could that shed that laughed with cracks all over it be called a church? Only partly roofed at first? Where the congregation sat on the ground?— He drove in the stakes. He set up the roof beams. He tied boughs together to support the bijao leaves. Watching him struggle alone, a few Santorontonians offered to help him. They began working together on Sundays. And they ended up doing it every night. After work. That was how the bamboo walls were made. The rough wooden benches. That table that was transformed into an altar. In addition, from the first days on, he had to take trips to surrounding villages. The Bishop had warned him: "There aren't any priests there. You'll have to be a kind of missionary. If you can, build a church. If not, fulfill your sacred ministry by seeking out the faithful wherever they are." He was doing both. Building the church so that they could visit him later on. And seeking out the faithful "wherever they were." Wherever his small boat and his courage could take him. The Santorontonians advised him: "Don't go too far away from shore, Father. You might get caught in a treacherous wind. A hammerhead might attack you and break a hole in the canoe. Or a contrary tide might drag you away... who knows where? Don't go too far out!" He paid no attention. He felt that his sacred function made him invulnerable. And if something unforeseen happened to him and he paid for his imprudence with his life, what more could he ask for? It would be a quick step toward God. That was why on days when the Sun squeezed him like a mango. Or on dark nights when the cold was a set of teeth in his bones, he was never absent from where he was needed. To all that he owed what was doubtless his most miraculous adventure. It happened one night when they came to get him for a stranger. He thought that perhaps it was the case of a premature voyager to the Land of the Bald. Four men came to get him. Four. Four evil-looking men. Four oarsmen in a lighter. Their speech was somewhat strange. They wanted him to come with them at once. Four. They said they had no time to lose. Four.

The Santorontonians were against it.

"Corvinas don't chase after harpoons, Father."

"Why don't they bring the one taking his last breath here to you?"

"You don't gather unknown eggs, Father. They might be snake eggs."

"Did you see their faces?"

"Aha! And their eyes."

"That's it. Their eyes are like dry blowfish."

"They talk with cemetery voices."

"And they have a smell about them. The smell of death."

"Maybe they've got some connection with Old Longtail."

"Don't mention him. Just mentioning him brings bad luck."

"Really and truly, Father. It would be best if you didn't go."

"It's best not to look for wrinkles on a shark."

The Priest calmed them down. What could happen to him? Would they beat him? Would they kill him? Would they throw him overboard?...They wouldn't dare mistreat a defenseless priest. Besides, there was no reason to prejudge things. The ones who did have good means of persuasion, on the other hand, were the strangers. When he said that he looked significantly at the weapons they carried: long daggers and double-barreled shotguns. He finally convinced his new counselors. He went off with the other men. They didn't exchange a single word during the whole trip. Not among themselves. Not with him. They rowed ceaselessly in a rhythmic way. They made the boat go very fast. After about three hours they drew alongside a sailing ship. It was an eerie ship. With three masts. Huge in size. They climbed up on deck along a rope ladder. His attention was drawn to the number of cannons and armed men. Most of all because it seemed to have been drawn out of another world. Another age. Could it be a warship? Or was it perhaps the ship of the pirate Ogazno who was sailing along the coast in those days? —Those days or a hundred years before? Had the Santorontonians told him? Or was it an old tale he had heard from his grandparents?— It was the pirate Ogazno's ship. They took him into the latter's presence at once. He was lying in a wide bunk. Half-dressed. When he heard the footsteps he raised his head. He opened one eye. Not the other. It was closed forever.

"Come closer!"

Cándido obeyed.

"Are you the priest?"

"Yes, sir."

He raised his voice in a menacing way.

"You must say: 'Yes, Captain.' I am Captain Tiburcio Ogazno!"

"Yes, Captain."

"Did you know that?"

"No, Captain."

"Well, you know it now."

"Yes, Captain."

He stood looking at him for a long time. He took out his good eye. He brought it close to Cándido's face, studying him minutely. Then he put it back into the empty socket.

"You're young for a priest. You're not tricking me, are you? You're not the sexton?"

"I'm the priest."

One of the men who had brought him intervened.

"He's the Priest, Captain."

The latter's face grew ironic.

"Do you have any idea as to why you're here?"

"To help someone die a..."

Ogazno interrupted him with a loud laugh.

"Oh, you dummy of a priest!"

He turned to his men.

"Didn't you tell him anything?"

They answered in chorus:

"No, Captain!"

He faced the priest.

"Mr. Dummy: you're not about to help anyone die a proper death here. The ones who were supposed to die are already good and dead. Do you hear me?"

"Yes, Captain!"

He laughed again.

"You can't tell, maybe we're the ones who are going to help you die a proper death."

He got goose pimples. He controlled himself. He lowered his eyes.

"The Lord's will be done."

"Lord? I'm the only lord here."

And to his men:

"Get everything ready! We'll soon see how this priest behaves! All hands on deck, right now!"

He got up with difficulty. He had bandages all over. He began taking wobbly steps. Cándido went over, attempting to help. He was refused.

"Leave me be! That's all I need! A priest to keep me on my feet! I can go by myself. Besides, I'm used to it. I've got more holes in me than a sieve. I always walk like this. It's part of the job!"

Limping. Stumbling. Leaning against the walls and whatever he had at hand. He went forward. He left the cabin. He went up the steps. And he went on deck. The Priest went with him, not saying a word. On deck, the Captain made a sign. Obeying him, they brought a stool over to the rail. He sat down on it and waited. Almost immediately several men emerged from the hold carrying something. Cándido saw what it was at once. But he thought it was a hallucination. No. What he was seeing couldn't be. His own eyes were deceiving him no doubt. Or could it be that he was dreaming while he was awake? Because that something was a Cross with an almost life-size Christ. They carried it over and stood it up beside the Captain. The tall Priest could bear no more. He fell on his knees and kissed the feet of the Nazarene.

"Stop acting like a clown! Besides... the Christ is yours!"

He was paralyzed with emotion. He gained control of himself. He babbled:

"M-m-m-m-i-i-i... n-e?"

"Yours!"

He stood up. He looked the image all over. Then he touched it in several places. As if to convince himself that it was real. He repeated:

"Mine!"

"Now it's only proper for you to know how it came into our possession."

Almost as if walking in his sleep, he agreed:

"Yes, Captain."

"Some time back we attacked a town. To the South. Far away from here. When we got there most of the inhabitants had run off. It was all quite easy. All we had to do was go from house to house picking up everything we wanted. We saved the church for last.

When we got there we went half-crazy. There were a lot of gold things. Jewelry. But most of all, there was a chalice. What a chalice, shit! I'll bet that all they ever did there was work to pay off that chalice. We carried on board all we could. This Christ among other things. The Cook had taken a fancy to it. Or, rather, he planned to send it to his wife. Since he was the only cook we had, I had to humor him. Because as far as I'm concerned, I never take images! They take up too much room and they're hard to sell. Besides, they're not worth very much. But the cook died yesterday. And I don't know what to do with that thing. Do you really want it?"

"Yes! Of course! But..."

"But what?"

"What if its owners want it back?"

"Oh, goddamn it! Do you want it or don't you?"

"Of course I want it. The only thing is..."

"So don't start begging! Now we're going to throw you overboard with it. If you get to shore it'll be because it's miraculous. And you'll deserve it. If not, give my regards to the sharks!"

Without another word he raised his arm. Lowered it. And The Crucified One and the Priest were immediately thrown into the sea. They still hadn't touched the surface of the water when the mocking voice of the pirate could be heard:

"Bon voyage!"

Cándido saw the three-master—with its rusty cannons and time-gray sails—immediately disappear into the mist. He swam the short distance over to The Crucified One. He said reverently:

"Forgive them, Lord, they know not what they do!"

Christ raised his head. He looked at him somewhat sardonically.

"As far as I'm concerned, they're forgiven. And since we do know what we're doing, let's hurry up so we can get there soon. I'm made of wood and it's no good for me to get all waterlogged."

"That's true."

"Get onto the Cross the way I'm going to!"

With an agile movement, the Son of Mary detached himself from the Wood. He hung over it. With hands and feet he began to move it. Cándido imitated him. And in a short while the little improvised craft slipped rapidly over the waves. Behind it a strange cortege had formed: everything from crabs to sharks. From that moment on Jesus and Cándido were blood brothers. That is, perfect comrades. Sometimes the priest had his doubts. Didn't he carry the Nazarene inside of him? In order to see him might he not be drawing him out of his own eyes?

The comradeship had grown deeper since the night of the fire. When that took place the church had already been completed for some time. Although it hadn't turned out to be luxurious or comfortable, it served its purpose rather well. Still, just because of that, Father Cándido hadn't given up his visits by canoe to neighboring villages. Whenever they called him he went. Almost always alone. As was his wont. The Santorontonians vainly kept on advising him: "You're going to lose your tail feathers on one of those trips. You're not up to this trotting around any more. You should ask for a younger priest to help you. One of these days you won't come back. And what would we do without you?" Sometimes he even tried to convince himself: "They're right. Don't go! Maybe because of one person you visit you'll never see the others for the rest of their lives. The worst is that you don't want anyone along. Not even your sexton, Romelio. What would happen if you had an accident? If, for example, you ran into a sunken log or a rock and your canoe sprang a leak? Could you bail it out yourself? Or if a hammerhead attacked and you overturned?" In spite of everything, he never stopped in the fulfillment of his duties. Even the Christ, who now occupied the center of the altar—that is, the table with a cloth and four lighted candles—kept on with his tirades.

"You live up to your name, Cándido."

"Eh?"

"It's time you enjoyed what you've managed to put together."

"Oh, yes?"

"Instead of exposing yourself to so many dangers, why don't you go kick up your heels at one of the fiestas they're always inviting you to?"

"Are you the one who's telling me to do that?"

"Yes. Me. What's so strange about that?"

"Well. Who you are. The reason you're in this Vale of Tears. All that you stand for. The symbol you are of..."

"Hold on! Are you forgetting that I went to the Wedding Feast in Cana? That I helped make it a success? That was where I performed my first miracle, changing water into wine!"

"You're right. But..."

"But you'll go in any case. I know it!"

The Martyr of Golgotha shook his head as if to say: "This fellow has got the best of me. There's no saving him." And yet, the one who did go to all fiestas, to make up for the absence of his godfather, no doubt, was Candelario. He had become Cándido's headache. Not content merely with being present at the merrymaking, once there he did whatever he pleased. He drank like a sponge. He got drunk. He wouldn't leave anyone alone. He made propositions to the women that did not always befit the circumstances. Provoking the men with words and deeds. Result: most of the time he would come back to the church early in the morning. He would pound on the main door with fists and feet. Sometimes Romelio the sexton was awake. Sometimes he wasn't. Then it was his godfather himself who had to get up and let his adopted son in. The youth answered words of advice, reproach, or censure with jokes. Those were the times when the good Cleric was lucky. Most of the time when he got in he didn't have the strength to stand up straight. Much less to put an articulate expression together. When—with all the fog in his head—he came forth with something to say, it would have unhinged the most level-headed of people.

"Godfather... You should get yourself a woman... to warm up your bones... What you need is a nice little ass... That way you'd see life differently..."

"Quiet, you wretch! Quiet! Have some respect at least for the one who died on the Cross!"

"Him?... He pretty near showed... his true colors... with Mary Magdalene..."

"Blasphemy! Sacrilege! You don't know what you're saying!"

Crossing himself. Nothing but blows. Dragging him. Sometimes alone and sometimes with Romelio. As best he could he got him to the room off the church. Where they lived. Sometimes early in the morning it was even worse. The young man would arrive all covered with the waste he had expelled. From the beginning or the end of his digestive tube. Or bathed in foul-smelling mixtures of liquor and spit. Or in blood, his own or that of someone else. He had to be undressed. Bathed. Put to bed. When the repugnant chore was over, Cándido would fall on his knees at the feet of his Comrade.

"Lord Jesus, what else can I do for him?"

"Get him away from here! Let him make a man of himself!"

"He's so young. And the world is so perverse."

"And you're such an idiot."

"What are you saying?"

"No. Never mind. Sometimes I can't help myself. You'll be sorry for having let him have his own way. Besides, it's all your fault. You take too much from him."

"It's the penance the Lord has sent me."

"Don't make Him your accomplice."

"Have you forgotten the Patriarch of Edom? Job said that the Lord giveth and the Lord taketh away."

"How nice and comfortable! Right? You sit waiting for my Father to take Candelario away from you."

Along with those and other small details, his work was increasing. Santorontón was still growing. And his church was getting better and better.

That was how everything was going until the night of the fire, which increased his comradeship with Christ. He was on his way back from giving extreme unction to someone who was dying. He promised himself that it would be the last time he would go out in his canoe. Both on the way out as well as returning he was on the verge of losing his way. Only his way? An optimistic thought. What he was capable of losing was "Number One," himself. On the way out, without realizing it, he got caught in a whirlpool. He only noticed it when he was in the eye of the spinning water. He was whirling around. He paddled desperately. His efforts were of no avail. The more he struggled, rather, the worse his situation got. The suction toward the bottom was stronger and stronger. He was worn out. Vanquished. He crossed himself. He waited calmly for the waters to swallow him up. Canoe and all. He closed his eyes. He took refuge behind his usual words: "Thy will be done, oh Lord!" At that moment three dolphins appeared. As if sprouting out of the liquid mass. Their gleaming skins and the quivering outlines of the waves seemed to turn them into crystal carvings. They leaped. One over the other. In graceful rhythmic acrobatics. They stopped. They saw the difficulties the Friend of Jesus was in. With a rapid decision they came closer. They arranged themselves in Indian file. Each took the tail of the one in front of his mouth. In that way they made a living chain. The last one bit onto the bow of the canoe. The centripetal force of the whirlpool made the bodies of the agile cetaceans tense. The boat and the Priest felt a strong shudder. Just as he was about to fall into the maelstrom he assessed the efforts of his sudden saviors. Would they resist the pull? Wouldn't they become detached from each other's mouth and tail? The canoe began to tremble. Convulsively. It gave a little. The living chain seemed to bend. Would it curl around the whirlpool? Would it be carried to the bottom by the sucking eye? Would he and the marine mammals take their last trip together under the waters? He was wrong. The cetaceans were not beaten. The pulling increased. His heart began to pound happily. It seemed to him that it had been lifted above everything. Higher than sounds. Higher than sights. Did he love life so much, then? Triumph over the whirlpool became possible. In a double vision he felt as if the liquid spiral were taking on a living form. It was a great octopus. A huge green octopus. Which had him squeezed in its countless tentacles. The eye of the whirlpool was its head. The spirals of waves, ever weaker, were the cephalopod's weakening extremities. Second by second it drew farther away. The chain of dolphins stretched out. The whitecaps bounced in harmony with the rhythm of their transparent bodies. They began to vibrate in a dance of colors. Could they have escaped from some iridescent aquarium? They soon had him out of danger. They put him back on course. With all his strength he began to plunge the paddle into the surface of the water. The living chain broke up. The magical cetaceans flipped their tails in a gracious farewell. The Priest blessed them after shouting with uncontained emotion: "Thank you, my children, thank you!" Later, on his way back, sleep overcame him. How much time had passed? Several hours? He had lost his paddle. He searched carefully in the bottom of the canoe. Not there either. The strange thing was that the canoe was moving ahead. At great speed. He could tell by the white mustache waves beneath the bow. By the spreading lines which the long keel of the boat was cutting in the water. He smiled within. It was the dolphins. Without a doubt. They had come back to help him. He looked forward. Alongside. Aft. No. It wasn't the small cetaceans. The water around him had the smoothness of molasses. A flapping of wings filled him with emotion. Could it be that his Comrade had sent him some angels? He looked up. They weren't angels either. They might just as well have been. They were pelicans. Five, all told. Their enormous spoonlike bills had picked up the chain of the boat. One behind the other, like an elegant fringe, they were carrying the row of links. They weren't flying very high as they towed him along. He smiled on the outside. Could his Comrade of the Cross have sent these and the dolphins? Or were they doing it on their own? It wasn't right to doubt. Couldn't the small cetaceans and the large fish-eating birds have free will too? In the meantime the pelicans' broad wings went on rhythmically with their slow flapping. It had an almost ritual solemnity. He shouted again, as he had the time before: "Thank you, my children, thank you very much!"

When they drew close to Santorontón he grew uneasy as he looked at the horizon. A red glow was spreading over the village. Could they be burning off some clearing? As they drew closer he was sure that they were not. It was a fire. A big fire. Right in the center of town. From what he could calculate, quite close to the church. His church! His heart gave a jump. Could it be his church? Impossible! His church was protected by God. Or at least by the Son of God. If in some remote case a fire started there, he was sure that Jesus would step in himself. He would get down from his Cross. He would get a bucket. He would fill it with water. He would multiply it by a hundred. Or more, if necessary. After all, hadn't he changed water into wine at the Wedding Feast in Cana? It would no doubt be much simpler to multiply the water. And if by chance he was unable to haul it himself, what difference did it make? He would ask his father, or maybe he would summon them himself, for a legion of Saints and Archangels to help him. And they would put out the fire in a minute. Obviously, therefore, it couldn't be his church that was burning. In spite of everything, as the flames made the outline of things clearer, he had to bow down before the irremediable. The fire was at his church!

He was drawn out of his thoughts and memories by the voice of the Burned Christ.

"We're getting to Daura, Cándido."

He replied with a certain sharpness:

"Yes!"

As they advanced they heard barking that grew louder.

"Does it upset you to see Clotilde Quindales?"

"No!"

"You can't fool me. She upsets you. Like most of the women in Santorontón. Like almost all women. Didn't you ever like women, Cándido?"
"What a question! Stop pestering me!"
"Answer me. Didn't you ever like them?"
"What do you think?"
"I'm the one who's asking the questions. Answer me!"
He remained thoughtful for a moment. Then he looked straight at him. In the eyes. He cleared things up.
"I liked them too much."
"Really?"
"And in a strange way."
"You don't say. Explain yourself!"
"Well, at first I saw them as a whole."
"I don't understand."
"It's perfectly clear. As a whole. Head. Body. Extremities. With clothes on, too."
"And later on you didn't?"
"No. I kept on seeing them as a whole. But completely naked."
"Ah, how about that!"
"In a little while they lost their heads. I mean I only saw them from the neck down. Later on..."
"You only saw their extremities."
"No. Only their sexes!"
"Cándido! What are you saying?"
"Just what you hear. As if the world were made up of whole men and of women who were only what they had between their legs. It got to be an obsession. It tormented me. I was becoming an idiot. Wherever I looked those visions rose up. Sexes. Sexes. Nothing but women's sexes. Just like a string of fuzzy shellfish. Spinning endlessly about me. I began to masturbate every chance I got. Like someone possessed."
"You've really kept your tastes well hidden!"
"One fine day, in desperation, I confessed. To the Priest of my village. He told me many things. That mine wasn't an unusual case. That most boys did it. The strange thing was the way in which the stimulus came about. Maybe I was being tempted by the Devil. In order to save myself I had to turn to the grace of God. He advised me to enter the Seminary. I had a lot of doubts. Finally I made my decision."

"And how did things go for you in the Seminary?"

"Well... We'd best leave that for another time. We're coming in."

The barking of Miss Victor—Clotilde Quindales' dog—was backstitching the shadows.

FOUR

Candelario Mariscal—in order to get hold of his memories—cast his eyes over the horizon.

"I had a lot to do with everything that happened to the Quindales that night."

"Everybody knows that around here, Colonel."

"The truth. Nobody knows the real truth."

The anthropoid eyes sparkled. He was getting ready for confidences. Because now he was quite sure that the famous Godson of the Priest would tell him what had happened. He only knew what evil tongues had spread around. Or what he imagined later on listening to Clotilde. That the Colonel had indulged himself by satisfying his haemophagia on the family. Was it only hunger and thirst for blood? Or was it the pleasures of haemoscopia as well? Blood. Always blood. The blood of the Old Ones. And the blood of the girls. Nothing but blood. First from the neck. Then from the sex. Those fountains of blood—both bloods—had burst forth because of the impulse of a hand. A single hand. The hand of Colonel Candelario Mariscal. Could all that be true? Mightn't he have been helped by The Evil One? Could Crisanta be right when she insisted—the same as the others, so many others, too—that the Colonel was the spawn of Old Longtail? If that was how it was, the Latter had probably helped him in his wild orgy of blood. Where did the truth lie? What could it not be? Everything was left floating in the air. A red dream embroidered on the crests of the waves. Or on the wavering treetops.

"You know all about it, Bulu-Bulu. I was after Josefa, Atanasio Quindales' older daughter."

The presence of Dominga and Crisanta made him stop. The Wizard was about to order the women to withdraw. He would make the coffee. The Old Woman was right. It was late for Minga. Besides, the girl was so nervous. Apart from her own problems, she'd worked hard all day. Making an effort, he held back. He thought that he would still be able to hear the Colonel afterwards. The important thing now was for the Colonel and his daughter to get to know each other. In that way the plan that had begun to germinate in his mind would progress.

Seeing her and saying to himself, "I'm going to have a bite of the watermelon," was almost instantaneous in Candelario. The girl, for her part, looked at him askance. With studied indifference.

"Good evening, Colonel."

"It's almost good morning, Dominga."

And then, after a pause:

"What a fine girl you're turning out to be! I would have barely recognized you."

"Really and truly?"

With studied indifference. But she pushed her breasts out more. She put a more provocative and rhythmic cadence into her hips. When the fire was lighted, the resinous half-burned wood sparkled with smiles. And the ripe girl's attractive profile was lighted up by the dancing of the flames. Since she had leaned over, the red fingers of the fire seemed to be going into the low neck of her dress. The Colonel was watching all that. He began to weigh every one of the young girl's parts on the scales of his eyes. A sudden burst of flame lighted up her chin. He thought of getting up. Beating Crisanta and Bulu-Bulu. Or sinking a shaft of steel into their bellies. Grabbing Dominga by the hair. Dragging her off to the first mat or deer hide that he could find. Pulling her down there. By force. Clawing off her clothes. And burying himself in her like a nail of flesh. He got a hold of himself. The heat subsided. What an imbecile! Why did he have to do it just at that moment? There was more than enough time for everything. He didn't have to hurry things. First things first. He had to solve the problem that was torturing him. Night after night. Without rest. Only the Wizard Bulu-Bulu could tear the "sickness" out by its roots. Why, then, not build up his patience and wait? Maybe sometime in the future he wouldn't even have to force the girl. And, who knows, not even the Old Ones. Maybe at some unexpected moment she herself would invite him in under her net. Or in the jungle. She would lie down peacefully. She would open herself wide. The way papayas split open when they ripen.

He continued speaking to her. With a voice that was having trouble remaining calm.

"Listen, Dominga."

"Yes, sir, Colonel."

"Do the boys flap their wings around you a lot?"

Maliciously, she showed her double string of teeth.

"Nobody flaps anything around me."

Candelario quipped:

"Did they have their eyes put out at birth?"

The girl sensed that she was being flirted with:

"Oh, come on!"

When the coffee was finished, the women went to bed. The men went down out of the house. They headed for the bank of the inlet. They sat down on the bow of the Colonel's boat. Inside their shells, the turtles waited. They stood out like gigantic stones. Half-sunken in the mud.

A clamoring hot coal, impatience, was burning Bulu-Bulu's behind.

"You were saying, Colonel..."

Candelario Mariscal served himself a mouthful of darkness. Then—with his look—he tried to penetrate the Wizard's spirit.

"As I was saying, I liked Chepa Quindales."

He saw her for the first time at Crisóstomo Chalena's. Chalena still wasn't the great son of a bitch he turned out to be later. He still hadn't got control over the rooftops of Santorontón. Nor had he become involved in the jungle or the swampland. Nor—still more important—had he signed that fearsome pact which brought about a complete change in his existence. Well, he'd met

Josefa Quindales at his house. He was interested in her in a proper way. Word of honor! He was going to say "Word of God," as they said in those parts. He couldn't. He couldn't ever since his godfather had driven him out of the church with kicks. That evening there'd been a big party at Chalena's house. It was an evening of dancing and merriment. The music of *amorfinos* and *pasillos* curled around legs. Cane liquor around throats. The heat around nerves. A smell of glorious bodies burned people inside and out. Down below, the sea was shattering its laughter on the shore. Its wave teeth bloomed. Sometimes, with lust, it would put out its green hands and caress the naked curves of its beaches. Up above, in the wooden house, the floor was swaying. It seemed to be keeping time to the rhythm of the dancers. Crisóstomo Chalena was handing out food and drink on all sides. Many guests—some by sea and others by land—were arriving all the time. Until it was the turn for the appearance of the Quindales in their shallow draft canoe. As always—which he discovered some days later—Atanasio, his wife Eduva, and their two daughters, Josefa and Clotilde, had all wielded a paddle. So that the family flew over the water like a flock of pelicans. They arrived all excited. When he saw the girl, everyone else became hazy. And as she came up the steps it was as if she were climbing up his body. Without realizing it, he went over. He took her by the arm. He tried to separate her from her people. Josefa resisted.

"Hey! What's the matter with you?"

He babbled:

"Come. Don't be afraid."

Josefa looked at him with her black eyes. As if two sharp points of chonta wood were through him.

"I'm not afraid."

She was wearing a broad-brimmed straw hat. Across the thin dress of multicolored chintz hung the machete, at a slant. She repeated:

"I'm not afraid. Of anything or anybody!"

Don Atanasio, who had taken a few steps forward, came back.

"Is he bothering you, Chepa?"

"No, Papa."

The Old Man went over to Candelario. He told him, calmly but firmly:

"You'd better not screw around with her."

For an instant he felt adrift. Everybody was in back of him.

Beside him, Chepa. Facing him, Don Quindales. Don Quindales wrapped in a horizon of shadows, lights, colors. Red predominating. The red of passion. Fire. Blood. What if he blasted him right there? Who did that old man think he was, getting in his way? He got control of himself.

"It's all right."

The Master of the House came over, staggering.

"Let the kids dance, Atanasio!"

The one addressed grumbled:

"You know what the Priest's Godson is like."

Chalena served him a glass of cane liquor and twisted about, having trouble keeping his balance.

"Toss down a drink and don't be a pest! Everybody came here to shake a little dust off, right?"

"Yes. But..."

"Let them dance!"

He took the drink. He shrugged his shoulders.

"Chepa knows how to take care of herself. If she wants to..."

His wife intervened.

"Come on, Chepa! Go ahead!"

Josefa looked at her mother. Then at the others. Finally at Candelario.

"After I've rested a little..."

Clotilde—who was still flat-chested and narrow-hipped—was devouring her with her eyes. She approved of everything her sister was doing.

Dancing with Josefa was like rocking in a hammock made of thorny buttocks. Strange thorns that wounded him inside and out. He could have sworn that he was exploding inside his tissues and his blood. A blood that wasn't any less murky and lukewarm because it was invisible. He moved, with an urge to squeeze her up against his body until he broke her apart. Or, instead, to carry her in his arms. To make his way through them all like a hungry shark. To run to the shore. To put her aboard the first boat he found. To take her out to sea. There to caress her. Not with his usual caresses. The ones he had learned from beasts in heat. Used several times already on other females. With preambles. Driven only to screw his sex into the other sex...No. He would lay Josefa down on the bottom of the boat. He would kneel beside her. He would look at her without doing anything. For hours.

Then he would lift her hair and let it fall again. Maybe—if she tried to defend herself—he wouldn't even dare undress her. Maybe he would kiss her. On the mouth. On the throat. His mischievous hands might wander down a bit. To her face. But nothing else. He would keep on kissing her. Looking at her. Caressing her. Making no advances with his kisses or his hands. Only where she would allow it. Not forcing her. Not trying to hurry things along. Everything would come by itself, an impetuous torrent of water. Without a doubt, finally—that day? another day? another week? another month? another year?—he would get to undress her. He would set up a siege without haste or respite. Until he felt in his body the total fusion with her body. Introduced. Integrated. Wiping out the limits between the two of them. That would come—of course it would come!—later. When Chepa wouldn't resist, but rather, would desire it...

Her voice brought him back to reality.

"Hey! What's the matter with you?"

It was a kind of awakening.

"What? What?"

"Watch where you put your feet. You've stepped on me twice."

"I didn't mean to."

She looked at him challengingly.

"What do I care what you meant to do."

She added, sarcastically:

"If you're tired out, we can sit down."

"No! When the piece is over."

"All right, if that's what you want!"

She smiled in spite of herself, with a touch of coquetry. She went on:

"Just as long as you don't step on my feet again."

They danced around again. Tense. Cumbersome. In silence. To the rhythm of the whining guitars and the drunken singers. He was furious with himself. He'd never been such a fool. He'd never hesitated like that. He felt like a sloop without mast or sails. Adrift and in danger of being swamped. He wanted to talk to her. To tell her so many things. So he could board her. Just like all the girls before. But nothing doing! It was as if they'd put a muzzle with seven knots on him. What did Chepa have that the others didn't? Was the real truth—contrary to what usually happened—that he was the one who was pissing with fear? He insulted himself: "You're acting like a goddamned fool! If you don't turn your dogs loose tonight, it'll be harder later on. Look how all the men have got their eyes glued to her stern! If you don't hurry up, they'll get ahead of you. Look at the hate and rage Don Quindales has in his eyes! Don't fall asleep. Get into the woman!"

His voice sounded weak, like someone else's:

"Chepa."

"What?"

"Uhh . . . when will I see you again?"

"Can't you see me now? Keep looking at me until you get tired of it!"

"No. I don't mean here. Later on. The two of us. All alone."

"No, indeed! With the reputation you've got? Do you want me to be ruined?"

"Just one little time."

"We've seen too much of each other already."

He said something he was sorry for almost at once.

"Don't be mean, Chepa!"

She became serious.

"You're the mean one, Candelario. News flies fast around here. Everybody knows everything."

"Evil tongues can even poison a pitahaya cactus, Chepa."

She became herself again.

"What do I care? You'd better stop bothering me."

"The fact is, I . . ."

The piece was over. The men all separated from their partners. Candelario made his last attempt.

"Chepa, I . . ."

She looked at him with eyes of ice.

"Don't you understand? Leave me alone!"

His voice broke. It was almost like a whisper.

"All right."

He was going to say something else. He held back. He repeated:

"All right."

And to himself:

"If that's the way you want it, Chepa."

From that moment on he didn't let a day pass without calling on her. He almost never used human form. Most of the time he appeared as a crocodile. It was his first metamorphosis. A nine-foot crocodile. He swam majestically. With indifference. He passed down through the inlets. His armor showed on the surface of the water. His long snout sliced through the tense surface. The fish fled. Only a few saurians followed him on occasion. He went along, sure of himself, paying no attention to them. Sometimes Santorontonian harpooners would chase him. They didn't throw a regular harpoon at him, but a double-pronged one. That sharp weapon with a double blade. It touched him. It didn't even leave a mark on his skin. Much less wound him. Some suggested going underwater. Hitting him in the stomach. The way professionals in the risky hunting of crocodiles do. Making him float and be still for a few seconds. Then the ones in the canoe could take advantage. They could hit him in the neck with an ax. Or stick the harpoon into some soft spot. Finally, one morning, they all agreed to try it. When they made their attempt, Candelario-Crocodile played a trick on them. He let them hit him in the stomach. He came to the surface. When they were ready to kill him with the ax he slipped back. He seemed to take a leap. He opened his great jaws. He displayed his dental artillery. The harpooners stood still in astonishment. They made ready to receive the attack of the fearsome beast. He would no doubt split the boat in two. Or simply give them a lash with his tail. Maybe they would lose their balance and fall into the water. They waited expectantly. They reacted. They were going to act. It was better to be ahead of any move on the crocodile's part. Something happened which stopped them again. The saurian half-opened his perverse little eyes. And he let out a guffaw. A ringing laugh. It hovered rocking on the treetops. On the distant mountains. On distant ships as their time-dried sails sliced through the fat-bellied clouds. The Santorontonians looked at each other in fright. They'd never heard a crocodile laugh before. They'd never known it was possible. Could crocodiles laugh like people? When they tried to recover from the sudden magnetic attraction, it was too late. The nine feet of saurian were rapidly sliding away. From that time on he had a name. They nicknamed him "The Fucker." Because they all swore that his laughter was meant to show them how he'd fucked them.

In Daura. Near the house of the woman who'd driven him crazy, he ran aground on the mud. He hid in the thick underbrush. From there he fastened his eyes on the steps, inaccessible to him. Hour after hour passed. When he couldn't see her he became furious. Would he forget all his calmness and go over to the base of the supports? Would he climb up to the trembling floor of cut bamboo? He held back. Most likely, if he did that, he'd lose her forever. How would she react when she saw him? In his human form, of course. She would be startled, certainly. Or maybe not. She seemed so brave! Maybe she'd tease him again. Maybe she'd ask him to leave. But what if she listened to him? What if her attitude toward him had improved? Why not give it a try? What would it cost him, in the end, to go up and lay his uncertainty to rest once and for all? He made up his mind. He'd do it. The first time she came out alone. Since she was always with her Old Folks. Or with Clotilde at least.

Master of his decision, he waited. He didn't wait for long. Josefa appeared, on her way back to the shore. She was carrying a pack on her back. Maybe she was going to fish for mussels or crabs. Not shrimp. She wasn't carrying a casting net or one for shallow water. He took on human form again. He came out of his hiding place. He took a few steps in the mud, drawing closer. Josefa raised her eyes at the sound. A mixture of confusion and rage flamed within them.

"You!"

He babbled:

"Yes. Me. Me, the one who can't forget you."

Suddenly she looked all around, frightened.

"Where did you come from?"

He pointed vaguely to the shore.

"From there."

The girl felt more and more nervous.

"How? There isn't any boat. Not even a raft."

He began to feel more secure. He said, a little mockingly:

"I swam over."

"Swam? Swam from Santorontón? That's a lie! Santorontón's on the other side. No man could swim this far. Besides, look how long it would take!"

She stopped. Looked at him. With real panic.

"Only if you're really what they say you are. That you're..."

"Who?"

"No! No! Nobody! And now get out of here!"

He tried to calm her down. He took a few steps forward.

"Don't act like that, Chepita!"

"Don't come any closer. Get out of here!"

"But, Chepa!"

He continued forward. With a quick move she grasped her machete.

"You get out of here... Or I'll make you sorry!"

He could have beaten her. Dominated her. Without using any weapon. By changing into a hawk. Or going back to his saurian appearance. Or in one shape or another. He didn't do it. What for? He still had a remote hope. What if she accepted him someday? He'd be patient. He'd still be patient.

The sun—a coral sea urchin—began to stick its barbs of light into the darkness. The horizon filled with incendiary smiles. Creatures and things reached out their tremulous fingers to tickle the dawn. The Colonel was silent. Bulu-Bulu looked at him eagerly. He had the urge to ask him a thousand questions. The obstinate silence prevented him. It was digging a moat the size of an abyss between the two of them. Finally the Wizard couldn't hold back. His curiosity became stronger than his prudence. His simian face filled with wrinkles.

"Now I can understand a lot of things."

But the Colonel was like a mute. He didn't even look at him. He looked, instead, at the mouth of the inlet. At the billions of tongues of the rising sun losing themselves in the crannies along the shore.

Bulu-Bulu persisted:

"So?"

Candelario finally deigned to look at him. His look was distant. Who can say where it was coming from? The Wizard insisted:

"So what happened?"

He answered, almost aggressively:

"What happened where?"

Bulu-Bulu smiled mysteriously. He persisted:

"What happened afterward with Josefa Quindales?"

The Priest's Godson spoke to himself.

"There are certain things that belong to the night. And night is on her way out."

"Ah!"

He looked at him again. After all, he was going to put himself in the hands of the Wizard. He explained:

"I'll come back later on today. When it gets dark. Then I'll tell you what happened."

He turned to the turtles.

"Let's go!"

The giant tortoises—with incredible steps—dragged their shells rapidly toward the water. The Colonel got on board. He made a slight gesture of farewell. And he left. Soon he was a dot getting lost in the shadows.

FIVE

As the Priest was about to knock on the door, a voice came out of the shadows:

"Go away, Cándido! It would be best for all concerned."

The voice was disguised. But he recognized it at once. Crisóstomo Chalena! No doubt about it. What was he doing there at that time? What did that bandit have to do with Clotilde Quindales? Why did he want him to leave? Why that veiled threat? Could he be the one who was flapping his wings over Josefa's sister? But didn't they say that Crisóstomo's bush no longer bloomed for women? That was all very strange. Very strange indeed. He didn't have time to go on thinking about it. He heard the hated voice again:

"Don't say later that I didn't warn you!"

At once—as he left—there was the sound of footsteps scratching in the night. He curled up with laughter. All that was needed was for Crisóstomo to say something and things would turn out just the opposite. That man almost always walked along sour paths. Most of the time his causes and his desires were unjust. So that if he had hesitated to approach the younger daughter of Don Quindales before, now he enjoyed doing it. Even if her behavior was hard to explain, she was acting on her own in this case.

He knocked. The girl opened. He'd only seen her a few times. More beautiful each time. That time her large eyes were shaken by tears.

"Come in, Father."

"Why are you out of bed? Aren't you sick?"

"Not me, Father."

"What is it, then?"

"It wasn't for me that I sent for you, it was for Juvencio. He's very sick. Look at him!"

"Yes, he is."

He looked into the corner of the miserable house. Dr. Balda was lying on a deerskin. The young man's appearance was truly discouraging. His clothing was in shreds. Dirty. Stained with blood. And there was a bloodstain on his face. His hands. Rough bandages covered his head. He had trouble breathing. He seemed to be asleep.

"What happened to him?"

"I don't know."

"He's been beaten."

"Yes. All over his body."

"How did he get here?"

The girl's face was upset.

"He came twice."

The Priest looked at her in disbelief.

"I don't understand."

"Well... I was asleep when I heard a wild pounding on the door. It woke me up. I went to see. Hundreds of fists pounding. I opened up. I was frightened. I closed the door right away. The pounding got stronger. I was afraid they'd knock the door down. I opened up again. There were dozens of monkeys. They were furious."

"Why did they come out of the jungle?"

"Who can say? What I do know is that they didn't keep quiet for a minute. They were screaming. They were moving from one side to the other. They were motioning, pointing something out to me. In a definite direction. I looked. And I didn't know what to do. Paralyzed. Mute."

"What was going on?"

"Finally a group of them came along. They were marching in formation. Walking sideways, their arms held out. Their hands joined. Making a kind of living stretcher. That was how they were carrying Juvencio. Without stopping for a minute they went over to my bed. There, very carefully, kneeling, they laid him down. Then they started screaming at me again, pointing to him. He didn't answer. The monkeys became silent. They stopped moving. Looking at it all."

"Didn't you call Dr. Espurio Carranza?"

"I ran to his place. I explained what had happened. He paid no attention to me. Even when I told him he should help Juvencio, considering, at least, that he's a doctor too. It was useless. He refused to treat him. He even said that everything that happened was just punishment for sticking his nose in where it didn't belong. Then I asked him to let me take him to him so that he could give him some kind of treatment at least. He wouldn't do that either. Because of that I went to Vigiliano Rufo's store. They didn't pay any attention to me there either. They even refused to sell me bandages and medicine. In desperation I set out for Juvencio's house. I was surprised to find the door open. I went in. The sight was horrible. Everything was destroyed: the medical instruments, bottles of medicine, furniture, books. The best I could do was find some bandages and disinfectant. I came back with it. But first I begged José Isabel Lindajón to go tell you. The monkeys were still here. Curiously, they didn't move, they were silent. Watching the doctor with sharp eyes. When they saw me come in, the older ones helped me take care of him. When we finished, one by one, without looking back, they left."

"You mean that if it hadn't been for them..."

"...Juvencio wouldn't be able to tell the story."

"What happened afterward?"

"There was a knock on my door again. This time the knock of only one fist. Afraid, I opened it again. It was Crisóstomo Chalena. With four men. He didn't try to come in. From the door he threatened me, warning me that he was giving me a good piece of advice. It would be best if I didn't get involved in what didn't concern me. I should let the little doctor there—he calls Juvencio that too—get what was coming to him. I answered him: 'Look at the condition he's in, Don Chalena. That poor Christian there can't even take care of his own soul.' He got even angrier. He told me to do what he was telling me. That I had enough troubles of my own. Why hadn't I left the little doctor where I'd found him? I cleared things up: 'It wasn't me, Don Chalena. It was the monkeys!' He thought for a few minutes. He seemed to have his doubts. He took off his straw hat. He scratched his bald head. As if muttering to himself that maybe it was true. Since early in the morning he'd heard devilish hollering coming out of the jungle. Afterward it seemed as if some animals—he'd thought they were birds—were traveling in regular flocks from one branch of the trees to another. In spite of it all, he looked at me with his harpoon eyes. He scolded me for having let them in. I shouldn't have even opened the door for them. I answered him again: 'Do you think I could possibly have done that, Don Chalena?' He seemed a little calmer. He said maybe I was right. I certainly couldn't have stopped them. Finally he said: 'All right!' He made a sign to the four men. They went over to Juvencio. They picked him up. Each one with an arm or a leg. They carried him. And they took him away. I stayed behind, not knowing what to do, all upset."

"But how did Juvencio get back here?"

"After a little while, there was knocking on the door again. Hundreds of fists. Like the time before. But stronger. I opened up."

"The monkeys?"

"Yes. They'd come armed with sticks, stones, pieces of iron, and anything they could find on the way. In the middle of them, carrying Juvencio—the same way as they'd taken him away—the four men. And behind them Don Chalena. If the situation hadn't been so serious I would have laughed. The Old Man looked like a tree with monkey blossoms. He had monkeys all over him. Stuck to him. Holding on with their tails. Or with their arms and legs. All over his body. One had his legs crossed around his neck. And when Don Chalena stopped or didn't do what they seemed to be telling him to do, the monkey would stick his fingers in his eyes. Of course, the Old Man didn't consider himself beaten. When his men laid Juvencio down where he is right now, he looked at me muttering: 'Don't think that things are going to stay like this! They'll pay for it! They'll all pay for it!' As if the monkey he was wearing like a necktie understood, he stuck his fingers in his eyes again. Without complaining, he told his men: 'Let's go!' The men seemed to hesitate. Or at least they delayed in carrying out the order. The monkeys, when they noticed, raised their weapons in a threatening way. When the men saw this, they hurried off. Only when they'd gone out the door did I realize that they were unarmed. Their pistols and machetes were being carried by the monkeys, who had stayed behind. They left too. In complete silence."

"I can understand. The monkeys can't forget all that Juvencio has done for them."

"And how much he's still doing."

"That's it. Well, tell me now. How can I help you?"

"Take Juvencio away!"

"Where?"

"To your place. It's the only place where he can be safe."

"Do you think so?"

"At least safer than here."

"What about you?"

"I'll wait here. To see what happens."

"You'd better come with me. That way you can take care of Juvencio yourself."

"But..."

"Your life wouldn't be worth a snatch-crab's claw here."

When they went by the church of Santorontón—the new stone church which Father Gaudencio was building and which, according to him, "would never be finished" so that alms and donations would go on *ad vitam aeternam*—he remembered the other church again. His church! The one that had died enveloped in flames. He relived that mournful night. When he realized that the fire was there, he helped the pelicans. He paddled with his hands as if a motor had been installed. The canoe flew along like a shark in heat. Even so he was too late. The whole village was there, throwing buckets of water on the walls. On the straw roof. It was burning like tinder. The Santorontonians knew it. Everything they did would be useless. Still, they kept at it imperturbably. Throwing water onto the humble house of the Lord. Cándido thought he was going to go out of his mind. He didn't care about the heat or the smoke. Or the strange crackling sound that came from the burning wood and straw. Or the falling of the beams and supports. Before anyone could stop him, he plunged into the reddened Church. They spoke to him. They shouted at him. What were they saying? He heard nothing. Someone tried to grab him by the arm. He shook himself free. He went ahead. Was his cassock on fire? He felt a lack of breath. His eyes were burning. He went on ahead. Where was he going? The others thought he was going to get his belongings, the ornaments. They were wrong. What he was interested in. Or what he was more interested in, was the Christ. His Christ! He got to the place. When he looked at it his heart broke in two. It was wrapped in flames. Part of the right arm was burning. His own fire was reaching his chest. If he'd had time, he would have asked him questions. Why didn't he stop the fire? Why, at least, didn't he stop the flames from reaching him? Or was it, perhaps, some new sacrifice for the salvation of mankind? He couldn't understand. The truth is that he was a poor ignorant Priest who couldn't understand many things. There wasn't any time for meditation. As best he could he climbed up onto the table under the Christ. He beat at it with his cassock. In an absurd drive to keep the fire from the Sacred Body. Then he embraced it. Was he burning? He felt the flames wrapping him up. His shredded clothes were turning to ash. He thought for a moment. How beautiful it would be to die like that on the Cross, embracing the Son of God! As if his fate were mingled with His! Jesus lifted up his head. He looked at him. With affection.

"Thank you, Old Man."

He answered, resentfully:

"Why didn't you save our church?"

"Don't you see that I can't?"

"Are your miracles all finished?"

He answered with another question:

"Why don't you save it yourself?"

"Me? I came of my own free will. To rescue you. Let's go!"

"It's too late."

"It's never too late."

He tried to get him off the Cross. Curiously, he began to feel less burning in his eyes. The tongues of flame were weaker. The tremendous heat was slowly diminishing. An aerostatic feeling came over his body. Was he dying? Had he lost consciousness? Or was it simply a loss of weight? He looked at Christ. He was still nailed to the Wood. There were no more flames. He did show some burns on his arm. On his chest. And also one on his face which he hadn't seen before. What about his own clothes? Had his cassock been on the point of turning to ash? He looked at himself. He lighted all up inside. The cassock, singed, had come together again. It seemed to have grown. It was open under the Cross, extending along the sides of it. As if it were a wing. Or, rather, a pair of wings. Two black wings stiffened by the wind. He looked up. The roof wasn't there. Had it fallen in? His eyes saw only the vastness of the sky. Speckled with stars. Fearfully, he lowered his eyes. All of Santorontón was receding. The church—with flames that were smaller and smaller—was growing smaller. Where were they flying to, then? Was the flight in his head or outside? Was he dreaming or alive? Was he living a kind of dream? He turned to Christ. The latter shrugged his shoulders.

"There are certain decisions that I don't make, my Father does."

The day after the fire he went back to the church. What was left of the church, that is. It was in ruins. They would need months to rebuild it. Years, maybe. The supports rose up like black stumps. The roof, without its straw, looked like a net to catch huge fish that was hung up to dry. There were no walls. A few benches bore testimony that of late the faithful no longer kneeled on the ground. From time to time the thousand mouths of the morning wind carried the ashes off to somewhere else. The Santorontonians had fought well against their unexpected adversary. There was no doubt about it. They could have won the battle. But they simply lacked the means to fight the catastrophe. And the firemen—with their hand pumps—from the nearest village had taken hours—days maybe—to get there. His faithful were still asleep from fatigue, most assuredly. The church was all alone. He went in. If you could call it that, walking under an open sky through the still smoking ruins. He began to calculate how much he would need to rebuild a part of it at least. It would most certainly be a lot...

He was interrupted by the voice of the Sexton.

"Father! Father Cándido!"

He hadn't noticed him. He was trembling. Pale. Feverish. He answered him ill-humoredly.

"What is it, Romelio?"

"How fortunate that your house didn't burn down!"

"You don't say!"

"Look!"
Only then did he notice that the one speaking to him was right. The fire had respected the modest building where he lived. It was blackened with smoke. Its walls were a bit cracked. But nothing else. The flames had stopped there. How could that have been? Wasn't it right next to the church? Wasn't it attached to it in the rear? Could that have been the miracle—another miracle, that is—that Jesus had granted him? As if the Sexton were reading his thoughts, he fell on his knees before him.
"It's a miracle!"
He agreed:
"Yes. It's a miracle."
Out of somewhere—from inside himself perhaps?—a mocking voice came. "Stop talking about miracles and get to work." Mechanically, he looked to where the Christ had always stood. Could it have been he? No. It couldn't have been he. He remembered that he'd left him on the shore. In the bottom of the boat.
He blessed Romelio, who was still on his knees. And he threatened him:
"Get up! We've got lots of things to do!"
The Sexton obeyed. They began to walk alongside each other. In silence. It was evident that Romelio wanted to tell the Priest something but didn't dare. Finally he decided to:
"Father Cándido!"
"What is it?"
"No. I'd better not tell you!"
He stopped short:
"What had you better not tell me? Speak up. Quick! Don't make me lose my time and my patience."
The Sexton summoned up his courage. With a barely audible voice he said:
"It was your Godson!"
"My Godson? I don't understand. What are you trying to tell me?"
"It was your Godson... who set fire to the church."
He reacted as if a snake had bitten him. He spun around furiously. He took him by the shoulders. He shook him.
"Don't lie to me! I know that you don't like him! That the boy doesn't get along with anyone! That he's got all the vices and none of the virtues! But this I don't believe. He wouldn't be capable of such a thing!"

Romelio crossed himself with two fingers. Kissed them.

"I swear by the Cross that lights my way!"

He turned him loose. His arms hung down. Like dead iguanas. He murmured as if to himself:

"No. It can't be!"

The Sexton explained:

"Yesterday, after you went out in your canoe, young Candelario arrived. He'd had more to drink than usual. He couldn't stand up. I only opened up for him because he was kicking at the doors of the church, crazy mad. When he came in he refused to go to his room. I tried to carry him by force, like other times. He wouldn't let me. He asked me to give him some sacramental wine. I refused. He hit me. Or he tried to hit me. When he tried it, he was the one who stumbled. He was about to fall. Just as I'm telling you, Father, he was moving like a sloop in a changing tide. Realizing in the midst of his drunkenness that he couldn't convince me by bad means, he began to promise me things. He was going to give me a lot of money. He was going to give me clothes. He was going to introduce me to women... Well, everything he thought would turn my head. When he saw he wasn't getting anywhere, he became furious. He threatened me. As God is my witness! I begged him to drop the matter. That it would be better if he went to bed. He paid no attention. He took out a cigarette. He lighted a match. He held it up for a while as if he was going to throw it onto the roof. He laughed. He lighted the cigarette. He dragged on it greedily. Then he blew out the match, which was almost burning his fingers. Once it was out, he tossed it away. He kept on smoking. He asked me again if I was going to get him the wine or not. Once more I said no. Then he took out the box of matches again. He lighted one. He looked up at the roof. And he lowered his hand, ready to throw it. I felt defeated. I promised to give him the wine... That I'd go get it. But that he should go to bed. I'd bring it right away. When he heard me, he let out a laugh: 'Do you think I'm such a damned fool? Bring the wine to me here. I'm going to drink a toast with Jesus.' Without knowing what to do, I decided to get the wine."

"There isn't any wine. It ran out a few days ago."

"I didn't know that. When I came back with the empty bottle, he wouldn't believe me."

"Why should he believe you? You wretch!"

"As much as I tried to hold him back, it was useless. He was crazy. Out of his mind. He got away from me. He let out a string of curses. And he ended up by throwing the cigarette over his head. Even if I'd tried to stop the fire, I wouldn't have been able to do anything. The straw was dry. And right away a flame started up. It grew rapidly, all over the roof. Soon there were hundreds of tongues of flame that were rising up all over the place. Your Godson looked at the spectacle. He laughed again. 'Let's see where they're going to hide the wine now.' And he staggered off to his room. I began to ring the bell. A lot of people came right away. We all tried to put out the fire. Impossible. Impossible to put it out with nothing but buckets!"

There was a brief silence, after which the Priest asked:

"Where is he now?"

"In his room. Sleeping."

He got there in two long strides. Indeed, as if nothing had happened, he was sound asleep. He couldn't stand any more of it. He grabbed one of his feet. He pulled him out of the bed. The other one woke up, startled:

"Wine! I want wine!"

That was when he got the first kick in the rear.

"Get out of here!"

He looked around, surprised.

"What happened?"

Another kick in the same place.

"I curse the hour I took you in!"

"Godfather, I..."

A blow identical to the previous one.

"I hope you die as soon as possible!"

Candelario reacted.

"Why do you treat me like this? What have I done?"

"Don't you know?"

He rubbed his eyes. He looked around disconcertedly. He seemed to remember.

"It wasn't me!"

Romelio didn't speak. But, from mind to mind, he transmitted to him, with all clarity, his accusation:

"Yes! It was you! I saw you. I swear I saw him with these eyes that will turn to dust and ashes."

A sudden spark lighted up his memory.

"I didn't know what I was doing! It was like someone was inside of me! Like someone else's hand moving mine!"

He got up. He received another kick.

"I don't ever want to see you again for all the days of my life! I could kill you! Get out of here! Get out!"

From that time on, the echo multiplied the choral phrases. In the nearby jungle. In the inlets alongside. On the sea close by. In the bamboo houses. In the sloops and canoes that came and went... It was like an unending gray vine rocked by the wind.

"It was a miracle."

"A miracle?"

"Yes. The Priest and the Christ were saved."

"What about the Priest's house? Another miracle?"

"No, not that. That was Old Longtail's doing."

"Why?"

"Because his son was there. Candelario Mariscal was there!"

SIX

On the night of the Quindales it was raining lust over the sea and over the jungle. Multimillions of zoomorphic eyes were weaving metaphors of phosphorus. Fastened on the sepia-green nerves, they sensed the coming. Was he really the representative of Old Longtail? Inside the saurian skin—an apocalyptic crocodile—The Spiteful One was bleeding arteries. *Caymantapachaca*. The water curls. *Caymantapachaca manajaycapi*. The blood boils. *Cayman-*

tapachaca manajaycapi canta. The dagger in his jaws. *Caymanta-pachaca manajaycapi canta tigrashpa ricuhuashachu*. The ivory dagger. —Wind lantern. Rainbow whirlwind. Magnet stones of sex.—Tongue of glass. Blood of smoke. Voice of metal. Candelario. Candela-río. Candle-river. Mar-iscal. Candela-río. Candela-mar. Candle-sea. —Fire-water. Sex-blood. Man-saurian. Candle-river-sea. Glowing tattoos. In his eyes: Chepa naked. In his mouth: boiling jaws. In his claws: the path to hell. In his sex: the fountain of evil. Chepa naked. His jaws boiling. The path to hell. The fountain of evil. —Dagger in his claws, fangs, and sex. Ivory dagger, of steel and coral. *Caymantapachaca manajaycapi canta tigrashpa ricuhuashachu*. From today forward I will never turn my face to see you.

The night of the Quindales. He was trembling, a tense reed at low tide. He had decided to find her. Make her his. Not bothered by anything that might stand in his way. In order to build up his spirits he had puffed himself up with liquor. He would tear everything to pieces. —Men. Animals. Things. Sea.— A sensual hurricane, he would wipe out everything that stood in his way. Even if the trees crossed their tangles of trunks, branches, and leaves. Even if the house twisted its walls and wove its props and beams together. Even if creatures—real or fictitious—knotted their claws and fangs. Even if harpoons, axes, and machetes tied dazzling chains between each other. A visible or invisible crocodile, he would climb the steps to the house of Josefa Quindales. The metamorphosis—his human presence—would take place up above. Opposite her. Or on her own deerskin. When she came to, she would already have him on top of her. Mounting her like a rider. And if she tried to protest. Oppose him. Or show displeasure in any way, it would fill his head with blood! His heart—did he have a heart?—he had stuck on a mangrove stake by the shore. The only thing that he carried in front like bait was his pair of testicles. They would guide him, the way pilot fish guide a hungry shark. Following them, the spite and rage that smothered him would disappear. As he thought about it, he advanced toward the Quindales place. A curtain of shadows fell over things. From the sea came the monotonous harangue of the dying waves. Not an eye was to be seen among the leaves. Could the inhabitants of the green country be asleep? Or was it simply that they did not want to see the erotic act? He went along stealthily, dragging his armored skin. Was he invisible at that instant? The wake of his belly on the ground. The four repeated tracks of his claws. Until a piece of snout came forth at the angular meeting of his eyes. No. He was not invisible. Couldn't he be? Was some unforeseen power opposing him? What did that matter! Nothing mattered! The important thing—the only important thing—was to perforate Chepa. To make her pay—with the price of a wounded sex—for all the snubs. When he tried to climb up it was difficult. His crocodile body was too heavy. What then? From there on he assumed his human form again. The dagger in his teeth. He climbed up with even more stealth. He reached the upper floor. He heard the Old Quindales both snoring. It was a strange snore. Could it be real? He didn't try to find out. What for, since it didn't matter if they heard him or not? Through the misty cloth he sensed more than saw the shape of both of them. He went into the other room. Two nets were hanging. One, small, in the foreground. Clotilde's, no doubt. The other, in the background, larger. Chepa's! He got down on all fours. He advanced, holding his breath. He wanted to surprise. She was the one he did want to surprise. So she wouldn't have time to dry out. Much less talk to him. He lifted up the netting. Curses! He saw only a bundle of clothing and bedcovers! Could she be sleeping on some other deerskin? In any case, she wasn't with Clotilde. Her bed was too small. The girl must have been only about thirteen. Could she be under the netting of the Old Ones? Without a doubt. So much the worse for them, if that was how it was. He'd take her by the hair. He'd drag her to her deerskin. And before her parents' eyes he would tear off her clothes. He would tame her. Until he nailed himself inside of her. Woe to them if they tried to stop him. He'd sew up their bodies with stitches of blood. As he thought that, he went back the way he had come. His rage grew as he did. Damned Old People! Had they thought they could fool him that way, that they could save their sprout? He'd make them see who Candelario Mariscal was now. Candelario Mariscal! The echo of that name seemed to burst forth under the netting.

"Candelario Mariscal! Curse you!"

The netting fell to the floor. The Old Quindales—husband and wife—got up. Don Atanasio snorted hoarsely.

"So, are you after Chepa?"

Fury blinded him.

"Yes, goddamn it! What about it?"

"You've been left with your stick in the air."
"Oh, is that so?"
Ña Eduva intervened:
"She's not here!"
"That's a lie!"
"Go look for her if you want to!"
He couldn't hold himself back. He threw himself on the Old Man. He grabbed him by the arms. He shook him.
"Is that true?"
"Of course it's true!"
"Where did you take her?"
"Far away from Santorontón."
"Where?"
"We won't tell you."
As the dagger made a metallic flash of lightning, he cut a fountain of blood on his face. He repeated:
"Where?"
"Up yonder. To a friend's house. On a ranch where the rivers start."
This time the knife sank into his stomach.
"But where, damn it, where?"
Don Atanasio bared his teeth.
"Go ahead and kill us! You won't get anything out of us!"
And Ña Eduva:
"We know who you are."
She crossed herself. She went on:
"And who your father is. The One Whose Name Is Never Spoken!"
He turned rapidly to her. He opened her face from top to bottom like a sliced watermelon. An explosion of blood.
"I'll find out."
"Only if The One We Know tells you!"
Clotilde had got up. She grabbed him from behind. She tried to shake him with her weak arms.
"Leave them alone! Don't kill them!"
With a fatalistic tone, he said:
"You're the ones who wanted it!"

He had the feeling of sinking into a whirlwind of intestines, muscles, and blood. A total bath from a thousand springs. Red. Red with liquid vapors. With endless strings of quin-quin ants.

His hand was getting tired from plunging the glowing steel into the conquered flesh. Parchment flesh. Somewhat dry from the accumulation of sunsets. Almost without defending themselves they had fallen to the floor. He, among them, bound by the steaming vapor of the lives in flight. He wasn't saying a word. He was looking without seeing. Or, rather, in two, three, four, or five superimposed exposures. Had they tried to defend themselves? Had they stretched out their clamorous hands, grasping the homicidal arm? Had they clutched the cutting blade itself? Had they embraced his legs when they fell? He was unhinged. Unhinged by shadows and blood. Blood. Wrapped in a tunic of blood. Smelling and tasting blood. Blood which came in through his pores. It bathed his eyes. It ran down all the paths of his body. It was a long, warm, and damp farewell. He no longer recognized the scarlet corpses. Wrapped in their red and frothy nets. Agglutinated in their elemental components. They were nothing but a shapeless mass. The dozens of steel bites had erased certain human characteristics. Unlikely concatenations of blood made monstrous spectacles arise. Pieces of feet coming out the mouth. A nose hanging from its owner's ear. Hands cut off. All by themselves. No arms. Crossed on the back. As with a new life of their own. And, slowly, in a high tide of ice, the wavering cold. The contagious white kisses that began to cover him. Only then the useless moan, the humble fright disappearing in Clotilde's eyes. Pupils widened. A tremulous quiver. Fright. Terror. Upset. Clotilde. Her breast flat as a plank. Her hips that had not expanded. Thin. Narrow. Minimal. Clotilde.

Crazed, he looked at her. He went over to her. She couldn't move. He picked her up. He laid her down on the deerskin. While the girl sank into the passive world of unconsciousness, he climbed on top of her. Leaping on a clover with green armor. Whirling about against the trees. Knocking them down with his tail. Destroying the trunk with his jaws. Pulling off the bark with his claws. The crocodile has gone mad. Woe to the jungle! Woe to the leaves! Woe to the tiny creatures whose dawn exploded in their insides! The crocodile has gone mad! Woe to the mortal circuits established along the shore! Woe to the bivalves crushed by the death-dealing jaws! Woe to the crustaceans massacred by the crashing tail! The crocodile has gone mad. Woe to the world the saurian's broad vision found in the water! Woe to the fish swept up as with an electric net! Woe to the waters beaten into whirlwinds of transparent scales! Woe to the astonished eyes encrusted in coral bushes! The crocodile is dressed in bloody light. The crocodile has gone mad. Mad, the crocodile.

In the night of Wizards, Bulu-Bulu sliced through the silence.

"Many people had reason to believe it was an invasion of crocodiles and men. Or Longtails. Or Cursed Ones. In the shape of crocodiles and men."

The Colonel stated, sententiously:

"It was only one man. A Crocodile-Man."

"Others thought that, too. They said that without a doubt it was you. You, in that form. Which hasn't been seen again for a long time."

"They didn't see the girls again either, right?"

"They didn't. They'd turned to smoke, too. Chepa forever. Only Clotilde came back. But the way she came back! It would have been better if she hadn't returned."

A smell of roasted plantains and freshly made coffee crawled up their noses. Dominga appeared in one of the windows.

"Would you like some coffee, Don Candelario?"

"You don't have to ask. I'm always ready for some."

"I'll bring it right down."

The presence of Dominga—Dominga lodestone-sex—was a parenthesis. She passed between them. Went back up. While he was savoring the coffee, Bulu-Bulu was still upset. What was the Colonel really after? To tell him what he, if he didn't know it detail by detail, at least imagined in general terms? Doubtless there were other facts. Why was he taking so long in getting to them? Curiosity got the better of him again.

"And was that all, Colonel?"

"No, Bulu-Bulu. Only the beginning. I've come to see you about something that's been happening during the past few days. Something which, if it hadn't happened to me—and kept on happening to me—I wouldn't have believed..."

"Ahhh!..."

"...and it has to do with the Quindales. With Chepa, that is."

"The way things turn out, eh?"

"You know that I was up in arms for several years. With my iron machete I punished sea and jungle."

"Yes. We've heard something about it here."

"From one side to the other. From the mountains to the Gulf. My bed was always a boat or a horse. And when I spent the night somewhere it was never the same place two nights in a row. Of course, sometimes I changed my bed to different places on the same night."

"I understand, Colonel."

"Well, then, two years ago on a ranch called 'The Fireflies' I was asleep. Suddenly I was awakened by footsteps. And a voice that I recognized immediately: 'Candelario! Candelario! It's me!...' Come, Bulu-Bulu! Let's see if you can guess who it was!"

"Chepa... maybe?"

"There's good reason for your being a witch doctor, Bulu-Bulu. Yes. It was none other than Chepa!"

He leaped to his feet. He picked up his machete. He waited. Chepa kept on advancing.

"Stop right there!" he shouted at her. "Or I'll curl your skin!"

She kept on advancing. She laughed, with a certain cynicism.

"Stop being a fool, Candelario. Don't you want me anymore? Or do I make you afraid?"

"Nobody makes me what you said. Just so you'll see, here's my blade. Take it! If my time has come, well, then I'll dance on my finger!"

He held out his weapon to her. She didn't take it. She kept on coming closer.

"Oh, you're still just as stupid as ever, Candelario! Haven't you figured out yet why I've come?"

"To get your vengeance, right?"

"Why?"

"Do you know what I did to the Old Ones and Clotilde?"

"I know everything!"

"So?"

"You did it because of me, didn't you? Because you loved me. Because you wanted us to wrestle with our pissy-places..."

"That's right!"

"What have I got to complain about? It was my fault for not paying any attention to you. At first you loved me in the right way..."

Without another word she got into the bed...

Candelario was talking without looking at the Wizard. Recalling the events as if for himself. Only at that moment did he seem to notice his presence. He turned to him.

"No matter what happens, I have to tell you, Bulu-Bulu, that

I never met a female like her. The she-devil seemed to have termites between her legs. So hard. So firm. Living rubber. At first, when she took off her last piece of clothing and stuck to me, I had such an attack of trembling that I don't have to tell you. I couldn't even touch her. So unexpected. So desired. So spirited she was, that it was enough to make the biggest ram of a man back off! I'm that kind of man, but I had goose pimples thinking that I'd be too small. That I wouldn't be able to satisfy her. That I wouldn't be able to calm her delayed desires. There wasn't even time to talk. She left at dawn. She refused to stay a moment longer. I begged her in vain. I threatened her in vain. Finally, she laughed: 'Oh, Candelario, you're still just as well-now-then as you were before. Didn't you like it? Be happy with what I give you...' On the next night the same thing. And the next. And the next. And the next. And so on, every night since then..."

"Every night?"

"Every one. Even now."

"And don't you ever see her in the daytime?"

"Never. No matter how much I try to find her. No matter how much I've asked her and asked people about her. Nobody knows anything. Nobody has ever seen her."

"How strange!"

"That's not what's strange."

"Is there still more?"

"A little more. A week ago, I had to pass by 'The Fireflies' again..."

There he found the same people who had put him up before. Among them the Foreman. A certain Casimiro Caliche. When the latter saw him he came over.

"I'm glad I found you, Colonel! I wanted to ask you..."

"Tell me, sir."

"Are you from Santorontón?"

"Yes, sir. Why?"

"Did you know the people named Quindales?"

He put himself on guard.

"I did. What about it?"

"Nothing. Just that I was married to Chepa. Chepa Quindales! May God keep her in his holy glory!"

He had made an effort to control himself.

"What's that? Has Chepa passed on?"

"Yes, Colonel. When you stopped the last time she was dying.

When she heard you'd arrived, she told me that you came from the same place. That she'd known you since you were a boy. That I should be careful with you. That you're the Son of The One We Know. The things people say in their last moments!"

Since he didn't believe him, he asked him to show him her grave. He said so he could put some flowers on it. The other one took him. Indeed, there was the little dead one. Or there she should have been, if it wasn't another trick of the she-devil. There was a sign nailed to the cross.

JOSEFA QUINDALES DE CALICHE

And the date. More than two years before...

The Wizard babbled:

"I never heard that dead people could do things like that."

"I never did either."

There was a brief pause. Bulu-Bulu broke it.

"After that, has she still come after you?"

"With more desire than before."

"And didn't it make you afraid?"

"Afraid? Never. Worried. Only worried. That when I found out she was dead I wouldn't be able to do anything with her anymore. I was wrong. I give it to her like a drum at a party. But I'm tired now. I swear to everyone, I'm waiting for the day when she'll go back to her hole. That's how ungrateful we are. When honey pours into our mouths we miss the stings..."

He looked at the Wizard anxiously. He went on:

"That's why I've come to see you, Bulu-Bulu. I want you to get her out of my bed. Let her go warm up the dead, if that's what she's good for. Get her to leave me alone. You, who are such a good witch doctor, Bulu-Bulu, you can get rid of her for me, can't you?"

The Wizard—Monkey Face, as his rivals called him—smiled mysteriously.

"If they're things from down here, of course I can get rid of her for you, Colonel! If not, the cure can only come from up above."

He pointed upward in a vague way. Perhaps beyond the bijao leaves of his house. Or, maybe, beneath the roof, on the floor that was warmed up, without a doubt, by the human fire irradiating from Dominga.

SEVEN

The zinc roof played a decisive role in Crisóstomo Chalena's existence. In the same way a role was played—according to what was spread about by viper tongues in low voices—by The One We Know. It was during the time the latter was still involved with Pancha the Mule. It was even stated that Chalena aided that abnormal love-making. Among other things, he let them have the corral behind his house. Some stated that he did it out of pure pleasure. Putting such a forbidden spectacle within range of his eyes. —Those frightful encounters between the Mule and The Malignant One must have been forbidden!— People with looser tongues or more morbid imaginations assured others that they had watched Crisóstomo Chalena in his deviant duties. He would climb trees. He would watch from on top of the walls. "I swear by the Crucified Lord!" It was a matter, in any case, of visions that were enough to raise one's hair. All things considered, maybe it would be worth it to swallow the sin—it must have been a sin!—if, in exchange, one could watch The One We Know in absurd congress with the Mule. How did it take place? Did he change himself into a Beast with a flaming tongue, with tail, wings, and horns? Did he grow in size until he became a giant? Or did only his tool grow so that he could work the Shameless One from behind? After all, what could Mandinga's tool be like? Black and sinewy like a chonta wood trunk? Long and bony like a plump viper? Did it light up, a torch on a dark night? Or was it smooth and slippery, like a big-headed mullet?... All in all, the majority of those who wagged their tongues were of the opinion that what was dominant with Crisóstomo Chalena was self-interest. A base interest. Perhaps it wasn't in the corral where Old Longtail rolled about with the Mule. It was in the host's own bed. Everything there was the fruit of sin. The Mule, for example, didn't stay on all fours like other mules. Rather, she lay down with her feet up. Just like a woman who had become a beast of burden. Or just the opposite. And in that way she let herself be ridden. Can you say ridden when Old Longtail was mounting her and beating at her insides with his tool? Can you say insides? Does the path to the insides with the Mule begin between her legs? Be that as it may—they reaffirmed—what was certain was that the monstrous thrashing took place in Crisóstomo's own bed. The latter received two compensations for it. First, the enjoyment of seeing those frightful nuptials from close up. And second, enjoying the benefits of the loan of the bed. The returns were soon evident. One day, for example, when the Santorontonians were facing the sea throwing their harpoons, a strange thing happened. Before Crisóstomo appeared on the beach there were no fish to be seen anywhere around. As soon as That One's Friend appeared, however, a huge corvina began to break water. They all tried to harpoon it. A vain effort. The corvina made his leaps. He sank into the water. And he only reappeared at the moment when Crisóstomo held a two-pronged harpoon in his hands. The fish came so close that it almost ran aground on the sand. The Lucky One raised the two-pronged weapon with both hands. He threw it. And it immediately reappeared, floating. He pulled it in and caught on those selfsame tips—silver encrusted with rose petals—was the beautiful denizen of the water. By a curious coincidence, three strangers were going about looking for corvinas, giant corvinas. And they paid—rather, they overpaid—for the catch.

That was how Crisóstomo Chalena started out on the gray itinerary of his fortune. The shadow of The Other One protected him at all times. Not only did the best-paying and biggest fish appear on his arrival. Not only was he surrounded by crustaceans coming out of their holes, raising their claws in clamorous reverence. Not only did bivalves renounce their existence with calcareous applause. Buyers also appeared on all roads and at all moments. Curiously, the other Santorontonians seemed to be following the opposite path. The more fish the Friend of Old Longtail got, the fewer they caught. And if by chance—through the latter's carelessness—they had an appreciable catch. Or pulled out hundreds of crustaceans, sinking their hands into the hollows of the mud. Or filled baskets with bivalves, letting them nap in the nooks along the shore . . . they would probably have to eat them all themselves! Or, on some occasions, give them back to the sea if they were still alive! Buyers no longer appeared. Or they had bought all they needed. From Crisóstomo Chalena, naturally. He began to fatten his purse. He no longer went along the shore very much. He hired a few hours of work from his former companions. They spread—for him—the nets in the coves. Or at the mouth of the inlet. Or they threw hand nets. Or they sank harpoons. But—everything was known in Santorontón—soon fishing didn't seem to be enough for the Partner's Partner.

One fine day—how many, how many years had passed?—the whole town was shaken by the news: a sloop had arrived. A large sloop. The kind that travels from the already brackish waters of rivers out to the green routes of the ocean. It didn't bring food. Or barrels of lard. Or sacks of rice. Or bunches of bananas. It came, however, riding low in the water. What could it be carrying? Curiosity made men and women prowl along the shore. The sloop was rocking like a sleeping pelican. It had anchored far out. Where there was no danger to its damaged keel. Or to its fat belly with who knows what kind of heavy material. Soon the Friend of Old Longtail was seen heading out to it. He was riding in a rudder canoe—the only one that could be found in the whole town. When he got to the sloop, he leaped aboard. He exchanged a few words with the Skipper, who came out to meet him. The Skipper turned to his men. He gave some orders. At once they began the operations to lift the heavy cargo out of the hold. It came in large wooden crates. Their weight must have been excessive. The sailors put the thick hooks that hung from the hoists around the metal cinches. They began to pull on the ends of the ropes. Little by little, they brought up the first of the crates. The Skipper moved the short boom from which the steel cables hung. The load swung toward the boat. As it dropped, it tilted dangerously. Don Crisóstomo took off his straw hat. He scratched his head. He showed displeasure. He looked all around with his tiny eyes, as if asking for help. And—as it seemed to the Santorontonians—he even made a signal to The One We Know. Of course, not even a shadow of the latter was to be seen. What is certain is that suddenly the fat-bellied sailing ship began to rise up in the water. As if it had been pushed from underneath. Soon the whole hull was out of the water. Until it barely grazed the water with its keel. The Skipper looked in amazement at what had happened. Then he looked at Chalena, whose tiny figure seemed to have grown taller. Don Crisóstomo didn't say anything. Then the Skipper signaled the sailors. They weighed anchor. They half-hoisted the foresail and the jib on the jib-boom. The Santorontonians looked at each other, worried. Was the sloop going to sail away? Had the crew become frightened? They were wrong. The sloop headed toward shore. The helmsman, gripping the tiller, turned to his men.

"Let's go, boys! So we can get away from here while it's still daylight! I don't like this at all!"

The sailors—not too sure of their actions—put the hook to another of the crates. How great was their surprise to find that they scarcely weighed anything now. They could lift them by hand, without using the apparatus or the cables. Just as if they had been changed into bundles of balsa wood. For their part, the loaders that Don Crisóstomo had brought didn't have to put the cargo in the rudder canoe. They only used it as a bridge. With their arms raised, each carrying a crate, they walked to the beach and put them down there. The spectators, for their part, crossed themselves. All of it, without a doubt, bore the mark of Old Longtail. The foolish dialogue drifted about just like canoes that move around in the sleepy waters when the tide changes.

"Look how well-sir-now Don Chalena is acting, right?"

"The worst part was selling his soul to The One We Know."

"Did he really sell? Can you sell your soul?"

"Who knows!"

"Would you sell your soul, Mister?"

"Not me. I'd only rent it."

"Anybody can do that. But what would Old Longtail say? Do you think he's satisfied with just a rented soul?"

"I don't know. What I do know is that I'd only rent it. And only if everything turned out the way it did for Candanga's Partner."

"Even if he's on the road to damnation."

"That's right. Right now, for example . . ."

"I wonder what he's bringing in behind those boards."

"God only knows!"

"I think it's zinc."

"You're right. Look!"

They had opened the first crate. Piled up, one on top of the other, were the sheets of corrugated metal. As soon as the last one was unpacked, Don Crisóstomo gave the impression of shrugging his shoulders and returning to his normal proportions. He came back over the canoe. It was untied from the sloop, which, in turn, hoisted full sail: the mainsail, the foresail, the jib, and even the topsail. It picked up speed almost immediately. And it dropped down beyond the horizon. As if hundreds of Longtails were hauling it below.

The collective dialogue kept bobbing around like a buoy in a heavy sea. "Word of God, it was The One We Know." Some asserted that the wind had brought them—at certain moments—bits of infernal conversation. Of course. Of course. Mandinga was guiding him.

". . . in order to do that you have to replace the bijao roof with zinc sheets."

"Zinc is very expensive."

"Don't be a fool, Crisóstomo. Do as I tell you. You'll soon see that you won't even know how to thank me enough."

That was all they had heard. Maybe the wind had changed. Or the Partners had lowered their voices. Or maybe everything had already been talked about before. It was sufficient, that was true, to keep on stimulating the chorus of Santorontonians:

"What would he want a zinc roof for?"

"What for? Well, who knows! It certainly stands up better, but it's hotter."

"And here by the sea it rusts fast."

"Maybe because it's more expensive. Since he's got money now. Lots of money!"

"He's not one to throw his money away."

"No. Not that."

They soon discovered the reason. Or at least the immediate reason. When it was put on, they saw that along all the lower edges of the roof he had large gutters placed. The slant would obviously make the water pour into the four pipes placed at the four corners. In turn, under each of the pipes they built large tanks. That bothered them even more. Could Don Chalena be going soft in the head? What did he need to collect rainwater for? Of course, Santorontón, like all that section of the coast, was very dry. Still, it had an advantage. Nearby—inland or on the neighboring island of Balumba—there were some freshwater wells. From there water was carried to the town in large wooden casks. Empty lard barrels. From inland by having the barrels roll down from the high points that made that possible. Or with an axle in the middle of the barrels to convert them into rolling stock, pulled by men or donkeys. Those wells were almost at ground level. On the other hand, the one on Balumba was a very deep well. It had a wooden plank across it. From there they dropped buckets down, swaying them, to pull out the water. Then they carried it in canoes. They, too, had large barrels in the center. Therefore, then, they couldn't explain what The Other One's Partner aimed to do—and was doing.

"He has all the canoes he needs."

"And the people. And he can pay well."

"That's right. Even people who don't want to work for him have to do it in order to earn a little more."

"What for, then?"

"Maybe it's just the opposite. Because he doesn't want to spend any more, not even for hauling water."

"In this way?"

"Of course. If the water falls out of the sky for him and he can store it up, why does he have to send out for it in the jungle or on Balumba?"

"Aha!"

"Besides, they say that sky water is the best there is."

In addition to that, their attention was called to the amount of zinc which had arrived. After they had roofed Crisóstomo Chalena's own house, there was a goodly pile left over. They put it in the yard behind the house. And that was all. Salustiano Caldera and Rugel Banchaca—among the most talkative of the Santorontonians—were worried, as is natural.

"I wonder what he's going to do with so much zinc?"

"That's right. What's he going to do with it? I don't think he's keeping it for when what he's just put on rusts or wears out."

"Is he going to build a bigger house or a shed?"

"What for?"

"With the ideas he's got now he might want to salt the fish and store it there. The way he monopolizes everything."

"I repeat. What for? Everything he buys from us they buy from him. Right here. Just the way it is. Fresh. Just caught. Sometimes even flopping in the nets."

"That's right."

Rugel Banchaca lowered his voice. Confidential.

"Do you know something, Salustiano?"

The one addressed imitated his tone:

"What?"

"I think Don Chalena wants to put roofs on other houses."

"What others? He's only got one."

"He wants to buy more. He's going around feeling people out. Hasn't he said anything to you yet?"

"Not to me. What about you?"

"He has to me. He wants to buy my house. And I heard that he's going to buy all the other big houses in town. To roof all of them with zinc."

"You don't say! What did you tell him?"

"No."

"And was he calm?"

"He laughed. 'You're all screwed up, Banchaca,' he told me. 'All right, all right, don't sell it to me. Just rent it to me!' 'I won't do that either,' I answered him. 'Where will I go with my Skinmate and the children?' He laughed, happily. 'Oh, Banchaca! You've always got something to say. Rent me your roof, then.'"

"Your roof?"

"That's what I asked him. And he nodded: 'Yes, sir. Your roof. To cover it with zinc and collect water.'"

"What does he want so much water for?"

"I asked him that, too. He got serious. 'That's none of your business.' He smiled again. 'Maybe to take a lot of baths. Or to do some planting. Or to do whatever I feel like doing...'"

"Don Chalena's changed a lot, hasn't he?"

"That's right."

"And was that all?"

"I still tried to get out of it. 'Zinc is very hot in the daytime and cold at night. My Skinmate and the children are going to roast when the sun is up. And we'll all freeze when it's dark.'

'Don't worry about that, Banchaca. Leave your bijao roof where it is. I'll put the zinc on top of it. In that way you won't be so hot or so cold.' "

"What did you end up doing?"

"What could I do, Don Caldera? You can't help but bite the catfish when it's put in your mouth. I accepted!"

"I'll be damned!"

"And I think that almost all the owners of large houses he talked to are either selling or renting them to him. Or at least they're renting the roofs."

"I don't like this foolishness one little bit."

"Don't you think they might be schemes of Old Longtail to mess us up? He's sticking his tail in everything."

"Aha! Because what Christian would ever think of storing up all the water out of the sky?"

"In Santorontón, at least, where there are so many freshwater wells close by."

The night of the day on which the last house was roofed with zinc, a strange thing happened: it rained heavily. It was still the middle of summer. In the afternoon there wasn't a cloud in sight. And nothing seemed to foretell what was going to happen. The Santorontonians woke up in a fright. The thick drops of water, as they fell on the corrugated metal, produced a fearful din. As if the skies were falling on the town. Some went to the windows. The slanting darkness—cut across by the spattering drops—was impenetrable. When they saw that, even if they couldn't sleep, they went back to their deerskins or mats. Only a few stayed looking out, trying to pierce the darkness with their anguish. At dawn, the Santorontonians were even more startled. It had only rained on the zinc roofs. The pipes were still dripping and the tanks were overflowing. On the other hand, the dry, thirsty leaves of the bijao roofs seemed to be leaning over to look at the strange spectacle. Not a single drop had fallen on them. They began to waddle from one side to the other. There was no explanation—there couldn't be—for what had happened. This time there were no comments. They simply looked and looked again at those enormous tanks where the water was still pouring out. One of those who had stood looking out his window seemed full of doubts. Finally he made up his mind. He told them that what had rained had not been rain. That the water there had been hauled in. He, in the shadows—with his eyes that one day would be dust and ashes—had seen dozens of giant birds come, each with a bucket in his claws. All at the same time, they poured out the contents. And then they went back to fill them up again. He hadn't mentioned it before because he hadn't been too certain. Certain that it wasn't rain, yes. Certain that it had been carried through the air, too. On the other hand, he couldn't say for certain that they had been birds. Sometimes they didn't look like birds. They looked, rather, like The Ones We Know. He couldn't tell—the night was so dark!—whether they had tails and horns—God protect us from the seven thousand horns!—though he could swear that he saw the wings, the buckets, and the water. And, also, that fire was coming out of their eyes. But aren't there birds that have fire coming out of their eyes? Or mightn't they have been bats? His words were received as the true explanation. Don Chalena, wasn't he the Partner's Partner? Wasn't he getting help from Him all the time? The only thing they needed to know now was what use the Partners—they were Partners, weren't they?—were going to make of the water they had collected. Conjectures flourished when several Santorontonians arrived back in town. Some came from the jungle, wherc they had gone to fill their barrels with water. They brought them back empty. They stated that the well had unexpectedly gone dry the night before. Others came from Balumba, Bulu-Bulu's island. They, too, brought back a barrel dry at dawn. When they listened to the ones who had just arrived, they looked at each other with growing fear. Even though it was brackish, could the well on the Quindales farm have gone dry too?

EIGHT

A spiral of ice and blood. Was it night? The Moon stretched out its wire claws. She saw them through the wild underbrush. A sweetish smell of death. Threads of halted blood. Garlands of broken muscles. Weariness. A wish to sleep. To keep on sleeping. Forever. The pain of a thousand teeth sinking into her body. Strongest halfway up her legs. Green cat claws in her eyes. To see or not to see. To see herself. Naked. A zigzag of torn clothing. Eyes. Teeth. Hands. The hands—butterflies of fire—turning her over. Seeing him on top. Not seeing him. Not seeing anything. And feeling him. Still feeling him. A dream? Seeing him. Seeing him? The Evil One! Was he The Evil One? No. The son of The Evil One. Dancing around her—lying down—on top of her. A dream? Still a dream? But what about the pain? The flames inside of her? A fire? A fire that was kindled in her deepest parts? There. Sinking into her. A bar. Iron? Fire? Flesh? Sinking into her. He, dancing—lying down—on top of her. Going off. Going off into the air. In tears. In death. To weep? To shout? Defend herself? The sweetish smell of fragmented viscera. Scattered intestines. Skulls slipping into premature laughter. Green dough. Red. Brown. Black. The volatile hair. The spasm in the hands. The bar driving in. Opening up her flesh. The bar of pins. Boiling pins. Opening a groove in her. He, dancing—lying down—on top of her. She, passive. She, wood. She, clay. Quiet. Mute. No flesh. No nerves. No tears. No blood. No sight. No ears. A dream? Nothing. Silence. An invisible fan blowing no's on her. A growing silence.

Sleeping clay. Dead clay. Had he left? Chase him. Arms. Find him. Tear him to pieces. Turn him to smoke. He, smoke? Smoke. Smoke. Smoke.

She got up. Staggering. She advanced. She trod, not realizing it, on the shapeless form of the dead ones. The two dead ones. The two dead Old Ones. Her Old Woman and her Old Man dead. From them she saw. From them she breathed. From them she anointed herself. From them she flooded herself. Not realizing it. Not seeing them. Smoke. Turn him into smoke. She went down the steps. She chewed on the new air. Was he walking? Was he flying? Was he crawling? A thousand tongues of earth. Licking her. Caressing her. Renewing her. A thousand green tongues. Jabbing her. Pinching her. Smoke. Turn him to smoke. "Clotilde!" Who? Where? "Clotilde!" She brought her eyes back. Or did she have them in the back of her neck? She looked. A crocodile. Out of the water. Advancing. A copper-ivory gesture. "Clotilde!" Coming closer. Another voice. A red-white-black voice. "Clotilde!" A jaguar. Breaking out of the green cage. The green wind. Other shouts. "Clotilde! Clotilde! Clotilde!" Two heads on each one: head and glans. Six heads: glans and head. "No! No more!" All trying to dance on top of her. Not sink in their claws, their teeth. Not to devour her. To dance on her. Only to dance on top of her. Lying down. Dance on her. Dance on top of her lying down. A bat? A Longtail? Many Longtails? Old Longtail, is he one and many? "No! No!" Smoke. Turn him to smoke. Run. From the zoomorphic jungle to the vegetable jungle. To the green heart of the jungle. Among the green teeth of the leaves. The trees? The trees, too? All and everything trying—lying down—to dance on top of her. All and everything colored sex. Crocodile-sex. Jaguar-sex. Monkey-sex. Tin-Tin-sex. Tree-sex. A rain of sexes. Falling on top of her. From everywhere. At every moment. Flee. Where? They would catch her. They were catching her. They were jumping on top of her. Lying down. "Clotilde!" Sexes in a garland. "Clotilde!" Sexes in a weave. "Clotilde!" A prison of sexes. Where to go? How to go? When to go? Impossible. They followed her. They were following her. They would follow her. A hundred crocodiles. A hundred jaguars. A hundred monkeys. A hundred Tin-Tins. A hundred bats. A hundred trees. They were jumping on top of her—lying down. They were climbing up her. They were dancing on top of her—lying down—one after the other.

How long? "Clotilde! Clotilde! Clotilde!!" Had she better go back to the house? What house? No. Better to seek refuge in San. Santo. Santoron. Santorontón.

In Santorontón. After vengeance. A single thought. A single orbit. After vengeance. On all of them. On all men. All of them are The Evil One. The Evil One is in all men. The Evil One is all men. On the beach. At night. Always at night. In the bars. Waiting for men. The men who come out—alcohol in their veins, a wave in their minds. Waiting for them at the end of the glass roads. Taking them—one by one—to dark places. The darkest. There to offer herself to the Man–Evil One—or Evil One–Man—by turns.

"But you're just a girl, Clotilde."

"Try me."

"But you haven't even got any teats yet, Clotilde."

"Try me."

"But you're a dry dugout canoe."

"Try me."

"But you don't even know how to wiggle your hips."

"Try me."

"You're going to break like a clay jar, Clotilde."

"Try me."

"What if Don Atanasio finds out?"

"He can't hear anything any more."

"Or Doña Eduva?"

"She can't hear either."

"Or Chepa?"

"What difference does it make!"

What could the Man do? What could he do? Alcohol sizzled in his eyes, hands, mouth. As he touched her it sizzled in other parts of his body. He didn't have to lay her down. Or make the least effort. She dropped first. She opened up like a fallen papaya. He danced on her—lying down on top of her—like The Other One. Like the Son of The Other One, rather. Isn't he in all men? Aren't all men he? When the lying-down dance ended—and the Man was lost in the void for an instant—she did a strange thing. A dagger flashed in her right hand. She put both hands under the person topping her. And before he had time to notice, she guillotined his testicles with one quick stroke. The one attacked tried to act. Enveloped in waves of pain and rage, he roared in despair. He reacted. He stood up in a red self-bath. "Curse you! You fucked me!" He tried to grab her. By the hair. By the arms. By the legs. "Curse you!" Impossible to grab her. She—leaping like a deer—dressed herself in shadows. Holding her trophy high. Toward the jungle. Facing the carrousel of astonished green eyes. The libido-sick flora and fauna no longer chased her. They made way for her instead. Radioscopy from up in the limbs. Through a million crossings of branches. In the zigzag of scales crawling along the ground. She walked through violet clouds. Holding the trophy high. They all made way for her. Following the long wandering path to her cave. She lived in a cave. From that night on—the night when the Son of Old Longtail had pierced her deepest flower—she lived in a cave. When she arrived she took the trophy. She ran a vine through it. She hung it from one of the stone outcroppings.

After the first trophy came more. More. More. Many more. As word spread through the region, men no longer wanted to go out alone. They avoided the night hours. Solitary places. The darkness. Since many of them did not know Clotilde, they were unable to give an exact description of her. Those who knew her, on the other hand, were ashamed of having climbed onto a young girl. So imagination and legend soon wove their nets of froth. A froth which, like night-blooming cereus, had different forms and colors. For some she was a huge woman. With hair of ebony twigs. Eyes like soapberry seeds. Absorbent lips. For others, just the opposite, she was a small woman. Hair of hedgehog quills. Honeyed eyes. A mouth of snow. All of them, it was true, agreed that she had breasts like gourds. Hard. Erect. And hips that swayed like a small boat. She went about naked. She attracted, like a living magnet of flesh. When she spoke to them and touched them, they lost their will. They had to surrender—lying down—to the absurd cumbersome dance. Whether they wanted to or not, they mounted her. They rubbed against her. There was no escape. In the end—when they least expected it—the demoniacal cut. Their virile parts forever lost. The sudden flight of the Headswoman. Could she be the Evil Woman? Or was it The One We Know who was taking on female form now to destroy them? Those who didn't know that it was Clotilde asked if it might not be one of the Old Quindales' daughters. Since their parents had been murdered they had disappeared. Candelario Mariscal had disappeared too, naturally. Couldn't he have been going about with his tail—because he had to have a tail—mixed up in all of that? Those who knew it was Clotilde acted like hipshot pigs and were silent. Or, on the other hand, helped the others' doubts increase. So men kept on falling between Clotilde's legs. As had been established, they paid their tribute with their own flesh. Now, almost always, they were outsiders. Come to buy something from Chalena. To do some business in Santorontón. Or simply passing through. To the Great City that nestled in the cradle of the Gulf. There the two rivers were that gave birth at their death to the Great River with long white locks and beard. Or toward the green-violet-gray horizons of the sea. Where sails sink down in a trice and disappear. Some were forewarned. They had been told about the mysterious woman—imagination and legend continued to drift along—who could change, as if she were many women. Who had an insatiable sex—how could it be otherwise, since it was made from several women superimposed? An entwining sex. Amphibious. A sex with brown-blue teeth. Teeth that bit, the way dogs bite the moon's reflection in the water. That produced a rosary of shudderings impossible to describe. To be with her was to be with a woman from the other world. But it had to be paid for. She had a price. Leaving one's virile parts behind in her hands. Unable to be with any other woman anymore. All of that rarely held back the man who had been warned. On the contrary, it produced a strong stimulation. Besides, a hope breathed deep down in everyone. What if it would be different with him? What if she responded to his caresses with caresses that rendered her harmless? If she left him unharmed and, even more, if she changed, from then on, into a woman like all other women? A vain hope. Nothing and nobody—as it seemed—would ever succeed in changing her. Days passed, weeks and months. And Clotilde kept on with her criminal cuts! Protected by the sinuous grimaces of the darkness, she sank back into the jungle every time. While she approached the refuge of her cave great odors sank their yellow fangs into her. When she was inside—holding her trophy high as always—the first thing she did was to look around. Hanging from the stone outcroppings—absurd Chinese decorations—were the male attributes. Satisfied, she draped the most recent one among the others. A feeling of triumph and happiness began to come over her. Sometimes her exaltation and joy would grow. Her eyes would dress themselves in a trim of colored knives. A hundred loud trumpets turned over in her mind. Her hands held vegetable cobwebs out. Soft flowers held the mutilated sexes. She dressed in them. She hummed melodies. A potpourri of strange melodies. And to the rhythm of her tangled notes—hot honey from a moquiñaña—she followed the absurd steps of an erotic dance. Fatigue—physical and mental—finally conquered her. She lay down. She slept. Wrapped in those sex pieces. When she awoke and took in the macabre spectacle she felt ineffable. Her vengeance continued. Her vengeance! Vengeance on The Evil One! The Son of The Evil One! And all men. Because The Evil One is in all men. Especially in the sex of all men. Suddenly a bell rang in her ears: "It's not out of vengeance." "Oh, no?" "It's for the salvation of womankind. All womankind. So men won't have things to harm them with."

The Santorontonians, those who were whole and those who no longer were, saw themselves in a situation where they would have "to take measures." If it had only been a matter of their wills, they might never have done so. But the problem of the Santorontonian women had arisen. What pretexts could they give them to avoid the fulfillment of their conjugal duties? How could they exhibit the ridiculous stump that was left them in a place where an instrument had stood erect before? There was nothing left to do but confess the misfortunes of a tragic adventure. When they found out, the women puffed up with hysteria. What upset them most was that it concerned Clotilde. So that little snot who'd never even squashed a clam was the cause of all their problems and misfortunes. For some—the incomplete men—it was too late. On the other hand, the others were at the point of being saved. Each one of the women, however, demanded that her man join the others. And that they do something. Their husbands, in the end, had to reach some decision. They met. The first thing, of course, was to make sure that it was Clotilde. It took a great deal to convince the disbelievers.

"It can't be. She's just a little girl. She hasn't got enough meat to make a tamale out of."

"You just wait and see!"

"I don't think it could be her."

"Oh, no?"
"It has to be The One We Know. Maybe she's got him inside of her."
"Could be. Well, then, what can we do?"
"First, tell everything to Father Cándido."
"Don't you think he already knows?"
"Maybe. We'll tell him in any case. To see what he thinks."
No sooner said than done. They went up to the door of the church in a troop. What was left of the church, rather. They knocked. The Priest came out.
"What do you want?"
They explained it to him in a few words. At first he couldn't believe it.
"Are you sure?"
"Quite sure, Father."
Since doubt still showed on his face, one of them hinted:
"Would you like to look at us, Father?"
"No. That's not necessary. I believe you. Wait a moment."
He went into the church. He went over to the Comrade of the Cross.
"Did you hear?"
Jesus turned his head, displeased.
"If they didn't have such dirty minds, they wouldn't be lamenting."
"The flesh is weak."
"Yes. That's true."
"And you should forgive them, shouldn't you?"
"That's true. Especially knowing how stupid they are."
"I'm glad you think that way, because I'm going to propose that you . . ."
"You're not going to ask me to intervene in something like this, are you?"
"What do you think?"
"I've done too much already by just listening to you."
"Aren't you the Son of God? Aren't you on this Earth to help us?"
"All right. All right."
And lifting his arms up to heaven, he called out:
"Father: Why don't you take me down from this Cross once and for all?"

It was Cándido who took him down, Cross and all, from the new table he had got him. He picked him up. Carried him to the door. There he addressed the Santorontonians.

"Let's go!"

"Where, Father?"

"To find Clotilde."

"Whatever you say, Father."

"Whatever you say."

"Whatever you say."

Some of the young men came forward.

"Can we help you?"

"That wouldn't be a bad idea. This Cross gets heavier every day."

Christ whispered so that only he could hear.

"I carried it all the way to Golgotha, remember?"

He muttered:

"Yes. The Cross. Only the Cross. But now, as a bonus, we're carrying you too, since you're nailed to it."

The women were joining them along the way. The strange procession headed by the Priest with the Cross on his back—helped this time by four young men—began to guide itself by Clotilde's tracks. The strange thing was that they weren't tracks marked on the ground. Rather, they seemed to avoid it. They were tracks opened in the brush. Trampled weeds. Torn bushes. Wounded branches. Could she be alone? Were there several women? Was she with Chepa, at least? They would soon know. The sound of their steps. The blows of machetes and axes which they sometimes used to open a way for the Cross. The thousand voices of the jungle announcing the arrival of the troop of people. All of it made the silence of the men more impressive. The majority of them were crossing themselves. They imagined the skinny girl's travels through the night. How was she able to go through the monstrous green tangle? Wasn't she afraid of the fangs and claws lying in wait along the way? How could she find her way through the gabble of darkness? Yes. They were more and more certain: Old Longtail was in her. He dominated her. She had to obey him. As if he had pecked out her eyes and sown her ears with mist. Who knows, maybe she was protected—by Himself—against everything! It couldn't be any other way!

When they reached the cave—wrapped in the nauseating sea-green cloak—nothing was there, nobody. Clotilde—or whoever it was—and the virile attributes were no longer there. Perhaps the cave was digesting them—or had already digested them—in its grim mineral intestines.

NINE

Candelario Mariscal rose up in arms in a way that was most peculiarly his own. He supposed that even his godfather would intervene after what he had done to the Quindales. His drunkenness—from spite, sex, and liquor—would never be an extenuating circumstance. For that reason he would try to spread distance between Santorontón and his person. To do so he took advantage of one of the swift canoes that carried fish to the city. The fishermen had barred the estuary of Los Nigüitos. The tide was already going out. Very soon, living silver, the scales would accumulate at the foot of the stakes. The canoe would draw near. In the blink of an eye it would fill up with fish. The fugitive didn't give them time. He drew near—crocodile—swimming up to the prow. The oarsmen were asleep. There were two of them. They were doubtless waiting for the fishermen to call them at the precise instant. Candelario—man—climbed into the boat. One of the oarsmen woke up.

"Is it time?"

"Sh! Be quiet!"

When he recognized Candelario he was frightened:
"Don Mariscal!"
"The very same. And hurry up. Let's get out of here!"
"Where to?"
"Wherever I feel like."
"What about the fish?"
"Hurry up!"
As he said it, his machete made the sound of death. The other oarsman woke up.
"What's going on?"
His companion explained:
"Don Mariscal wants us to take him away from here."
"Where to?"
"Anywhere! As far away from here as possible! Right now!"
The other looked at him out of the corner of his eye. Mocking.
"Give us a break!"
Candelario's machete collected a life. With a leap, it sank into his head. No explosion, no moan. The head fell like a rock into a well. The attacker turned to the survivor.
"So! What do you say?"
"Whatever you want, Don."
"That's fine! First help me throw him overboard."
The two of them picked up the dead man. They threw him into the water. A splash was heard that made the taut surface boil with scales and bubbling. Then nothing. The Priest's Godson gave another command:
"Now, let's go, let's catch the wind!"
Each one picked up a paddle. Clutched it, stabbing the water. The canoe gave a leap. It took on a mustache of foam. It seemed to rise up on that side. And then it shot forward—a huge harpoon—into the womb of the darkness.

By dawn they were already far away. Neither one had slept. They hadn't stopped rowing. The oarsman seemed dead with fatigue. He stopped for a moment. He stretched his arms. His naked torso, a sweaty mangrove trunk, tightened up. The voice of the Fugitive rang out, angrily:
"What tick is biting your balls now?"
"None, Don Mariscal."
"What's wrong, then?"
"I was drinking in a little air."

"You don't drink anything until I tell you to."
"All right, Don Mariscal."
"If not, you'll stop drinking for good!"
"Yes, Don Mariscal."
"And stop calling me Don. From here on I'm Colonel. Colonel Candelario Mariscal."
"Yes, Colonel, sir."
He immediately picked up the paddle again. They rowed in unison, as in the beginning. The oarsman on the middle seat. Candelario in the stern, steering. They went on in silence for a while longer. Without resting or slowing down the drive of the sinewy paddles. The Colonel broke the silence.
"What's your name?"
"Nicasio Canchona. They call me One-Eye. One-Eye Canchona."
When he said it, he turned his head. Indeed, he left eye was missing. Without stopping his rowing, Candelario commanded:
"From today on you won't be One-Eye Canchona anymore. You'll be Captain. Captain Canchona."
"Yes, sir, Colonel."
After a period of silence, the dashing Captain dared ask a question:
"Colonel, sir."
"What is it?"
"Can you tell me now where we're going?"
"I told you before."
"Oh. That's right, Colonel."
"Besides. It's none of your concern."
"Of course not, Colonel."
He was hungry.
"Have you got anything to eat?"
"No, sir, Colonel."
"Let's take a break, then."
"Yes, sir, Colonel."
They laid the paddles down in the bottom of the canoe.
"Haven't you got any fishing gear either?"
"No."
"I might have known, goddamn it! What have you got, then?"
"Nothing, Colonel, sir."
He tried to explain:
"We're not fishermen. We're only boatmen, that's all."

"Yes, that's true!"

He paused. Went on:

"Let's see if the mullet are biting."

Canchona looked at him in surprise.

"Have you got a hook?"

"No."

"Or bait?"

"Where would I get any bait from?"

"How are they going to bite, then?"

"Let's see if they bite at nothing."

"Ahhh!"

Captain Canchona saw his chief put his hands into the water. He began to stir it up. Just like the splashing of a heavy shower. Was he in his right mind? Catching mullet in the daytime without a casting net? If there was only a shoal at least. Because mullet . . . not even with a hook! The damned things won't bite. So you can give them all the bait you want. And trying to do it with his hands! He'd just finished with those thoughts when he saw a school of mullet approaching. There were hundreds of them. They looked like little silver bells drawn along by a maniacal tuna. In self-selection the larger ones began to group together. Not even at night, in the light of a lamp, a lantern, had he seen so many. Fins of a net network netting. Lamplighting lamp lighting up. And now under the sunlight sunning sun. They passed like arrows, piercing the water in several directions. To make things worse, they were in the River. The Great River. The Old River. "The Bearded Patriarch." The River with a greenish-gray face and a white beard. And mullet are inlet fish. From the mangrovey nooks. He was still startled. The larger, big-headed mullet grouped together, came over to the Chief's hands. Their speed diminished. Finally they stopped. The Colonel was gathering them in. Throwing them into the bottom of the canoe. When he thought he had enough he spoke to the ones waiting.

"Fine. All right. Beat it!"

The mullet seemed to be revived. They reacted. They wiggled their fins and tails. They rejoined the school. And with the same speed with which they had come, they went away. Canchona was getting afraid. Or, rather, he was even more afraid. That man wasn't a man. At least no man could ever do the things he did. Might it not be true, perhaps, that he was the Son of Old Longtail? Even though he wasn't a great believer, he felt like crossing himself. He didn't. What good would it have done him? For the moment he would wait for a good chance to flee. Because the company of Colonel Candelario Mariscal wasn't good at all. Could the one just mentioned be reading his thoughts? Who knows! He'd smiled the way crocodiles in bogs smile. He'd spoken to him in formal address.

"I want to warn you, sir, about one thing, Captain Canchona."

He, too, make an effort to smile.

"Tell me, Colonel."

He addressed him in the familiar form again.

"Don't think about trying to horse around with me."

"Don't say that, Colonel."

"You screwed yourself up by coming with me. You'll never be able to get free! Unless I want you to!"

His fierce crocodile smile was even sharper.

"It's as if I had you chained by the balls."

One-Eye shuddered. In spite of all, he didn't want to keel over.

"What's to be is to be, that's all, Colonel."

In the little stove used to smoke out termites and drive off blight, they smoked the mullet. After they finished them, they picked up their journey again.

The wild waves of the Gulf shook them, skittish deer on blue coal burning white. The Sun seemed to bathe the shores with gold cloudbursts. Soon he would hide his trembling head behind the horizon. A sloop was cutting distances with its sails, a flowing together of grasped machetes along the River.

"Do you know where we're going now?"

"No, Colonel."

He pointed to the low-slung boat that seemed halted.

"There!"

He didn't try to ask him why or what for. Did he have to ask? Wasn't he getting to know the Colonel better and better? Didn't his sinister intentions seem to flower in his tiny eyes? He nodded:

"Aha!"

"The tide will change soon. It will have to anchor near the mouth of Dead Man's Inlet. That's where we'll go."

"Yes, sir, Colonel."

A short time later the shadows matured. The tide stopped. The sloop dropped anchor near the shore. The Colonel warned:

"Whatever happens. Whatever you see. Whatever you hear, don't fall back!"

"No, sir, Colonel."

"Even if you don't understand sometimes."

"Of course, Colonel, sir."

"The only thing you have to do is obey me."

"Yes, sir, Colonel."

Without adding another word, Candelario Mariscal leaped into the water. As soon as he touched it, crocodile. He turned his head. Green now. Snouty. Horrible. He opened his toothy toothed toothladen jaws. Frightful.

"Get on my back!"

"What? What are you saying?"

"Just what you heard. Hurry up!"

On the verge of soaking his loincloth with his dregs out of simple fear. He got up. Trembling. Would he do it? Wouldn't he do it? If he stayed in the canoe he probably wouldn't be left to tell the tale. The Colonel would take his life, the way he'd done with the other one. Without hesitation. Besides, could he really do what he wanted to do? Wasn't he under the impression—even before it had been said—that he was tied by the balls? The crocodile-crocodile. Crocodilic crocodile. Crocodiled again:

"Are you coming or aren't you?"

"I'm coming, Colonel, sir!"

He leaped into the water. He got onto the back of the huge saurian. Only then did he realize that it was carrying a machete in its jaws. Without knowing why, that cheered him up.

"What about the canoe?"

"We're leaving it behind."

"But . . ."

"Don't be a horse's ass, Canchona. With me you're going to have all the sloops, canoes, and anything else you want."

"Yes, sir, Colonel."

He took a last look at the small boat. Then he looked ahead. The speed with which the saurian swam made him hold onto the almost mineral bumps of its skin. The hull of the sloop seemed to be growing. They were already alongside it. Now he was swimming near Colonel Mariscal. Now he had his human characteristics. Now they began to climb up the chain that went from the bow to the boom. One-Eye hesitated again. What if he shouted? What if he warned the sailors? If he told them it was the Colonel and what he was up to? Maybe just with the mention of his name the others would know what his aims were. He halted. Would that do him any good? Could they defeat him? Would they come under the occult power that the runaway seemed to have? Because nobody could take that away from him. The Colonel wanted room to breathe because he was running away. And without doubt the cause of his flight must have been very serious. Hadn't he killed his companion without hesitating for a single instant? Hadn't he done it because he hadn't decided to obey him at once? And he was bossy. That was the truth. Would he escape, he himself, from that invisible chain that held him prisoner? In order to convince himself, one more time, he tried to draw back. At once he felt a tug on his testicles. It was true, then. He had him tied by the most delicate of all places. He couldn't do anything. Even if he wanted to, everything was useless! Since he'd held back, the Colonel turned around, hissing at him:

"Goddamn it! Are you going to stay glued back there?"

Again he felt the painful distemper between his legs.

"I'm coming, Colonel."

He went rapidly ahead, still saying to himself:

"Now you really are screwed up, One-Eye! Screwed up for good!"

The sloop had only two crewmen: a very young sailor and the skipper. They were eating when the attackers appeared in the bow. The skipper, in spite of the fact that he was puzzled at not having heard any sound from the water, didn't wish to show any fear. He leaped to his feet.

"Hey! What's going on? Who are you people?"

One-Eye answered:

"Colonel Candelario Mariscal and his people."

"And what do you want?"

"For you to beat it."

He didn't seem to understand.

"To what?"

"To beat it and give us the sloop."

The skipper drew back. He leaned over. By the stove was a cut-off machete. A stump. He grasped it.

"Well, old chum, I'm not afraid of the quick or the dead!"

Candelario seemed impassive. He simply looked at One-Eye to see how he would settle things. Canchona advised:

"Come on, Don. Why throw coals on the fire? You people had better go."

This time the Sailor stood up. He already had a pointed machete in his hand. He advanced toward One-Eye threateningly.

"Why wouldn't it be better if you people left?"

Mariscal intervened.

"Don't waste words, Captain. Get rid of them!"

He handed him the machete. As he grasped it, Canchona had an unknown feeling. The same blood began to circulate between the machete and him. As if the weapon were alive and were only the prolongation of his arm. And yet, it didn't obey him. Paradoxically, it seemed to have a will of its own. Or was obeying outside commands. The truth is that he began to whirl it around wildly. He looked at his Chief. It could have been said that the latter was kindling an ironical smile in his little eyes. He turned his sight back on his new-found adversaries. They leaped on him, ready to do him in. A vain enterprise. Oar-machete. More machete. Whirlwind-machete. Whirlwinding machete. Whirlpool machete. Whirlwind. Wind. Grind. Whirlwinding. Windmilling. Milling. Machete. The machete was like a dynamic wall protecting Canchona. The Skipper tried to take stock of the situation. To guess who they really were and what they intended to do. He slackened his drive a little. The Sailor, on the other hand, made a supreme effort to get through that wall of acrobatic steel. All useless. The machete leaped out of his hands. He tried to grab it. Absurd. The weapon—suddenly elastic, rubber maybe?—got away several times. Until in one last drive it leaped over the rail and into the sea. Furiously, he tried to use his body. To die rather than face shame. Curiously, the whirlwinding weapon turned over. And instead of using the edge, it began to swat him with the flat. The Skipper ordered:

"Enough!"

The boy didn't obey him. He tried to put his arms, his head, his whole body into the whirlwind of metallic blows. The Skipper went over. Took him by the arm.

"Enough, I say! Can't you see that the machete has wings?"

He turned to Candelario.

"Colonel: the shore is far away. And sharks suckle here. Why don't you put us off closer in?"

"All right."

One-Eye gave the machete back to the Colonel. The latter went on:

"And now give us something to eat."

"Yes, Colonel."

They sat down around the small stove. They began to eat. Suddenly the Sailor, leaving prudence behind, started fighting again. He leaped on Canchona. The Captain, surprised, couldn't defend himself in time. He took a few blows. That was all. Almost instantaneously, without Mariscal's making an expression or gesture, the elastic machete took flight. With a clean blow, it sliced off the attacker's left ear.

"That's the last warning, boy. And that's because you've made a good impression on me. You've got balls. But the next time don't count on it."

He smiled, the way a jaguar can smile at a badger.

"Now you know."

The Sailor turned around. Looked at him. Before they could hold him back he ran to the rail. He shouted, superstitious:

"I'll take the sharks!"

And he leaped into the night and the sea.

Hours later the Colonel took the Skipper into his confidence.

"Does the sloop belong to you?"

"Yes, sir, Colonel."

"It will still belong to you."

"Yes, sir, Colonel."

"All I ask is that you do what I tell you. You'll take me wherever I order you to. Back and forth. That's all."

"Yes, sir, Colonel."

"You're going to make money, of course. Lots of money. All the money you want."

"Yes, sir, Colonel."

That was how Candelario Mariscal began the maritime phase of his campaigns. Soon, in the Gulf. In the inlets. On the Great River that poured into the sea. The tales of adventures, deeds, and legends circulated. As they passed on from mouth to mouth they kept on growing. The way the liquid masses that the Moon gathers in everywhere grow with the tides.

"The Colonel's got more than a hundred men now."
"More than a thousand."
"And all with balls. Hard-souled like him."
"They say they're well armed."
"Aha. Axes. Machetes. Shotguns. Carbines."
"They've even got cannons."
"And sloops."
"More than a hundred sloops."
"More than a thousand."
"And he travels in one that flies."
"They've all got wings."
"And the men who go with him have got wings too."
"Wings. Horns. And tails."
"And fire comes out of their openings."
"That's right. Ears. Eyes. Noses. Mouths."
"And they've got lots of money."
"Lots and lots of money. They've all got lots and lots of money."
"And they screw the best pussies around."
"And they don't just attack sloops anymore."
"Aha. They attack ranches and even villages."
"They all must be partners of The One We Know."
"Every last one of them."
"Can it be true that the Colonel is the Son of That One?"
"Who can say, Don!"
"That's right. Who can say!"

TEN

Juvencio Balda woke up. His body ached. His mouth was terribly dry. He opened his eyes. Beside him, on the bamboo floor, the young girl was sitting.

"Oh, it's you, Clotilde."

"Yes. It's me. How do you feel?"

"Fine."

"That's good!"

She sat up a little. She leaned over him to get a closer look. Poor thing! His face was black and blue from all the blows. He had trouble breathing. His look was a little vague. Distant.

"I'm going to get you something hot."

"Don't bother."

"I'll be right back."

She got up, agile. The doctor tried to follow her with his eyes. As he did so, he ran into the face of the Priest, who was observing him.

"Do you really feel better?"

"Yes, Father. Although a little sore."

"Luckily you haven't got a single broken bone. But they gave you a bad beating. Were they Chalena's men?"

"Yes, Father."

"Why?"

"They want to get me out of Santorontón. He. And others like him."

"Oh! So you're going to leave us?"

"Now less than ever."

He looked at the priest with thanks. He added:

"I have a lot of friends here."

"That's true. If it hadn't been for them you'd be on the Other Shore already. In the Land of the Bald."

Going on, he told him what had happened with the monkeys. He pointed out that Clotilde had sent for him. That, for the moment, she was taking care of him. She'd spent two sleepless nights. Juvencio listened to him attentively. He nodded:

"She's a good girl."

The Priest wouldn't make an out-and-out affirmation. He murmured:

"So it seems."

"She's suffered a lot."

"And still suffering."

At that instant Clotilde came back. She was carrying a steaming cup in her left hand. In the right one, she was holding a spoon with which she was trying to cool the mixture.

"Let's have some of this. It will help you get your strength back."

She sat down beside him again. He protested:

"Why are you going to all this trouble?"

"It's no trouble. And it'll be good for you. You'll see."

With her left arm she raised him up a little from behind. He sat up slightly. Spoonful by spoonful—which she put into his mouth—he began to drink. Whether because it was more comfortable that way. Or because he didn't have the strength to hold his head up, he rested it on Clotilde's shoulder. She had a sudden feeling of displeasure. She felt the dark urge to hold him tightly against her breast. To tell him new words, that she didn't know very well. They could have been the ones mothers use to rock their children to sleep. It made her afraid. How could she have thought that? What right did she have? What illusion? Why and for what reason? She gave him the last spoonful. She made a great effort not to weep. Not to run out. Not to disappear from his side forever. She controlled herself. She put the cup down on the floor. And, delicately, she helped him lie down again.

Juvencio looked at her with a warm feeling.

"Thank you, Clotilde. Thank you very much."

Father Cándido, who was observing the scene, suggested:

"You should lie down for a while, child."

"I'm not sleepy, Father."

"Even if you can't sleep. At least you should get some rest. Don't let yourself get sick."

"It really . . ."

"It's the best thing. I'll take care of Juvencio."

"All right, Father."

The Priest watched her leave. How strange! In the time that had passed since the murder of her parents, she had become transformed. Especially since she'd come back from the city. She'd grown. Her look and her manner were no longer those of a child. On the contrary, she looked like a woman older than she was. She still had, it was true, that mysterious and fatal look that the tragedy had plowed into her. Perhaps he'd misjudged her. Could it have been because of what they'd told him? Or could it have only been from what he'd been given to see? His thoughts were interrupted by the sound of strong, rhythmical rowing. He went to the door. A rudder canoe was approaching. A big one. With a canvas canopy. Four oarsmen were moving it along. Two on each side. Its speed made it approach quickly. Soon he was able to identify those on board. They were sitting in the middle of the boat on wooden benches. It was the big-boss high command of Santorontón: Crisóstomo Chalena, Father Gaudencio, Dr. Espurio Carranza, Vigiliano Rufo, the shopkeeper, Salustiano Caldera, the Political Lieutenant, Rugel Banchaca, the Chief of the Rural Police, and two armed Rural Guards.

Cándido had the impression that they were strangers. They looked so different from the ones he'd always seen. Chalena rose up like a monstrous spider spinning webs to catch whatever was within reach. His face was all mouth. Or, at least, his eyes, nose, chin, forehead, and ears looked like nothing so much as the appendages of that toothed pit. Father Gaudencio was dressed in burnt red. He gave the impression of a cooked crab, all full of prickles. Naturally, everything about him glowed. Everything about him smelled of incense. His hands were moving like a tiny whirlwind, as if he were beating eggs. But those most changed were Espurio Carranza, Vigiliano Rufo, Salustiano Caldera, and Rugel Banchaca. Espurio—who, in addition to medicine, was in charge of the useful trade of Funeral Pomp in Santorontón—looked like a black-painted carob tree. In spite of his sweet barbershop smell, he couldn't get rid of the fragrance left by his daily dealings with the dead. Vigiliano—with his hump that was worthy of a greater cause—carried a cane that was taller than he. That's why he almost always held it as if it were a shepherd's crook. Salustiano and Rugel—something strange for them—were wearing shoes. Half-cured cowskin boots. They walked as if they were crushing glass with their feet, carefully. Although both were wearing straw hats, these had strings of snail shells as bands. The rural guards were the only ones barefoot. They carried, slung over their shoulders, Winchester rifles. They smelled of cane liquor. With an identifying odor. The smell of people whom nothing or nobody can knock down. Just like the smell of those wooden barrels where they brew that liquid staircase used by people who want to flee themselves.

Suddenly the sand on the shore rose up. It began to spin with dizzy speed. The sand on the shore. In the midst of them. Wrapping them up. Enveloping them. In ascending waves of corkscrews of teeth, eyes, hair, torsos, hands, feet . . . Little by little, in the foreground, the figure of a three-headed snake was taking shape. The head in the middle belonged to Rugel Banchaca. The ones on either side to the two rural guards. Behind the trident-looking ophidian, five crocodile heads, without tails, were turning about. Five crocodile heads joined at the trunk. Five crocodile heads with two feet. Five crocodile heads moving like a carrousel, spinning on the axle that joined them. Five crocodile heads in a living five-pointed star. Five crocodile heads that were five human heads: Gaudencio, Chalena, Rufo, Caldera, Carranza. A grafting of their facial traits onto the characteristic traits of the saurian. Five-headed. A five-headed crocodile approaching. Behind the three-headed serpent. When they got to the foot of the Priest's house, they changed again. They recovered their anthropomorphic appearance. They greeted Cándido respectfully but drily.

"God has given us a good day."

"God has given us a good day. To what do I owe this honor?"

Chalena turned to Caldera. The toady smile arched his mouth.

"You speak. You're the one in charge."

The Political Lieutenant cleared his throat. He assumed an air of acute importantitis.

"Father Cándido. On behalf of the civil, military, and ecclesiastical authorities of Santorontón, I come to ask you to hand Dr. Juvencio Balda over to me."

A mocking look decorated the old Cleric's face.

"Might one know why?"
Salustiano Caldera turned to the others. As if asking for orders. Chalena suggested:
"Tell him what it's all about."
"All right."
He turned to Father Cándido again.
"He's been accused of killing the cripple Timoteo Ruales."
"Oh, yes? When did he kill him?"
"Two nights ago."
The Cleric's face hardened. His voice hammered.
"The night you people almost killed Dr. Balda?"
The Political Lieutenant looked around in order to get his courage up. He straightened up his body. He released some fluty sounds.
"I don't know what you're talking about, Your Reverence. Besides, it's none of your business. The only thing you have to do is turn the accused over to us."
The Priest assumed his sarcastic tone again.
"Is that all?"
"That's all. And the quicker the better."
He turned to Banchaca.
"Do your duty."
In his turn the Chief of the Rural Guard turned to his men:
"Let's go!"
The policemen came forward. Cándido stood in their way.
"You're not taking him away from here."
Chalena asked, in a belch of innocence:
"And why not?"
"He's in no physical shape to be moved."
"Oh, no? What's wrong with him?"
"You know that quite well."
"Me?"
"Yes. He's badly hurt. Very serious. All covered with bruises. From the beating you people gave him."
"How can you say a thing like that, Father Cándido?"
Espurio Carranza intervened.
"I, as a doctor, can examine him."
"Why didn't you do it the day before yesterday? Maybe he wouldn't be in the shape he's in if you'd attended to him in time. At least he wouldn't have lost so much blood."

"I didn't know about it."

"That's a lie!"

"Don Cándido!"

"Clotilde went to get you, the same as Vigiliano Rufo. Everybody refused to do anything for the doctor."

Father Gaudencio's syrupy voice could be heard.

"Reverend Father Cándido."

"Go ahead, Most Reverend Father."

"Don't you think it would be better if you obeyed the law?"

"Who said otherwise?"

"We're men of the cloth. Our duty is only to save the souls of the faithful."

He lifted his eyes to heaven beatifically. Cándido half-closed his.

"That's what I'm doing, Father Gaudencio. Except that Dr. Juvencio Balda's soul is still sticking rather tightly to his body. And I don't think that anyone—least of all we—has the right to unstick it before its time."

Chalena intervened again. Without subterfuges. Master of the authority that he was assured of exercising.

"All right. That's enough. We're going to take the little doctor out in any case. No one, not even you, can stop it, Father Cándido. If we were in your church, perhaps it would be something else again. But you haven't got a church anymore."

The Cleric's six feet of height trembled.

"That's true. I no longer have a church. But you're not taking Juvencio out of here. First you'll have to make mincemeat out of me."

Father Gaudencio raised his imploring hands. Then he made a vague gesture with them. As if absolving the civil and military authorities of Santorontón.

"May the Lord's will be done."

Just as if it were an order or a command, the others advanced. Cándido tried to stop them. A vain gesture. With no consideration for his age or his habit, they shoved him. They tried to move him to one side. He reacted. He regained his place. They hit him. He defended himself. First, simply by trying to cover himself with his hands, in the desire to stop the successive blows. They grew more frequent yet. In spite of his determination, they began to make him fall back. As if in a dream, he heard Chalena's voice.

"Don't hit him with your carbines."

Could they have lifted them up? Were they ready to beat him with the butts? He couldn't have thought it, not even for a second. The blows grew stronger. He wasn't sure of the moment when he began to return them. Since he was a giant and led a healthy life—in addition to his daily exercise with a paddle—every punch of his made the adversary stumble in turn. The worst part was that he had to fight off several of them. So that for every blow he returned, he received five or six. He was already half-dazed. What kept him on his feet was his decision to stop them from eliminating Dr. Juvencio Balda. He was slowly losing his strength. He had the feeling that he wouldn't be able to resist much longer. It was likely that in a few brief seconds the others would throw him to the ground. Senseless. Walk over him. And carry off the injured man. That would be killing him outright. Who knows, maybe that was what they meant to do! A blow in the stomach made him hesitate. A punch on the ear changed it into a bed of sparks. He half-closed his eyes. Night drew eaves of shadows over his eyes. Was he going to fall? Was he falling? He felt that he wasn't alone. Somebody beside him was helping him. Could it be Father Gaudencio? Had a sudden solidarity with the one who wore the same habit been awakened in him? No. It wasn't Gaudencio. He heard an identifying voice.

"Damn you all!"

It was Clotilde! She was crazy! They'd tear her to pieces. He thought in confusion. With the rage and the hate they had for her. They'd take advantage in order to satisfy their dark vengeance on her. He tried to tell her to leave. To leave him alone. Those were things for men. Because he, even though she might not think so, was a man as well as a priest! Very much a man! He knew how to defend himself. He could defend himself. And if not, what difference did it make? Wasn't it part of his mission to fight for a cause he thought just? The price he might have to pay was not the question. When he tried to do it, he barely opened his lips. He let out no sound. In the meantime, the blows were increasing. He stumbled again. He couldn't keep his balance. A blow on the forehead knocked him down. He fell with the sound of a dry bag of oysters in the shell. He tried to get up. Banchaca hit him in the chin with his knee. He fell again. This time unconscious. Clotilde, in turn, also fell under similar conditions.

In view of that, Chalena urged:
"Go ahead!"
Jumping over the fallen figures, they went in. Juvencio, lying on the floor, looking at them, made vain attempts to get up again. He muttered fiercely:
"Swine!"
They leaped on him. They were going to pick him up. Or drag him. They were stopped by a stern voice that came from behind them.
"Back!"
They turned, frightened. Giving them the command was the Burned Christ. He was looking at them serenely, although not taking his eyes off them. He repeated:
"Back!"
The men, disconcerted, looked at each other. Then they looked at Jesus. He was nailed to the Wood, standing on a rustic table. As they took stock of his misery, they recuperated. They grew bold. Chalena raised his singsong voice.
"Why pay attention to him? It's just an image. It isn't even whole since the church burned down. Isn't that so, Father Gaudencio?"
The latter had some doubts. He looked at the Martyr of Golgotha. As if studying him. The truth was that the Christ wasn't favored too much by his appearance. He was going from bad to worse. Paint peeling. Splinters. In addition to being burned. To top off his misfortune, he had lost some of his facial characteristics. The only things that distinguished him clearly still were the number of wounds and the blood that poured out of them. His eyes, too, had kept a vital glow. The Priest—in view of it all—agreed:
"That's right, Don Crisóstomo."
"Go ahead, then!"
They went to where Juvencio was again. Banchaca took his head; Caldera his legs. The injured man offered no resistance. What was the use? When they were about to lift him up, they heard a sharp sound from behind them which made them turn around again. They were paralyzed with fear. The Son of Mary had detached himself from the Cross. He had come down from the Cross. He was holding the Cross in both hands. He was lifting the Cross with an incredible effort. The Cross was a huge mace. The Cross raised over their heads. The cyclopean Cross.

The punitive Cross. The weapon Cross. Threatening. Implacable.

Impelled, as it seemed, by an invincible force, they fell to their knees. Chalena, without getting up, recovered from his fright a little, argued:

"We only came to carry out the Law."

Without lowering the Cross. Without changing his tone. Christ shattered him with his look:

"Be still, you evil creature!"

Father Gaudencio, in turn, recovered. He thought it was his duty to Latin it with a little flourish:

"*Adhuc sub iudice lis est*."

Christ became angrier. His eyes seemed to light up. His voice became slightly hoarse.

"*Vade retro*, Satan!"

And to the rest, threatening them with the Cross.

"Now, out of here!"

Without waiting for any more arguments and without adding a word, they stood up. They ran. Father Gaudencio in the rear, holding his cassock up with both hands. He kept on shouting:

"Wait for me! Don't be like that! Wait for me!"

They were into the rudder canoe in a trice. The four oarsmen began to move their long poles. They sank them into the water with great rapidity. They seemed motorized. The canoe leaped across the water like a big-headed mullet.

The first to open his eyes—the one they had left in good shape—was Cándido. He made a slight gesture of pain. He was aching from the blows. In spite of everything, he was able to look around. Clotilde was still unconscious. Juvencio had risen a little, seeing that he was coming to. Up above—nailed to the Cross again—Christ was observing them with an affectionate smile.

"Old Man: you were almost done for."

The Cleric expressed a little resentment.

"Naturally! Friendship doesn't count for anything anymore. Even when they see someone dying, comrades fold their arms and leave him to his fate."

Juvencio—making an effort—explained things:

"Don't be unfair, Father Cándido. If we're still alive, we owe it to Him."

The Priest remained doubtful. What could really have happened?

ELEVEN

When Colonel Candelario Mariscal rose up in arms on the mainland, blood flourished on the four horizons. It was a war without quarter. Without distinction. "They're all my enemies," he would assert. That was how he dealt with anyone he found in his path. It was the same whether aiding a guerrilla band or a revolution; civil strife or an international war. "We're on one side, Captain Canchona; everybody else is on the other." In that "everybody else" he included rich and poor, children and elderly, men and women, peasants and city folk. He preferred, of course, to ally himself—whenever it was possible for him to choose—with evil causes and perverse individuals. "What can I do, Canchona? That's what happens to me. I like to screw the underdogs now, the people who can't defend themselves. Something's made me bow-legged, because I like to trample on people who are down." He had his own stamp. After an encounter with his occasional adversaries, he would visit the field of battle. If there was still someone left wounded, he would liquidate him with a bullet or with his machete. He preferred the latter. The crisp, heavy noise which the steel produced as it opened a path through the bones gave him a strange satisfaction. Especially the bones of the skull. "It sounds like splitting a pumpkin, Canchona." When all the dead were good and dead, he would have them buried with their right hands sticking out. "In that way they look as if they're waving good-by to me. And if I come back they're saying hello." When that return was delayed. And all that could be seen were equidistant rows of first, second, and third phalanges, he was happy. "The way things turn out, eh, Captain Canchona? Even the buzzards have respected the wave. They ate everything right down to the last nerve, but they left the bones nice and comfortable." On the other hand, if families, friends, or comrades of the deceased had buried their hands, he would become furious. "Sons of bitches, don't they want Colonel Candelario Mariscal to have his greeting? Well, they're going to have to greet him a lot now. A lot more now." Without further ado, he would attack those who lived in nearby villages. It didn't matter whether it was a village, a settlement, or a simple farm. When they saw him coming, the cowards shat in their pants. The brave ones gritted their teeth. They knew it was useless to resist. Their machetes or shotguns would fly out of their hands before they could use them. No one begged for forgiveness, no one begged for anything. When some woman tried to start up with her dirty words, her husband would silence her. "Don't waste your spit, Old Woman. You know what the Colonel's after." He made them dig their own graves. He would bury them alive, with their right hands sticking out too. Once underground, the unfortunate ones would wave that hand—at least that was the only thing seen of them—until their last death rattle. The Colonel would hold his stomach from laughing so much. "Can you see them waving to me now, Canchona? If they'd let the other dead ones keep on with it, these here would still be eating their manioc." He fell more and more in love with weapons. Knives as well as firearms. When he got a new one, he would test it in his own way. Machetes—"Only the machete is good for cutting, Mr. Dummy"—against the slim branches of the trees. Carbines or pistols always on living targets. Usually he did it in villages. "People are all teat by teat together in towns and there are more than enough to choose from, Canchona." He would go in on horseback. Sometimes a platoon of men would follow him. Sometimes not. He would go alone. Or with his inseparable One-Eye. When he thought the time was opportune, he would start his test. He would empty his cartridge belt on the first people he passed. Without distinction, as always. "Why should I, they're all my enemies." His happiness had no limits when, with a single bullet, he could cut down several lives. Canchona was almost certain that sometimes he had heard him say: "I send these souls to my father. To see what he can do with them." The truth was that his Colonel upset him. What was he after? What did he aim to do? What were his ambitions? It was certain that he gave himself a good life. In everything. He got what he liked: the best horses, boats, clothes, etc. Females he didn't even have to conquer or even make a show of conquering. Saying "I'm going to eat me this little pitahaya" and digging in his spurs were one and the same. If they were single girls or widows, there was no problem. He put them right into bed. He laid them down on the bottom of a canoe. He mounted them in the grass. He enjoyed them in the straw netting of a hammock. Or on the back of a horse. "Did you know, Canchona, there's nothing like gobbling up a female on horseback. The horse helps sometimes when its skin quivers." If they were married women, the thing became a little complicated. Either he would put them into bed and the husband had to take off on the run. Or he would dispatch the man to the Other Shore. Would it be to send that soul to his Daddy? Sometimes Canchona had his doubts. Perhaps he hadn't heard that business about souls. He'd made it all up. A product of the gossip that covered them like an ebb tide wherever they were. Maybe The Evil One. Maybe the Son of The One We Know. "You're going to do yourself harm, Canchona, traveling around with That One. That One is 'That One.' Have you ever seen him take a bath? Of course not. He has to keep his horns cut. Or filed down. Or hides the stubs under his hair. But what about his tail? Keep an eye out for it! Even if he goes into the River with a loincloth on, you'll see his tail. He has to carry it all curled up. Like the coils of a snail shell." "Oh, you must be pretty dumb, Canchona! When you learn all about it you'll already be roasting in the Five Hells." The Colonel could read him from a distance. Or was he putting it in his head so he could read it? "So your ears are burning, eh, Mr. Dummy? Well, if you want to take off, sir, go ahead! But don't forget that I've got you tied by the balls." It was true. He was still in chains down there. Everything he did to free himself was so much straw. If he deviated just the slightest bit when they were going together, he felt the painful ache between his legs at once! Sometimes it enraged him. Was he or wasn't he Captain Canchona? Wasn't he as brave as his Chief? Well. Not that brave. But brave enough. Enough to stand up to the one who made his men the best paid in the region. So? So, it's one thing with a harpoon and something else with a casting net. He simply couldn't. He was fucked up—fucked over and under and up—for good. The only thing he could do was resign himself to his fate and see things through the eyes of Colonel Candelario Mariscal. And what if he really and truly was the Son of The One We Know? Oh, what the hell! How long was he going to keep hanging back? When the line was cast, corvinas had to be caught! There wasn't any other way out! When he became resigned—which was most of the time—he set out to enjoy things. The way the Colonel did. Eating. Drinking. Wearing his Sunday clothes every day. Laying females. Getting his pint at wakes. Having a beautiful time. Naturally. All of this in the parentheses between battles. Which was what lasted the least time of all. "Because, for my part, Canchona, what I like to do is fight. I wouldn't exchange a good spray of bullets for the best bottom in the world." Why shouldn't he like it, since bullets and knives respected him? Since it was like watching a cloudburst falling on a donkey's indifferent skin? Not him. He preferred anything else—plantain ball soup, a drink of cane liquor, a good dance spiced with the music of *amorfinos*—to the rain of projectiles and the rattling of knives and swords. And there was something else. The dead. In spite of the fact that he saw them all the time, he didn't like dead people in the least. He didn't enjoy it, the way the Colonel did, every time somebody fell. Of course, they didn't fill him with as much fear as they used to. At first, the dead wouldn't let him sleep. He'd see them coming closer to his shelter. Making horrible faces at him. With the faces they'd left in the ground. Broken up. Wrapped in the matter that came out of all their wounds. Not anymore now. He'd got used to it. And, furthermore, there were so many of them that he couldn't identify them. In order to bring them all together a huge corral would have been needed. Or lots of houses.

In the meantime, the prestige of Colonel Candelario Mariscal was growing. He was already considered one of the most assiduous of grave planters. It climbed up from the marine tangles of the brackish coast to the frozen crests of the high mountains. The legend braided its glass rattlesnakes in the persevering homicidal drive. The Son of The Evil One emerged from the shadows. Some probably doubted his tangible presence. So absurd was everything they attributed to him! Still, they had to give in before the daily milestones. Especially because the criminal acts bore his personal stamp more and more. For example, he'd hit upon the trick of "preparing the terrain." He was no longer content with threatening small and poorly defended villages. On the contrary, he besieged those that had the air of being cities. He commanded a regular army. He had plenty of equipment, arms, and rations. "Someday I'm going to treat myself to the pleasure of turning a city into a cemetery, Canchona. Can you imagine what it would be like, leaving them all eternal-grinning skulls? You'll see, Canchona!" When he attacked an important place he would send his message on ahead. A barbarous message—that was what he called "preparing the terrain." It was inspired by something people said they did farther to the north. According to what he was told, in order to prove that he had conquered a city, the ears of the inhabitants were cut off—so many ears, so many conquered people. He kept the fleshy appendanges in a sack. And he would send them on as evidence of a mission accomplished. He liked the procedure. Although he made a slight change. His message was not one of ears. It was one of hands. Sometimes he would cut them off in some neighboring village. Sometimes on the outskirts of the very village he meant to conquer. When he sent them to the Town Fathers, he would offer a mocking commentary: "In this way they've got no reason to be resentful. Right, Canchona? It's like sending them a greeting ahead of time."

All that villainy had already put the police and the military authorities on the alert. They organized groups, ever larger, to hunt down the disruptive Colonel. At first he eluded them. He would disappear from right under their noses. Was he a ghost? Was he the creation of popular gossip? But all those deaths? All those rapes? All that sacking? All the misfortune he left behind like a kind of personal wake? He continued to elude them. He didn't even have to make use of uncommon procedures. He knew the terrain like the hilt of his machete. Besides, he could count on the complicity of the inhabitants of those parts. Willingly—with him it was always better to do it willingly. Or unwillingly. Which was like taking a one-way trip. When the hunters grew in numbers and began to use more modern equipment, the Colonel was no longer content to disappear into smoke. He still eluded them. But with tricks that bore the bloody stamp of Candelario Mariscal. On certain nights, he would capture several soldiers. He would take away their rifles. He would fasten them to the floor by the butts. There they stood with the bayonets sticking up. Then he would drop the poor devils from a very high beam. In such a way they were strung out on the sharp-pointed weapons.

Their comrades awoke to their shrieks. "That way they'll realize that I take things seriously, Captain Canchona." At other times he would "return" the prisoners to their respective forces. He returned them in his own way. Naturally. He would look for several tall trees. With flexible, elastic trunks. He would bend them down until their tops touched the ground. He would seat a soldier on them. With a single slice he released the trees, transforming them into real catapults. The "returnees"—human projectiles—flew swiftly. They fell in pieces among other trees and onto stones or into the midst of their own people. "What else do they want me to do but return them? Whole or in pieces, but they go back to the place they came from." When he found out there was a Colonel among the officers pursuing him, his tricks took a different tack. He thought it was a trick worthy of their rank. He didn't care whether or not his Colonel adversary was a career officer. Or whether he'd been graduated in the joyful heat of bullets. The important thing was that he had to make them know that no other Colonel but Candelario Mariscal was snorting about there. He would start his joke by taking off the military kepi with the point of his machete. Then he would use it to comb his hair—that is, he would make a line on his hair without touching his scalp. And, finally, he would leave him a memento: a diagonal line drawn in blood across his face.

The news was reaching the cities. The fearsome image of the improvised officer was rising up everywhere. According to the very fantasy of those talking. The people almost always adorned him with the general attributes of The Evil One.

"He's got seven thousand horns."

"Really?"

"And seven thousand tails."

"There can't be that many."

"Rivers of sparks flow out of his eyes."

"Ah! And does he have wings?"

"Twice seven thousand wings."

The expert would extend his hands, trying to take in a great space. Adding:

"Just like that."

"Enough to give you a scare, right?"

"Just imagine!"

"His ears are pointed, aren't they?"

"Of course. As if they had sharp nails on them."

"What about his hands and feet?"

"His claws are like daggers. With webbed fingers. That's how he can hang down from any branch or roof he wants to."

"He must look like a huge bat."

"And that's when he has his normal looks."

"Can he change?"

"When he changes he's covered with heads. They come out of his belly. His back. His arms. His legs. Naturally, seven of them come out of his neck. Each one more horrible than the next. With flaming vipers' tongues. And thousands—thousands and thousands—of arms and legs. Each one with a machete. Or a pistol. That's why nobody can stand up to him."

"We're lost! What can you do against the Devil?"

"Don't use his name. His name brings bad luck."

Others knew a little more.

"No. It's not Him in person. It's a Son of His. He looks like any one of us. He only looks like us."

"And you think he's going to attack the city?"

"Who knows? He's getting stronger every day. He's got more people and more weapons. The worst is that wherever he passes, he leaves ruins. Just as if a million fireshitting giants had passed through."

"What's the Army doing? The Government?"

"What they can. What else can they do? They've got their hands tied. These things are not of this world."

"What about the priests?"

"Well, we'll see. I think they're going to have to do something. I've heard that if things keep on getting worse, they're going to organize a procession. They'll take all the images out of the church. All the churches, that is. And they'll start sprinkling holy water in all directions."

The truth was that the soldiers were all upset.

"If he was somebody like us, maybe . . ."

"That's right."

"But lead slides right off this Somebody."

"I know that better than anyone."

"You? How's that?"

"I fired point blank at him. He spat in my eye. As if he was the Jaguar. I took good aim. The bullet hit between his eyes.

And the lead, it bounced off! As God is my witness!"
"So how could you live to tell the tale?"
"Because our commanding officer was a Colonel. And Colonels make Mariscal go crazy. He likes to show them up immediately. He caught ours with a machete right on his drawers."
"Goddamn it, that's a hard man to please!"
"After the guy's pants fell down, he gave him a stroke on the nose. He sliced him right down to his roots. Leaving only the bones on the front of his face. 'So you'll remember what a real Colonel is like,' he hollered at him."
"We're all fucked up."
"Fucked up beyond recognition."
"What are we going to do?"
"There's a rumor that Colonel Epifanio Moncada himself is coming to face him!"
"The Minister of Police?"
"The very same."
"And don't they say that That One is another Son of the Devil?"
"That's why. Maybe they'll understand each other."
"I don't think so. The Minister's got a lot to do. Just getting rid of idealists. Students. Intellectuals. Grumblers. The Opposition. The ones who don't think the way he does. The ones who don't get along with him. The ones who know who he is and what he wants."
"I can only tell you what I heard. So, if it doesn't turn out that way, the only thing left to do is say our prayers and commend our souls to God!"

Candelario had already heard the news.
"Captain Canchona. Our uprising is over."
"Why, Colonel, sir?"
"Colonel Moncada is coming looking for me."
"What's that got to do with it?"
"Colonel Moncada is Colonel Moncada, don't you know that?"
"Oh!"
His Chief took a long look at him. He spoke as if One-Eye were on to everything.
"Where I strike, no hair grows. And where I spit, a jaguar is born. Still, you more than anyone else know why I can't fight him . . . Besides, I get the feeling that I wasn't the one who brought

off this uprising. As if ever since I killed the Quindales I had some other man inside of me."

Canchona averted his eyes. He said as if to himself:

"That's the way it has to be, that's all, Colonel, sir. What now?"

Candelario grew hoarse:

"The caracara hawk I made these dummies dance to has gone."

He got control of himself. Went on:

"Divide everything up among our people."

"Everything? . . . What will be left for you?"

"I don't need anything, Canchona."

"All right, Colonel."

He carried out the orders he'd received and was back in a short time.

"It's been done, Colonel."

The latter cast his look out at the horizon.

"The way things turn out, Captain Canchona! It seems hard to believe that I planned to turn this whole land into a cemetery."

His aide babbled.

"You were still on the point of doing it, right? And there's still time . . ."

"No, Canchona. I've lost my feeling for it. Besides, the only one who could cut me off. The only one who's just like me—or like what I was until just now—has finally made an appearance. And he's doing a good job. On a grand scale. In a legal and organized way. He can bury more people in a single day than I can in a month. I can't cross paths with him. I never talked to you about him, did I?"

"Never, Colonel, sir."

"Maybe I was afraid that if I mentioned his name he'd appear."

There was a moment of silence. One-Eye broke it, not without certain emotion.

"What about me, Colonel, sir?"

"You, what about you?"

"What am I going to do?"

"Whatever you want. From today forward, I set your balls free. You can go wherever you feel like going."

A feeling of freedom glowed throughout his body. He was moved deep down inside. He looked at his Chief. Could he really be the Son of The One We Know? Or not? He was the worst of men—could he call him a man in his thoughts?—the worst he'd ever known. A murderer who killed for the sake of killing. Who enjoyed other people's deaths. Doing away with him would have been a benefit for all. Why didn't he do it? Why didn't he try to? He was free. Could he shoot now? Would his finger on the trigger of his pistol obey? Wouldn't the bullets slide or bounce off him? No matter what. The important thing was to try it. He held back. He couldn't. Something higher than his reason filled his spirit. Besides, the Colonel had been good to him. —Could the Son of The Other One be good to anybody if he really was the Son of The Other One?— He'd saved his life many times. He'd helped him enjoy as he'd never dreamed of doing. Of course, always wrapped in a cloak of blood. But He thought that was the best way to live. "Look at the sea or the jungle, Canchona. The largest or strongest are the only ones who survive. In order to do it, they have to devour or exterminate the smaller or the weaker." He wanted to answer that they only did it out of hunger or self-defense. What for? It would have been useless. It was useless to try to convince him. As if in spite of himself—with the solidarity of a domesticated wild animal with the one who fed him—he said:

"I want to stay with you, Colonel. Wherever you go. To be like your shadow. I..."

A stray bullet—stray?—perforated his skull, cutting him off. Candelario, a short time later, with his own hands, dug him a grave. Buried him—unlike what he did with everybody else—without his hand sticking out. What for? "Canchona will keep on waving good-by from under the earth."

That was how Colonel Candelario Mariscal's military adventures came to an end. As was natural, the tide of words kept on ebbing and flowing.

"He left just the way he came."

"It had to be like that, didn't it?"

"He turned to smoke."

"So much the better. Can you imagine what would have happened if he'd stayed up in arms?"

"And they say that all thanks are due the Minister of Police, Colonel Epifanio Moncada."

"Well, He's the Son of That One."

"Of course."

"And since the Other One is too."

"Of course."

TWELVE

The news that the wells had gone dry caused consternation among the Santorontonians. It was only at first. Later on they consoled themselves. Why had Don Chalena collected so much water? It might even be better now. They wouldn't have to go into the jungle or out to Balumba to get it. They had it right there. Within reach. Saving the waste of time and effort. The difficult trips overland, rolling the casks along by man or animal power. The same as the trips on the sea, in canoes, cutting through currents and waves.

"He had good reason to get a lot of houses. And he bought or rented the roofs of most of them."

"That's right. Of course. The Partner advised him what was going to happen."

"It's good it turned out that way. Just imagine if he hadn't saved up water! All of Santorontón would have died of thirst!"

"The way things turn out, right? Sometimes it's good to snuggle up to Old Longtail."

"Aha!"

"Do you want me to tell you something?"

"Let's hear it!"

"I used to think bad things about Don Chalena. I thought he'd turn into a damned bloodsucker. That he was climbing up onto men the way the Witch's Broom hangs onto cocoa pods until it leaves them dry."

"We Christians almost always fool ourselves."

"Yes. Now we can see that he's not so bad. He was worried

about Santorontón. Who would ever have thought to store up water?"

"You're right. Who would have?"

"What we have to do now is carry our casks to the houses with zinc roofs. And draw water from the tanks."

Soon, the sandy, dried-out streets of the town were all filled with people—Santorontón was still growing. They were rolling the casks along. Or carrying buckets and pots. They went along in silence. Full of hope. With the certainty that all would turn out as they thought. When they got to the houses roofed with zinc, they had a surprise. The water tanks were closed. Locked.

"I wonder why Don Chalena put locks on them?"

They gave it more thought.

"So they'd be closed up tight."

"But what for?"

So vermin won't get in. Or so birds and animals from out of the jungle won't come to drink from them.

"Of course, isn't that it? What shall we do, then?"

"Go find Don Chalena."

The man had changed overnight. He had yellow-green bullfrog stripes. His arms and legs had become thin and shriveled. His turtle-shell stomach was heaving, a living bellows. He could barely open his eyes—slant-eyes, slit-eyes, sluice-eyes. The part that had continued growing on him was his mouth. Was his head becoming nothing but mouth? He was outside. By the door of his house. Stretched out in a hammock hung between two stakes. The Mute Woman was rocking the hammock. Her son by Crippled Timoteo Ruales, Tolón, seven years old—the only one she had managed, for the rest, always by unknown fathers, had died at birth—was shooing the plague of insects. The delegation of Santorontonians—headed by Rugel Banchaca and Salustiano Caldera—came up. They all made the ritual greeting.

"God has given us a good morning, Don Chalena."

He half arose.

"Good morning. What can I do for you?"

Salustiano came forward. He was becoming the most pushy. "We'd like for you to lend us the keys to the padlocks."

He didn't seem to understand. He sat up farther.

"What did you say?"

The other man become a little disconcerted. It was only for a second. He recovered:

"We'd like for you to lend us the keys to the padlocks on the water tanks."

The frog face showed an infinite sadness.

"Don't you see that I can't?"

"What?"

"I can't. I'd be glad to give you all of the water. After all, Santorontón belongs to the Santorontonians. Almost all the houses belong to you people. But you can see. It's not up to me. I can't."

They looked at each other, troubled. They repeated the two words as if an invisible mussel were jumping from mouth to mouth.

"He can't..."

"He can't..."

"He can't..."

Crisóstomo went on:

"It costs money. A lot of money. It shouldn't have been spent. I know. But where would we be now without water? Something here inside told me"—he touched his swollen blowfish belly—"that someday what's happening now was going to happen. Wells don't last a whole lifetime. Wells go dry. And somebody has to worry about taking care of Santorontón's thirst."

"Yes. That's right."

"That's why buying the zinc didn't bother me. Hiring the sloop and the workmen. Building the roofs. Putting up the gutters and drains. Building the tanks. A lot of money. An awful lot of money."

"Of course, Sir."

"I'd give you water. Why shouldn't I give it to you? You need water for everything. But I've spent an awful lot of money. And it wasn't my money. It belonged to the people who own the zinc roofs. The gutters. The drains. The tanks. And they want it back. Or, in any case, they want to be paid something for their help."

They looked at each other, disconcerted.

"What are we going to do, then?"

The Batrachian showed great sadness.

"Help those who have helped you."

"Where will we get the money from? We don't even have enough to die with."

"It won't be much. Practically nothing. Free...free. No, naturally. I want to help you. Why shouldn't I help you? I'm one of you myself. I live here too. I arrived here when there were only four houses in Santorontón. Help me to help you with the ones who are helping us!"

The rolling phrase was repeated from house to house. The same as the malaria outbreak that comes with the first rains—the goddamned rains that weren't falling now! "We're fucked up backwards and forwards." They hadn't swallowed what Don Chalena had told them. They were sure that if he'd had any help it had come from the Partner. And what did He care whether he got more or less money? Is money worth anything in his Kingdom? What he wanted was more souls. A lot more souls. So he could lug them in sacks to his Selfsame. They got the feeling that Don Chalena wasn't Don Chalena anymore. He was the Toad. That Toad in the center of the village square. The one into whose mouth they tossed bits of iron. Except that you had to throw money. Lots of money. For him to release a cask. A bucket. Or even a pot of water. They had to economize with their water. It got so that they almost only used it for drinking and cooking. Other things were taken care of with sea water. At first they'd tried mixing the two so as to get more casks of fresh water. All they got was sick. So they had to give up the idea and resign themselves to using fresh water only for certain needs. Since their catches of fish had been bad. And when they caught something there was almost never anyone to buy it. Everything was going from bad to worse! Finally they had to go to the "Administrator"—he said that was all he was, an administrator—of the zinc roofs of Santorontón. He bought their fish for almost nothing. People did come to buy from him, no one knew from where. Strange men—were they really men?—would arrive by night. In silent ships. They would anchor broadside along the shore. Far from the dock. Or they would drop anchor closer in. And from there they would come in a canoe. They never strolled through the village. Never went to bars. They went directly to Chalena's house. And they would leave, after a few brief moments, in the same way. Crisóstomo himself rarely went out anymore. Most of his "commercial operations" were handled from his hammock. By the door of his house. Always rocked by the Mute. Always with Tolón shooing the bugs away. After all, why should he move? He had trustworthy people who did things for him now. They were none other than Salustiano Caldera and Rugel Banchaca. The evening of the day they went to ask him for the famous keys, he'd spoken to them. In private.

"Naturally, the water won't cost you two anything."

They were startled. Rugel Banchaca, mistrustful, tried to guess his thoughts.

"Oh, no?"

"No. I told you to stay behind so we could talk about that."

Salustiano seemed interested.

"How's that?"

"I'm going to recommend you to the owners."

"What for?"

"You'll have the job of controlling the water. You'll take care of the keys. You'll collect. And then you'll give me the money."

Rugel scratched his head.

"Shit! It sounds like a lot of crap to me and I don't like it too much!"

Salustiano faced him.

"It'll be worse if you haven't got water for anything, won't it? What are you going to use to pay for it?"

"That's right! What are you going to use?"

Chalena cut them off, impatient.

"Well. Do you accept or not?"

Salustiano insisted to Rugel.

"We accept, right?"

His companion twisted all over. Unwilling. It was just an instant. He recovered. What could he do?

"All right. All right."

That same night, later on, Espurio Carranza and Vigiliano Rufo arrived. They looked ugly. They didn't even say hello. Chalena, when he saw them, sat up in his hammock. He put on a merry face.

"You finally got here! I was going to send for you."

The doctor-undertaker and the storekeeper were getting more and more furious. The first spoke.

"Is the rumor running through the village true?"

Chalena put on an innocent air. He lowered his eyes.

"What rumor?"

"That you're going to sell the water. We..."

He interrupted him:

"You two have nothing to worry about. You'll have all the water you need free."

The storekeeper intervened.

"That changes things."

"That would be awful! My cheating the most important people in Santorontón out of their water! I'll give orders to Salustiano and Rugel so they'll give it to you themselves. The only thing..."

The others frowned again. In unison:

"What?"

The face honeyed them with smiles.

"We'll have to stick together no matter what happens. I think this is going to get ugly. There are a lot of people who haven't got anything to pay for the water with. Thirst might even cause some damage. And then it would be good for you people and me to stick together."

Vigiliano nodded.

"You can count on me in everything, Sir."

Espurio did the same.

"Me too."

When the deal was closed, the owner of the zinc roofs—Administrator, for the other Santorontonians only—invited them to have some cane liquor. They were drinking when Chalena commented:

"There are two other people I'm going to give free water to. Father Cándido, so he doesn't stir the people up against me. And Candelario Mariscal... because he's Candelario Mariscal."

The Doctor-Undertaker asked, with a certain hope:

"What about Bulu-Bulu?"

"Of course. Him too. We have to keep on good terms with witch doctors."

"Wouldn't it be better to refuse him? That way he won't be able to take care of the patients in his open-air hospital. And he'll have to go sing his tune somewhere else."

Chalena looked into the shadows. As if he were afraid that the Wizard's hundred eyes were looking at him.

"No, doctor. I can understand your feelings. After all, Bulu-Bulu is your competitor. But a Wizard is a Wizard. And Bulu-Bulu is the best wizard in these parts."

As the others were leaving, he said to them:

"Tell the Colonel I want to talk to him."

"All right, Sir."

"All right."

The next morning Vigiliano Rufo's shouts awakened him:

"Don Chalena! Don Chalena!"

He came to the door, ill-humored.

"What's the matter?"

"Colonel Mariscal says for you to come see him. That if you don't go right now, he'll drag you there by the tongue."

"Tell him I'm coming."

A while later he was facing Candelario.

"Good morning, Colonel. How can I be of service?"

He didn't answer his greeting. He looked at him through eyes teeming with rage.

"You mother-fucking son of a bitch! What's all this business about my having to send for my water?"

"Well... You see..."

"Don't give me any bullshit. You have them bring it here to me."

"Of course, Colonel. If that's..."

"If not, you'll have to bring it to me in person. And with your pants off, so I can give you a whack on the ass now and again."

"You like your little jokes, Colonel!"

"Try me and you'll see if it's a joke."

He cursed the moment Candelario had come back. Why hadn't he stayed away and done his things somewhere else? Why hadn't Colonel Epifanio Moncada wiped him out in time? Before, when he was away, everything was peaceful. Peaceful? It was just the same. The Colonel had come back completely changed. He kept out of everything. He almost never went around. They said he spent the whole day sleeping. And that at night strange noises could be heard in his house—a solitary one, on top of a rise. In spite of the fact that he lived alone, he always seemed to be arguing with somebody. Could it be that he had visits from his father, the Partner? What was for certain was that he didn't show up in the bars any more. He didn't look for fights. They didn't even know if he'd raped any women. Or killed any men. In the end, what difference did the water business make? It would be sent to him. It was just a matter of giving an order. Besides, you had to keep on the good side of the Colonel. Why try to find a fifth leg on a Crocodile? All things considered, he couldn't shake off the thought. The Colonel didn't seem to be the Colonel any more. Sometimes he would go off in his canoe. And he would head off in some unknown direction, always pulled by four enormous turtles. Where could he be going? What could he be doing on those trips? Could he still be sowing skeletons and broken cherries on distant islands? It had been said lately that he was going out to sea. Along the open Gulf routes. At last! Let him go. He rubbed his hands, happy. Outside of those few thorns, everything was going just the way he wanted it. Even Tolón, the little son of the Mute and the Cripple, had consented to carry a fistful of earth—for some time—in his right hand. He would let him sow a rosebush there. He would receive a little colt as a reward. One colt! He would give him ten if he asked for them. He would soon have the colts he wanted. On the other hand, no one else would have a rosebush growing in a boy's hand.

Little by little, all the possessions of the Santorontonians passed into the greedy hands of Crisóstomo Chalena. He never made exceptions. "If a bird can fly, he goes into my pie." First it was live money. Ringing and singing. The rosebush and the boy. Then, everything they had: furniture, clothing, tools. The colt. The Golden Colt. In the rooms of the house of the Owner of Water, stacked up in a haphazard way, were chairs, cots, hammocks, harpoons, axes, machetes, barrels, stoves, bathtubs, casting nets, hand nets, hooks, etc. The Mute Woman, deep in her silence. Later on some people gave the most valuable pieces they owned: doubloons that the tide had spat upon the sands of the beach. Pieces of prehistoric goldwork found in the tombs of their aboriginal ancestors. Jewels that lighted up the femurs and tibias of skeletons huddling in funerary urns. Old objects fished out of sailing ships sunk close to shore. Pearls that slept in an iridescent dream inside bivalves. A fistful of earth in a hand. There came a time when the Santorontonians had nothing more to give. They had handed over the very last of their family jewels. Even their engagement rings. Their houses were half-empty. In order to conserve water, they were drying up. Carob trees at summer's end. Their skin revealed the mysterious anonymity of their bones. Desperate. Distressed. Tops spinning in anguish around Chalena.

"We haven't got anything left to give you, Sir."

He would look at them, squandering his sticky smile.

"Search hard. There must be something left around there."

Tolón had the earth in his right hand.

"We've already searched. All we have left is the skin on our bones."

"See if you can think of something. The water can't be given away for nothing."

"Just give us one little barrel on credit."

"One little pailful."

"One little potful."

"We'll pay you later, Sir."

Tolón was dreaming—asleep or awake—about the Colt. Golden Colt. Pearl Colt. Foam Colt. Winged Colt. Light Colt. Wind Colt. A colt in his eyes. Inside and out. Colt. Little Colt. Tiny Little Colt.

"Not even if I was out of my mind. If you can't pay me now, what are you going to pay me with later?"

"Don't be mean, Sir."

"Do us a favor, Sir."

"God will remember you, Sir."

His pasty smile. Earthen. A footprint.

"I'd love to. It's just that the water doesn't belong to me. You know that. I only administer it."

Tolón had his rosebush, planted.

"Oh, that's not like you, Sir!"

"Don't let us die of thirst, Sir."

"We're dying of thirst, Sir."

"Don't you see that I can't? I administer the water. Other people own it. I only administer it."

As on every day—in front of them—he would keep on watering his rosebush. His rosebush in Tolón's extended hand. Colt-Rose. Rose-Colt. Tolón-Colt-Rose. He would keep on watering his rosebush.

"What can we do, then, Don Chalena?"

"How should I know? That's your business."

"Try to think of something you still want from us, Sir."

"What could we give you, Sir?"

"Maybe our houses, Sir!"

"Of course, why not? A lot of you only sold me—or rented me—your roofs. Say, that's not a bad idea. No. Not a bad idea at all."

He kept on watering the Rosebush. In front of them—withered body withered dead-oyster eyes—in front of them. Tolón was dreaming—asleep or awake—about the Colt. Chalena was dreaming—asleep or awake—about the Rosebush. The Mute was dreaming—asleep or awake—about Tolón in bloom. The Santorontonians—asleep or awake—kept on dreaming about water. Water. Water.

When all the houses had passed into the power of the Owner of Water, the long laments returned.

"We haven't got any houses anymore, Sir."

"Or water either, Sir."

"We're dying of thirst, Sir."

"What are we going to do now, Sir?"

"We haven't got anything else to give you, Sir."

A voracious smile of rapacity rocked the batrachian's mouth.

"There's something you still have left."

"Us? We haven't got anything left, Sir."

"Yes. There's something you still have left. Yourselves!"

The Rosebush was growing. Growing. In the earth. In the hand. In the earth clutched in the hand.

"Ourselves? What do you mean by that, Sir?"

Chalena kept on watering the Rosebush. The Rosebush was sinking its roots into the flesh. Into the muscles.

"Yourselves. You can give me your arms. Your legs. Your eyes. Your ears. Everything. Everything you have. I can give you water for yourselves. Lots of water."

Tolón was weeping. Wailing. The Mute was also weeping. Wailing. With her hands open. Her arms uplifted. Her eyes lined with fear and fright.

"What are you saying, Sir? Will we have to cut ourselves up? Will we have to go cutting pieces off our bodies to give them to you?"

"No. You'll still keep them. Right where you have them. But they'll belong to me. I'll lend them to you to use. You'll ask my permission to use them. I'll give it to you or I won't. According to how I feel. They'll still be mine. Only mine. You won't have charge of your bodies. No part of your bodies."

"Not that."

"We can't do that, Sir."

"No."

"No."

He kept on watering the Rosebush. In front of them, he kept on watering the Rosebush. Tolón—bathed in water and tears—kept wailing. The Mute also kept wailing. The cries of silence.

The Colt was green. The green of wrath. The Colt was crystal. The crystal of tears and water. The Colt was red. The red of fire and blood.

"Then you'll have to leave your houses. You won't have either water or houses."

The Santorontonians said nothing. They turned their backs on him. They left. A while later they returned. Chalena kept on watering the Rosebush. The Rosebush kept on growing. The Mute kept on wailing. Tolón kept on weeping. The Colt kept on flaming.

"Here we are, Sir."

"Here are our arms."

"Our mouths."

"Our legs."

"Our eyes."

"Everything we have."

"Here is everything you wanted from us."

"What can we do?"

"We're thirsty."

"And our old people are thirsty most of all, our wives, our children!"

Rubbing his hands. Opening his mouth—Mouth. Maw. Moray. Mailbox-mouth. Well-mouth. Crater-mouth—he drooled:

"I'm so glad you made up your minds! Salustiano and Rugel will give you all the water you want. But don't forget. You belong to me. To eat. To work. To drink. To wrestle pissy-places with your women. Everything. You've got to ask my permission! You're only on loan to yourselves! Remember that always! Nothing that you have belongs to you! Everything is mine! Only mine!"

"All right, Don Chalena."

"All right, Sir."

"All right."

Some Santorontonians escaped. At least they tried to escape. They were unable to. The waves of the sea, hands of foam, threw them back onto the beach. Or they were driven by the invisible gallop of a million wind stags. Or the gray-green dogfish grown into floating mountains. They couldn't get away. Even if they wanted to with all their strength. They had to stay santorontoning in Santorontón.

"How can we escape? He has a pact with Old Longtail."

"If we got away, he'd bring us back again."

"It's all useless! We have to give him what he wants!"
That's why even the most recalcitrant gave in. Themselves. They ceased being owners of themselves. Their owner was the Owner of Water. He wanted more. Always more.
"Now we really don't have anything, Sir."
"Even if we wanted to, what could we give you?"
"Now that we've given you all of our bodies in exchange for water."
The Barrel-mouth. Pipe-mouth. Tank-mouth curled. Malevolent.
"What about your women?"
"Never that, Sir."
"We'd rather die of thirst."
"Or anything."
The monstrous Mouth closed its eyes.
"Have it your own way! It's your affair!"
When the women learned about it, they became furious. Not at Chalena, but at their men.
"Since you've given him everything."
"Since you're living on loan from him."
"Since he owns you and everything you have, why not us?"
"Certainly. Why not us?"
"Besides, what can happen to us?"
"Really. He can't make use of women anymore. Not even if his soul demanded it."
The men stuck to their guns.
"From us, everything. From you, nothing."
"What about thirst?"
"We need water for everything."
"We can 'see' thirst. Do you know that?"
"Thirst is dark green."
"It has the eyes of a dead fish."
"A snake skeleton."
"Flesh of sand."
"It comes together and falls apart with the wind."
"We can't go on like this."
"Even if you don't want to, we'll go see Don Chalena!"
Don Chalena watering the Rosebush. Damned Rosebush! The Colt of Smoke. Damned Rosebush! The root in the flesh. Damned Rosebush! Tolón half-crazy. Damned Rosebush! The Mute Woman nailed down hand and foot. Damned Rosebush! Damned Rose-

bush! Rooted in the earth. In the hand. In the dreams. Damned Rosebush!

Only a few women resisted. They preferred to die of thirst. Or whatever. Humiliate themselves like that? Never. The majority agreed:

"Here we are, Sir."

"To trade ourselves for water."

"Lots of water."

"To last for us."

Puffed-up Frog. Laughing. Rubbing his hands.

"Starting when?"

"Right now."

"Let's go in, then. Let's go in."

"Go in? What for?"

"I'll tell you inside."

"If you don't tell us why, we won't go in."

"If you don't go in, there won't be any water."

The women exchanged looks. They made up their minds.

"All right, Sir."

When they were inside, Well-mouth.

"Take off your clothes!"

"What?"

"What are you saying?"

"Take off your clothes."

"No!"

"Not that!"

"Never!"

"No water, then!"

They hesitated.

"Why do you want us bare naked?"

"You can't even make it with one of us. Much less the whole lot!"

Almost with anguish:

"To see you! Just to see you!"

"All right, Sir."

"All right."

The poor rags. The humble rags on the floor. They were more ashamed—among themselves—of their rags. Miserable. Blossoming with stitches and patches. Than of their own bodies. He was looking at them with the eyes of a different zoological species.

Or of a being from another world. Finally they were exposed—a blooming of dark skin—to the impotent optic voracity. He made them line up by the wall. First facing him. Then with their backs turned, so that they wouldn't see him. He got undressed in turn. A toad swollen with toads. Monstrous abortion of an absurd ventropod. He went over to them—one by one. He observed them. He smelled them. He tried to touch them. He had second thoughts. He was even impotent in intent. He gave a shudder. He laughed. Gelded monkey. He drew away. Got dressed again. Gave a couple of small claps.

"Put your clothes back on. Go get your water."

He laughed again. Looking at them. Crumbling them with his eyes. With his nose. Laughter on the outside. Laughter on the inside. As if his innards were laughing up in his mouth.

That was how things were going in Santorontón when Rugel and Salustiano began to bring him news every day:

"The ditches are drying up."

"And the sprouts on the trees."

"The ceibos are full of holes."

"The young pitahayas are disappearing."

"And the sour prickly pears."

"The animals are dying."

"Because of dryness, nothing more."

"Without a drop of blood."

Chalena—even though he had already suspected it—asked:

"So, what about it?"

"Nothing. The thirst is starting to strangle the jungle."

"The animals are coming in closer."

"Some fine morning we'll find them right in Santorontón."

"To fight with us over the water."

A cave with teeth smiled again.

"We'll fight. I'm ready for a fight!"

There were two pieces of news that killed his smile:

"A new priest is coming, Father Gaudencio."

"And a new doctor. A certain Juvencio Balda."

THIRTEEN

Bulu-Bulu's hospital was quite a distance from his house. On top of a hill. The wind combed it everywhere. It had a roof but no walls. There—lying on the ground, one beside the other—were his patients. His sufferers, as he called them. Only a certain few rocked in hammocks hung from hooks in the stakes. There were not many sick people at this time.

"Ever since Dr. Balda came, this has been going downhill. Not many sufferers come to see me anymore."

"Why is that?"

"Because he's half a wizard himself."

Candelario was puzzled.

"Don't say that. He's a doctor."

The simian face put on a look of mock rage.

"Don't come to me with any stories, Colonel. What is it he does? He uses herbs. Earth. Or animals. He brings them here transformed into drinks. Powders. Or pills. In little bottles or boxes that he buys in the city. Or at Vigiliano Rufo's. I prepare mine myself. That's the only difference. Sometimes he sticks a needle into the sufferers. And puts his brews in that way. I prick them too sometimes. To get the sickness out of them."

"He's studied. You know. He's gone to the University."

"I don't have to study, Colonel. I was born knowing. Or, what I mean is, my father taught me. My grandfather had taught him. My great-grandfather him. My great-great-grandfather him. And so on for hundreds of years that are lost in the long night. If that's not enough, they're still teaching me."

"I don't understand."

"We Bulu-Bulus are one and we're many. I've existed ever since the first Bulu-Bulu came into the world. And from that Bulu-Bulu on down, they all exist in me. They're me. I'm them."

"Oh, is that it?"

"Anyway, I don't mean to take anything away from Dr. Balda. For sicknesses of the body he's as good as I am. In patching up sufferers he's a champion. He's even shown how with animals. Do you remember when he sewed up the bellies of all those wounded monkeys? When he set the broken arms and legs of so many of them? He put on splints and treated them just like people. He's very good, that doctor is. If somebody cut me with a machete or put a bullet in my body and took away one of my lives, I'd go to him! And even though we're not friends I'm sure he'd take care of me! On the other hand, I'd never put myself in the hands of Dr. Espurio Carranza!"

"Isn't he any good?"

"He's a bad doctor and he's got a worse heart. Besides, he's got the business of burying the dead. The more people that die, the more money he makes."

There was a brief silence. Candelario spoke.

"Are you better than Dr. Balda in something?"

"Not in something. In lots of things! In the first place, people with one foot in the grave come here. The incurables, according to the doctors. No matter what the disease."

"And you cure them?"

"Almost always."

"What if you don't?"

"When they come here they know that they're closer to the Other life than to This one. If they're saved, what more do they want?"

"But you've got your specialties, right?"

"Of course. Sicknesses that aren't of this world. Ones that are hard to find in the body, at least. Or that can't be cured with drugstore medicines: among others, the evil eye. Unrequited love. Betrayal of love. Dying without knowing why. Bad vapors for plants, animals, and people. Hexes. The harm done by enemies. The wish to die. The fear of something or of everything. Dealings with the dead. Having a ghost, a witch, or a creature stuck in your body."

"That's why you have your cures and your practices, right?"

"Not just for that. I've got my prayers. My allies. My talks with saints, black and white. —Because you should know that ever since we came from the other side of the ocean we've run aground on white saints.— And my sacrifices. Animals. In some cases even people. I'm not going to tell you about that, Colonel!"

"I know a lot of things."

"There are other things you don't know."

"Do you think so?"

The Wizard nodded. He looked at him bat-eyed. He explained:

"For example, you don't know that I had Clotilde Quindales here."

"You did?"

Bulu-Bulu nodded again.

"I found her one night, in the jungle. She didn't recognize me. She couldn't have recognized anyone. She was way up on the Moon. Completely out of this world. She said that in order to save women, it was necessary to geld men. That she, every time she had one on top of her, would cut his nuts off. Beyond that she told me a lot of things that would make your hair stand on end."

The Colonel felt a corkscrew in his groin.

"That's strange! Isn't it?"

"I tried to get away from her. I couldn't. She kept on following me. She wanted to do her things with me. She talked to me about what a good female she was. She showed me some parts of her body that the rags barely covered."

"And?"

"The fact is that during those months she'd changed completely. She'd become completely woman. Everything there was that had to swell up on her had swollen up. If I'd been someone else and not the Wizard Bulu-Bulu, I would have jumped on top of her."

"Weren't you afraid?"

"Of what?"

"That she'd cut yours off too?"

"It was all a big lie. I think that even though she'd become a woman, she hadn't crossed her legs over anyone."

"What was it, then?"

"Didn't I say she was walking on the Moon? She was carrying a whole string of pinecones around. She was almost wrapped up in them. They hung down both sides of her body. They were what she said were men's balls. From the men who had covered her and that she'd gelded. A little old lie!"

"Did you cure her?"

"A little bit. The Moonstruck girl had too big a Moon. In her head. And who knows where else! I fed her. I prepared some brews to calm her down. Make her sleep. That did her a lot of good. Besides, the sea breeze that blows here carries off ideas, as good or bad as they might be. The sufferers who were in better shape helped me too. All of that was very good for her. But that's all. The one who cured her—or made her be cured—was Dr. Balda."

"How did he know what was going on? How did he run into her? Did he come over here?"

"I sent her to him, Colonel. Clotilde didn't have anything to pay me with. And—in any case—in a short while my sufferers were getting all roused up."

The Wizard didn't speak of other things. Besides, everybody knew about them. The sicknesses he cast. The songs and dances he offered by night. The horrible masks he put on. His absurd costumes. Feathers. Dry leaves. The bark of trees. Animal skins. Especially jaguars or crocodiles. The paint he covered his body with, strange cabalistic signs, living geometry, ancestral totemic symbols. He soaked himself in strange oils that had aggressive odors. He would set fire to himself. The flames surrounded him. Without burning him. He leaped. The flames leaped in time to the rhythm. A percussion of distant drums snaked through the jungle. Other sounds—xylophones, metallic sounds—echoed the vibration of the hollow trunks. And, finally, human voices coming from who knows where, seemed to stimulate him. He would offer whole vines of words pulled out of his remote origins. Or invented by him. He would repeat them over and over with onomatopoeic monotony. —Sea? Wind? Thunder? Battle? Incantation? Spell?— He whipped himself. He whipped his victims. And he offered sacrifices of vermin mixed with fragrant resins. Nor did he talk about the fact that he made dolls to "harm" certain people. Nor that he sent those who wanted a good harvest to fornicate upon the earth, into it. Nor that he advised women to put banana leaves on the virile member of the one they didn't want to lose. Nor of his calls to the Tin-Tins to calm women with the urge. For his part, the Colonel didn't ask any more questions. He was sure. He wouldn't say anything about "that." He would show his canine teeth in an ironic smile. He would turn the words around. And on to other things. That was why he was just content to listen.

The two of them had gone off alone. Ña Crisanta and Dominga stayed behind. They never came. In the family of the Bulu-Bulus—Monkey Face had explained—women never took part in witchcraft. Not even in cures. Even less in caring for the sufferers. They didn't know the smallest details regarding those things. They dedicated themselves exclusively to household cares. Sometimes, as in the case of Dominga, they learned a little more. He had sent Dominga, when she was quite young, to the city. To some of her mother's relatives. The girl couldn't get used to it. And as soon as she was able, she came back to Balumba. As much as he tried to persuade her to leave the island, she resisted. She made up a whole series of reasons. What was she going to do in the city? She didn't feel natural there. She wanted, instead, to be with her Old Folks. Take care of them. Live in the open air. Bathe in the inlets. Fish. Cook. She couldn't get used to streets cluttered with houses. Houses stuck one against the other. Strings of enormous hives inhabited by gigantic bees. Anthills that boiled over with the coming and going of people and vehicles. He'd threatened her. He'd even tried to use force on occasion. She had to study. Learn a different way of life. More civilized. If she were a man, well. She could go on being a wizard like the Bulu-Bulus before her. Even though Wizards were on the way out. But she wasn't a man. She was a woman. And women, in things like that, were practically useless. She had to go back to the city. She'd made threats in turn. If he insisted, she'd leave Balumba for good. He'd never hear from her again. That's why he saw himself obliged to give in. Let the girl do whatever she had in mind.

As one who didn't like the idea, the Colonel hinted:

"You should have married her off."

The Wizard feigned displeasure:

"She doesn't like anyone in these parts."

"Oh!"

The image of Dominga—with those undulating hips—came back to lie in wait for him. Why was he waiting so long to get her into bed? Would Bulu-Bulu let him do it for the business of curing him? Or was he afraid of the Other One, the dead one—so dead—Chepa Quindales? The truth was that the female just mentioned was getting hotter every day. He'd never imagined that a dead woman could have those insatiable drives. That was it! He was afraid of that goddamned big dead whore! Ever since she'd taken him on he hadn't been able to get close to any other woman. He'd gone so far with some— in the daytime, of course!—as to get them bare naked. Even get them on their backs. Legs spread. Waiting for him to show himself. He, for his part, was armed and ready. Suddenly something fearful would happen. He would feel a cold kiss on his virile parts. His member would deflate like a punctured bladder. And, suddenly, he'd be left in the slimy unseen jail of impotence. It was She! He was sure! The Damned Woman was only content to caress him and in doing that she sank her cold teeth into his glans! On the other hand, at night, why did she try to wrap him in sheets of fire? Why did she seem to brand him or, at least, tattoo him with irons that marked him deeper inside every time? He was screwed! He! Candelario Mariscal. Breaker of asses. Sower of fear. Upraised lash to bite into all flesh. He couldn't get free of that corpse! Ring-corpse! Chain-corpse! Lodestone-corpse! Vessel-corpse! Corpse-corpse-corpse. A corpse he had there stuck inside him. A corpse where he was stuck in turn.

He turned to the Wizard with wrath.

"Well. When are you going to free me of the dead woman?"

The Wizard took on a mysterious tone.

"I've been consulting all the Saints. The Black Saints and the White Saints."

"And?"

"They've told me that the only cure for you is . . ."

"Out with it!"

". . . to get married!"

"Shit! That really is good. Me get married? You can lead a horse to water, but . . ."

Bulu-Bulu became jaguar-in-a-rainstorm serious.

"Look, Colonel. I respect you. I assure you! I'd never tell you something I didn't believe."

The Colonel frowned.

"Say whatever you want, Bulu-Bulu. But some things make a person laugh just thinking about them."

The Wizard took a chance and played his whole hand.

"Colonel. You'd better leave. Pretend I didn't say anything."

Candelario became furious.

"What? Leave? Say it again and you'll see me shut you up for good!"

The little man seemed to huddle all together. He remained rigid. His eyes became dead. There was a smell of dimness all over him. He changed his voice. It was a voice from beyond the grave. Wrapped in earth that came from some clay jar buried for hundreds of years.

"You can do what you want, Colonel. Or try to. I'll still respect you. But if you don't believe what I'm telling you, we don't have anything to talk about anymore. I repeat. You'd better leave!"

The Wizard's attitude disarmed him. He opened his small sleepy eyes a crocodile-little-bit.

"I didn't think you were such a tough little man, Bulu-Bulu."

"Appearances deceive sometimes."

A minimal smile peeled his few teeth. He went on:

"Besides, you can't kill the dead. And many dead men live in me. I already told you, Colonel."

The latter didn't pay any heed to the last words. He was worried about something else.

"Is what you said true, Bulu-Bulu? That I have to get married for the dead woman to stop fucking me?"

The Wizard nodded.

"And completely legal."

The Colonel went back to his previous stand.

"Stop your horseshit, Bulu-Bulu! Talk serious!"

The one addressed kept his dignity.

"Are you going back to your old tricks?"

He got hold of himself.

"No. No. It's all right!"

He seemed suddenly worried. He went on:

"Where am I going to find a female for that?"

"It's a matter of looking for her. Maybe closer than you think."

The Colonel looked at him fixedly. A suspicion glowed under his skull. Could he be thinking of Dominga? Would he try to tie him to the girl forever? The Monkeyface eyes were still dead. Could it be that? Couldn't it? Did he—Colonel Candelario Mariscal—have the face of you-can-pass-off-a-badger-on-me-for-a-pig? He said, like one who didn't like the idea:

"You're right. Right back there in the city I might find a woman made to my measure."

The Wizard seemed to come alive. He put on the most innocent face in the world.

"Of course, Colonel. The women titty around there."

"I'll go next week."

"The quicker the better, Colonel."

Could he be telling him the truth? Couldn't he be fooling him? Didn't he want to stick him with Dominga? Dominga. She was good, damn her. Dominga. Every time he saw her, she looked better built. Sturdier. More wiggly. More twisty. Dominga. Like making a mussel jump out of his bellybutton. Dominga. He had to hold himself back from throwing her down in front of everybody. Stop from doing to her what he'd done to Clotilde after making filets out of the Quindales. Dominga. All things considered, he couldn't do it. Rather, he shouldn't do it. Not just because he liked the Wizard, precisely because he was a Wizard. And Wizards are always Wizards. No one can even suspect what might happen with them. Especially a wizard like Bulu-Bulu. Didn't he say that he was one and he was many? That a whole string of dead men were alive in him? Who knows, if he killed him—or tried to kill him—maybe all the others would come back to life! Better that their paths didn't cross. Goddamn it, he was changing! Why was he thinking all of that? Could he be getting old? Before he would have gone through the driest inlet. Without worrying about the consequences. He would have rolled around with Dominga on her mat lots of times. And let's see who'd tread on his crocodile tail! Now, on the other hand...

He repeated, as if to himself:

"Maybe you're right, Bulu-Bulu. What I need is a woman. A woman who can keep me tied up with every knot in the book."

Bulu-Bulu—in a surge—remembered Crisanta's recommendation. "If we marry off Dominga, it has to be with a Priest and everything."

Since he felt the same, he made himself clear:

"And in Church."

"Do you believe in that, Bulu-Bulu?"

He gave an evasive answer:

"We Wizards don't have to believe or not believe in those

things. We believe in other things. If the Saints order it that way, it's because that's the way it has to be."

A short time later they were on the shore of Balumba. By the Wizard's house. Dominga's wandering urges made their appearance almost at once. The Colonel looked her up and down. As if thinking her over. As if evaluating her. The girl, as if realizing it, snuffed out the lamp she had between her legs.

"Some coffee, Colonel?"

"Thank you. It's always been good for me, we might say."

The sinuous hips moved about. This way, that way. That way, this way, the paddle of a canoe. Was the woman already rowing inside of him? Would she keep on rowing until she turned him into her sea, her river, her inlet? All of a sudden he thought. Why look in the city—the Great City-of-Two-Rivers. Of two Rivers in one River. Of one River that makes a Sea. Of one River that makes a Gulf—which was dancing in front of him, shaking his roots. If he had to marry someone in order to frighten Chepa off, why not Minga? Of all the women in Santorontón, Minga was the best. He was sure. Even without having tried her. Besides, the city had marked its invisible tattoo on her. She'd never be like the others anymore. And she seemd to light up when she laughed. Deviltry stirred steadily in her eyes, a two-pronged harpoon. That made it hard to free yourself from those eyes. All that, not to mention the white fabric that gave hints—in front of her legs and behind—under her chintz clothes. He concluded. Yes. Why not Minga? At that moment she was coming over. The eddy of temptations that burst forth from her made him half-nauseous.

"Your coffee, Colonel."

"Thank you. Thank you very much."

He stared at her. The force of such a look paralyzed her. She remained anxious. Waiting. He threw it at her point-blank.

"Listen, Minga."

"Yes, sir."

"How'd you like to marry me?"

She became disconcerted.

Ña Crisanta and Bulu-Bulu pretended not to notice. They didn't even look at the couple. Rather—the Wizard from a piling, the Old Woman from the window—"observed" the countryside. The Giant-River. Sea-River. Gulf-River. Opening up in a huge fan toward the west. Three sails of a sloop—a hand with three fingers—tickling the clouds.

Candelario insisted:

"I'm not teasing, Minga. Seriously. How'd you like to marry me?"

She stopped laughing. Became emotional. Fell apart a little.

"Yo . . . u?"

"What's the matter? Am I all that bad?"

She hastened to answer:

"No. Not that!"

She looked at him intensely. She explained:

"Just the opposite. The fact is . . . What they say . . . and I . . . I . . ."

He remained calm. He spoke with a tranquil voice.

"I can see that they've told you a lot of things about me, right? They probably told you that if I like a woman, I rape her. And that it's all over then and there. That if she doesn't have a man, there's no problem. And if she does, that's no problem either. Because right there the man meets his end. That, in the same way, if I get the urge—good or bad—I'll carry you off with me."

He smiled. Added:

"It's not all true. Or all a lie either. You can see. I'm asking you, how'd you like to marry me?"

His face turned crocodile.

"I'm asking you for the last time."

She answered, hurriedly:

"Of course, Colonel."

Candelario turned toward the Wizard, laughing openly.

"You see, Bulu-Bulu. I screwed you. You've got to give me the medicine along with the prescription."

The Wizard shrugged his shoulders, with feigned indifference.

"Minga will give you the medicine, Colonel. What else are women for?"

He looked toward the window.

"Right, Crisanta?"

The Old Woman answered grudgingly:

"Of course! Of course!"

The decision made, Candelario Mariscal went to find the Political Lieutenant. As soon as the latter saw him, he came forward to greet him, all rolled up into a ball. He was going to say: "What a miracle to see you here!" He stopped himself in time. The word "miracle" was out of place.

"To what do I owe the honor of your visit, Colonel?"

"I'm going to get married!"

Salustiano Caldera showed great surprise.

"Married? You?"

Candelario frowned.

"What the hell! Is there anything wrong with that? Can't I get married if I feel like it?"

"I was only talking, Colonel. Why shouldn't you get married? You can get married as many times as you like. I was only talking."

"Aha!"

"When do you want to get married?"

"Tomorrow."

"At what time?"

"At whatever time I feel like it."

"Fine, Colonel. Fine. I'll have all the papers ready. Whatever you say."

"Naturally, whatever I say."

He gave him all the information. He went to the church immediately after. When Filemón saw him cross the threshold, he crossed himself. It was as if the old sexton had seen The Evil One in person. He was about to run away. Or hide. The Colonel didn't give him time. He let out a shout that echoed throughout the church.

"Hey, there! Wait a minute!"

The other one stopped, as if he had just noticed him. There was the glimmer of a forced smile.

"What can I do for you, Colonel?"

"Tell Father Gaudencio I want to see him."

"He... he's resting."

"Have him get up. I've got to see him right away."

"But I..."

He became impatient.

"Oh, shit! Are you going to do what I tell you or not?"

"Yes, Colonel. Yes. Whatever you say."

Running—as fast as his strength, which wasn't much anymore, would allow him—he went off to carry out the order. Candelario, while he was waiting, looked around. How different this church was from his godfather's! It was built of reinforced concrete. Or, at least, it was going to be. The beams were even covered with wooden molding. The iron supports stuck out everywhere from the already hardened mixture. The bricks formed high walls, still not cleaned. The paving stones included many white ones. In front —almost at the foot of the altar—an inscription. With gold letters, too. He went over. Read:

FOR THE SAKE OF HEAVEN
CRISOSTOMO CHALENA
ESPURIO CARRANZA
VIGILIANO RUFO
SALUSTIANO CALDERA
RUGEL BANCHACA

Could they have paid for that? Was it simply a tribute rendered to the bosses of Santorontón? In any case, from what he saw, it was a question of a priest who was on the ball. He thought back. Almost from the first day he'd arrived in town, he'd begun to build the church. He charged for everything. Baptisms. Oils. Last rites. Saying mass. Marriages. And burials too. He had his own private cemetery—holy ground—behind the church. The farther away the deceased was buried, the cheaper the price. On the other hand, those whose crosses were near the walls of the church paid very large amounts. All, of course, for the building of the House of God. The house that was taking so long to grow. That seemed as if it would never be finished. His reflections were interrupted by Father Gaudencio's presence. The eyelids were puffy. As if he had just got up. He went arrogantly over to Candelario. He spoke to him in a fluty voice. Like that of a thirsty vulture.

"What do you want?"

A look of mockery hovered on the Colonel's cheeks. He bowed.

"Good morning, Father Gaudencio."

"Hello. What do you want?"

The bridegroom's voice sweetened into a honeycomb of aroused moquiñaña bees. With apparent timidity, he stammered:

"I . . . I want . . ."

The other one shouted at him, haughtily.

"What?"

"To . . . to get . . . to get married."

Indignation and surprise seemed to go beyond the limits of his tolerance.

"What? What did you say?"

Candelario pretended to make an effort. He smiled pleasantly.

"Just that. I want to get married."

The Priest looked at him. As if he hadn't understood. He repeated:

"Get married?"

Then he looked at him steadily. Coldly. In anathema.

"It would be sacrilege!"

"Sacrilege? Why?"

"Because you're..."

The pleasant smile grew broader.

"What?"

"The son of..."

He corrected himself quickly.

"The one who set fire to this church. The other one, rather."

Candelario darkened.

"Yes. My godfather's."

He refused to explain anything. He didn't feel to blame. Another hand had moved him. He'd lost his will that night. He was drunk. He didn't realize what he was doing. Why did he have to explain? It would have been a waste of time. The Priest wouldn't understand. How could he understand, if his godfather hadn't even understood? Whether he was actually guilty. Would Father Cándido have treated him so badly if he hadn't thought so? Well. The main thing was to get him to marry him as soon as possible. To solve the problem that had him flat on his face. All the rest was water under the bridge. Would he explain himself? Or wouldn't he? Maybe with time.

Father Gaudencio suggested:

"Why doesn't your godfather marry you?"

He became upset.

"Him? Never! I wouldn't even ask him."

The Priest felt himself master of the situation. He spoke in a definitive way.

"Then you'll have to go somewhere else. Here, in this church, I can't marry you."

The Bridegroom reacted. He laughed again. This time a crocodile laugh.

"Oh, no?"

"No. That's all. Good day."

He turned his back. Went off. Only two steps. An unexpected question stopped him.

"Do you like to dance, Mr. Priest?"

He turned around. Indignant.

"How dare you!"

"I'm going to give you a lesson."

The Cleric fell apart. He showed it. In a rage.

"How dare you! Sacrilege!"

The Colonel pointed to the sign. The sign with the large golden letters.

"What have you got to say about that division of shares in heaven? Do you think those bastards deserve it? Aren't they the ones who are bleeding Santorontón dry?"

"Go away and don't bother me!"

"It doesn't matter to me, of course. What matters to me is for you to marry me. For the last time, are you going to marry me or not?"

"Never!"

The word wasn't out of his mouth when the Colonel was by his side. He clutched his machete. He hummed a tune. He began to beat the flat of the blade against the floor. The metallic tone accompanied the melody. Without pausing in the maneuver, he turned once and then again around the Cleric. In a vain attempt the latter tried to get out of that moving encirclement. He stepped to one side. There was Candelario. He stepped to the other side. The same thing happened. In view of that, he stopped. He folded his arms. He lifted his eyes to heaven. As if begging for divine justice. Or to show indifference. Soon the circle became tighter. The machete blows were getting closer to the satin slippers. Longer and stronger sparks burst from the pavement. Candelario. Candela-río. Candle-river. Candle. Candlelight. The metallic squeals kept getting closer. They weren't on the ground anymore, they were on his feet. He leaped. He reacted. He tried to maintain his composure. Could he have cut his foot off? Was it with the flat of the weapon? No. They were sharp sounds. Maybe with the dull edge. Another blow. Another leap. Should he lift up his cassock so as not to fall? He would look ridiculous. Like a woman lifting her skirt to tap dance. Another blow. Another. Another. Another... Naturally, the leaps that accompanied them. All of it to the rhythm of the song the Colonel was still humming, imperturbably. The pain was becoming intolerable. Was he mashing his toes? His heels? His instep? They grew more frequent. Sharper. Or could it be because he kept hitting parts already touched? Little by little they were climbing up. Not just on the feet anymore. They were climbing up his ankles. Along his calves. Each time they became more difficult to bear. Was he going to keep on like that? Better do something. Shout. Call for help. Tell the sexton to ring the bells. Maybe his parishioners would come to his defense. He thought otherwise. What good would it do? He knew it was useless. No one would come to help him. They were all afraid of the Colonel. Even Filemón had refused to come back in. So? The pain was unbearable. The blows alternated between his feet and his legs. They were already climbing up to his knees. He didn't have the courage to continue resisting. In spite of all, he would make an effort. A supreme effort. He would show that madman what a Priest is when he defends his faith and his beliefs.

Suddenly the song stopped. What didn't stop was the exasperating rhythm of the blows. The mocking voice asked:

"What color is your blood, Father?"

The one addressed didn't answer.

"Well, let's find out."

Gaudencio, unable to contain himself, shouted:

"No! Not that!"

"Are you going to marry me, then?"

"Never!"

He lost the tip of a slipper. A well-aimed blow of the machete cut it off. The piece flew several paces away. Immediately the same with the other slipper. He felt he was a martyr. He lifted up his eyes again. At that instant he felt a prick. Like the sting of a fireshit ant. He looked. On the tip of his great toe—with a watchmaker's precision—there was a tiny cut. A small stream of blood was flowing. Then he looked at the Colonel. He felt an awful fright. In his place there were crocodiles. Colonel-crocodiles. Many colonel-crocodiles. Turning about him. In a series of superimposed figures. Some blending with others. Nor was the machete one machete. There were dozens of them. Hundreds of machetes. They were beating on the floor. They were drawing sparks. In time to the song that the multiple mouths had begun to hum again. He wailed:

"Enough! Enough!"

"Are you going to marry me?"

"Yes. Yes."

The deadly music ceased. The machete went back to its belt, the crocodile-colonels became a single one. Crocodile-Colonel metamorphosed into Colonel. The voice of the latter echoed peacefully. As if nothing extraordinary had happened.

"I'll see you tomorrow, Father."

"Tomorrow. Tomorrow."

The Bridegroom took two or three steps. Stopped. Turned.

"Oh. I forgot to tell you."

The Priest looked at him. Nervous.

"What?"

"People don't fool around with me."

FOURTEEN

Native and alien ghosts—some alive, some transitory, the worst kind—forced him to leave the city. "Where will you go to rattle your bones now, Juvencio Balda?" He picked up a pencil and a map of the province. He closed his eyes. He spun his right hand around several times. Stopped. Lowered it. Marked a spot. By chance. He opened his eyes. Looked. He was surprised. The sharp point had hit an arm of the Great River—the Sea River—almost where it becomes a Gulf. The map showed no settlements. The closest must have been many miles away. "What are you going to do, doctor? Stay where your enemies bloom? Will you offer up to them what's left of your liver in one final hiccup of tribute? Or will you follow your bitter impulse and go live in that desolate spot?" He decided on the route marked out by the sharpened plumbago. Once decided, he found the best way to get to the unknown spot. No one could direct him at first. He was filled with anguish. Was that tiny little exit going to be closed to him too? He got hold of himself. The smart thing would be to go down to the shore drive that ran along the River. Go into bars near the docks. Maybe someone there could tell him. He was wrong. The regular customers of those dens knew little about routes like that. If he went up River, they told him. Or, rather, up Rivers, since the Great River divides in two up there, he might be able to get directions. On the other hand, down River, impossible! All in all, they pointed out to him, there—there where he was showing them—there weren't any motorboats. Only sloops. And, according to their speculations, most of them passed it by. They were going somewhere else. Further inland—where the islands are like papaya seeds. Or outward bound. Toward the north or south of the Gulf. He could probably take one of those sloops. From there they would put him in a canoe. And they would take him to the mouth of the estuary.

On hearing the word "canoe," someone advised.

"Why not go in a canoe? There are canoes that come and go. Every day."

Another explained it:

"That's right. Bringing fish!"

And another:

"They come to the back part of the city."

Juvencio was puzzled.

"How's that?"

"Don't you know, doctor? The city has two Rivers. Two Rivers that become one in front. And the Sea, behind..."

"Of course. Everybody knows that."

"Well, people travel on that Sea too."

They abounded in explanations:

"Along the thousand canals it forms."

"Through the estuaries where they find currents."

"Some go, others come."

"Among the thousand islands."

"That's where the fishing canoes go."

"And the rafts."

"But you can never get there on a raft."
"Sometimes it's better never to get there, right?"
The Doctor explained:
"The worst is that I don't know where I'm going."
"Oh, hell! That really is hairy."
An Old Man put in his word. He was drinking his cane liquor right from the bottle.
"From what you say, where you want to go is Santorontón."
"What's that? A town?"
"It won't ever be that."
"A ranch?"
"Something more maybe. A settlement. Or maybe it's grown. Maybe it can be called a village now. It's been a long time since I've heard anyone mention Santorontón. Since things started to happen."
"What things?"
"Things... Things that aren't good for Christian people."
He looked at the doctor through the unreality of his alcohol.
"If I were you, I wouldn't go!"
"Why not?"
"Maybe Santorontón doesn't even exist."
"What do you mean?"
"Or never has existed."
"How's that?"
"Or what happens there doesn't happen."
Juvencio smiled:
"Maybe it's up to me to find out. Besides, I've got a tough hide as it is. Inside and out."
The other gave his opinion:
"To each his own, Doctor. And don't be offended, I'm not saying it because of you. I'm just saying it. It's a saying: An ass that wants a whip will go looking for it himself."
"I repeat..."
"Have it your own way!"
He downed a goodly amount of the flaming cane juice.
"So you've got to arrange your trip over on the backside of the city. With the canoers themselves."
The fishing canoes were returning to the islands with only a few provisions. Rice. Lard. Plantains. Beans. Sometimes they also carried equipment they could use in their work: Casting nets. Lines or sinkers for them and larger nets. Hooks. Tips for gaffs

or harpoons, etc. So they were almost always traveling empty. That's why there was no problem in arranging his trip. "And even if we were all loaded up," the Helmsman assured him, "we'd find some way to fit you in. Even easier now since we've got enough room to have a dance on board." So Juvencio was able to board with plenty of room—in addition to his personal belongings—for some of his medical instruments and a few pharmaceutical products. When he asked about the cost of the trip, they told him they'd settle that later. Not to worry about it. They put him on the seat in the middle. And almost immediately the oarsmen started rowing. There were four of them. They did it vigorously. In a rhythmical way. He noticed that one of them had a look of pain every time he made an effort.

"What's the matter?"

"A damned ray stung me on the foot. It's swelling up on me."

"When was that?"

"Last night. While we were gathering in the fish in the blocked inlet."

The Physician went over.

"Let's have a look at it."

"It's nothing, doctor."

Juvencio gave him a quick examination.

"It's starting to get infected. I'll fix it up."

The oarsman expressed himself evasively.

"If you want..."

"Stop rowing. Come to the stern."

The other one seemed doubtful.

"Well..."

The hoarse and mocking voice of the Helmsman dropped in.

"Do what the doctor says. It's best that way. If not, you'll have to go to Bulu-Bulu's tonight. It might be too late by then. And you might lose your leg."

When he stood up, the wounded man's face contracted. He muttered.

"Goddamn it! I didn't think it was so bad."

The doctor took care of him. Recommended:

"Lie down for a bit. You've got to rest."

He went back to his seat. He looked around distractedly. They were already into the intricate labyrinth of the islands. He got the impression that they were going round and round in the same place. Only the dimensions and the configuration of the inlets—

more or less wide, more or less straight, more or less curved—indicated to him that they were going through different places.

Behind him the voice of the skipper was heard.

"A little rice and dark conch, doctor?"

He accepted, smiling.

"Thank you very much."

When he turned around to take the plate, he saw the one stung by the ray. He had evidently got a little relief. He was in a deep sleep. He recommended:

"When he wakes up he'll feel better. He'll be hungry. Give him some rice. But no conch."

They arrived at sundown. So, did Santorontón exist? Or was he the one who had ceased to exist and that was why he was able to go meet the nonexistent? Whatever it was, the truth is that he was looking at that village. His informant had underrated it. It had a lot of houses. Here and there its kerosene lights could be seen, yellowish. In the center gasoline lamps stood out, bluish. The outlines were confused. Only a few human shadows walked about slowly. Amidst the sporadic barking of street dogs.

Juvencio was about to jump onto land. The Helmsmen stopped him.

"Where are you going?"

"To look for a hotel. Or an inn. Any place to spend the night. And to put away my things until daylight."

"Don't even dream about it, doctor. Here, for good or evil, no one will put you up."

"It doesn't matter. Leave me on the shore. I'll stay on the beach. Tomorrow I'll see what I can do."

The one stung by the ray had awakened. He heard part of the conversation. He suggested:

"Why don't we go see Father Cándido? He lives alone. The doctor can probably stay with him."

The Helmsman approved of the idea.

"That's true."

And without consulting the passenger, he ordered:

"Let's go there!"

They arrived after a few minutes of rowing. The Helmsman shouted:

"Father Cándido! Father Cándido!"

The door of the house by the shore opened. The light that came from inside outlined a figure.

"What do you want?"

"Lodging for a friend."

Without hesitation he made the invitation:

"Have him come in."

All the canoists—except for the wounded one—unloaded the doctor's belongings. The latter went over to the priest.

"Thank you, Father. I'm Juvencio Balda, a doctor."

The Priest smiled broadly. Shook his hand. The young man shook his, effusively.

"Glad to meet you. You already know who I am. Make yourself at home."

"If it wasn't for you, I probably would have had to spend the night on the beach! And with all this cold!"

The oarsmen finished their chores. Juvencio asked:

"How much do I owe you?"

The Helmsmen explained:

"We're not in this business, doctor. They pay us to carry fish, not people."

The young doctor felt a sudden emotion.

"Thanks for everything."

"Thanks to you, doctor. For healing our oarsman."

That one showed the corncob of his teeth.

"I'm already feeling as good as new again."

With no further ado, they sank into the night. In the midst of the tireless symphony of the waves. Little by little the steady rhythm of the oars faded away. Juvencio looked around. A house of bamboo. Mangrove beams and a bijao roof. It stood a few inches off the ground. There were two rooms. In the one that served as a living room, a table and two chairs. Over the table, the Burned Christ. In the other room, a cot and its netting. In addition, a stove made of bricks, inside a box. The doctor's belongings were piled in a corner. The Priest followed the newcomer's gaze.

"You were wrong to get enthusiastic. It's the hospitality of a poor priest."

He was almost a giant. Athletic. In spite of his years—"How many? How old could he be?"—he stood straight. Like a palm mangrove. He wore a threadbare cassock. With patches all over.

Very clean, that was certain. Thinning gray hair. Brown eyes. A sharp nose. An expressive mouth. Prominent cheekbones. Big ears. Bony. Sinewy. Infinite goodness: such was the cleric.

His voice tense, the young man gave an opinion:

"I wish there were a lot more priests—rich or poor—like you."

Cándido turned to the Burned Christ.

"What would Gaudencio think if he heard those flowery words?"

The Son of Mary put on an expression of doubt.

"Who knows? Maybe he would die of envy. Or maybe of rage. He'd think that you were competition for him. And, what's worse, all for nothing."

"Who's to blame?"

"You're not going to say that I am, are you? That would be too much!"

"Who else, then?"

"Cándido! Remember, we have a guest!"

The Priest was furious.

"If you don't make miracles anymore, why don't you ask your Father to? Why do you let this imported monk convert the church and all it stands for into a marketplace? Why don't you send him and his music somewhere else?"

"Don't prod me into violence. One of these days..."

The doctor intervened.

"Is there another priest?"

The Priest answered:

"Didn't you know? Of course! How could you, you just got here. Well, yes. There is another. A certain Gaudencio."

The Crucified One advised:

"Calm yourself, Cándido!"

"How can I be calm when I talk about that person... the one who kicked me out of the church?"

Juvencio was more and more puzzled.

"Out of the church? You?"

"Yes. Out of my church. Rather, out of my half-church. Because mine—the one I built with my own hands and those of the Santorontonians—burned down some time ago. I hadn't rebuilt it yet."

Jesus insisted:

"You can tell him later. Don't be abusive. Now, offer him something to eat."

"You're right."
And to the Doctor:
"You must be tired and hungry. Well. Whatever there is in this house is yours."
He smiled. Added:
"Including a cot and some netting."
"Don't put yourself out on my account."
"No one will be put out. We'll share some smoked mullet. Some plantain cakes. And a little coffee."
Juvencio was feeling more and more peaceful. He smiled.
"The service is as good as the price."

The next day the Priest took him to Santorontón. In his canoe. He paddling as always. He tried to convince José Isabel Lindajón—one of his most faithful parishioners—to put him up. It wasn't easy. The affection and the respect he felt for Father Cándido were obvious. But, no doubt, he was held by an invincible terror.
"You know. As far as I'm concerned there's no problem. But outsiders aren't welcome here. The bosses are afraid they'll find out the things they're doing."
The same word again! He wanted to know.
"What things?"
José Isabel—old and skinny, a sucked-out cane—replied evasively.
"Many things."
The Priest explained:
"A handful of men have taken over the village. One especially. A certain Crisóstomo Chalena. He controls the rainwater. Ever since the wells dried up, it's all we have. For that reason those who oppose him go thirsty."
"Haven't they found a solution to it?"
"They haven't been able."
Lindajón ventured:
"Speaking of Don Chalena . . ."
"What?"
"Tolón—the boy with the rosebush—is all one big moan. He cries and wails day and night."
Juvencio became interested.
"Why?"
"He has a rosebush stuck in his hand."

"How can that be?"
The Priest, in a few words, explained it to him again. The Young Man seemed very concerned.
"There's no time to lose. He has to be looked after right away."
José Isabel explained:
"If you go alone you won't even be able to get in."
Cándido nodded:
"I'll go with him. But first let's unload the doctor's equipment. Because he's staying here, right, José Isabel?"
Lindajón shrugged his shoulders. Fatalistically.
"Yes, Father Cándido. No matter what happens."
A short while later they were before Chalena. Lying in his hammock. As always. He half sat up on seeing the Priest. After saying hello, he asked:
"What miracle brings you here, Father Cándido?"
"I've come to introduce Dr. Juvencio Balda."
The little man observed him. The medical man was of average height. Chubby. Quite young. Careful of his dress. Courteous manners. Affable face. He irradiated pleasantness. He made a bad impression on him. He got control of himself:
"Welcome, doctor. Especially since Father Cándido has brought you."
He stopped. Before the other one had time to thank him, he added:
"Although I have a feeling you're not going to last long here. There's practically no work. We already have our doctor. A good doctor. Dr. Espurio Carranza."
The Priest joined in.
"Another doctor is always welcome."
He went on. Jokingly.
"Besides, Santorontón is still growing. More people are being born and dying every day. Pretty soon Dr. Espurio will have enough to do with burying his dead. His own and outsiders. Because once in a while Bulu-Bulu sends him some too."
Chalena smiled with his great frog mouth. His eyes seemed to disappear.
"I was just talking, Father Cándido. Just talking."
A shriek interrupted him. An invisible viper tore the air. Almost ultrahuman. They shuddered. Then the weeping of a child. Mixed with guttural cries. Strange. Growing. Finally running. Coming

close. Mixed with the wailing and weeping. Chalena stood up. With difficulty. Maybe he wanted to stop what was happening. He didn't have time. On the doorstep a monstrous group. The Mute Woman, Tolón. She pulling on her son's left arm. Tolón bag of bones. His eyes seemed larger. Pain. Insomnia. Desperation. Labeled on his face. His hair long, tangled. A wild look. His right hand outstretched. Decomposed. —His arm purple.— Wrapped in shoots and dead leaves. A living bush. The Rosebush. Rosebush-hairshirt. Rosebush-root. Rosebush-dagger. Rosebush-fang. With a sudden movement, Juvencio leaped forward. Beside himself he pulled out the shoots. The leaves. He scattered the earth. With care he extracted the roots. They had not gone in very deeply. Perhaps not at all. They had barely scratched the skin. He did his curing. Chalena—a chromatic palette—showed astonishment. Rage. Pain. Fear. Desperation. Upset...

He roared:

"What are you doing?"

Juvencio did not answer. He didn't even change his expression. Chalena shouted, even louder:

"What are you trying to do?"

He went forward. Stumbling.

"Let go of him!"

Cándido intervened:

"Leave him alone."

"What about the rosebush?"

"You were going to lose it in any case."

He fell apart.

"No. No! Please! Don't kill the rosebush!"

Juvencio turned around. He had bandaged Tolón's hand.

"There it is."

The Mute stopped weeping. She fell on her knees. Kissed the doctor's hand. Crisóstomo looked—out of control again, idiotically—at what was happening. Two tears ran down his batrachian cheeks. He fell onto the hammock. Moaned.

"My rosebush."

He recovered. Became furious again. Faced the doctor.

"You'll pay me for that. You'd better leave. Or you'll see what will happen to you!"

He looked at Father Cándido with rage and hatred.

"You too. Busybody! You'll all pay me! All of you!"

Juvencio explained:

"If we had delayed, the roots would have sunk into the child's flesh. He would have lost his arm. He could have died."

The other one didn't seem to understand.

"I won't give you any water! Not a drop! And anyone who does will lose his. Forever! You'll see. I'll make life impossible for you. You'll die of thirst!"

The young man looked at him. Coldly.

"You're not alone in the world, Mr. Chalena. Santorontón either. A few hours from here we can still get justice."

These words seemed to calm the homunculus a bit. Nevertheless, he didn't consider himself defeated.

"We'll see! We'll see! In any case, it would be better if you went away. Ever since you've come you've started to cause problems. It would be better if you went away!"

Again the voice took on its plaintive tone.

"My rosebush. I lost my rosebush!"

Tolón's shining eyes. A colt of glass and froth. Of glass and blood. Of black glass. Of green blood. Of smoke and jungle. A colt with wings. A colt with wings on wings. Four. Ten. A hundred wings. Going off. Going off off. Going off off off. Turning. Glass ball. Turning butterfly turns. Soap ball. Young mangrove butterfly. "Oh, my rosebush." "Oh, my colt, little colt, little colt! Oh, my black-green little colt! Oh, my air-moon little colt, sea-moon! Moon glass colt! Sea froth colt!"

Days later—when he was already settled in the village—Clotilde arrived. Wrapped in her net of pinecones. Held by her testicular dreams. Bulu-Bulu had sent her. A traveler from a world of glowing stalactite suspended sexes. A Moon graft in her great eyes. Sea in her open lips. Serpent in her mental distortions. Half-naked breasts of invitation and things of offer, she appeared on the threshold. She was mostly dressed, perhaps, in dream caresses. She had something of a miraculous image left from a trance. The half-shadow light that directed her steps seemed to sparkle at every instant. The fleeting hospitality of the Wizard had transformed her. She still passed along through evasion and distance. Above it all, her body smiled springtime. Her bones did not hint at bitter angles under her skin. She was growing curvy. A slight attraction that was marginal to her consciousness seemed to surround her. The one who brought her explained:

"Bulu-Bulu sends her."
Juvencio looked at him in astonishment.
"What for?"
"For you to cure her. She's a sufferer."
He pointed to his head with his forefinger. Turned it around his temple. Added:
"In the nut."
The doctor attempted a feeble protest.
"She's a girl. I can't have her here. I..."
The other one shrugged his shoulders.
"You'll see what to do. I'm doing what the Wizard told me to do. That's all."
And he left.
Clotilde entered quite naturally.
"Do I give you urges?"
She tried to get even more undressed. Rather, to take off what little there was left to cover her. The doctor stopped her.
"Wait. Come here. Sit down."
She obeyed.
"What's your name?"
"Clotilde."
He looked at her more intensely. Suddenly he felt a double tenderness. As a doctor and as a man. Psychically she seemed so despoiled.
"Do you want something to eat, Clotilde?"
"Good. And whenever you want to cover me..."
"Cover you?"
"Yes. Mount me...you can do it. Only you know already what will happen to you."
"What will happen to me? I don't understand!"
"Yes. I'll have to geld you. That's what I've done to all the others. Look!"
She showed him the garland of pinecones. Continued:
"Men are evil. They do harm to women. And these I have to save."

FIFTEEN

At first Ña Crisanta was out of control.

"How can you hand Minga over to a Son of The One We Know?"

"Nothing but talk."

"Are you sure?"

He answered with another question.

"Would you rather have the girl burying X-Bonetails every night?"

"She'll get over that."

"Or if the Tin-Tins get her pregnant first?"

"The Tin-Tins don't come this far."

"That's what you think. I've seen their tracks underneath her window. Especially the first night."

"Oh, yes?"

"That's why it's better if the Colonel takes her."

He didn't say so. But he thought it inside: "Even though it's just medicine." The Old Woman was resigned.

"What can we do, then? I hope it all turns out well! I'm afraid."

He was afraid too. Why shouldn't he be afraid, knowing Candelario as he knew him? Of course, the man had changed. A great deal. That Chepa Quindales, with her urges of a dead woman, had made him turn completely around. Earlier he never would have given him his daughter. He would have preferred her being taken by any one of the Santorontonians and not the Priest's Godson. Now, on the other hand, he was sure that the latter would cling to Dominga. As to a balsa-wood log in a stormy sea. For the Colonel, his daughter would be the best cure. Would she? Would the Dead Woman beat a retreat? Or, on the contrary, would she stay there naked between the newlyweds? Would he try to roll around with her and not with the other one? If that came to pass, he, the Wizard Bulu-Bulu, would intervene! He would use his powers—the good ones and the evil—so that Minga would not have to keep on burying snakes night after night. Otherwise, it looked as if everything was going to turn out well. The Colonel had the turtle-drawn canoe moored by the house. From it—as from a command post—he was organizing the last details of the wedding. Among other things he asked Ña Crisanta to invite all the bosses there were in the village. She had resisted. With her teeth showing, of course. But inside she was moving like a restless curiquingue hawk.

"It's useless, Colonel. They won't come."

The Colonel bared his teeth.

"You're so beaten down, Ña Crisanta! Invite them! Tell them that Colonel Candelario Mariscal wants them to attend his wedding!"

"What if they say no?"

"Then warn them that they'd better go talk to Espurio. For their plots in the cemetery. The burial will be free. I'll provide that and I'll provide the corpse."

The Old Woman wrinkled up like a squeezed rag.

"And."

"What?"

"Should I invite your godfather too?"

"No, Ña Crisanta. Not him or his friends."

The Wizard's wife didn't even name them. What for? In addition to the Burned Christ the "friends" were Dr. Juvencio Balda, Clotilde Quindales, José Isabel Lindajón, and a few more. Without pushing the matter, she got ready to carry out the order. She began to think well of the Colonel. It seemed that this time he wanted to do everything "trulytrue." For her it turned out to be an exceptional occasion. In Santorontón they had never forgiven her for going off with the Wizard. They looked down on her. "Just imagine! Marrying a Wizard. A Witch Doctor, and a black one at that!" In most cases they wouldn't even speak to her. When she went to the market—or any other public place—the other women would avoid her. As if she had Yellow Fever or Bubonic Plague. They would whisper among themselves. Throw looks full of disdain or mockery at her. It was the same with Dominga. Happily, she didn't care about anything. She went about wrapped in her red whirlwind. Pricked by her intimate problems. By the feverish explosion that was kindling her drives. With the fierce anguish of every day as night drew near. Sensing the daily presence of the X-Bonetail that was to coil about her. The one she would bury later so she could sleep. Through all of it, the Old Woman could taste the yellow and frothy corn wine of vengeance with anticipation. In order to do her duty better, she started to fix herself carefully. Old loud-colored clothes that she had buried in the bottom of the drawers. Funny-looking squeaky shoes. Creams the Wizard used for his spectacular nighttime makeup: none of which made her ceremonial appearance very impressive. When she was ready and walked in front of Bulu-Bulu, he couldn't hold back his laughter.

"You look like a drunken parrot."

She gave him an angry look. Got control of herself. Even put on a little smile.

"The parrot and the drunk are your mother."

The Wizard let out a loud laugh. He watched her leave in her canoe. She paddled herself. She headed for Santorontón. She didn't turn around a single instant. The truth is that she didn't have much time to face the people. The first one she saw was Chalena. He sat up in his hammock. Although he already had an idea of what she was coming for since Father Gaudencio had spread it to the four winds, he assumed an innocent air.

"What a miracle to see you, Ña Crisanta!"

"Well, it really is a miracle, Don Crisóstomo. I've come to invite you to my daughter's wedding."

"Oh, is she getting married?"

"It's time, isn't it? Or was she supposed to spend her life dressing saints?"

"No, of course not. Who to?"

"Candelario Mariscal."

"So she caught the Colonel. Who would have thought that of Minga! It would have seemed she wouldn't crack a plate."

"Sometimes eyes are no good to see things with, Sir."

"When's the wedding?"

"Tomorrow."

"Tomorrow? That's quick!"

That was too much. The face of Bulu-Bulu's woman became ferocious.

"What? Is there anything wrong with it?"

Chalena reacted. He realized he'd gone too far. He tried to be pleasant. A quick transition.

"No. I think it's fine. I'll be there! It would be awful to miss the marriage of Colonel Candelario Mariscal to the daughter of Bulu-Bulu!"

Ña Crisanta said good-by and went to the house of Dr. Espurio Carranza. He came forward to receive her. He didn't want to or couldn't hide the fact that he knew all about it.

"We've already got the news, Ña Crisanta. Congratulations. The Colonel is the best catch in Santorontón. Of course, Dominga has a lot of attraction on her side too. Congratulations again. And please congratulate Bulu-Bulu. I wish all the best for the wedding couple."

"Thank you, Dr. Espurio. Thank you very much. That's precisely why I'm here."

"Please explain, Ña Crisanta."

"I've come to invite you and your family to the wedding."

The doctor smiled with great friendliness.

"There's no problem as far as I'm concerned. I'll be among the first to arrive."

"What about Ña Jovita?"

Espurio scratched his chin.

"She won't be able to come, I'm sure."

"Why not?"

"My wife never goes to such affairs. Never."

The Old Woman smiled. With the most pleasant face she could put on.

"We want her to come. Her and the girls."

Espurio's face grew a touch sarcastic. He half-lifted his head.

"Uhmmm, Ña Crisanta. You're asking the impossible!"

The feminine smile grew stronger.

"As they wish. That's your business, doctor. But before I go I have to give you a message from the Colonel."

"Tell me, I'm listening."

"He told me that those who don't come to the wedding can start arranging for their plot in the cemetery. That he'll provide the corpses and the funeral. In your case everything will be easier.

Since most of the cemetery belongs to you. Since you run the funeral business. And since it will be several people at the same time—Ña Jovita, the girls, and you—it will be that much cheaper."

The other repeated mechanically.

"Yes. Of course. Since it will be several people it will be cheaper."

He reacted suddenly.

"What are you saying?"

"What you heard."

He reflected quickly. Calmed down. Tried to appear as calm as he could.

"You're right, Ña Crisanta. I think I can convince my family. We'll be there. Don't worry."

The news spread rapidly. The mandatory invitation to the Colonel's wedding has its effect. They practically wouldn't let Doña Crisanta speak. As soon as she began to put her words together, they were already accepting. So as the cases repeated each other, she began to feel surer of herself. So she could enjoy the humiliation of the others more thoroughly. The women, of course. As she went from one house to the next, she thought not only about what she would do in those moments and on that day but what she would get to do later. They would have to pay her back. Those few moments were not enough to compensate for the long days, months, years that she had suffered. Ever since she started following Bulu-Bulu. The first to turn their backs on her had been her very own parents. When she tried—already married and living with the Wizard—to beg their forgiveness, they had rejected her. Or, at least, the Old Man had prevented her mother from forgiving her. "He's not just a witch doctor. His whole family are witch doctors. If she has a son someday he'll follow the tradition of his relatives too. He'll be a wizard." They say that the mother had attempted a weak defense. "So what? Aren't wizards people too? Does your daughter stop being your daughter because she's the wife of Bulu-Bulu now?" "I don't care what you think," he had argued. "The Wizard has probably bewitched you already. While I live and have all my five senses, that witch will never set foot in this house again." The witch was she, his daughter! If that was how it was with the ones who had given her life, what could she hope for from the others? From then on she practically shut herself up. She only went to the market. Sometimes—very rarely—she went to mass. Always in a corner. Marginal.

Away from everything and everyone. Without anyone's saying a word to her. As if there were an invisible barrier between her and the others. Even when she went to buy something, the vendors sold to her with fear. Were they afraid of contracting some unknown and incurable illness? Through it all, then, she would find the way in which the others—especially the women—would pay her back. Attending her daughter's wedding was just a start. A first payment on the substantial debt. All in all, she was enjoying every detail of what was happening. After her visit to Dr. Espurio, she no longer went for the men but for the women. These received her immediately. And even though they may have been dying with rage inside, on the outside they forced a smile. Ña Crisanta hefted that smile carefully. She knew that if they didn't drive her off with clubs. If they didn't pile wood around her and set fire to it, it was because of the Colonel. The Colonel didn't say things just for the fun of it. Besides, he was still wrapped in the black-red cloud of his homicidal legend. It was as if he always had his cortege of corpses. Starting with the old Quindales couple. And continuing with those whom—according to what people said—his footsteps left behind in a macabre wake on land and sea. Why play around with razor-sharp machetes on all sides? It was better to smile. While it was possible, it was better to smile. Meanwhile, smile. Smile. You could smile. Smile. Better to smile. Smile.

When the news reached Cándido's ears he exploded with fury. His usual interlocutor received the impact.

"You already knew, right?"

"Who in Santorontón doesn't?"

"How dare he, that wretch, profaning the house of the Lord?"

"Cándido!"

"It's a sacrilege! It won't happen! I'll go kick him out of there!"

"Calm down!"

"And to whom? To the daughter of Bulu-Bulu! To a witch. It can't be!"

"Cándido! Listen to me!"

He raised his eyes to the Burned Christ.

"Speak!"

"First of all, calm down."

"Are you going to stick your nose in where it doesn't concern you?"

Jesus smiled.

"Who started it first? Besides, everything concerns me."

"Oh, is that so? Then do something to stop the wedding."

"Why?"

"You know quite well that my godson... I mean that Colonel ... is a criminal. Besides, he burned down the church. And even you yourself got burned!"

"Are you forgetting that I forgave the people who crucified me!"

"This one... he's worse than they!"

"What's wrong? Would you rather he didn't get married then? That he just carry the girl off? Don't you think it's one of the first good things he's done?"

"That wretch doesn't fool me! He's got something up his sleeve. Even if you're against me, I'll stop that wedding!"

"Do you even know her?"

"Dominga?"

"Who else? She's the bride, isn't she?"

"Yes. I know her. I've seen her from a distance."

"What do you think of her?"

"Well, a woman. A woman... like all the others."

"Don't you think she's got the same right as the others to find happiness?"

"Yes. Of course she does. That's just why I have to stop her from being joined to that man by the Law of God."

"What if she loves him?"

He stopped in perplexity.

"That's true. I hadn't thought of that."

He looked at the Christ. As if trying to read his thoughts. He realized that what he wanted to do was absurd. He muttered:

"The truth is that sometimes I don't know what to do with you. Whatever looks good to me, seems bad to you. What is it? Am I so far away from your Father's hand?"

The Crucified One smiled mockingly.

"No, Cándido. It's not that. It's just that old age is turning you into a fossil. A grumbling old fossil."

Mockery also came to the lips of the Priest.

"Look who's talking about old age! How old are you?"

His comrade went along with him.

"Almost two thousand years old."

The Priest went on in the same vein. But without changing his previous aims.

"All right, 'young fellow.' For the last time I tell you that this time you're not going to have your way. I'm going to the church. I'll do everything in my power. Even if it means pulling Father Gaudencio out by the ears. Or with kicks from my boots driving out Colonel—Colonel, huh!—Candelario Mariscal."

Jesus shook his head, worried.

"What a hard head you've got, Cándido! I'm sure that neither ax nor harpoon could ever penetrate it."

SIXTEEN

The arrival of Father Gaudencio had turned Santorontón green. Most of the inhabitants waved ornaments made of palm leaves: Branches. Crosses. Woven figures. They put on their Sunday clothes. They went down to the shore. And they waited for the launch—a specially rented motor launch—that was bringing the priest. The whole reception was mainly the work of Father Cándido. Of course, when he heard of the arrival of that outstanding shepherd of souls he had become upset. This was how he put it to his soul friend:

"Don't you think that two priests are too many for a village like this?"

"Yes. Especially considering the conditions in Santorontón. And for a church which, in spite of your optimism..."

He interrupted him, worked up.

"What? Isn't it a church like all the rest? Just because it's the way it is does it stop being one? You yourself, burned and faded, aren't you still the Crucified One?"

"Let me finish! I'm saying that in spite of your optimism the church is getting too big for the village."

"Oh, well! That's different. So what?"

"So nothing. We can't prejudge the Bishop's intentions. The only thing you have to do is prepare a reception worthy of the new priest. Then we'll see what happens."

"You're right."

First of all, he had the nasal-sounding bell tolled strongly. Ever since the day Romelio had left—the fateful day of the fire—he had taken care of that and all the other duties in the church. The echo of the clapper on the bronze spread out. It hit the mountains and came back, multiplied, down to the village. A good number of his parishioners came to its call. They surrounded him. He talked to them:

"My children: Another priest is coming. Father Gaudencio. We must receive him properly."

Some grumbled:

"What do we want more priests for?"

"You're more than enough for us."

"What can we do with two when we can't even support one?"

He got cocky:

"What's this about supporting me? Nobody supports me! I do almost everything for nothing."

"That's true."

"And you even—sometimes—help us out."

He cut them off.

"All right. Enough. Whatever we say, Father Gaudencio will be here tomorrow. We have to get ready to welcome him."

"All right, Father."

"If you want it, all right."

"All right."

On the following day—when the launch bringing the new Priest docked—they were all surprised. He was rather young. Although tall, not as tall as Father Cándido. He was stouter. He had light eyes. White skin. Pink cheeks. He spoke with a peculiar accent.

Different from theirs. You could tell a mile away that he came from distant lands, where they spoke a different language. Where? Where could it be? From over the sea, maybe? He almost always maintained an air of superiority that humiliated people. He wore new and expensive clothing. When he arrived he was carrying a fine handkerchief, embroidered with lace. The crowd answered the greeting by waving their palm ornaments. That lasted for a few brief seconds. Then the Cleric stepped on a laurel plank that led him to dry land. Behind him, protecting him from the sun with an umbrella, came Filemón, the Sexton. The people waited respectfully. Father Cándido—very clean but very threadbare, as always—went forward to greet him. He even had a few words in mind. The other did not stop. He gave a quick nod. And he kept on greeting the Santorontonians. With the rhythmic waving of his handkerchief. The big man was disconcerted for a moment. He shrugged his shoulders. And without noticing the slight he had been given, he turned around. He walked with long strides until he was beside the newcomer. The crowd was parting to let the two of them through. At no moment did Father Gaudencio stop waving his handkerchief or the Santorontonians their palm ornaments. Suddenly he stopped, put away the handkerchief. He gave some blessings to the town. And turned to the host Priest.

"Where is the church?"

"Right in front of you, Father."

The other looked everywhere for it.

"Where?"

Father Cándido put out his right arm, pointing it out. The humble structure of wild bamboo still showed the marks of the fire. Only a small part had been rebuilt.

"There!"

Gaudencio looked in the direction indicated. He could not conceal an expression of displeasure.

"That? That's a church?"

His colleague began to feel his blood boiling. The speech he had prepared was being replaced by a collection of phrases. The kind that start arguments. He had a hard time holding back. Still he managed. He said humbly.

"I've said mass in that church. I've heard confessions. And I've baptized babies for several years in this village. It used to be better. Much better. Until it burned."

"Why hasn't it been rebuilt?"

"Santorontón is a poor village, Father Gaudencio."

The latter looked around. With a rapid calculation he made a kind of evaluation of the surrounding buildings.

"Still I see some well-built houses. Quite a bit better than the House of the Lord. That cannot be. They will all have to help me build a church. A real church worthy of Him. Of reinforced concrete."

Father Cándido kept himself under control still.

"Yes. Maybe you're right."

They went into that kind of broken-down barn. It still showed the black grimaces of the fire. The stumps of the roof barely covered by bijao leaves. The walls wrinkled and wavy. The floor with an accumulation of ruins everywhere. The mannered one could not contain himself. He made a gesture of disgust and disdain. He took his handkerchief out again. He tried to cover his face. Withal he didn't say a word. Only when he saw the Nazarene—faded, with cracks and burns all over his body—did he explode:

"And this?"

The other's voice became hoarse.

"It's Christ! Our Christ!"

The displeasure and distress were even more pronounced on the face of the young Priest.

"What a lack of tact! Now I understand everything! His presence is harmful to us. We have to get it out of here immediately!"

The Old Priest shook like a harpooned corvina. Should he or should he not sock him? Kick that scoundrel out of the church or not? Or drag him by the ears to the launch so he could go back where he came from? He made a maximum effort to control himself. He mumbled:

"Jesus? The Crucified Jesus?"

"Yes. This one. It's a disgrace to religion!"

He was about to leap on the cassocked young man when, by chance, he looked at "his" Christ. The latter gave him a joking wink. Cándido—in view of that—gave in to the circumstances. He said:

"Don't worry, Father Gaudencio. I'll take care of it myself."

The other one looked at him fixedly. As if trying to penetrate his thoughts. Should he tell him what he had to tell him? Or wait a little while, when the crowd had emptied out of the church? It was beginning to fill up as if there were a tidal wave. Why wait? Better to say it immediately, taking advantage of the situation. Besides, in that way he would eliminate one of the problems he had to resolve in Santorontón. Having made the decision, he said:

"Yes. That's best. That way you can start fulfilling your new duties."

In spite of the fact that he was prepared for the worst, Cándido was puzzled.

"New duties?"

Friar Gaudencio nodded. He explained briefly the Bishop's decision. In brief, he—Gaudencio—would take charge of the pastorate of the souls of Santorontón. For his part, Father Cándido would take care of the numerous souls who were spread out through the extensive region. Even on the side where the sea filled in around the seedbed of islands.

He babbled:

"What about my church?"

"You'd best forget about it, Father Cándido. I'll build another one in its place. Different. Bigger."

He went on, savoring the picture:

"Of reinforced concrete!"

"The Bishop's order will be carried out, Father Gaudencio."

They said no more. Even if they had wanted to, they couldn't have. The public was finishing their invasion of the broad "nave" of the church. Cándido watched them come in. He read great enthusiasm on the faces of most of them. In a few hours they seemed to have changed their standards. They looked at each other. They gave the impression of saying: "This is a real priest." According to what they were thinking during those instants, Father Cándido had been all right for the early days of Santorontón. Now his figure denoted old age. His physical aspect. His gestures. His expressions. His clothing. Everything seemed out of a past age. Nonexistent. Whose validity had passed. On the other hand, the new priest breathed youth. Agility. Elegance. Distinction. When the parishioners had all come in, he raised his right hand and with it blessed the gathering again. He kneeled. They followed him. He prayed aloud. It was a metallic voice. Agreeable. Haughty. It hung vibrating in the air. The sheep followed his prayers. Then he got up. With brief words, but very much to the point, he thanked them for their welcome. He made them various kinds of promises for the salvation of their souls. He told them that God's mercy is infinite. There is no sin—no matter how mortal—that cannot be forgiven. He asked them, at the same time, not to cease visiting the House of the Lord. If possible, every day. Here the tone of his voice became plaintive.

"...Although the Lord is in bad shape in Santorontón. He does not have a House worthy of Him and of the Santorontonians. But don't worry. We shall build a church that will be the pride of these parts. A fireproof church. Eternal. Let us begin building it as soon as possible. Not next week. Not tomorrow. Not this afternoon. Right now!"

He called the sexton:

"Filemón!"

As if conjured up, the latter appeared. He was already carrying a tray in his hands. Father Gaudencio addressed the faithful:

"Those who want to help in the building of the church can do so now. Those who give larger contributions will see their names engraved beside the altar when it is finished. In letters of gold!"

Filemón and the tray began to circulate at once. In an ostentatious way, Crisóstomo Chalena—who was in the front row—dropped in a handful of large-denomination bills. Almost all the prominent people of the village followed suit. The poor people gave only coins. Some nothing. When the tray came back to Gaudencio's hands his eyes filled with jubilation.

"Thank you, my children, thank you very much. Thank you very much for this demonstration of faith. In this way our church will soon be a reality. Since I have seen that many of you cannot—although I know that in your hearts you really want to—give your support to this holy work, I ask you to offer your hands. Only your hands. With them you will be lending great support to the building of the New House of the Lord."

A short time later the church was empty. Father Gaudencio was found settling into the old rooms which until that day had been occupied by Father Cándido. The latter went over to his Christ. He didn't say a word. He went over to the Cross to take it down. He was sad and furious. He couldn't resist it. He had an anguished feeling of impotence. Of having to let himself be stepped on. Or dragged along. As if he were being borne along by the impetuous current of an eddy as it carried him off. For a moment he contemplated his comrade. With his fists clenched. Two tears of wrath and grief struggled to make an appearance in his eyes. He dried them with the sleeve of his cassock until they finally overflowed.

"Old Man!"

He looked away without answering.

"Old Man!"

He raised his eyes.

"What?"

"Don't act that way."

"I'll never forgive or forget this, never."

"This is nothing, Cándido."

He looked at him reproachfully.

"Oh, no?"

"Remember what they did to me!"

He smiled, with a certain bitterness. He added:

"And what they're still doing to me. Even those who have dedicated their existence—at least that's what they say—to propagating and protecting our faith."

In a wave of images his friend's whole odyssey passed through the Cleric's mind. From manger to Calvary. He felt as if they had stuck seven harpoons into his chest. He fell to his knees. He covered the feet of The Crucified One with kisses.

"I'm an incurable idiot, Jesus. Forgive me!"

What was happening? Was what he was feeling true? Two hands were gently lifting him. Two arms went around his neck. He heard a voice whose tenderness went right through his backbone.

"My Brother. Sometimes we all need to be forgiven. Have you forgotten about the Olive Grove in Gethsemane already?"

He raised his eyes, which he still had lowered. The Christ had descended from the Cross. He was by his side. Joined to him in a fraternal embrace. The emotion smothered him. He insisted:

"In any case, I need to be forgiven."

The Son of Mary smiled.

"So be it, then. I forgive you!"

Then his child-with-a-new-toy look lighted up his face.

"And now to sow optimism, Father Cándido! Faith cannot remain shut up within four walls!"

"You're right."

"Besides, have we seen ourselves in worse shape, or not?"

"Of course. And we'll get out of this just as well as we did the other times."

The two of them carried the Cross. They took it out of the church. It was growing dark. The lights of Santorontón were already beginning to blink weakly. They went to the shore. They got into the canoe. They didn't put the Cross in the hole in the center as on other occasions. The Son of Mary asked:

"Aren't we going to use your cassock as a sail?"

"What for? We'll be staying close to the village. Very close. Where we can find a place to build our house. Right by the shore, that's it. I don't imagine that Father Gaudencio will take much time to minister to the poor. They'll be left for us. For you and for me. On the other hand, he'll be busy at other things. Especially in the building of his church."

He turned his eyes back to look behind. The village—or whatever—the village he loved so much, was getting farther and farther away. It was already almost nothing but a string of fire beetles on the horizon.

In spite of himself he murmured:

"Who knows what will become of the Santorontonians!"

Jesus turned his head, smiling.

"They'll do quite well. Santorontón is a lucky village."

"Oh, yes?"

"Of course. If everything turns out just the way they want it, so much the better. Otherwise, during difficult times they'll always have us."

SEVENTEEN

The bone dryness of the jungle cut the landscape with black crosses. The presence of aggressive fauna grew closer. With the drying up of green plants and trees with liquid substance in their trunks, the march toward Santorontón was becoming imminent. It could already be noticed that some beasts had reached the edges of the village. The dogs—with their warning barks—had taken it upon themselves to frighten them off. In spite of everything, the visitors didn't draw back very far. Their anxious roars could be heard. At night a belt of phosphorescent eyes seemed to surround the cluster of houses. Some creatures—the vipers especially—managed, without doubt, to cross the border. Perhaps by their silent snaking. By the magnetism of their staring eyes. Or because their breath became mingled with the thousands of breaths come from the jungle, what is certain is that they were able to cross—or circle around—the village. They went to the shore. They coiled around the tall, knotty trunks of the coconut palms. They climbed up to the tops. From there they threw many coconuts down onto the ground. Or had they detached whole bunches of them, knotting themselves together, ophidian to ophidian, to form a kind of rope of living loops? Or did they wrap their tails around each fruit and begin to beat them against the stones at the entrance to the sea? Or did they steal an ax, coil their tails around it, and split the fruit to get at the milk? Or did they sink their sharp fangs in until they perforated the hard shell and extracted the liquid? Or weren't they serpents but monkeys? These monkeys with long tails and swaying limbs. Who left no track. Who, instead of walking, "flew" from branch to branch in the trees. Or between the eaves of the houses. Or between the peaks of the crags. Or between the fence stakes. Or between any of the high parts of the mountains. What is certain is that the Santorontonians were perplexed. At every instant the civil and military authorities, that is, Salustiano Caldera and Rugel Banchaca, carried the latest news to Crisóstomo Chalena. They spoke one after the other, almost like a single person. That was doubtless due to the community of their interests and proposals.

"We've got them here now, Sir."

"They're walking among us."

"That's right."

"They don't attack us because they don't feel like it."

"Some have approached the water tanks."

"What about the coconuts?"

"Of course. The coconuts are giving out."

"People are beginning to be afraid."

"And they blame you for everything."

"That's right! They say that if you hadn't warehoused the water the wild beasts wouldn't have come here."

Chalena heated up. He arose in his hammock. He roared:

"Haven't I told you that if I hadn't collected the rainwater we'd already be dead from thirst?"

Salustiano explained:

"We told them that. But..."

"Go on."

"They think that you ordered the wells dried up so that there wouldn't be any other water except what's stored in the tanks."

Rugel put in again.

"And that way we'd all be in the palm of your hand."

The little man grew furious.

"Ingrates! Even after I've saved them from drying up and dying! How could I have done any harm to the wells? I didn't budge from here. Besides, I don't think anyone's gone near them. Much less plugged them up."

Salustiano spoke again.

"We told them that too."

"So?"

"The fact is they think..."

"Say it. Don't be afraid."

"They think that your Partner helped you."

"My Partner? What Partner?"

"The One We Know. That he's the one who does everything you need or want."

He raised his head. He hesitated for a moment. Which would be better? For them to believe that he had a pact with Old Long-tail or not? Maybe the most favorable thing for his ends would be to leave them with their doubt. Neither to affirm nor deny it. He looked at them, challengingly. He was sure that they would spread it to the four winds.

"All right. Even if it were true... For the moment the only thing we can do is prepare. For when the beasts attack us."

Rugel agreed:

"That's what I think. If they catch us off guard, there won't be anyone left to tell the tale."

Chalena smiled, mysteriously.

"Don't worry. I've got a plan that can't go wrong."

Salustiano ventured to ask him a question:

"In this too... will you be helped by your Partner?"

He answered, evasively.

"Maybe."

To himself he thought no. Something strange was happening. It had been a long time since The One We Know had answered his call. Nor did he come, as before, to pay him a visit from time to time. Could it be that he was getting bored? Could he have thought that he and all of Santorontón were already digested bread? Could he be cautious because now there were two priests in town? Could he have thought that with the return of his son, Colonel Candelario Mariscal, the family was sufficiently represented? Who knows! What is certain is that he hadn't seen him for a long time, not even from a distance. Not even the smell of sulfur reached him.

Clotilde came to him with the news.

"Juvencio! Juvencio!"

She woke him with shouts.

"What's going on?"

"Get up! Hurry!"

He got dressed as fast as he could. He went to the door.

"Tell me!"

"They're burning the jungle."

"Who?"
"I don't know. Look!"
He turned his eyes inland. There. Where the hills began to climb. Great flames could be seen in different parts. They were growing rapidly. Perhaps because of the double dryness of the summer's end. Also, of course, because of the dehydration that had caused the thirst of the zoomorphs. Small lights could be seen running, hither and yon. In the tender dawn—as it grew lighter—they became less and less identifiable. The curious part is that where they stopped, fire rose up immediately. Is it a case of pyromaniacs doing a job? Santorontón was on its feet. Some of its inhabitants, looking out from their various houses. Others wandering through the streets. Trying to get a better look at the unusual spectacle. Soon, in great waves, a smell of smoke and burned wood began to arrive. A short time later, this smell was grafted onto another, even more penetrating. The smell of roasting meat. Obviously, the inhabitants of the jungle were already being trapped. The wall of flames prevented their escape. In the meantime, Father Cándido—early riser that he was—had noticed all that was happening very quickly. Somewhat discouraged, he approached his Friend.
"Come see what's happening."
"It's not necessary. I know."
"Do you know who's doing it?"
"Don't you?"
"Yes. But why are they doing it?"
"Don't you know?"
"Frankly, no."
"Maybe they're trying to prevent the thirsty animals from attacking the village. And taking over Chalena's water tanks."
"Do you think they're going to deep-fry it indiscriminately?"
"What a question!"
"Answer me."
"Did you doubt it for one minute?"
"And are we going to stand around with our arms folded?"
"We could go. In case something occurs to us."
He looked at him. With reproach.
"I, in your place..."
"What?"
"I'd bring on the rains ahead of time. Aren't we quite close

to winter? That would put an end to the problem. And the majority of us would be happy."

"You think that changing everything is in my hands, don't you?"

"What are you good for, then?"

"Cándido, Cándido. Don't be abusive!"

"You're right. I'm sorry. This has put me in a bad mood."

"That's obvious."

Controlling himself, the Priest helped Christ down from his Cross. The two of them carried it and headed for the village. While they were approaching they realized that the fire had grown on all sides. Flocks of birds of all different kinds were taking flight. The smoke was putting fog and bite into the eyes of some. Suddenly they stopped. As if their wings had become immobilized. They fell—spinning over each other—into the flames. Others struggled, desperate, among the millions of gigantic red or gray claws. In most cases they overcame the adverse conditions and managed to escape. Then they flew at high speed in the direction the wind was taking. In order to flee that inferno as fast as possible. For their part, the Bosses of Santorontón had gathered at Chalena's. The last to arrive was Rugel Banchaca. He came surrounded by his rural guards. Armed to the teeth. Without saying hello he went straight to the heart of the matter.

"As you all can see, they've set fire to the jungle."

Chalena made a hypocritical fuss.

"Are you sure of what you're saying?"

"Yes, Don Chalena. Quite sure. We got as close as we could to the fire. It was too late. The arsonist had already taken off. We did see their fresh tracks."

Salustiano intervened:

"We will have to make an example of them."

Chalena agreed:

"Of course!"

He exchanged a look of understanding with the Political Chief. He continued:

"So it will serve as a lesson. So nobody will try to repeat this infamous thing."

Rugel suggested:

"For now, we should arm ourselves. With whatever there is: Shotguns. Carbines. Harpoons. Machetes. Axes. And the ones who don't have any of those, well, with sticks, stones... anything!"

The shopkeeper made a gesture, with his right hand raised, as always. He wasn't in on the plan. Or they hadn't had time to tell him about it. He asked, ingenuously:

"Who are we going to arm ourselves against? Against the arsonists?"

Espurio explained impatiently:

"We'll grab them later."

"So?"

"Now we'll get rid of the wild animals."

"Oh!"

"Soon some of them will want to break out."

"What have we got to do with that?"

"They'll probably try to attack us."

"Why?"

Chalena cut in. Raging.

"To take over the water. Just imagine. If they were all dried out before, how do you think they are now that the fire is toasting them?"

Vigiliano Rufo finally understood. He immediately took their side.

"Then we'd better hurry and have the whole village arm."

"That's it. Let's go!"

"Let's go!"

"Let's go!"

The Bosses spread themselves out in the different parts of Santorontón. In a few minutes the whole village had armed itself with what was within reach. As Espurio Carranza had predicted, soon they saw that—at the edge of the jungle—in an absurd mixture of breeds, sizes, and colors, the various denizens of the jungle were trying to escape. Insects. Herbivores. Carnivores—all half-singed—were struggling to get out. Some tight against the others. Sometimes squeezing against each other. On occasion climbing on top of the rest. Trampling them. Breaking them into pieces. Sometimes traveling over the bodies of others. It was a strange spectacle. Animals who would have devoured each other. Who never would have been able to be close to each other. Those who lived at soil level. As well as those who grew under the earth. Or those who sought shelter in the trunks or branches of the trees: all were trying to find the empty spots that might have been left by the fire. These were very few, of course. The flames were growing. Becoming agitated. Separating. They approached until they blended with larger ones. They went along devouring everything with their millions of insatiable tongues. There was a moment when it seemed that multiple rivers were being born in the heart of the jungle. Multiple zoomorphic rivers. With millions of different aspects. With millions of multicolored changes. The men—as soon as they had them within their reach—proceeded to liquidate them. The animals—even the most voracious and aggressive—didn't try to defend themselves. The larger ones were shot. The smaller ones hacked up with knives. Clubs. Or stones. They were doing that when a strange thing happened. It seemed suddenly as if the jungle had begun to rise up by itself. In an uncontainable wave. It rose up to the tallest treetops. There where the fire had not yet reached with its full strength. When they noticed it, the Santorontonians remained paralyzed for a few seconds. They only had eyes for that. What was happening? What could be happening? Suddenly deafening shouts dominated the thousand noises of the crackling wood. Of the falling trees. Of the gusts of hurricane wind that the change in temperature moved toward the sea. Of the uneven march of the animal world in its torrential flight. And from the accents of desperation, pain, and protest that rose up from that world at the unexpected aggression of which they were victims. The shouting was growing. Growing. Stronger and stronger. Ever stronger. From every chest a shout of astonishment and fear escaped:

"The monkeys!"

"The monkeys!!"

"The monkeys!!!"

In fact it was the elastic anthropoids. Had they turned to rubber? Using their long limbs and tails they now began to leap. In a kind of impossible flight. From branch to branch. Toward the salients of the jungle. When they got there they began to swing, pick up momentum and leap to the houses. To the tips of the stakes. To the masts of the boats. To the peaks of the crags. With eyes rolling. Open mouths toothed from fear. Denoting fright. Some of them touched the ground from time to time. It was to gather more momentum. To go up again and continue the long leaps. It was as if they had turned into springs. Every time a part of them touched something solid, it was to jump higher and faster. Dominating, finally, the transitory human paralysis, a shout was heard. Was it Chalena? Yes. It was Chalena.

"What are we waiting for? At them!"

The others seemed to wake up in sequence. They shouted in turn:

"Yes!"

"At them!"

"Kill them!"

"Before it's too late!"

"Before they attack us!"

"Before they take over the tanks!"

"Kill them!"

They aimed at them. They began to shoot them. Many of them were caught in flight. Others when they reached the ground. Or when they stopped for a second to work up momentum. Death made them take absurd leaps. As if they were doing their last acrobatic tricks. Taking their last swings. Others were wounded. They fell to the ground. When they saw themselves perforated in some part of their body they began to poke the wound with their upper limbs. Especially if it was in the stomach. They pulled out their intestines with great curiosity. They showed them to their attackers while they shrieked, frightened. The shots continued. The number of those lying lifeless on the ground grew. Or of those wounded who tried to drag themselves away. While they continued to pull out what they had discovered in themselves. The Santorontonians seemed possessed with a zoocidal madness. Their faces had become demoniacal. They were going wild. Now they were killing just for the sake of killing. Enjoying the destruction of life. Then a haughty and vibrant voice was heard:

"Enough!"

Did they hear it? Didn't they hear it? They went on with their killing unperturbed.

"Enough! Enough!"

Since they still paid no attention, the voice became stronger. It dominated all the noises.

"Enough! Enough!"

Only at that instant did they look. With his hands held high—just as if he wanted to hold them back—in front of them Dr. Juvencio Balda rose up.

Salustiano intervened:

"Who invited you to the funeral?"

The young doctor asked in turn:

"Why are you killing those inoffensive creatures?"

Chalena—bursting with rage—thundered:

"You stick your nose into everything! We're sick and tired of you!"

Espurio advised:

"Don't pay any attention to him. He doesn't come from here. He doesn't feel these things. Let's keep on defending 'our' village."

"Yes. Let's keep on."

"Let's keep on!"

A few more shots were fired. More anthropoids—dead or wounded—fell to the ground. Another voice, still stronger than the one before, tried to hold back the murderous voracity.

"How long are you going to go on killing?"

The accent dominated them. They looked at the one speaking. Hair disheveled. There was Father Cándido, his cassock floating in the wind. His face severe. A strange authority radiated from him. That wasn't all. Clutched against his chest he held the longer beam of the Cross. What herculean strength let him do that? What drive so intense helped him left that Christ, almost life-size, so high? What is certain is that above him—above them all—the figure of Jesus with his arms open was raised. As if asking for clemency. There was a moment of expectation and silence. Chalena broke it:

"Why should we pay any attention to this Priest? For church matters we've even got our own Priest, Father Gaudencio. But now it's not even a question of matters of our religion. We only want to defend our lives and property. We have to do what we think best."

Some backed him up:

"Yes. We have to get rid of the monkeys!"

"They're the worst."

"Before they attack us."

"Before they take our water away!"

"Yes."

"Yes!"

"Let's keep on killing them!"

"Let's go!"

They picked up their weapons again. They fired again. Once more the simians began to fall. They hadn't stopped leaping to escape that inferno. Father Cándido—in view of that—couldn't contain himself. He let himself be carried away by his warlike nature. He grabbed the Cross, Christ and all. In a threatening way. The men halted. Then they began to retreat. Clotilde—who had accompanied the doctor but had remained half-hidden behind a house—thought that she was dreaming. Or that she was starting to see things that didn't exist. That weren't occurring. That were happening—like things from some time gone by, a fearful time—only in her imagination. Father Cándido continued advancing with the Cross held high. He went over to Juvencio to be with him and give him support. A few Santorontonians also did so. Suddenly, Crisóstomo reacted. He stopped. He turned to his people.

"Are we going to let an old Priest stop us from defending ourselves?"

Espurio seconded him.

"Besides, look at that lack of respect! He's threatening us with the Cross itself. He's capable of trying to hit us with it without worrying about smashing the Christ to bits!"

Salustiano:

"He can't stop us from defending ourselves!"

And Banchaca:

"No one can stop us!"

Chalena suggested:

"Why don't we take the Cross away from him and ship him out with it to where he came from?"

Dr. Carranza added:

"And we'll do the same with the little doctor."

And Chalena with hatred:

"We should send that one even farther away."

The rest in a chorus:

"Yes!"

"Yes!"

"Take the Cross away from him!"

"Ship him out in the canoe!"

"Get rid of the little doctor once and for all!"

"That's right!"

"Let's go!"

"Let's go!"

In a mass. Their courage up. They hurled themselves at Father Cándido. He drew back. Somewhat disconcerted. It was only two steps. He reacted. He stood firm again. In place. At the same time he moved the Cross back a little. In order—if necessary—to give it momentum and use it like a gigantic mace. The others kept on advancing. Now they were quite close to him. Almost within reach of their hands. They reached them out. Several dozen men were about to take the Sacred Wood away from him. Now they were about to... A third voice held them back.

"Just a moment!"

They looked up. A shudder of fear shook most of them. On the top of a hammock. Standing. His arms crossed. There was Colonel Candelario Mariscal. He seemed to have grown. A strange, almost demoniacal smile creased his lips. His eyes threw off sparks. He continued speaking calmly:

"Whoever touches a hair of my Godfather's head... can consider himself a corpse!"

There was an instant of stupor. They felt a kind of whiplash in their eyes. A wave of countless corpses and crimes formed a kind of halo around the military man. Some could even identify those who made up that carrousel of dead and wounded. Would they dare take a chance with the Son of The One We Know? Only Chalena—could it be because he had or had had a pact with the Selfsame?—dared mouth:

"But, Colonel. We only want to defend ourselves."

The one addressed looked at him, coldly.

"Don't come to me with your horse's ass ideas, you shitty queer. I know damned well what you people want. And I know who the ones are who set the fire too. The ones who are causing all this. But what the fuck do I care? To hell with all of you! The only one who matters to me is my Godfather. And you don't mess with him. You heard me!"

Father Cándido turned to Candelario, furious.

"And who are you to defend me? Butting in! I'm enough and more than enough to defend myself. I don't want anything from you. Evil born! Get out of here! That's the only thing you can do! Get out of here!"

The Colonel remained impassive. He didn't even look at the Priest. He looked around in an aggressive sweep. His face began to change a little. He showed a smile full of disdain. He warned again:

"You heard me!"

He turned his back. He began to walk. With great slow steps. Everybody—this time even Cándido himself—remained petrified. As if part of a great sculptured group. The first to react was, again, Chalena. He wanted to say something. Do something. When he was about to initiate the gesture or the word, an unexpected event occurred. Lightning flashed. Thunder rolled. A monstrous black cloud, come from who knows where, settled over them. A drop of rain fell. Then another. Then a hundred. Then a thousand. Then how many? Little by little it was becoming a torrential cloudburst. A chilling squeal broke the fire. The flames were humiliated. The zoomorphic flow fought with the liquid flow as it tried to ascend against it. The anthropoids began their leaps of return. The men lowered their weapons. The Master of the Water looked at the sky, full of rage.

"Goddamn it all!"

He was the only one who felt such rage. The others felt a kind of liberation. From the Bosses on down to the most humble. Especially the latter, of course. Men and women threw their heads back and opened their mouths. They drank in a few swallows of the marvelous liquid. Clotilde did the same. It wasn't for long. Juvencio called her:

"Clotilde! Clotilde!"

"I'm coming!"

"Help me!"

She went over quickly. The doctor, with two poles, reeds, and interwoven vines, was trying to build a stretcher. She helped build it quickly and efficiently. With great care they placed the wounded monkeys there. An infinite wonderment and gratitude was pictured in the almost human eyes. Those who were better, stretched out their long arms and legs as if to help the ones carrying them. Those who had been badly wounded simply let themselves be carried. None made the slightest sign of protest. They seemed to understand that everything was for their good. In the meantime, the Santorontonians withdrew to their houses. To collect the water in what they could. Buckets. Pots. Tubs. Barrels. They were afraid that this rain might be the first and only one of the season. That a short while later they would find themselves in the clutches of Crisóstomo once more. Minutes later, Juvencio and Clotilde realized that they had been left alone. They were the only ones who—instead of collecting water—were transferring anthropoids to the improvised clinic. Soon they realized their mistake. They were not alone. There were two more people helping them. Cándido and the Nazarene—with another improvised litter—were also transporting simians.

EIGHTEEN

When he saw Clotilde for the first time he became disturbed. That terrible world into which she was sunken. The contrast that existed between the monstrous things she expressed and her timid, almost innocent appearance was inexplicable. What extraordinary shock could have unhinged the unfortunate woman like that? It must have been something ultrahuman. Beyond the limits of the most feverish imagination. Otherwise there was no explanation for why she wanted to mutilate all men. —Could she have had that desire before sinking into that sea of shadows?— Or why she believed she was wrapped in a cloak of testicles. The testicles—as she maintained—of all those who had possessed her. And, much less, having just met him, wanting now to go to bed with him. Could it be that she had an urge to mutilate him too? Had she really castrated some man? Weren't the imaginary testicles—in reality only pinecones strung together on a branch—nothing more than the continuation in her mind of something that had happened in principle sometime? Would he get to find it out?

Would she tell him? Would it be worth the trouble to pull her out of that world of transitory punished lovers? Would the everyday and rational world turn out better than that night of sex and blood? It was his duty as a doctor. What about his duty as a man? If he'd had such a specialty, he would have seen more clearly. He didn't have it. The most he could do would be to make her better physically. Beyond that limit it would be hard for him. Maybe it would be advisable to send her to the city. Was that possible? Would he have the means to follow through on that proposal? The first thing he did after she had something to eat was to consult with José Isabel Lindajón, at whose house he was still staying.

"Could Clotilde stay here for a few days?"

The one addressed was disconcerted. He scratched his head. He looked inside his rooms.

"You see, doc. As far as I'm concerned it's all right. For me, at least. But who knows whether my wife would let her. Maclovia can be so screwy..."

"It won't be for long. Until we can send her to the city."

"The fact is...Besides...The things that girl says. She wants men to mount her. So she can geld them afterward."

"Don't you understand that it's all a lie? That it only takes place in her imagination?"

He took off his hat—which he always kept on. He scratched his head.

"I know, Dr. Balda. Of course I know. But if she says it, she says it. I understand that too. Clotilde's off her rocker. What happened to her wasn't just nothing."

"What happened to her?"

He told him in a few words. From what happened the night the Quindales were murdered. Up to what he knew. That is, the quartering of the Old Folks and the disappearance of the girls.

"How long did they stay lost?"

"Clotilde, a few months. Until the Witch Doctor Bulu-Bulu found her in the middle of the jungle."

"What about the other one?"

"Nothing more has ever been heard of Chepa. As if the earth swallowed her up. The last thing was talk that she was wandering around up country. That the Old Folks had sent her away in time."

"Poor girls."

He paused. Continued:

"So, can Clotilde stay until I can get her to the city? I've got a friend there who was my classmate and treats cases like this. He's very good. He has a fine clinic. He's made surprising cures."

"I repeat what I said before, doctor. As far as I'm concerned..."

It wasn't difficult to convince Maclovia. Besides, Clotilde, outside of her sexual obsession regarding men, was normal in everything. When she was among women she worked, the same as they, at the tasks that befitted her. She spoke about general matters with surprising saneness. Sometimes she even went somewhat beyond what one would expect for her age and circumstances. She would laugh. She played with those the same age as she. She forgot about the obsessive theme that made her different. Only if one of the others began to ask questions about that matter did she become transformed. She would refer again to what, according to her, had happened to her. Her questioners were horrified at first. They couldn't even conceive of the absurd scenes that she retold. When they remembered the real circumstances—known by most—of the death of the Quindales, and the time Clotilde had been alone in the jungle, they shuddered. Who knows how the girl got through it! Only then could they appreciate the horrible limits of everything she'd suffered! Nervous, they encircled her with questions:

"What happened after your Old Folks were killed?"

"Where did you go?"

"How could you be alone for such a long time?"

"What did you eat?"

"Where did you sleep?"

"Didn't the wild animals attack you?"

"Didn't the Tin-Tins get close to you?"

She remained looking at them with anguish. She made efforts to remember. It was like passing through shadows. She replied simply:

"I don't know...I don't remember...I don't remember anything..."

The questions went on. With relation to her sister.

"What about Chepa?"

"Did they kill her?"

"Is it true that they carried her off 'up there' where the rivers come from?"

Didn't she really know? Did the Old Folks keep the secret even from her? Didn't she want to tell? Was Chepa still alive? Was she under the earth already? Had somebody else buried her? Had she buried her herself maybe? Caught by doubt and desperation, she almost always answered:

"She went away."

Or sometimes she repeated:

"I don't remember. Word of honor, I don't remember. I can't remember."

Little by little the women were growing accustomed to her ways. To her mental flights. To her sudden changes, when someone—sometimes she herself—made reference to men. She would become transformed. She would repeat the same stories. Her face hardened. Her pupils dilated. She fell apart physically. It seemed that in an instant one woman had replaced another. When the allusions continued. When she began to give details, the transformation went into its crescendo. Her hair seemed to stir and stand on end. Her gestures and expressions became automatic. More and more they obeyed the dark, uncontrollable impulses than they did her own will. Could she have preserved something of her free will at those moments? Wasn't she the other being—injected temporarily into her being—who dominated her and obliged her to act in an absurd way? After some time had passed the women were growing accustomed to that kind of double presence of hers. They even laughed at her a little. Perhaps with the feeling that she would feel less worried. They joked about her. She didn't notice. Or she didn't want to notice. It was an uneven dialogue. Of a double tessitura. While the questions implicitly had a playful tone—and sometimes even a mocking one—she always answered seriously.

"So you go around wrapped in men's balls?"

"Yes."

"They all had something to do with you?"

"Yes."

"And afterwards you gelded them?"

"Yes. Yes. Yes."

Her behavior with men was different. She didn't stop making up to Juvencio. And to José Isabel Lindajón too. But especially the doctor. In view of the fact that he paid no attention to her. That he didn't respond to her amorous invitations—no matter how much stimulation she put into them—she began to impute bad reasons to him. Wasn't he a man? Didn't he have something to answer her with between his legs? Or wasn't what he had good for anything? Was it only for appearance? The stimulation had begun with words. Insinuations. Agreeable, at first. Then angry. Raging. And all of that had only been the prologue. Soon she passed from verbal proceedings to deeds. To wearing down by force. Taking him by the arm and trying to lead him, almost dragging him, to the deerskin. Since everything had turned out in vain, one night her plan came to a crisis. She appeared in his room. Completely naked. She went over to his bed. He was asleep. When he woke up, he already had her by his side. Rubbing him with her quivering, warm skin. He had to commit two acts of violence. One, with himself, so as not to let himself by conquered by the attractive presence. To overcome the impulse of his own libido exacerbated by abstinence. And another with her. To make her give in. To oblige her, against her will—suffering blows, scratches, and attempted bites—to leave his room. To make her get dressed. And, finally, to lead her afterward to where José Isabel Lindajón's family was, in the upper part of the house. On the following day, she—still floating in her world of mist—when she met him asked:

"Why don't you want to?"

He tried to distract her, by changing the subject.

"Did you get to sleep last night?"

She didn't pay any attention to him. She insisted:

"Answer me! Do you think I'm not good enough for you?"

"You have to eat well. What did you eat this morning?"

"Or don't you feel man enough?"

"And rest. Get as much rest as you can."

"Are you afraid of me?"

"And bathing. You have to go to the inlet every morning. With the other girls. And swimming."

Clotilde looked at him. The rage began to light up in her eyes. For a moment she seemed beside herself.

"What's hanging between your legs is going to be mine. You'll see!"

Maclovia couldn't keep silent. She spread the news. She added details. Many of them of her own manufacture. Soon all of Santorontón was gossiping about the matter. As always, the chorus bounced along, from one side to the other, a crazy wave in the windless afternoons.

"Did you hear? Clotilde..."
"What? Oh."
"Crazy like a fox."
"Yes?"
"Yes. José Isabel Lindajón and Maclovia caught her naked in the doctor's cot."
"Ah, that Dr. Balda!"
"Yes! He looked like a harmless goat. And he's turning out to be a wild-dicked old ram!"
"She's rubbing him all the time."
"Where did Clotilde come from?"
"God only knows!"
"They say Bulu-Bulu sent her to the doctor."
"In what gully could he have found her?"
"Maybe in the Five Hells."
"Could be."
"When the Old Quindales were killed they evaporated."
"What about Chepa?"
"That's right. What can have become of her?"
"Is she dead?"
"Well, who can say."
"Or did she just beat it away from here?"
"Probably."
They concluded:
"Anyway Clotilde is a danger for everybody."
"Of course. They say she's made up to José Isabel too."
"Really?"
"That's what they say."
"That really twists the tail on the pig."
"Aha! Just imagine, here in Santorontón she wants to make it with all the men."
The latter, for their part, were licking their chops. On sultry days when the Sun snaked through them inside and out, they would lie down on the sand, on the edge of the sea. The waves reached their feet. They didn't move. The image of Clotilde bare-assed hovered over them—reed with a hundred knots boat of soft chirigua wood torturing flame that came and went cat's claws hooked in all over their bodies perennial groundswell infected in the blood hot waves foam all the senses dying. Clotilde, Clotilde, Clotilde.
"The little devil's turned out quite good."

"Enough to beat around in her oyster bed."
"Hour after hour."
"Day after day."
"But she's off her rocker."
"What difference does that make?"
"It's always getting in the way, isn't it?"
"What does craziness have to do with the other thing?"
"What if it's true that she gelds men?"
"A crock of shit."
"What if it's true?"
"Can't you see that she says the pinecones she carries are the balls of the men who went you know where?"
"So you think it's all in her head?"
"Where else, then?"
"What about the doctor?"
"That, yes, who knows! I'm not taking anybody's side!"
The women, in the meantime, were still aroused. It was like a wasp's nest beaten with a stick. They came and went, buzzing. The doctor-undertaker's wife captained them to a certain point. It seems that Doña Jovita had finally found a reason to justify her existence. Still squelched in the almost sepulchral environment created by her husband, she slipped like a bony shadow through the corners that he'd left open to her. Anonymous. Silent. Dead in life. She herself was surprised that Espurio hadn't already put her six feet under in one of the plots in his cemetery. The Clotilde business was as if the Sun had come out for her for the first time inside her own courtyard. Her minimal domestic destiny—inhabited by husband and children blood-sucking vampires—had, finally, a chink of light.
Like someone casting a hook to see what's biting, she stated:
"We can't stand around with our arms folded."
Some bit.
"Yes. We should do something."
"The best thing would be to get her out of Santorontón."
"What if she doesn't want to leave?"
"We'll get her out in any case."
"Of course, right. We can ship her off in a canoe. Give her some food and water. And let her take off for wherever she pleases."
Somebody argued:
"But she's crazy. She doesn't catch a lot of things. Where could she go?"

"That's her business."
Another proposed:
"Why don't we ask the Priest?"
And another, playing the innocent:
"Father Cándido?"
"No. Father Gaudencio."
Espurio's wife intervened again.
"He'll agree with us. He's an immaculate man. A real saint. How could he allow Santorontón to become perverted?"
"Especially now that the church is almost finished."
"And we're going to give him a festival in honor of the Patroness of the Village."
"That's right."
"Let's go, then."
"Let's go!"
"Let's go!"
When they returned with the consent of the Young Priest it was too late. Juvencio—finally, after some epistolary inquiries—had succeeded in sending Clotilde to the city. He sent her with the same fishermen who had brought him to Santorontón. Although he had given her an injection so that she would sleep during the trip, he managed to get Doña Maclovia to go with her. He gave her all the details. Dr. Carlos Alaya himself, his old classmate, would meet them. He had agreed to take charge of the patient. He had even shown an interest in the case. Especially because of the girl's background. The special circumstances that had caused her illness. And the original obsession that she showed. The psychiatrist would have everything necessary at the dock to take her to his clinic.
As was to be expected, this caused a fury among the feminine upper crust of Santorontón. The target of their harpoons had been stolen away! It was manifest—in addition to the bitter gestures and expressions—in angry and violent words. The first outburst was from Jovita's throat:
"It can't go on like this. Oh, no! Dr. Balda is going to have to pay!"
"Indeed. Why did he stick his nose in where it was none of his business?"
"The minute he arrived he got mixed up with the Mute's son."
"Maybe he made Tolón and his mother disappear himself."

"Of course, don't you think so? Ever since that day nothing has been heard of them."

"Do you think he sent her to the city, Doña Jovita?"

"Who knows! The truth is he sticks his nose into everything. You can see now..."

"Maybe he wants to cure her."

"Clotilde doesn't need a cure, she needs punishment."

"Maybe if she's cured she'll want to come back."

Someone gave the timid opinion:

"Well. Now she's the owner, the sole owner, of Daura, the Quindales' little island. She might come back to claim what's hers, mightn't she?"

Espurio's wife was burning. She grunted:

"We'll see."

For her part, Vigiliano Rufo's mate had maintained a discreet silence. She listened to the commentaries. And she thought it was time to intervene.

"The little doctor can say and do all he wants. We're not going to allow a woman like that to be around us. What an example for our daughters!"

"And ourselves!"

"What shame for Santorontón!"

The one who had expressed Clotilde's rights to Daura insisted:

"What if she's cured?"

"How can she be cured?"

Doña Jovita threw a challenging look around her.

"I see it as something hard. That woman has got something much worse than what we think."

They looked at her anxiously. Worried. They asked in a chorus:

"What, eh?"

"She's got The Evil One. The Evil One inside her body."

NINETEEN

Snail under the gale. Snail with prickly bones showing. Sunken shrunken trunk in its gray armor. Snail under the gale. The wave dancing over with its million melodic eyes. White ring on fingers of sand. Snail under the gale. Prickly curved dwarf sticking his teeth into the cone-roofed wind and face-up barbs spines of a bony stalagmite. Juvencio. What do you want Juvencio?

"I was saying, doctor."

"What, José Isabel?"

"We ought to do something."

"What thing?"

Juvencio. Fashioner of phantoms. You left yours—alive and piercing, who accompanied you since childhood—encrusted in the niches of urban asphalt. And now you've got new ghosts swaying on the line fences of your insomnia. You carry a dizzy whirl about a team of them. Are they alive or dead? Do they exist or are you creating them on your own springboard of dreams? Do you go with them? Are you one of them? Are you passing through Santorontón and its vertical rain mirror? Or haven't you left your crackling city cage city where you crumbled your cadaver inside its bars of anguish?

"Something that would save us from what's happening to us. And from what could happen to us."

"Are you talking about the fire?"

"And the water, doctor. Especially the water."

"Oh, yes! The water."

You survive yourself, Juvencio. You no longer are who you are.

Or are you still a corpse among corpses? Aren't you inventing this microworld? Has it ever existed at some other time? Does it belong to yesterday, today, or tomorrow? Don't you yourself project it outward a bridge to the infinite in order to walk it through your questions? After all, what difference does it make? You're still a snail, rocked by the gale. Dragged along for stretches by the swirl of rains that take over the thousand routes of the wind.

"When the rains end, what will become of us?"

"You've all handed everything over to Chalena, right?"

"Everything."

"Yes. We've got to do something."

Juvencio. Oh, Juvencio! What do you want? What do you propose? Where are you? Are you still in your doctor's office in the city without friends and without patients? Do you still believe that Medicine has turned into a business? That it—meant to serve only as a fight against death—doesn't always fulfill its functions now? That a lot of money is needed to work in the field? Do you still think that Quixotes and Samaritans get screwed in this one and in the next? Tattooed with rebellion inoculated with disinterest, your fate is to eat your own hunger. To drink your own thirst. To love your own impotence. Oh, Juvencio! Little glass tinkle bell destined to be shattered by the hooves of oxen! What are you going to do? What can you do in Santorontón? Cure eternally the monkeys that Chalena's men wounded?

"I think you're the only one who can help us, doc."

"And I want to help you, José Isabel."

"Since Clotilde got back from the city she tells a lot of things about you."

"Good things?"

"Very good. Dr. Alaya talked about it all."

"Dr. Alaya thinks everybody's like him."

"That's the way it should be, doc. But you have to help us."

Your breasts, Diamantina. Your breasts. All of you, but your breasts. Do you know that at one time I saw the world through your breasts? When you crossed my path your breasts pierced my eyes. Since then I've been Daltonian. Living in a labyrinth that didn't belong to me. I spent whole nights dreaming about your breasts, Diamantina. Prison of breasts. Fetters of breasts. Kaleidoscopic blindfold of breasts. Alabaster balloons I have flown in them. With them. Now they are green. Green and yellow.

My whole city has turned green. Green and yellow. What She is. What is in Her. Green. Yellow. From a green banana. From a yellow banana. The fruit I baptize on teeth rotted with premature riches. Green when green. Yellow when ripe. Your breasts without use. Without use then. Only to humiliate a meeting with avid people. Avid ones like me. Without use. Then you used them—it runs in asphalt gossip—on the lips of many men. Only on the lips of your children now? Your children who should have been mine. That's why I attacked you on the street. A day of cocoa boiling in the sun. Sepia-gold city. Do you remember? Crossing through the columns. Protection of doorways. Avoiding my anxieties. "What do you want? Why are you bothering me? Stop following me!" I really wasn't following you. You were following me. You were persecuting me. Aggressive. On the border of the geared vigils of insomnia. I was working in the School Library. I lived among books. And I didn't see any books. In the stacks. Up. Down. All over. Your breasts. They turned many colors. Changing. I drank in them. I drank from them. I lived drinking as if one lived drinking. As if every book—every breast—were to live drinking vivifying drinks or dribbles of a drunken draught. Spirals of cherry-pink nipples spun about me. A tiny wave roller coaster the polyphoneme magnet of curves. Magnet on magnet, magnet. Obsessed bedazzled daily befogged palpitating in your tracks. "Why do you persecute me? Let me go!" Magnet under magnet, magnet. Meta metamor metamorphosis. Microrubrics of flame in your blood. Orchestra of nerves symphonizing your pupils. Changing pentagram on your cheeks. Magnet toward one side magnet. Diamantina! Diamantina! Why didn't I climb up your blond stairs? Why didn't I rock in your hammocks of golden webbing? Why didn't I embed myself crazy dream-sap-sucking vampire transplanted in tissues of muscles and arteries? Magnet, magnetized magnet. "What do you want, Juvencio? What do you want?" "I want you." Magnet. You laughed your amphibian necklace teeth magnent half moon warm petals trim magnet. Diamantina magnet. Magnet Diamantina.

"Couldn't we open up the wells again?"

"Don Chalena would cover them right up, doc."

"Bulu-Bulu's too?"

"I think that one too."

"What if all the Santorontonians joined together to defend the water in their wells?"

"It might have been possible before. From what I see now, it will be a touch difficult. We're divided. There are a lot of people who gain when the rest get screwed."

"The ones who gain are a few. Only the ones involved with Chalena."

"But Don Chalena's got help. A help against which nothing is any good."

"What help?"

"The One We Know."

"That's your imagination, José Isabel."

"Maybe so, doctor. But when it comes to help, he gets help!"

"You, José Isabel? How are you going to defend yourselves when even you think like that?"

"You can't do anything when you can't do anything."

"Are you going to fold your arms? Are you going to let Chalena finish you off?"

"Not that."

"So?"

"That's where it's at. That's why we want you to advise us, since you know so much. Clotilde told us."

"What?"

"That only you can save us."

"Oh, what ever will become of Clotilde!"

Oh, what ever will become of you, Juvencio! The city wasn't green. Less yet, yellow. Maybe that's why you got on board a carrousel of precipices. A little marsupial swinging on Diamantina. Intoxicated by her, you followed up to the threshold of her caresses. Hanging from her window. Living street light screwed in at unreachable distances. In a perpetual autophagy of silence. Perhaps some time. Maybe one time you reached her hands. And at a School dance didn't you cover all the letters of her body alphabet? Only in torturing intuition. Separated by the Chinese wall of others' eyes. You stayed on the threshold. Gathering courage to cross that wall. You felt that her breasts no longer pierced your eyes but your torso. Something else came between. A Teacher. Treacherous tie of woven snakes, he snatched her from your arms. He bore her in the delirious spirals of music. Mixed in among the—for you—sonorous knives that came out of the pentagram. Pulling your heart like an elastic trophy. When the wind devoured the last rhythms, you wanted her to come back. Vain desire. With his green key the Teacher had her in enchained enchantment. Green key. Green lock. Green Teacher. Green. Green whole. The houses, too, green? The city, green too?

"Well, you'll see, José Isabel."

"Tell me, doc."

"The best thing would be to build a reservoir."

"What's a reservoir?"

"Well, there's a large gully near here. Right?"

"Yes, doc."

"It can only be reached through a pass. Between two hills."

"That's right."

"If we bring those two hills together. If we build up a wall of stones, sticks, and earth, a lot of water can be collected. The water of a whole winter."

"Ah! You mean a bog."

"If that's what you people call it. A bog! With it there'll be water for all summer."

"That's right, doc! We hadn't thought of that."

"And Don Chalena will be left with a long nose."

Long nose. Toads don't have long noses. Nor can their noses grow. Only their bellies grow. Until they burst. Fluted belly. Green. Yellowish green. Are you left with a long nose, Juvencio? Diamantina and the Teacher. Did the Teacher teach Diamantina? Did Diamantina diamondize the Teacher? "No, Juvencio. I intend to explain it all to you. I tried to explain it all. I couldn't say no because he's the Teacher. Teacher. You know that. You don't know the rest because you left. I looked for you when the dance was over." Dance. Dance. Dance. "I want to explain the whole thing to you, Juvencio. Wait for me this afternoon. In painting class. Late in the afternoon." The afternoon. Trembling with solitude and fear. The wreath of silence hanging from their tongues. Full of multicolored strangled phrases. Rocking with their honey torches polychromatic windows to drink in grafts of anguish. Unborn phrases nocturnal aphasia carnations blooming in the neurons without extending their smallest tentacles to the vibration of the throat. Suddenly, the Teacher hedgehog of jealousy. The Teacher stalagmite of snow. "What are you doing here all by yourselves?" "Nothing." Nothing. We weren't even talking. We were looking at each other. Intuiting in ourselves the paths of the spasm of the flames that are being born from the tattooed caresses. No words. No acts. Just looking at each other. He repeated. "What are you doing here all by yourselves?" "We already said, nothing."

Immediately, the denunciation. The microinquisition. The betraying lips of lust. The path of erect pins. The foolish wave of excrement rocking in midget throats. "They were all by themselves. Diamantina and Juvencio, all by themselves. The two of them, all by themselves. All by themselves in a classroom. Painting class. The farthest away of all classrooms." The insidious hidden blowgun with small doses of curare to kill drop by drop. Were they kissing? Had they explored through their clothes, the brackish angles of their bodies? If they were innocent why did they seek out the solitary symphonies of mirrors without glass eyes without lids? All by themselves. Themselves—Good Heavens—in a classroom! The painting room. The most distant of all rooms. The commentaries boiled with coral and sulfurous veins. First, among Teachers and students. Inside the School. Then, crossing through, horsemen of the furies, on their mad beasts, all thresholds. "Diamantina and Juvencio in the painting room." "Yes. In the lonely and distant Robinson Crusoe room." "It was late afternoon." "No. It was nighttime and they were all by themselves." "They were necking. Half-naked." "Completely naked." "Ten eyes saw them. Ten. Ten eyes." "No. Twenty eyes." "No. A hundred eyes." "Shameful." "Corrupt." "Alone." "Naked." "And they were." "What, eh?" "Doing that." "That?" "That!" In the School the tidal wave grew. They had to be punished. An exemplary punishment. Kill them? Roast them? Have a cannibal feast so that everyone can sink his teeth into them? It wasn't possible. Unfortunately it wasn't possible. So, then? Expel them from school. But hadn't Juvencio just represented the students in an international contest? Wasn't he one of the most promising students in the past few years? The microinquisition microinquired. At least it was necessary to hold back his diploma. Let several years pass. One at least. What about Diamantina? "Let her lose a year too." She already had the INRI hanging between her breasts. Or maybe lower. Between her legs. Everybody should know that she and he. All by themselves. In an empty classroom. In an empty night. Naked. Doing "that." What about you, Juvencio? What could you have done for Diamantina? You hadn't even ever kissed her. On that day you didn't even take her hand. That afternoon you didn't even have a conversation. Afterward even less. You were imprisoned. Rather, you were both imprisoned—each on your own side—in the invisible jail of a great guillotined love. A great love? And the city still wasn't green. Or wasn't completely green. Maybe a bit sepia. Smell of cocoa. Were they still made of cocoa, men and things? Diamantina, too, made of cocoa? You, Juvencio, also, made of cocoa?

"The only bad thing, José Isabel, is that to make that bog we'll need a lot of men."

"A lot?"

"Just imagine! Raising a wall of wood, stone, and earth! And raising it in a short time. In a blinking of the eyes. When there's an Indian summer. Because if not, the rains themselves won't let it be built! They'd drag the material into the sea. We'll need a lot of men, José Isabel!"

"I'm beginning to see that."

"We've got to cut the stakes. Carry them. Sink them. Lay them crosswise. Put the stones between them. The stones will have to be brought from here, from the shore. And then add the earth, behind, so that it will hold."

"That's right. Plenty of earth!"

"I shouldn't be talking to you about these things, José Isabel. You know a lot more about it than I do."

"Don't you believe it, doc. God always made the bogs here. Never men."

"And if there aren't a lot of men they can't do it either. Even supposing that the water doesn't destroy the wall, they'd spend the whole winter working. Summer would come and there'd still be a lot to do. We'd have to have all of Santorontón working."

"Impossible, doc. Most of them have been sold to Chalena. He won't let anyone loose."

"Then it looks hard to me, José Isabel. Except that Father Cándido might help us."

"Before, maybe. Now, who knows!"

"That's right. The one in charge now is Father Gaudencio. Aside from Chalena, of course."

"Sometimes I think that Don Chalena isn't Don Chalena."

"What do you mean?"

"He's not the partner of The One We Know. He's the selfsame Longtail!"

"How's that?"

"The Evil One also likes to get into the skin of Christians."

"Oh, the things you people believe, José Isabel!"

"That's the way things are when things are that way, doc!"

"Then I don't know what we can do."

"What about Clotilde?"
"What's Clotilde got to do with this?"
"She can probably help us. She knows a lot about the jungle since she lived there so long."
"You're right. Maybe she can help us."
What about us, Diamantina? Nobody can help us. Don't leave. I want to keep hanging on your breasts. Yes. Maybe Clotilde can help us. Nobody knows what she did when she was alone in the jungle. Maybe she learned to communicate with the animals. Sometimes I think they obey her. At least I've seen some of them following her. Maybe too she knows some friends of her parents. They say that the Quindales were respected. And liked. What could have happened to the other one? It's as if the earth had swallowed her up. And why didn't they do anything to the Colonel? Why didn't they inform the authorities? Couldn't they prove anything? Was there an investigation? Could it be that they're protecting Father Cándido without his wanting it? Or is it just all talk? Don't go, Diamantina. I want to stay hanging on your breasts. Hanging on the corner, a wandering lantern. Hanging on your silence. The battalion of microbes who are impelled to defeat us doesn't matter. Sepia inquisition absurd microbes unconscious green myopia. We will conquer in the city sepia avatar that ambers chelonian nacre. We'll meet again closer by. Why are you silent? Why have you coiled around that Teacher blooming with pockmarks—he already a green walking custard apple? Why do you draw that long parallel line that keeps us equidistant? A great love? Never closer but never farther away, Diamantina. I keep on flying in them balloons of foam that I whip up myself. Balloons of smoke that I blow myself. Soap bubble balloons that I string together with my toothed reed. A great love? Diamantina. A great love?

"Here's Clotilde, doc."
"What is it, Clotilde?"
"José Isabel told me what you're thinking of doing."
"Can you help us?"
"I think so, doctor."
"Call me Juvencio."
"Yes, Juvencio."
"Are you sure you can help us?"
"Yes, Juvencio."

Diamantina poem encircled by wind. Do you exist? Did you exist? Weren't you scribbling made of sighs vines of looks? In reprisal for insomnia without vigil I plunged my heart into the Anatomical Amphitheater. There I have left it in the hair-raising world of the dead. Dead? My heart—a piece of cadaver—in an orgy of cadavers. For them it's the same as a bloody ball. At night they'll play strange games. Meanwhile, along the now greenish streets, I keep on greening. The theobroma goes on leaving its dominion to a musacea, the paradisiacal sapientum. I keep on greening. The giant crustacean houses are also greenish. Green river green moon green inlet green street. Everything is turning green. And I a cadaver greening. My hands and feet made of jade? My hair flames of emerald? The swirling of musaceae? The night paradisiacal? The Moon sapientum? The entire city paradisiacal musacea sapientum? In reprisal streamers of bile. Bile wake long thread of rage cobweb of cold green *chiri lumar. Achachay! Huagllichina. Huagllichigrina. Huagllichicuna. Huagllichimuna. Huagllinacuna*. Oh, Juvencio Balda, *runa lumar! Cambag llaquita huacaypagni cangui!*

"I think so, Juvencio. I think so."

TWENTY

That night Dominga waited almost happily for the arrival of the X-Bonetail. Would it be the last X-Bonetail in her life? Everything seemed to indicate so. On the following day her marriage to Candelario would take place. Just thinking about it made her tremble. She really didn't know what newly discovered feelings were knotting up in her breast. She had a mixture of fear and anguish. Of attraction and repulsion. The truth is that before then few men had approached her either with good or evil intent. When she was in the city she still hadn't become a woman. On Balumba or in Santorontón because of other reasons. Sometimes she had been pursued from a distance by litanies of bittersweet phrases: "Damn it, Bulu-Bulu's daughter is starting to look good." "Looking better every day." "Too bad her father's a witch doctor!" "What's that got to do with it? Are you going to catch witchcraft if you lay her?" "No. That's not it." "What, then?" "You've got to be extra special careful with witch doctors." "That's right." "They can get you all screwed up for good." "Are you telling me? In Melao Chico an upland halfbreed got on the bad side of a Witch Doctor. Poor guy! The Witch Doctor changed him into an iguana. And he tied him to the prop of his house so he could give him a beating every day." "He got off easy. Some witch doctors changed another one into a rat. They threw him into a cesspool. So that shit was dropping on him all the blessed day long." "Aha! That's why Minga's asshole has to wait for her father to stick a candle in." "Or so the jungle animals can have a good time." "Or the Tin-Tins. The way the blasted devils do their harm and run." "Sure." She pretended not to notice. What good would it do her to turn around and insult them? They were probably seconded by all Santorontonians and even her father's patients. And what could she do against the whole village? Or against the sufferers in the open-air hospital on Balumba? Sometimes she'd catch a different look from among the young men. One of sympathy. As if they wanted to tell her: "We understand what's happening to you, Dominga. We'd like to approach you, invite you out for a canoe ride. Throw the harpoon. The net. Or leave the cage with a hundred hooks out to sea. Cast the net at night to fish for schools of mullet. Or stretch out the cove or inlet nets. We'd also like to take you into the jungle. Swing on the mango trees. Or pechiches. Look for ripe pitahayas in the underbrush. Get inside a sack to knock down the honeycombs of the moquiñañas. Or simply go swimming together. In the inlets or on the shores of the sandy beaches. But you can see it's not possible. Our families won't let us. They've forbidden us to talk to you. You're Bulu-Bulu's daughter! And nobody wants anything to do with Wizards! Especially a Wizard like your father. Hog-crackling head, thick monkey lips, and black as ebony!" On a certain occasion one had dared follow her. He was a sailor from outside. One of those who only came to Santorontón from time to time. She'd stepped up her pace. Since the other one had done the same, she'd stopped short, turning around: "Look. You don't want to mess with me." "Why not?" "It's best for you and for me." "Why?" "Because it's best." "The fact is I like you a lot. I swear to God." "All the same, leave me alone." "But why?" "Because I can't have anyone liking me." "Don't you like men?" "No. That's not it." "What is it, then?" "I'm Bulu-Bulu's daughter." "The Witch Doctor?" "Yes. The Witch Doctor." "So what's that got to do with it? Witch Doctors are nothing to me." Then she had begged him: "Really. For the love of God. Go away! Leave me alone!" And suddenly she'd turned and run toward her canoe. He couldn't catch her.

With the Colonel it was different. Her own father had put him under her nose. Even Ña Crisanta seemed to agree. And usually it was the Old Woman who was most opposed to her getting tied up with any man. Of course, she would have preferred someone else besides the Colonel. For example, that sailor from outside who chased her one day. What can't be, can't be. Besides, Candelario didn't displease her. He looked so strong. Especially inside. He gave the impression that he had muscles even on his words. She almost couldn't look him in the eyes. When she tried to an ant tickle went all through her body. It started in her hands and feet. And it was concentrated between her legs. Besides—since the Santorontonians had humiliated her too—she shared Ña Crisanta's vengeful joy in a certain way. She would see them the next day—in their best Sunday clothes—attending the wedding. They would be dying with envy. Especially the marriageable girls. They all would have liked to have hooked Candelario. Would they have liked to? Wasn't it said that he'd been to bed with hundreds—or thousands—of women? Wasn't it known that his hands were soaked with blood? But what did they have to do with it? Something like that showed that he was the most male in those parts. In the end, then, she ought to feel satisfied. And yet she couldn't. On the contrary, she was flooded with doubts and hesitations. Everything was all right for the moment. But what about later on? The next night. When he'd start caressing her.

When he'd climb on top of her and sink his flesh strut into her. Would she still be satisfied? Would it please her? Yes, indeed. She was almost sure it would please her. She would finally discover the secret—was it a secret?—that shook her so many times. And beyond that? Beyond what? Let it come! The wiggling. The pleasure. The discovery. Nobody could take them away from her! Besides, there was something important. The most important. The farewell to the X-Bonetail! Even though she'd grown accustomed to his visits—how many, how many visits had the damned rattler paid her?—what's for certain is that it was preferable that he not visit her anymore. Getting accustomed didn't mean that she'd lost her panic, her revulsion, her anguish. All that was greater every night. She still felt as if she were walking by leaps over harpoons with their tips up. Any hesitation. Or loss of control. And she would be doomed forever!

For her part, Crisanta wasn't all there. In the last moments the wedding preparations had dulled her wits. She went her way like a boat adrift being dragged along by unknown forces. She wasn't aware of what she was doing. As if she weren't taking part in things. And were looking at everything from outside. At dusk the imminence of events seemed to awaken her. Suddenly she recovered her awareness of what was happening. "Your daughter's getting married tomorrow. Your Dominga. She's going to marry Candelario Mariscal—the evilest man in these parts. Woman-chaser. Murderer. And if that's not enough, son of The One We Know." How had it happened? At what moment had everything been arranged for that absurd marriage?

Under the effects of what witchcraft—because it had to be a piece of witchcraft—had she accepted it? And not just that. She'd also taken part in the preparations.

Next to her Bulu-Bulu was snoring like a saint. She leaned over. Shook him. The Wizard opened his eyes immediately.

"What? What is it?"

"Wake up. I want to talk to you."

He sat halfway up.

"What's the matter?"

"Nothing."

"So why don't you let me sleep, then? It's very late and at midnight and in the morning we've got a lot to do. We'd better leave it for tomorrow, don't you think?"

"It has to be now."
He opened his eyes all the way. He immediately suspected what it was all about.
"Anything you say, Old Woman."
He stretched. He sat on the edge of the bed. His wife stared at him. Studying him.
"I want you to tell me the truth."
He played the innocent.
"The truth. The truth about what?"
She let him have it point-blank.
"Why do you want to marry Minga off to the Colonel?"
"Me? I haven't got anything to do with it. It's their doing. You saw it."
"Yes. I saw it! You were mixed up in everything! Playing possum you brought things to just where you wanted them. Tell me why you did it."
"I swear to you, Crisanta, that..."
"Don't come to me with any tales. I want to know everything."
"Really, you're fooling yourself."
"If you don't sing now, I'm going to Candelario and tell him the wedding's off tomorrow."
The Wizard got all tangled up. He went through a series of absurd gestures. Finally he decided.
"All right, then."
He paused. He went on:
"You were the one who gave me the idea."
"Me? Don't make me laugh."
"The night you said that Minga needed a man. A man so she could get rid of the serpent and the moon. That was exactly when Colonel Candelario Mariscal showed up."
The Old Woman muttered, as if to herself:
"Colonel Mariscal! Do you know who he is?"
"Who in Santorontón doesn't?"
"And all that he's done?"
"You know that I know much more than the others."
"So how can you hand your daughter over to him?"
"He's a man, isn't he?"
"Of all men he's the only one who can't marry Minga!"
"Why didn't you say so before? Why did you do everything possible to set up this wedding?"
"Why? Because you bewitched me. I wasn't myself. I was who

knows who. I obeyed your orders. That's all over. I won't let myself be led along by witchcraft anymore."

There was a silence. The Old Woman spoke again.

"In the first place, how did you get the Colonel to marry Minga?"

"How should I know? I repeat. It was their doing."

"Aren't you going to tell me he's doing it because he likes the girl?"

"So maybe it was like that. Wouldn't any man like Minga?"

"Oh, Bulu-Bulu! You think my mother just dropped me, don't you? All right. If you won't tell me, I know what I have to do."

"Why don't you think he..."

"If he'd wanted the girl, he'd have carried her off. Willing or unwilling. Without even telling us."

The Wizard's face wrinkled dry custard apple.

"That would be something to see... All right. I'm going to blab everything."

In an abbreviated way, he retold the whole matter, from stem to stern. The Old Woman, as she listened, was growing more and more infuriated. When the Wizard finished, she looked at him, full of hate.

"You did that with Minga?"

"It was the best thing, wasn't it?"

She calmed down a little. She even felt a little pity.

"Wizard or not, you're getting dumber every day, Bulu-Bulu. The only thing this is going to do is bring trouble. I have to have some words with Minga. Right now."

"Crisanta..."

She paid no attention to him. Dominga had finished burying the X-Bonetail. Her last X-Bonetail! She stood up. She went back to the house. As on the other occasions she was naked. Rampant. Head high. With quick steps. They thought she would keep on going, the same as always. They were wrong. The girl stopped. She smiled at them. Resplendent.

"Good night, Papa. Good night, Mama."

They answered laconically.

"Good night!"

"Good night, daughter!"

For a moment Ña Crisanta hesitated. Should she stop her? Should she ask her to forget about the wedding? That—no matter what happened—it was better not to go through with it? It was a farce worked out by her father. With the best of intentions. A farce in any case. The Colonel certainly didn't have any interest in her. For him she was just medicine. He was getting married to get rid of a dead woman he had to please every night. Bulu-Bulu thought that if he had a legitimate wife—married in Church and all—the dead woman would go away forever. That turned out to be dangerous. What if the dead woman didn't go away? What if the Colonel continued to give her pleasure? What if in front of the new bride she got undressed and obliged the brand new husband to take care of her first, ahead of everyone? What if he wore himself out from covering her so much and became useless for taking care of anyone else? What if she lay down between the newlyweds and prevented them from even touching each other? The best would be to get out in time. Later on it would be hard. On the other hand, if the Colonel really loved her, he'd face any danger. She and the Wizard—she was sure that the latter would do the impossible—would help her. They would even take care to see that the dead woman didn't bother them. They'd remain every night—both of them or taking turns—at the foot of the matrimonial deerskin to fight off Chepa. Because—didn't she know?—the dead woman was none other than that Chepa Quindales people mentioned so often. In everything. They would help her in every little thing if the Colonel loved her. The worst part was that he didn't love her. Candelario could love nobody. At least nobody who was of this world. Those of this world only served him for his criminal acts. Especially to gain more souls for Old Longtail. Because—didn't she know that either?—he was the Son of Old Longtail. She had to forgive her, her mother, for not having told her before. But maybe Bulu-Bulu had bewitched her. Or Old Longtail himself had stuck his tail into these matters. Only that night did she begin to realize how much harm she'd done to her. Without realizing it . . .

She made up her mind. She had to tell her. No matter what happened she had to have some words with her. It was better to stand up to Colonel Mariscal. And not ruin Dominga forever.

"Child!"

The girl stopped.

"What is it, Mama?"

"I want to talk to you."

She bloomed in smiles.

"Whatever you say."

"Let's go to your room."
"Let's go."
Bulu-Bulu, fearful, tried to intervene.
"Crisanta... I..."
"What?"
"Umm... No. Nothing. Just give Minga good advice."
The Old Woman reasoned, sourly:
"When have I given her bad advice? It's other people who've done that."
The Wizard looked at his daughter. A strange emotion spiraled in his throat. Suddenly it hurt him to be Bulu-Bulu. The Witch Doctor. Monkey Face as his colleagues called him. He would have liked—at that moment—to have been a different man. Or, maybe, a frail woman. Then he would be able to weep out loud. He held back. Looked at his daughter. Serenely. In full control of himself. Only his voice flowed more irregularly than at other times.
"Sleep happily. And may everything go well for you."
"Thank you Papa. I wish the same for you."
When they went into the next room, Dominga took Ña Crisanta's hands:
"And thanks to you too, Mama. Thanks for all you've done so I can get married."
"But, if I..."
"If you know how happy I feel."
"Oh, yes?"
"Tomorrow, when I go into the church, they won't humiliate me anymore. They'll forget who I am and who my father is. I'll forgive them for all the time they looked down on me."
"They—and especially the women—will never forgive us for what's taking place tomorrow."
"What difference does it make? What I go through in the church can't be taken away from me by anybody. The church will be full of lights. Colors. Music. It will never have looked so pretty. It'll be like a dream, Mama. I never imagined that something like that would happen to me."
Should she tell her? Shouldn't she tell her? Supposing she did, would she pay any heed? Would she thank her? Would she believe her? And even if she believed her, wouldn't she go right on ahead? Wouldn't she go through with the wedding, even in spite of what they wanted? Even knowing that she was going to pay very dearly

for that happiness? On the other hand, did she have a right to take that little piece of happiness away from her daughter? Before making up her mind, she asked her one more time:

"Are you really happy?"

"Very happy, Mama. I don't think I'm going to be able to sleep tonight. I'll be counting the hours that are left. Very early, at dawn, I'll go to the inlet. To take a bath. So when the sun warms up it'll dry my hair."

There was a silence woven with the dissimilar thoughts of mother and daughter. Finally the former dared at least to ask her a question.

"So?"

"What, Mama?"

"Do you love the Colonel?"

"I don't know, Mama."

"What then?"

"I like him, Mama. I liked him when I first saw him. He's so strong. So sure of what he says and does. And in spite of that..."

"Go on."

"I don't know why, he seems to be hiding something. Seems to have a scorpion stinging him inside. Sometimes he grows sad, for no reason. He looks far off, as if he sees things that the rest of us don't."

"What if it's true what they say about him?"

"That he's the Son of The One We Know? I don't believe it. But if I did, what difference does it make? I'd try to help him. Can't he be saved? Does he have to be in trouble forever, without any hope? Besides, there are people he's good with. With his Godfather, Father Cándido, for example. And—like it or not—he's helped Dr. Balda several times."

Why contradict her? It would be useless.

"Of course, Dominga. Of course."

The only thing she could do was defend her. Bulu-Bulu and she had to defend her. She and Bulu-Bulu. Immediately she began to give her advice. More intimate advice. The advice mothers give their daughters when they're going to get married. Bulu-Bulu and she. She had to do this. And the other thing. And still another thing. Only in that way would she be able to defend her marriage. Especially with a man like Colonel Candelario Mariscal. She and Bulu-Bulu.

And Bulu-Bulu was like a madman. He went down the steps in two strides. He went around the house two or three times. He stopped by one of the braces. He urinated. He did the same thing on each one of the other braces. He lighted a cigar. A long, thin cigar made from several leaves of rolled tobacco. He blew out draughts of smoke. Through his nose, ears, and eyes. He peeled these last as they shone white in the darkness. He ran into the jungle. He looked for a trunk. The trunk of a very tall tree. The tallest of all trees. He climbed it. He grasped it with his legs and his tail. He had a tail now. To the highest of the branches. He sucked on the cigar several times. He dressed himself once more with the smoke of the six puffs. With his mouth, seven. Seven puffs. Then with the lighted tip he sketched whirlwinds of light. He raised his arms. Jaguar arms. Black and gold arms. His body rocked. Black and gold. His legs rocked. Black and gold. His tail. Black and gold. His jaws. Black and gold. Jaguar. Jaguar black and gold. Dagger teeth. Red and white. Black and gold. Coral red. Sea-foam white. Ebony black. And gold gold gold. He roared. The leaves of the tree shook. The leaves of all the trees. And the eyes in the leaves. Green leaves polychrome eyes. The Jaguar roared again. Silence. Silence in the leaves and in the eyes. Black and gold. "Balumba. Bulu-Bulu. Bulu-Bulu on Balumba. Minga on Balumba. Bridals on Balumba. Bálumba-Balumba Balumba-Balumbá. Jaguar Bulu-Bulu. The Jaguar on Balumba. Minga at the bridals. The bridals on Balumba. Bálumba-Balumba. Balumba-Balumbá."

TWENTY-ONE

"I think I can help you, Juvencio."

"How?"

"By getting the inhabitants of the jungle to help us."

"Do you mean the animals?"

"Yes, Juvencio."

"I hadn't thought of that, Clotilde."

"The monkeys especially."

"Are you sure they'll do it?"

"No harm in trying. I can try to convince them."

"If you did that, there'd be no problem. We could be ready for the first Indian summer when it comes."

José Isabel intervened:

"But could we do it all in one day?"

The doctor replied:

"Who knows? We'll work day and night if we have to. Until we finish."

"Fine, doc. Besides, the Indian summers come with a full Moon. That way we'll have light till we're ready to quit."

"Light till we're ready to quit." And yet, Juvencio, you, how long will you be in the dark? With night tattooed on your soul. Night fell ahead of time in you. If you were vain—or, perhaps, vainer—you could apply to yourself the phrase that ran from mouth to mouth in Incadom after the murder of Atahualpa, *chaupi punchapi tutayacu*. Night fell in the middle of the day. After the microinquisitions tried to pulverize you, you sought a way out. Medicine. Medicine stood out for you like a luminous thread leading out of the labyrinth. But the labyrinth wasn't green. It clung to your lips. Like a leech. You appeared in the phantasmal phantom Morgue of another planet. An everyday phantom. The difficulties of scalpels were your own difficulty. Diamantina? Paradoxically, all that helped you resurrect yourself. Diamantina? Diamantina began to be part of a carrousel of truncated memories. She sank in the whirlpool of silence and shadow. Little by little you felt that your heart was no longer alien. The dead had stopped playing with it. At midnight. When they arose from their icy slabs. Sometimes already cut up. Lacking one of their members. Or with windows—marks of dissection—on all four sides. Or with absurd slashes on their faces or stomachs, showing their bony laughter. Or some psychedelic polychrome caused by the anatomical incisions. Or perhaps already changed into only a part of someone. Into active pieces automatically scattered by inertia. But they gave you back your heart. Maybe each one of them, in turn, took out his own heart. And played with it, that macabre football. Those viscera of others were probably superior. Because yours lacked the elasticity they required. Owner of it now, you placed it—like everything that was yours—at the service of science. Your love, at that time, was Medicine. When you could—when your time came—you left that fascinating world of sliced-up dead. You sank into the absorbing peripateticism of hospitals. It's true that the cadavers pursued you for a long time. You'd familiarized yourself with their look for too long. With their aggressive smell. With their gradual decrease in size. While the cutting steel sank into them. At first you even thought it strange that human beings—live ones—could move. Act. Speak. Express ideas. They seemed less real to you than those other human beings—ex-beings?—silent. Passive. Tranquil. Incapable of doing anything. Neither for good nor for evil. You only harmed one dead woman. Diamantina? She looked too much like Diamantina. Young. Beautiful. A suicide. There was a moment when you thought she moved. Or did she move? Completely naked as she was, she got up off the slab. Put her arms out to hug you. You asked to work on her. On her. They let you. When you approached with your surgical instruments you were overcome by a strange trembling. Was she breathing? Did she move her face to see you? Were her eyes lighted up? Was she trying to embrace you? When you went out—the few moments you had outside the necrocomium—you were assailed by doubts. Hesitations. Was necrophilia trapping you inside its absurd nets? Was your libido becoming deformed? Didn't coitus with living women attract you anymore? Was that passion for the decedent dominating you? You should hurry to get the necropsy over with. The quiet necropsy might lead you to the tempestuous environment of mortuary orbits. It was best to withdraw. Not return. Control that aberrant impulse. Look for sexual encounters with other females. It didn't matter who they were or where. What you needed was exhaustion. Total annulment of the libido. You were going back! You were clutching the cutting steel. You were ready to use it on her. Still, you remained motionless. Discontented. Disconcerted. Not knowing what to do. Your boiling blood beat against your senses. Voluptuous prenecrophilic waves were rising up in you. You would have liked to have dressed her with kisses. Run over her with your mouth. Tattoo yourself onto her. Even sink into her, or, rather, blend into her! As if you were making love to a marble body. "Indian summer starts tomorrow, doc." If it hadn't been because the others were beginning to watch you. At every instant. The watchmen—especially when the other students had left—were hanging on your movements. You were the first to arrive. The last to leave. One afternoon the Teacher called your attention to it: "Juvencio, when are you going to start the dissection of that cadaver?" You held yourself back so as not to attack him. Calling her a "cadaver." It was a lack of respect! Cadaver! He and his whole family were cadavers! "Doc, doc. Indian summer starts tomorrow."

José Isabel shook him:

"Doc. Doc."

"What? What's going on?"

"I'm talking to you and you don't seem to hear me."

He reacted.

"I was thinking about something else. What is it, José Isabel?"

"Indian summer starts tomorrow."

"Oh, yes? Then there's no time to lose."

Clotilde intervened—only at that instant did he notice Clotilde—with a certain worry.

"Don't you feel well?"

"I feel all right. I was just remembering..."

She smiled.

"It's good that you're all right. Because we have to be ready. For what's coming."

"Of course!"
"As of now I think the monkeys will help us."
José Isabel added:
"I've talked with a lot of humans too. Those we can count on."
"What did they say?"
"Even though they're afraid, they've agreed!"
Juvencio became enthusiastic.
"Very good. We men will take care of cutting the logs. Looking for stones. Directing the work."
Clotilde assured them:
"The monkeys and all the animals that help them will haul the material. And they'll drive in the stakes too. They'll lay the stones. And gather earth from the hills."
José Isabel scratched his head.
"I'm just worried about..."
"Who?"
"Don Chalena and his people. They'll try to stop the work at all costs."
Juvencio calmed him down.
"Things have changed, José Isabel. In the first place, everybody has water now."
"That's right. And it'll last them until after the rains are over."
"Of course. They've saved some. And they know that winter is going to continue."
"That's right, doc."
"Besides, Chalena's main weapon against Santorontón was the fact that all the water belonged to him. If the water belongs to everyone, he can't threaten them anymore. I can assure you that if some of them help us, the majority won't interfere. They'll let us build the bog, as you people call it."
Clotilde agreed.
"Juvencio's right, José Isabel."
Clotilde! Clotilde has been completely cured. Look at her eyes. Her pupils are no longer dilated. She's serene. Tranquil. She seems to have forgotten the absurd ideas that dominated her when you first met her as if they'd never existed. She lives in her house. The house that belonged to her parents. Alone. Completely alone. Or, to be more precise, along with a dog, Miss Victor. A white bitch. Old. Bony. All eyes. Honey eyes, a little sad. One day you asked Clotilde to settle in Santorontón. She smiled. "No, Juvencio.

I'd rather keep you at a distance." You were startled a bit. "Why?" She looked at you, teasingly. With a kind of innate coquetry. "Because on any given day you'll send me back to the city." "Didn't you like the city?" "Yes, but I want to be where I am." "Aren't you afraid?" "Afraid of what? I'm better protected than ever. Besides Miss Victor I've got my other friends. They watch over me. The ones I don't see, but I can feel them. Maybe they don't let themselves be seen so as not to bother me. I hear their cries. Their clapping. Their running. Or their flying. Sometimes they even leave me gifts by my door. Especially things to eat." "That's the way it should be, Clotilde. If you think it's best." Clotilde! Every day you're more of a woman. Better shaped. I notice that the looks of all the men follow her. The women, for their part, have had to accept her. Since she returned she hasn't become involved with anyone. And if any man said something to her, she cut him off cold! Besides, she doesn't come to Santorontón very often. When she comes she only visits José Isabel and his family. And me. You're thinking about Clotilde too much, Juvencio. The same thing is happening to you as happened with that beautiful dead woman some years back. But that one was dead. Loving her. Wanting her was rolling around face down on your index finger. You realized in time. That's why you asked the Teacher one day: "Look, doctor. Give my dead woman to somebody else. Something strange is happening to me." The medical man smiled. "Are you falling in love with her perhaps? Don't worry about it. On certain occasions the same thing has happened to a lot of us. It's a mixup of feelings. What must happen to certain sculptors. From observing their statues so much as they make them. From wondering how much they're going to work them, they put something of themselves into them. Their own passions. By reflection they receive in turn what they put into their work. And by loving them, they love themselves. Or they love their creative passion. Or the dissatisfaction with what they didn't obtain in everyday life. I repeat. Don't worry. I'll give her to one of your classmates." When he saw them make the first incision in her he shuddered. And when they began to dismember her, he was on the point of hurling himself at the one doing it. He was barely able to hold back. He left the Morgue. Crazy. He ran to the nearby cemetery. A cemetery with white arches and green palm trees. Green palm trees to fan the postmortem sleep under the broiling sun. There he burst into tears.

Desperate. He had the feeling for an instant that the ones who were under the ground. Or in the polished mausoleums. Or lying on the slabs of the Anatomy Amphitheater—especially his dead woman—were the real living. Those who already had an eternal life, without any zigzag, definitively made. On the other hand, those who moved, wriggling like worms in order to find the destiny of the others and their own destiny, were the authentic deceased.

To-u. Ad-cug. Toad-ucug. Green toad. Black toad. Yellow toad. Bloated toad. Not little-jambatu toad. Big-ucug toad. Lying in his hammock. Without the Mute rocking. Without Tolón fanning. Toady toad. Not jambatudy. Ucugy. Not jambatu. Ucug. Chalena the toad. Chalena not jambatu. Chalena ucug. Rurruillag Chalena? Capon Chalena? Rurruillag Ucug? Big capon toad? Chalena capon. Self-made capon. From sinking into himself. From his virile parts' sinking inside him. From philo-auto-atrophy. From minimizing all that made his thirst for power less. His hunger for money. Although nobody—not even he himself—knew that he was a capon. Oh, the caponing! Oh, rurru surcushca chugri! Chalena hammocking. Without the Mute rocking. The toad ucuging. Without Tolón fanning. Oh, the caponing! Oh, rurru surcushca chugri!

"Don Chalena! Don Chalena!"

Ill-humored.

"Ah! Salustiano! It's you!"

"Yes, Don Chalena. I was coming..."

"For what? Out with it, quick."

"Well...A lot of Santorontonians are getting together with Dr. Balda."

"What for?"

"To build a bog."

He got up, furious.

"Goddamn it! That doctor will get me yet! What do they want a bog for?"

"So you won't control the water anymore. With a bog they'll all have water until the end of summer."

Chalena lay down again.

"And how are they going to make the bog?"

"They're going to bring two hills together."

"Those dummies are crazy. They'll spend all summer and they

won't even have the wall finished. And that's if all the Santorontonians are working!"

"A lot of them have got together, Don Chalena."

"Don't worry, Salustiano. That still has to be seen!"

He gave a little swing in the hammock. He himself. Without the Mute rocking him. Without Tolón fanning him. He. Ucug ucuging. Salustiano shrugged his shoulders.

"I was just saying, Don Chalena. But..."

"Go on."

"Last night the dogs were doing a lot of barking over by the jungle. I looked out. It looked like the trees were moving. The leaves and branches were making a lot of noise. Like when the wind blows from the southeast, one gust after another."

He sat up again. Green toad. Yellow toad. Black toad.

"Didn't you go see what was going on?"

"Yes. We went this morning. Rugel Banchaca, me, and some rural guards."

"What did you find?"

"Nothing! Not even tracks. There were only a few fallen limbs."

"Oh, damn it! I'm beginning not to like this."

"Could it be things done...?"

"By who?"

"By The One We Know."

"I don't think so. It must be the monkeys."

"Maybe. Since they don't leave any tracks. They always get around up above. Leaping from branch to branch."

"When we had the fire we should have finished them all off!"

"We would have... if Colonel Candelario Mariscal hadn't butted in."

"In any case we've got to get prepared. Tell our people to get their weapons ready. It can't be! They can't make the bog right under our noses!"

"All right, Sir."

Salustiano leaving. Chalena hammocking. Without the Mute rocking. Without Tolón fanning. Ucug ucuging. Capon caponing. Rurruillag rurruillaging.

TWENTY-TWO

The night before the wedding Santorontón looked the same as ever. The lights winked from the street lamps. The dogs streaked the silence with their atonal signatures. The nasal claws of the sea scratched the sand white. Only from time to time did the jungle let the polyphony of its millions of throats be heard. This, of course, in the part beyond the houses. Along the streets bereft of footsteps. Along the belt of reeds that bordered the village. On the naked beach. On the other hand, inside most of the homes everything was quite different. Santorontón—curiously—was boiling. An unaccustomed movement whirled the women. They went from here to there. From there to here. In a hurry. They got dressed with an unknown rapidity. They didn't worry—unheard of!—about the clothes they were wearing or their physical appearance. What they were after was to save time. The strange thing is that this spectacle didn't even spare the bosses. Not even the highest police authority of the village, Rugel Banchaca. Dumbfounded, he contemplated the unusual preparations. His wife, a fleshless female, Doña Prudencia—who ordinarily lived up to her name—and their daughter Petita—innocent and pure for lack of opportunities—didn't even look at him. As if he didn't exist. That's not all. They hadn't given him a single bit of information regarding it all. Feeling wounded in his triple authority—as husband, father, and chief of the Rural Guard—he couldn't contain himself. With his voice of a startled turkey, he shouted:

"Prudencia!"

Not even the echo answered his words. He buttoned his fly and tightened his belt. When he relaxed he always had one open and the other loose. He stood up. The tone of his voice rose:

"Prudencia!"

His wife—a harpoon at the ready—without stopping her movements, answered. Did she put honey or nettles on her tongue?

"What is it, Rugelito?"

"What's got into you two?"

"Nothing."

"So what all this bustle?"

"We're going out."

He was blind with fury.

"Where to?"

"I can't tell you."

"And what for?"

"I can't tell you that either."

The Chief of the Rural Guard remained thoughtful for a few moments. He suspected that this had something to do with the wedding of the Priest's Godson and the Witch Doctor's daughter. But, actually, what was it all about? Why that mystery? What were they aiming at? Could it be some headstrong thing that would bring disagreeable consequences down on all the families? In Santorontón the procedures of the aforementioned Mariscal were quite familiar. If he was challenged, he would carry out his threat. If necessary he would bury the whole village. The women didn't realize exactly how much danger they were exposing themselves to. There was no doubt that the Colonel would make no exceptions because of age or sex. So? The best thing was to hold them back.

"You're not going anywhere."

"Who's going to stop us?"

"Me."

Doña Prudencia stopped for a moment. She looked hard at the Chief of the Rural Guard.

"Don't make me laugh, Rugelito."

The latter didn't want to put his triple authority into play. He was sure that the Old Woman would have the last word. He softened.

"I'm doing it for your own good."

In any case, Ña Prudencia looked at him with mockery.

"Are you going to call your rural guards to hold us back by force?"

He drew himself up again, even knowing it was useless.

"I've got more than enough pants to give the orders in this house."

"Oh, yes? Couldn't it be that you're afraid something's going to happen to you?"

"Don't push me, Prudencia."

"If you really were a man, you'd have stopped a lot of things in the village."

"Are you talking about the Colonel's wedding?"

"That. And everything else."

Banchaca scratched his ear. He always did that when he was at the height of his fury.

"Say whatever you want, tonight you're not going to get your own way. So you can start taking off those rags, you and Petita. You're not budging from here."

His wife sat down next to him. She changed attitudes. She became serener. More understanding. At the same time more sure of herself. She did, as always, live up to her name more. In the end that was how she would conquer her husband.

"Look, Rugel. It's better if you don't get involved."

"Why?"

"All—or almost all—of the women in Santorontón have agreed on what we're going to do."

"What is it that you're going to do?"

"I repeat. We can't tell."

"Are you going to the Colonel, maybe, to ask him to hold off the wedding?"

"What do you want me to tell you?"

"Are you going to beg the Witch Doctor to send his daughter as far away as possible?"

"Why do you insist?"

"Or are they going to ask Father Cándido to stop the wedding?"

"Why wear yourself out? Besides, you know very well that Father Cándido doesn't count for anything anymore in Santorontón."

"Then are you going to Father Gaudencio to convince him not to marry them?"

"You refuse to understand. I can't. I mustn't say anything!"

Rugel Banchaca shrugged his shoulders.

"All right. All right. But I warn you that even though all the women may have agreed, I'm sure that the men haven't!"

"You're wrong, Rugelito. The majority of the men are backing us up. Even your own rural guards."

"What about Salustiano?"

"Him too."

"And Don Chalena?"

"Him too."

"And Vigiliano?"

"Him too. And also Dr. Espurio. And also almost all the other men. The only ones who don't know—they don't know a thing about it and maybe that's why they're not with us—are the ones on Father Cándido's side. Of course the ones who back us up are doing it just because. They don't know exactly what it's all about either."

He shrugged his shoulders and scratched his ear again.

"It's your affair, then. Go ahead! But just let me warn you once more that you're putting your head in the jaguar's mouth."

Prudencia stood up, eyes flashing.

"We know that. But anything is preferable to having them make a mockery of us."

The woman had put it precisely. In most of the houses in the village the scene had been similar. Only at Dr. Espurio Carranza's was it different. The Medical Man had noticed the coming and going of some women in and out of his home. He had noticed, too, that his mate was turning, overnight, into something like the feminine leader of Santorontón. During a moment of respite for her, he asked:

"Well. What's up with you, Jovita?"

"Nothing. Why?"

"So many visits have some reason behind them. Tell me what you're all planning."

Her artichoke face contracted.

"Don't you know?"

"No."

"Can't you guess?"

"Not that either."

An angry pity flooded her.

"You're a little angel, Espurio."

"Explain yourself."

"Do you think we're going to let the daughter of the Witch Doctor and the son of The One We Know profane our church?"

Panic and fury beat on the bile of the Doctor-Gravedigger. He roared:

"You're not mixed up in this, are you, dummy?"

"I am."

"Fine. Then I'll get your coffin and your grave ready."

"You'd like that, Espurio. But you won't be able to."

"Oh, no?"

"No. Because I'm nobody's fool. Even though I've got the village stirred up, I'm staying right at home! Keeping you company!"

That didn't calm the Doctor.

"You know damned well that you don't fool around with the Colonel."

"I know that. That's why we've prepared things well, so that everything will turn out naturally."

"Just as you wish. As for me, I wash my hands of this. Like Pilate."

"You're the luckiest one, Espurio."

"You think so?"

"In the worst of cases, if it all fails. If the Colonel steps in and kills half the village. Who's going to end up making some money?"

"I don't know."

"Why you, Idiot. Don't you own the cemetery? Don't you have the Funeral Business? So? Who will have to bury all of them?"

"Say. That wouldn't be bad. You're right."

He reacted. The shadow of the Colonel seemed to be cast on everything around him. He looked at her steadily.

"In any case, I don't like it. What if not even I am left to tell the tale? It's a business where your life is at stake."

Jovita laughed.

"Don't be a coward, Espurio. The only lives at stake are those of the others."

She closed her face. Continued:

"In any case, I won't allow that Colored Witch Doctor and his family—his family especially—to walk all over us. I'll risk my own life in order to stop it if that's necessary."

Little by little the last lights of Santorontón were dying out. First, the candles and lamps that lighted up the inside of the houses closed their lids. Then the street lights quieted their amber laughter. A battalion of shadows took over all the houses. Only at that instant, like white spirals, did the women begin to appear. Tributaries of silent rivers, they thickened the human current on its way to the church. They knocked. It didn't open. They insisted. Filemón, ill-humored, asked:

"What do you want?"

Since Doña Jovita wasn't with them—under the pretext of a headache, generally not feeling well, fatigue, etc., etc.—Prudencia assumed command.

"To talk to Father Gaudencio."

"He's already gone to bed."

"You have to get him up. It's urgent!"

"Why don't you wait till tomorrow?"

"We've no time to lose. Hurry up!"

"But..."

"No buts about it. Or do you want us to go get him ourselves?"

The tone of voice of the wife of the Chief of the Rural Guard had taken on an unexpected authority. The Sexton gave in.

"No. Not that, Doña Prudencia. Come in! I'll go get the Reverend Father!"

The tidal wave of women entered the nave of the church. They remained waiting in silence. In a short while the Priest appeared. He came wrapped in a cloud of rage. He made an effort. He got control of himself. Before him stood the cream of village feminine society.

"God's good evening, Father Gaudencio."

"May you have a good and holy evening, my children."

He faced the wife of the Chief of the Rural Guard.

"Doña Prudencia, to what do we owe this visit to the house of the Lord at such a late hour?"

"Forgive us, Father Gaudencio. We want to make a request of you. And it can't be put off."

The Priest rubbed his hands.

"You know you can count on me. What's it about?"

There was a deep silence. The women didn't even move. With a somewhat emotional voice, Prudencia expressed her wish:

"We want you to pay a visit to Bulu-Bulu. The Witch Doctor."

As if he hadn't understood, he babbled:

"Go to the house of... the owner of Balumba?"

"Yes, Father."

He exploded. Unable to contain himself, he lost control.

"Have you gone mad?"

He recovered immediately. He underwent a transition. His voice became honeyed, arpeggioed again, as always.

"Do you realize what you're asking me to do?"

"Yes, Father. You've got to prevent tomorrow's wedding!"

"That... That's impossible! In the first place, I've already promised the Colonel."

"It would be a sin, Reverend. Worse still, a sacrilege!"

The Priest didn't pay any attention. He went on:

"Besides, even if I hadn't given my word as a Servant of the Lord, the Colonel would make me do it! You people don't know him very well. I do. He has some very convincing arguments. Nothing can stand in his way!"

"Him, no. But Dominga, the Wizard's daughter, yes!"

"I don't quite understand. Explain it to me!"

"That's why we ask you to go to Bulu-Bulu's house. There you can talk to Crisanta. To Dominga. Or, if necessary, with the Witch Doctor himself. You have to convince them of the kind of man the Colonel is. Of the dangers that the girl will face if she marries him. That even though you bless them it would be forced by Candelario Mariscal's threats. Threats against you and against the village. That a marriage like that isn't valid. In short, anything that might occur to you."

"I don't think it would get any results."

"You have to try it at least."

"Maybe they'll refuse to see me."

"You? They'll receive you with open arms, Father."

He swept his gaze over the broad group of women. Could he deny that wish of theirs, proper or not? They were his main strength in the village. If he turned them against himself, his mission would be difficult. Maybe impossible. Perhaps he would never preach another sermon. Nor say a mass. Nor practice other religious offices. Of the smallest degree. Or of indeterminate degree. He had to accept. There was no other way out. *Ad maiorem Dei Gloriam*. If worse came to worst he would say that he was forced to. All the women in the village put pressure on him. He was forced to. What if the Colonel didn't believe him? If he threatened him the way he had before? His feet were still like bushes.

Ad maiorem Dei Gloriam. No. The Colonel would probably act in some other way. It would be different this time. The women of Santorontón backed him up. The women. Before killing him. The women. Or wounding him gravely. The women. Or trampling on his dignity. The women. Heee waaas suuure. Were his teeth going to chatter? Was he afraid? Very much afraid. The women. What could he do against the wo the men? Wowowo mememen. "Get hold of yourself, Gaudencio." On the other hand, could he convince Bulu-Bulu and his family? Maybe he could. Especially Ña Crisanta. He would glue reasons together. Reasons. Veiled threats. Veiled. He also agreed that the wedding shouldn't take place. He would do everything possible for it not to. He would pick up what Ña Prudencia had said. And he would add things from his own throat. From his jawbone. *Stultorum infinitus est numerus*. Of a religious nature. Of course. Very certain and just besides. There had been no preparation. The banns had not been posted. Everything had been hurried. Skipping over the precepts of Dogma. Could a marriage of that stripe be valid? And if it were to men, what about divine approval? His scruples woven together, he decided. It was obvious. It couldn't be denied. The request of the ladies was most adequate and opportune. Ladies? That description made him laugh inside. He remembered that in the gossip he was an Atlantic priest. Atlantic. From overseas. Women. Women of Santorontón. Atlantic. Only because of an absurdity of fate was he there. He yearned for another distant world. More in tune with his background and his aims. Would he return there someday? Wouldn't he remain a Santorontonian forever? Atlantic.

He pondered.

"All right. I accept. And I'm only doing it because you people asked me. Perhaps God is speaking through your mouths."

The feminine chorus puffed up like a nest of chonta bugs. A bell of muscles rang. The green fangs creaked in their accent.

"Thank you."

"Thank you very much, Father Gaudencio."

"Thank you very much."

Ña Prudencia warned:

"That's the way. It has to be right now, Reverend. Minutes are precious. Afterward it will be too late."

The young cleric puffed up his cheeks. He repeated in his way.

This time, anointed. Sacred.
"Immediately! *Vox populi vox Dei!*"
And to himself—thinking about the women of Santorontón and the Witch Doctor and his family—*Stultorum infinitus est numerus*.

TWENTY-THREE

Lying there. Wounded there. Suffering there. There. Looking at her. Eyes large. Very large. Become all eyes. Feverish. Frightened. Following her with lasso looks. Wrapping her up. Drawing her in. Wall pupils. Chain pupils. Where to go? Where to escape? Where to seek refuge? Tied. Hands and feet. Soul. Tied to a pair of eyes. On the ground. In the air. In him. Tied. "Clotilde. Clotilde." Was he talking to her? Without words. Without moving his lips. With his eyes. Tied. With fear. With suspicion. With anguish.
"Clotilde."
"What is it?"
"Are you here?"
"Yes. Here."
"Come closer!"
"I am close."
"Closer."
"I can't get any closer."
She couldn't get any closer. Closer to the jaguar. I run. And

he behind me. Then? He has a different kind of hunger. I run. And he behind me. Let's see if he can catch me or not. Let's see if I can climb the trees. Or wrap up in the reeds and bushes. I'm small. I'm weak. I'm afraid. The Son of The One We Know killed my Old Folks. He climbed on me because he didn't find Chepa. Now the jaguar wants to climb on me too. I run. And he behind me. His eyes make me sleepy. I'm going to lie down. I'll remain motionless. Like dead. He'll come closer. He'll give off a roar of defiance. The two hungers will fight inside him. The hunger of desire will win. He'll dance the whirlwind of fire and ebony on me. Then he'll stick in his claws and teeth. A hundred white knives will make furrows in my flesh. Or, more than the female-food, will he respect the female-female? I'll go to sleep. I'm going to sleep. I'm asleep. The jaguar dances. The jaguar dances on me. His whiskers tickle my throat. His eyes pierce mine. His enormous face grows in my retina. He roars and laughs. And dances. Dances his demonic dance on me. "Clotilde!" Am I dreaming it? Have I dreamed it? "Clotilde! Clotilde!" Will I have dreamed it? Is it a memory? "Clotilde! Clotilde! Clotilde!"

"Clotilde!"

"Tell me, Juvencio."

"I'm thirsty."

She passed her arm under his neck. She raised his head. She pressed it, softly, against her breast. Poor thing! Lying there. Wounded there. Suffering there. For a moment she rolled up everything around her. Emotion flourished in her throat.

"Drink."

He drank looking at her. The eyes. The great thirsty eyes. If she could only turn into water to calm the thirst of those eyes!

"Thank you, Clotilde. Thank you very much."

She smiled. She smiled all over. Lips all over.

"Try to sleep."

"Don't go, Clotilde."

"I'm not going."

I'm not going. I no longer can go. It's too late. Here I am waiting for the jaguar to tear me apart. What difference can it make? After the Son of The One We Know did to me what he did, it's all the same to me. Has the jaguar torn me apart? Am I missing something? Am I complete? Behind the jaguar comes the crocodile. Or can it be the Son of The One We Know again? Don't they say he always takes the form of a crocodile? Or is it a crocodile crocodile and not a man crocodile? This one is really coming to eat me. I can hear the grinding of his two jaws resonant fangs. I can see his two tiny eyes pursuing me. Why move? Why run? Why try to resist? Everything would be useless. Soon I will be vibrating in his jaws a steaming ball of twisted, ground-up flesh. Or maybe he's coming to mount me too. Only to mount me? If I get away from him, won't the Tin-Tins pursue me? Won't the Tin-Tins attack me in strings? And if I get away from the Tin-Tins, will the trees stop coming? They want to sink their roots into me too. Grow in me. Enjoy in me. Live in me. Shake their green hair while they dance in me. I'm only earth. A piece of earth. In the earth. They all stick their hooves into my belly. Between my thighs. Will they stick them? Do they stick them? Have they stuck them? Are they sticking them? "Clotilde." I've got salt rain in my eyes. An anthill of quin-quins on my tongue. "Clotilde. Clotilde." They stitch up my ears with vegetable needles. Earth. That's what I am. They stitch me up with threads of sap. Earth. Where all have gone. Have come. Or have remained. Earth. Earth.

"Clotilde!"

"What is it, Juvencio?"

"Thanks again."

"For what?"

"For saving me."

"I don't understand."

"If you hadn't called Father Cándido, I wouldn't have lived."

"The monkeys would have saved you. They would have killed Chalena and his men."

"What can monkeys do against people?"

"Who knows! Maybe some night they would have come to Santorontón. They would have taken over the village. And they wouldn't have left a Christian with his head on."

"You think so?"

"And not just the monkeys. The other animals too. The monkeys have many allies in the jungle."

"Yes. That's right."

"Facing danger. Or when they want something, they all join together. Friends and enemies."

They all join together. Friends and enemies. If it hadn't been for the monkeys, she wouldn't have told the tale. It was the only thing that came to her, a wave of images, from time to time.

The monkeys saved her. Of that she was almost sure. The monkeys. Did they stop the jaguar from mounting her? Did they snatch her away from the crocodile? Did they defend her from the Tin-Tins? Did they protect her from the serpents? Did they wall her in with their bodies against the other animals of the jungle? Did they cover her against the trees themselves? Did they carry her to the cave, where—in those waves of memory—she saw them? Almost certain. Not entirely certain. Had they saved her? What had happened during the time that was all night? Or almost night. Did weeks, months pass? Was she completely alone in the jungle? Or during that time—elastic time—did the monkeys take care of her? Or didn't anyone take care of her and even the monkeys were only in her night? A night of many nights. A night of many days and many nights. The dawn of those nights, had it been when Bulu-Bulu found her? Had the light begun to penetrate her in the Green City? Juvencio's presence, had that been the true light? Since her arrival on Balumba he might have had news. He had had news. Something had been told him—from asking questions—by some of the women. Especially Maclovia, José Isabel Lindajón's wife. Especially that she wanted to castrate men. All men. Even if she had given herself to them first. Then to castrate them. To save the women. Only in that way would they have nothing to do them harm with. They had explained to him later that nothing happened. What she took for testicles were only pinecones. She propositioned everyone. That's true. One of those propositioned was Dr. Balda himself. She'd got into his bed naked. With no consequences, of course. The castration business was nothing but a lie then. What about the other thing? What had happened in the jungle? About which he hadn't heard at all? That's why it's better if I go away. Better for me to leave you, Juvencio. I do you harm. I do harm to all who get close to me. I should leave you now. You're better. You've got someone to look after you. Father Cándido is good. And Christ defends you too. Our Christ. I no longer have anything to do here. It's best that I leave. Lest night come back to me. A flood of night. And what I think and do would be a cobweb of nights. It's better that I leave, Juvencio.

"Clotilde."

"What?"

"Where are you going?"

"To fetch water."

"Don't take long."
"Do you need anything?"
"Just having you near."
Juvencio half-closed his eyes. She took advantage. Not to go inside. To the kitchen. On the contrary, she went to the door that opened on the sea. The shore of the sea. She went on tiptoes. So they wouldn't hear her. So that he especially wouldn't hear her. The Nazarene followed her with his look. A slight smile of kindly irony parted his lips. He advised his chum:
"The dove wants to fly away, Cándido."
"What, what?"
"Clotilde's running away."
The Priest, who was reviewing his prayers so that he wouldn't forget them, caught up with her. She was crossing the threshold at that instant.
"Were you looking for something?"
"No, Father."
"So, where were you going?"
"To wash. To wash a piece of clothing."
"I see. But you forgot."
"Forgot what?"
"The piece of clothing."
"I'm going for it."
She turned half-around with her eyes lowered. She didn't have time to go away.
"Wait, Clotilde."
"Yes, Father."
"In the first place, don't go out alone. Without telling us. Chalena's hundred eyes are lying in wait. Everywhere."
"The monkeys are looking after us."
"Nobody. Not even the monkeys can stop a stray bullet. Or the flight of a harpoon. You already saw what happened to the cripple Timoteo Ruales."
"Of course, Father."
"Also capable of putting the blame on Dr. Balda afterward."
"I hadn't thought about that."
There was a brief pause.
"In the second place, you shouldn't lie to me."
"I'm not lying to you, Father Cándido."
"So why don't you tell me... that you were running away?"
"Just that..."

"You weren't running away?"
"You know that I..."
"You weren't running away? Answer me. You weren't running away?"
She lifted up her eyes. She looked at him. Fixedly.
"Yes, Father."
"Why?"
"It's the best for everyone."
"Who's everyone?"
"The Christ, you, Juvencio..."
"I don't see the reason."
"You people have already got too much with your own things. All I do is make it worse."
"With you or without you the problems will go on. Besides, the doctor needs you. He has to be taken care of. Given his medicine. Get his treatments. I can't be at his side all the time. Even if I wanted to. I have to go out and take care of my faithful. I've only got a few of them left. For that reason they need me more than ever. I can't abandon them."
Yes. It's true. Everything Father Cándido says is true. I shouldn't leave. I shouldn't leave Juvencio. I have to take care of him in everything. The way he is he can't take care of himself. He has to be cured. Helped with his necessities. Even with his smallest necessities. It's true. Everything is true. But what if I can't hold myself back? If this thing boiling inside of me fire crab scratching me all over comes out? If one day I clutch him against my breast? If I begin to stroke him? If I cover him with kisses? If I say "my Juvencio, my lovely boy"? If I tell him I can't be without him? That I am of him, in him, for him? I need to die dying without stopping dying. To die dying living deaths. To die dead alive. Dying dead from those days weeks months that I died living in the cave. Or wasn't it in the cave? Or did I dance a live coal under the green eyes of the trees? Or did I live in the fangs of the jaguar? Or did I sleep dying in the crocodile's jaws? Or did the monkeys bury me and then dig me up? Did they take me later to where Bulu-Bulu was for him to revive me? Or am I dead? I continue dead. What exists for me today doesn't exist. Have I invented Juvencio? I don't know what to do. I don't know anything. Where to go? Where to sink to recuperate myself? Only in death. I'll seek it in the sea resonant liquid coffin. Or I'll go to the jungle. Shall I call the sharks or the vipers? Shall I lie

down on the earth—earth myself—so that the hawthorns can grow in me? Shall I go bleeding in it rejoining it until the end? To die. To die dying. That's what can save me. The only thing. What should I do, Father Cándido? What should I do?

"I'd stay. If it were up to me, I'd stay. How couldn't I stay? I can't. Don't you see that I can't?"

"Why not?"

"I have to take care of my things. My dog Miss Victor. She's all alone. And the farm. The planting. What will I live on afterward? I have to work. I don't have anyone to help me. I'm alone in the world."

"Oh! That's why..."

"How could it be anything else? Something's got to be planted. Not to sell. Who's going to buy anything from me? Just for me. You can't just live off fish. And sometimes the fish don't bite. They get skittish. Besides, the house is falling in. It must be all in ruins. I've practically had no time to fix it. And my dog. Poor thing. I wonder how she's making out."

"Yes. Of course."

"You have to explain it to Juvencio. Dr. Balda will understand. He has to understand."

"That's how it is. He has to understand."

He looked at her. As if he wanted to pierce her with his eyes. He added:

"We all have to understand."

"Then... can I go?"

"You can. Why not?"

Running—as if in order that neither of them would repent—she went to the shore. With a leap, as she launched it she fell into the canoe. She picked up her oar and began to paddle. She paddled as if everything depended on it. Cándido looked at her, until she was just a dot growing smaller at sea. Then he turned to his friend.

"You were right. The dove wanted to fly away."

"Did you let her go?"

"She had to go. She's going to look after her planting, her house, her dog. Besides, she thinks her presence just complicates things for us all the more."

Jesus moved his head from side to side, as if thinking: "There's nothing we can do."

"Oh, Cándido! The way you live up to your name!"

The Priest's face turned sour.
"Why?"
"Really, don't you realize?"
"What?"
"That it's all a lie?"
"I don't understand."
"Clotilde didn't run off because she's afraid of harming us. Or because she wants to take care of her things."
"Why, then?"
"Clotilde's running away from love."
The old Priest scratched his ear.
"You know. I think you're right. What a jackass I am!"
He paused. Added:
"What if I go after her?"
"It would be useless. The hardest part for her was breaking away from here. It's too late now."

TWENTY-FOUR

Bulu-Bulu jaguar, in the top of a tree. The tallest tree. Bulu-Bulu coral graft in the night. The Jaguar smoking. Bulu-Bulu smoking. Orchestras of smoke dressing the leaves. Ghosts of smoke traveling in the air. Bulu-Bulu Jaguar moving. Letting go. Dividing. Bulu-Bulu Jaguar one and many. Whirlwind of Bulu-Bulu Jaguars. Jaguar Bulu-Bulus. The Wizard in fragments. Bulu-Bulu arms.

Bulu-Bulu legs. Bulu-Bulu tail. Heads with eyes of fire. Body arms legs ears and tail. Of ebony and flame. Bulu-Jaguar-Bulu. Jaguar-Bulu-Jaguar. Flying pieces of Bulu-Bulu shouting: "There are bridals on Balumba." "The daughter of the Wizard has bridals on Balumba." "Bulu-Bulu calls the wizards to see it on Balumba." "Bulu-Bulu gives his daughter as a bride on Balumba."

To the north and to the south. To the west and to the east. Pieces of the Jaguared-Wizard keep on flying. Of the Bewitched-Jaguar. Especially toward the north. There where rivers wind ribbons of roaring foam. From the top of the sky to the sea. They went sowing the fresh news: "Bridals on Balumba." The distant Witch Doctors—from mountains and coast, from near the sky and from shores by the sea—were picking it up. Breaking it up. Spreading it around. "Monkey Face is marrying off his daughter on Balumba." "Bear us to the bridals!" "Bear us to Balumba!" Bálumba-Balumba Balumba-Balumbá. Some were already sleeping their dream of death inside the earth. Ten generations. Yet they heard the drilling voice: "I'm marrying off my daughter Dominga on Balumba!" Bálumba-Balumba Balumba-Balumbá. They awoke out of their dream of death. They clad their bones in flesh. They cleaved open the ground. Their grandfather faces appeared. Their look of centuries. And on paths of wind they undertook their journey to Balumba. On the four paths. On the four horizons. On the four arms of the floating cross. "Bear us to Balumba!" Without touching the trees. "Bear us to Balumba!" Bálumba-Balumba Balumba-Balumbá.

When he felt that he had notified all of his own, Bulu-Bulu–Jaguar took shape again. Remaking himself. The pieces of body blended together again. His tail went away. The red-black splotches on his skin also went away. His enormous head. His feline whiskers. Only the lighted cigar remained. The clothing of smoke webbing. The Wizard Bulu-Bulu. The peerless Monkey Face. That seemed tattooed with a perpetual smile. That bent its back before everyone. Bálumba-Balumba Balumba-Balumbá.

He wasn't like that before. Before—gray-haired four-hundred-year-old before—he arrived on a slave ship. With beams and boards in sonorous grimaces. Slaver. With sails and masts and sea saliva. With a hull decorated with the living mother-of-pearl of bivalves. Bulu-Bulu among slaves—princes, warriors, virgins, artists, artisans, wizards—chained by the neck. Among many slaves. The distance devoured half of them. The other half, were they alive? Slaver. Flapping of the sails. Laughter of the wind. Bite of the roasting sun. Insides dried out from hunger and thirst. Bodies clad with lash marks. Slaver. Pushed. Sunk. Brought down. Cataract of blood and tears. Slaver. How many suns and moons, piled up, pressed together, dying in the floating jail of motionless nights? How many times seven? With the iron ring around their necks. Joined by the thick chains of iron and anguish. How many suns and suns? How many moons and moons?

At that moment Juvencio's voice was heard, clear, precise:

"Clotilde! Clotilde!"

The Priest looked desolately at the Christ:

"What shall we do, then?"

The Thorn-Crowned One observed him, ironically. A slight mocking smile crossed his lips:

"Don't get me involved in it! Let's see what you can do! I want to hear what you're going to tell the doctor!"

"Why don't you help me? Aren't we such good comrades?"

"I'm tired of helping you."

The Priest grew irritated.

"And aren't you such a miracle-maker? Didn't you multiply all the bread and wine at the Wedding Feast in Cana?"

"Yes. So what?"

"Why don't you multiply Clotilde into two? While one goes home, the other stays with us. With the doctor, rather!"

"You'd like to solve everything with miracles! As if it were that easy! That age is past."

His companion looked at him with reproach.

"Don't tell me that!"

The doctor's voice took on more strength:

"Clotilde! Clotilde!"

Cándido, as if it were he who was being called, answered. To his own surprise, his voice had taken on a slightly higher pitch.

"I'm coming! I'm coming!"

Clotilde hair disheveled torn clothing tight around her body. She was paddling. A vertigo of oars water sky wind. Paddle an extension of herself her hands her eyes her love her anxiety to flee. Vertigo. Sinking in her body and in the canoe fastened in space. Canoe harpoon canoe thirst for water canoe heart thrown into the distance. Vertigo. Buzzing of words of caresses of sinkings. Vertigo paddling. Where to? Toward flight? Toward oblivion and silence? The claws of the night night night. Night inside her. Tearing her dress of shadows. Better dying. Dying in claws of dead wings of nocturnal ebony. Dying. There. Vertigo. Night. Death.

She threw herself into the sea. The green dark light white hands lifted her up. Returned her. Threw her back into the canoe. She took the paddle. She hit her head with it. Flower of the wind. Staff of twisted petals. Entwined. Pink viper. Smoke blow. The paddle didn't seem to touch her. Couldn't she die? Did she have to go on dying alive day by day? Or living dead night by night? Or had the monkeys wrapped her in curtains of light, balsa logs made of laughter? Were they taking care of her for themselves? Because she could still do them good and they didn't want to lose her?

At least to flee, then. Between two waters an erect sea plant, she began to paddle furiously. She stuck a long tortoise shell machete into the green white belly of the marine laughter. Once more she returned to the world of rotted teeth and taciturn turtles. With more fury. As if she were digging moving ditches in the water in order to soak her final efforts. She should continue living dead. Or dying alive. She felt every stroke of the paddle sinking into her blood pushing the red current inside her dilated veins. As if she were traveling toward her own conscience. Am I paddling backward? Have I changed directions? Is there something superior on my horizon that is carrying me against my own prow? Above the water there were no longer only waves. The scribbling of the foam began to place its signature on the beaches. Where was she going? Was she going back? Yes. She was going back! The house of Father Cándido, the Burned Christ, and, provisionally, Juvencio was already looming up. What could she do? Change her own heart into a tomb.

When the canoe began to kiss the shore, she was shaken by the anguished shout.

"Clotilde! Clotilde!"

Burning—burning again with life—she answered:

"I'm coming, Juvencio! I'm coming!"

One day they heard a slight sound. They looked. They looked. A green sword smiling in the belly of the ship. How miraculous! An emerald sword! They moved to get closer. As close as the chains hanging from their necks and eyes would permit them. It was impossible. A new sword appeared in the belly of the ship.

And seven! And fourteen! And twenty-eight! And sevens of times seven, seven, seven! All sharp-pointed. All emerald. The slaves were absorbed, motionless. Unable to speak. Unable to laugh. Just like statues of tucuma or ebony. They just kept on staring with astonished eyes. Suddenly the jewels were growing teeth. Teeth green too. And then they began to move. They came and went. In and out. They were sawing the planks of the ship's hull. They opened enormous mast holes. Through them the water inserted its millions of claws of foam. The swords swam into the ship. It was seen that they were fish. Agile swordfish the color of hope. The slaves trembled with fear. The slaves—Bulu-Bulu, the first Bulu-Bulu, and the last, and the same as always among them—thought their final hour had arrived. The ship trembled. The ship was sinking. It trembled and was sinking. All the slaves—princes, warriors, virgins, artists, artisans, wizards—asked their gods for help. Chains around their necks. Sunken in roaring waters. They tried to raise up songs. To exhibit acrobatic ritual dances. They didn't have time. The fish surrounded them. They used their tiny teeth. They sawed through hard chains. The slaves could move once more. Feeling themselves free, they tried to go up on deck. To confront the grim torturers of endless days and nights. They couldn't do it. The fish opened their legs. They put themselves between them. And just like marine horses they made them cut through the ocean. Were they swimming? Were they flying? Caravel calabocse was left behind. Caravel with bearded whites aboard. Left behind. With bearded white men the color of ivory. The color of the tusks of aged walruses. White men dressed in iron—hearts of iron too. Sometimes turned into bicephalic octopod monsters. Left behind. White men who kept fire and the voice of lightning in metal tubes. Sowers of death and anguish. Dealers in bodies and souls. Left behind. The sails erect. The rigging dressed in mourning. The oars exhausted. Without fever of Gospel or gold. Submerging. Bouncing. On the greenish salty hammocks. When they saw the amphibian procession of slaves reaching shore, they shouted in rage. Quaking. Their senses were confused. They grasped instruments of panic. They vomited homicidal terror through the mouths of the nasal iron. They grew. Harsh. Unreal. Absurd. Flashes of fire wove their beards. Their livid faces became streaked with light. Their metal clothes. They seemed to be rising. On the stern. They were rising up at the stern. The caravel was sinking at the bow. Seesawing. The poop deck rising up. The bearded men oblique. Firing. Some, when they saw the black slaves, escaping, leaped into the water. They swam anxiously. With fury. Vibrating agonic death rattles. Whereas, the rest stayed nailed to the deck. To wicks and powder. To cannons. Lombards. And poetry. See-Saw-See. Saw-See-Saw. The bearded white men now almost on the line of the gray horizon. Without letting go of their weapons. Without letting go of the deck of the caravel. The bow inclining. The bow drawing them. The bow descending. The bow submerging. In endless flocks of foam camels. Then all very quick. As if someone—from above—were pushing the ship to the bottom.

On Balumba again. —How many? How many years was he on Balumba? Rather, perhaps, how many centuries?— In those days, when they reached the emerald land, they identified first the trees. They learned very quickly the ones that were friends. And also, needless to say, those that were not. What flowers, roots, and fruits could help them. The same, or equal to all they had left on distant shores across the sea. They were once more what they had been before. They revived their old customs. Their arts, legends, and myths. Their tattoos and masks. Their dances. Their songs. Their multiple secrets in all forms. It was a piece of the past world encrusted in the future world. The blacks in other nearby regions who were still slaves were integrating themselves into the Emerald Kingdom. Those who continued to flee. Those who were castrated for having fled. Those who simply heard about the place where one was still free. All. All. All were merging—with blood and with dreams—into the people of the Hope Kingdom. The bearded white men, on the other hand, never came close. They couldn't. Even if they were chasing some fugitive—black fugitive, eunuch fugitive. The green walls kept them on the edges. The natives, on the other hand, also began to join with the newcomers. They gave them help so that they could learn hundreds of secrets of the new land. How to domesticate useful animals. And cultivate the plants that cure. The plants that kill. They also showed them their best weapons. And their musical instruments. Made from leaves or elastic wood.

One day the unforeseen happened. The jungle seemed to tremble. The sea leaned toward the shore. It was broken by masts, by sails. By yardarms and rigging. Could it be the caravel that had brought them from Africa? Could it be the caravel they had seen sink? The one they thought was sleeping at the bottom of the sea forever? Yes. The caravel. Yes. "Their" caravel. The awakened ship came to touch ground. When they least expected, it was beached, a giant whale of old weepy wood. Intact. Its poop deck and windows. Its rib frame nailed to the hull. Even the tight ropes that held the bowsprit. Even deck, waterways, and bridge were whole. On the sails a few crustaceans were writing amphibious words in the clouds. The fearful ex-slaves left the jungle. They whitened the shore with their astonished eyes and teeth. They went closer. The foam came down stairs of waves. The caravel—"their" caravel—seemed to keep on coming. Toward the shore. Toward dry land. Only there did it seem to stop. The blacks went on board. Hope went through their senses. It could be said that the ship had never been in the maritime depths. Could it have never sunk? Everything they found aboard was in perfect shape. Since it was a memorable occasion, they chose a King. The King immediately ordered that it be embedded in the jungle. In the center of the place where the huts were. They obeyed. They unloaded it. They took off the grim cannons. They stuck them in the ground, mouth up, like enormous statues. And those were the first monuments of the brand new kingdom. Although they knew that thunder and lightning bloomed in their hands, they wanted to keep them. The same as defeated, humiliated, chained gods. Over them one day they would place their authentic gods. Later they brought off the pikes, the lances, the muskets, the crossbows. Also the munitions and powder. Next the liquid fire of wine. The provisions: chick peas, beans, flour, biscuits. A few animals—that came to life again as soon as they were touched—and who served for the propagation of like species. Finally, the clothing. Civilian garb and costumes of war.

The caravel was dragged along by sheer human effort. Pushing it with shoulders, arms, heads. The whole body. It was moved along skids. Little by little. Into the jungle. A monumental proboscidian belly up. As it went trees were felled. Separated. Branches and leaves broken off. Cleaning the reeds. The tall or tiny grasses. A kind of absurd voyage on the polymorphous vegetable ocean. The eyes of the jungle opened in madness. Never had they seen such a spectacle before. The multibillionary fauna remained static. With panic. The dark men—a tireless team of monster ants—continued dragging the ship inland.

When everything was ready, a symbolic festival began. The ship remained erect, sustained by dozens of stakes on both sides of the hull. The inhabitants of the Emerald Kingdom went to get dressed. They put on the newly obtained clothes. An indescribable carnival in the jungle, everybody making use of different outfits. The plated metal coverings. The gaudy court costumes. Sometimes parts of one were mixed with those of another. The women covered their bodies with silks. Only at certain spots. Where it didn't prevent them from showing the beauty carved into their bodies. Once dressed in these garments, they began dances of epileptic pleasure. Stentorian onomatopoeic songs. Kaleidoscopic banquets. Which blended ancient culinary customs of their ancestors. With those they learned from their newly made aboriginal friends. And with what they had found in the belly of the caravel. Up above, on the bridge, sitting, the King of the Emerald Kingdom could be seen. The King was smiling. The King witnessed the triumphal acts. He felt one and many. He himself and also each one of his subjects. Therefore he immediately stopped the music. He stopped the songs. He stopped the dances. He stopped the banquet. And through the mouth of the first Bulu-Bulu—and the same as always—he gave them news that filled their senses with astonishment.

The multiplied accent of the hollow trunks made the news pulsate even in distant places: there, in the heart of the Tropics, a small country of free men had been born. All of its inhabitants would come to be Kings. They would take turns every seven days. One after the other. Until all, all of them had reached the honorable hierarchy. Then the first King would be King again. And so on forever, in an infinite chain.

Sevens of days passed. Seven, seven, seven. The sonorous rains glass daggers arrived. Gold daggers of innumerable suns arrived. The old caravel began to smile. Seven, seven, seven. A smile born in its belly. Then it laughed all over. It broke out in guffaws. Seven, seven, seven. The King in turn fell. The ship showed its ribs to the air. Its twisted masts filled with splinters. Its beams and rigging woven with nets of branches and neighboring leaves. Its sails flying—gray bats—in the direction of the sea. Seven, seven, seven. The Kingdom was being diluted. The magnet—freedom—attracted other men of various colors. Other men already a mixture of bearded white men and bronze aborigines. Seven, seven, seven. The former slaves scattered. The times changed. They lost the fear of finding themselves castrated. Of wearing the heavy iron rings as neckties. Of the red tattooed bars that the lash leaves on the body and the soul. Of slave ambition and the cruelty of the slaver. Seven, seven, seven.

One night Bulu-Bulu left—the first and the last, and the same as always. Bulu-Bulu walked until he came to the vegetable orgy. Did they give him that name there? Or was it he-they who gave him his? Bulu-Bulu. The Wizard Bulu-Bulu. The wizards Bulu-Bulu. Bulu-Bulu-Bulu. Bulu-Bulu-Bulu. Bulu-Bulu-Bulu. Bulu-Bulu, who was having bridals. Bulu-Bulu, who was marrying off his daughter Dominga on Balumba. Who was still weaving the news on the traveling needle of the wind. "There are bridals on Balumba." Bálumba-Balumba. Balumba-Balumbá.

He was already beginning to see the wizards from time before. They were arriving now. From the four horizons. Walking flying rising up. The wizards from before and from always. He received them with an equal's greetings. They were arriving now. They were reunited now. They came as Jaguars. Dressed as Jaguars. With teeth and claws of Jaguars. Whiskers of Jaguars. No, Jaguars. Wrapped only in Jaguar skins. Outwardly feline and inwardly wizards. In the midst of them, living, an authentic Jaguar. A jaguar in his cage of woven sticks. Caught with an invisible weapon. With a magic weapon. Authentic Jaguar. Bulu-Bulu caught him on returning to Balumba. Without wounding him. Without even scratching his skin. Throwing out puffs of smoke into the triangle face. Transporting him on thin hammocks of smoke to the cage. Authentic Jaguar. Bulu-Bulu caught him on returning to Balumba. When all the witch doctors sat down around the cage. Bulu-Bulu went into it. He looked into the Jaguar's eyes briefly. The Jaguar remained like a statue. Bulu-Bulu advanced. He put the sharp-pointed machete in the hard foreleg of the Jaguar. The Jaguar roared. Hanging his eyes, his teeth, his claws on that roar. Bulu-Bulu made shreds of the cage. A totemic communion, the witch doctors threw themselves onto the Jaguar. They tore him apart. With hands and mouths they were tearing—Bulu-Bulu among them—pieces of flesh. Of nerves. Of bones. They also drank the foaming hot blood. A totemic communion. Afterward, the outside visitors left. The visitors carried away new images of the peerless MonkeyFace. A distortion of his dance in a disintegrating zigzag. Cohesioning. In what parts of the body of the Wizard were they separating and joining to the rhythm of the voices and blows? "Oh, Jaguar! Oh, Jaguar, help us! Bulu-Bulu's daughter has bridals on Balumba! Oh, Jaguar! Make her fruitful from the first night on! A big bulky canoe is her body! Oh, Jaguar! May she have seven children! May she live to see them! And also see her children's children! Oh, Jaguar, help us! Oh, Jaguar!"

Were they his family? Was it only he himself become a multitude? Or were they the diverse dead Bulu-Bulus? Before rejoining their graves had they come to look at him? Whatever it was, the others went back to their deep destinies. To take off their Jaguar skins. To take off too the human skins that a few hours before had covered their bones. And, finally, to inhabit the earthen vessels where they were sleeping their dream of centuries.

TWENTY-FIVE

One day Timoteo Ruales appeared in Santorontón with the light of dawn. He came on his little four-wheeled cart. Made out of boards and four wheels. He crossed his legs on it. Rather, what he had left of legs. Which wasn't much anymore. Barely a quarter left from where they began. Ever since an alfajía tree—in the jungle, when they were starting to fix up Crisóstomo Chalena's house—fell on top of him. Flattening everything in its path like a pancake. Now he pushed himself along with both hands on the ground. Getting onto solid ground took great effort. Had it been hard for him to cross the wet sand? Because he'd come from the sea. There was no doubt about it. He was advancing perpendicular to the shore. From where the waves bit the moving border, to the bank. Could he have dragged himself along—snail snail—a gastropod with four extremities? Two complete and two almost incomplete. On his back his little cart of boards and four wheels. Could he have come swimming? On the back of a shark or a cetacean? Or in a boat? What kind of boat? Canoe, sailboat, or raft? Who knows! If it had been that way the sound of oars would have been heard. Or the flap of sails. What is certain is that he was there. Breaking, with his presence, the violet casting net of dawn. One of the first to spot him was Espurio Carranza. The doctor-gravedigger gobbled up dawns. He liked to taste tender young horizons. To see if some new client was arriving. Because every time a newcomer cut his figure against the sky, Espurio considered him a candidate. First, a candidate for patient. Then a candidate for corpse. Which amounted to the same thing, sooner or later, a candidate for inhabitant of the domains. When he saw Timoteo he showed him his four yellow teeth.

"Did you get here by swimming?"

The cripple looked at him furiously.

"Yes, I got here by swimming."

Then his walrus mustache seemed to tremble. He added:

"On top of your mother."

The other one didn't bat an eye. His smile mellowed him for nasty remarks.

"That's Timoteo Ruales! The foulest tongue in town."

The double cripple paid no attention. He made an effort as he got close to the bank. He tried to climb it by sheer digging in of hands. He couldn't. He got off the cart. He practically lay on the ground. He raised himself up a little on his right hand and the two stumps. With the left he grasped the edge of the cart. The little platform on wheels moved a few inches. The effort was tremendous. Timoteo raised his head. He looked around in desperation. There was nobody. Only the doctor-gravedigger observing him mockingly. What could he do? He overcame his instinctive revulsion. He grunted:

"Well, goddamn it! Aren't you going to give me a hand?"

"Of course! Why not?"

He went down the bank. He helped him up, taking him by the

right hand. Ruales stood on what was left of his legs. He had them covered with some pieces of tanned leather. Wrapped up. As if they were boots for a tiny elephant. When they got to the top of the bank, Espurio's smile grew larger. His stereotyped smile. Of a saurian.

"All right, now. Let's go!"

The Cripple looked at him, with a mixture of rage and anguish.

"What?"

"You're on land now, aren't you? Let's go!"

"What about the cart?"

"Oh, yes. The cart!"

With two leaps he went down the bank. He went over to the small artifact. He stepped back a little. He got set. And he endowed it with a kick, sending it toward the sea. The little cart stopped right by the edge. The advancing waves gave it a few licks. He advanced a few steps. Got set again. The Cripple's voice held him back.

"I see you're the same son of a bitch you were before."

He tried to explain something. He became disconcerted. He couldn't. He recovered. He didn't have time to act. With strange leaps. A mixture of gigantic worm and cricket. The Cripple—an improvised acrobat doing somersaults—was approaching. He tried to run. Impossible. The human whirlwind had taken on the speed of vertigo. He felt a painful blow on his calves. He tried to respond. Another blow made him stagger. Another brought his corpulent humanity to earth. Before him. Standing on his stumps. Timoteo. Dwarf—absurd huge dwarf at that instant—Timoteo. The enormous head. Out of proportion. The ferocious bulging eyes. He laughed diabolical fangs of a beast.

"The same son of a bitch as before."

The fangs grew larger.

"As punishment you can carry me."

Afraid. Of the ridicule he would be exposed to among his people if they saw him. Of the plans for his person that might be flying around in that half-crazy cripple. He mumbled:

"It was a joke."

"This is a joke, too. Get up!"

Espurio obeyed. Timoteo took the cart in his left hand. With a leap he climbed up onto the shoulder of the doctor. With incredible strength he wrapped his arms around his neck. What he had left of legs he used to squeeze his waist, like a pair of tongs. The doctor seemed to hesitate. He hit him with the stumps wrapped in leather.

"Giddap!"

The owner of the cemetery—half-owner, because Father Gaudencio was already appropriating the best plots—stammered:

"Where are we going?"

"To see my wife."

"The Mute?"

"Have I got any other?"

"That's true!"

"And my son, too. Tolón must be quite big by now."

A winch with poisonous hooks dug its barbs into Espurio's mind. With the greatest of innocence he mumbled:

"Who knows where they are!"

He squeezed his neck tighter.

"What are you saying?"

"They left some time ago."

"Where?"

"God only knows!"

"You're not tricking me?"

"By the cross that lights my way, no!"

He remained pensive for a few moments. Espurio stopped. The upset and the anguish painted the Cripple's bronzed face green. Almost in spite of himself he murmured:

"Goddamn her! So why did I come?"

He recovered.

"Tell me! Tell me everything! Don't lie to me, by God. It'll cost you if you do!"

"Let go of me!"

"No, sir, goddamn it! I'll let you go when you puke out what you know!"

Seeing that there was no other way out, Espurio turned his guts into a heart.

"Well, you'll see. A doctor arrived here some time back. A certain Juvencio Balda."

"What's that got to do with me?"

"He's the one to blame! The one to blame for everything that's happening in Santorontón. He's got the village and all the people in it upside down. Nothing here's the way it was before."

"Stop beating about the bush! Tell me about my wife and my son! I don't give a shit about the rest."

The doctor told him. All in his own way. Of course. According to him, Juvencio had treated Tolón professionally. He'd done him harm. So much harm that the boy was at the point of dying. No matter how much he was against it—he, Espurio Carranza. No matter how much Crisóstomo Chalena was against it. Tolón worshipped Chalena. Chalena was going to give him a colt.

Timoteo was puzzled.

"Chalena? A colt?"

"Yes. He'd already given him a rosebush..."

It was a rosebush that everybody took care of. Chalena himself watered it. The Mute stayed on as Chalena's servant. She lived in his house. With her son. There wasn't anything they didn't have. "Chalena's good with those who are with him." He was going to give him a colt. He'd already ordered it. They were bringing it from "up yonder." There where the trees and torrents share things. A little colt so that Tolón could play. But the little doctor butted in. Could he be a doctor? And the Mute and Tolón disappeared overnight. They didn't leave a trace. Chalena looked for them in person. Then the rest of them looked for them. The Political Lieutenant and the Chief of the Rural Guard.

"Do you know that they're Salustiano Caldera and Rugel Banchaca?"

"Don't fuck around bringing in other people. Tell me what happened next!"

"They all crossed themselves thinking where your wife and son could have gone off to. When they stopped searching in Santorontón they went to the jungle. Then they went to Balumba. To the Quindales' Farm. Nothing. Absolutely nothing. As if the earth had swallowed them up."

"A big mess, eh? And what did the doc say?"

"That he knew nothing. He hadn't seen them either. They'd probably gone to the city. To the city! How could they get to the city? Who with? With what money? In what? To whose house? Just imagine! A woman who can't talk with a kid who almost doesn't talk!"

"And that doctor... is he still here?"

"Still."

"Then, take me to him!"

"But... I won't go in. I don't want to see his face!"

"Nobody's asking you to do that. Why should you go in? The one who's looking for him is me."

Juvencio was still sleeping. Ruales the Cripple knocked on the door. As if he wanted to knock it down. In a while he heard the sleepy voice of the medical man.

"Who is it?"

"Your father, you bastard!"

"Wh-what?"

"Open up or I'll knock the door down!"

Almost at once steps were heard approaching. The doctor opened the door.

"What's going on?"

He didn't have time to say more. Timoteo—with a trip—already had him on the ground. He held his neck with both hands.

"Where are my wife and son?"

The doctor looked at him, frightened.

"What are you talking about?"

"Don't play the damned fool. About Carmen! The Mute who was with Chalena. And Tolón. My wife and son!"

Juvencio recovered. He tried to get his ideas together. The Mute? Tolón? At first he didn't remember. A sudden spark lighted up his memory. Yes. It was when he first got to Santorontón. The first day he'd set foot in the village, to be exact. He was the boy with a rosebush in his hand. A rosebush that was beginning to sink its roots into his muscles. All he did was take out the rosebush. Nothing else. He learned later that the boy and his mother weren't around anymore. When he asked they told him that they'd gone off with some relatives. Where? Who knows? Other bits of gossip reached him too. He didn't bother to investigate them. They had to do with other people. Many of whom he didn't even know. That was when, for example—now he remembers—he heard about Timoteo Ruales for the first time. He tried to get up. Some misunderstanding, certainly. Maybe he could clear it up for him.

"I..."

The other one wouldn't let him. With great strength he pushed him. The doctor fell back onto the ground. He hit his head. Half-dizzy, he caught a look of hate.

"You know very well what I'm talking about."

The doctor—getting over the impact of the blows—tried to calm down. Yes. He had to clear everything up. While he had time. If he delayed just a little it would be too late. That possessed creature had the devil in him. He seemed to have decided on the worst. What had they told him? No doubt something very bad about him—Juvencio Balda. Something suggested, in all probability, by Crisóstomo Chalena and his henchmen. He hadn't managed to collect his thoughts. The Cripple gave him a tremendous shake.

"Let's see if you're going to tell me where they are. Or what's become of them. If not you can start saying the best prayer you know."

"I don't know where they are."

He hit him in the waist with the right stump. At the same time he exclaimed:

"Oh, you don't?"

"I really don't know."

"Didn't you heal my son?"

"Yes. That I did!"

"Didn't they take off afterward?"

"Yes. But..."

He repeated the blow. The doctor didn't complain. Even though he made a gesture of pain.

"Go on."

"I didn't have anything to do with that. What interest could it have been to me? I'd just arrived in Santorontón. I didn't know anybody. I'd just landed in the village when they told me what was happening to Tolón. They wanted to take me to him. Right away. Father Cándido went with me. I went..."

"Father Cándido? Do you know him?"

"Yes. Of course."

A sudden idea occurred to him. He continued:

"Why don't we go see him? He can explain it all to you." Ruales muttered, as if to himself:

"You're right. Father will tell us the truth. Let's go. Get up!"

Juvencio obeyed. Instantly—in the same way as before with Espurio—the Cripple mounted him. He repeated:

"Let's go!"

The doctor protested.

"Like this, like a horse, I'm not going!"

The other one tightened even more around his neck. He repeated, with both stumps, the blow on his waist. The doctor winced a little. He didn't move. Timoteo assured him, in a rage:

"You'll go any way I feel like."

Juvencio half-turned his head around—as much as he could. His voice was tranquil. Firm.

"You're wrong. Like this. I won't go!"

The gesture and the tone conquered the Cripple.

"All right, then. All right!"

He got down with a leap. He went over to the cart. Got up onto it.

Still, while he pushed himself along with his hands, he warned:

"Don't think you're going to have your way. Everything depends on what Father Cándido says."

"I know."

They went to the shore. There, in a canoe—the doctor had a dugout canoe now—they went off in the direction of Cándido's house. As it had to be, everything was cleared up. Timoteo believed—he had been one of his good faithful—in the word of the Priest. He knew him well. He was one of the few who had been good to his son and Carmen. That woman who had arrived like a ship adrift. He took her in and kept her by his side until the alfajía fell on him. He had to leave her when they took him to the Hospital in the city—in the service of Chalena. Chalena! He should have guessed. That's why the bastard sent him to a fish-packing plant. Far away from there. In a place where he could work sitting down. Certainly to prevent him from coming back to Santorontón. He looked toward the place where the village Boss' two-story house stood. He threatened:

"You'll pay for this! You bastard!"

TWENTY-SIX

"We told them, Don Chalena."

"Yes, Sir. They were only waiting for the first Indian summer."

"Indian summer's already started."

"It started yesterday, Sir."

He sat up in the hammock. With his Panama hat he shooed away the plague of mosquitoes and güitife gnats. He looked at them angrily—toad capon capon under the hooves of a bull. He croaked:

"And you didn't stop them?"

"We couldn't, Sir."

"Why not?"

Salustiano stammered:

"They've got the whole village together."

And Rugel:

"Not just the village. They've got all the animals together too."

"It was the little doctor, wasn't it?"

"And Clotilde, and Lindajón, and Don Cándido and others . . ."

"I think that even the Holy Christ is helping them."

He ran his bandanna over his neck. He was sweating buckets. It must have been from emotion. He muttered:

"Don't talk nonsense."

"You don't think the Holy Christ is involved?"

"No. That's not it. The Holy Christ is the one that Father Gaudencio brought. The other one is a Burned Christ. Nothing more."

"That may be, Sir. But what they've got together, they've got together!"
"Now we've got to do something. We can't stand around with our arms folded."
"Whatever you say, Sir."
"That's what we're here for."
"Let's go, then."
"Let's go, Sir."
"Let's go."
He stopped. Asked:
"Have we still got some people we can count on?"
"Yes, Don Chalena. The rural guards and a few Santorontonians. Most of the rich people in town."
"All right, then. Move it!"
A cumbersome barge, he advanced. A toad graft growing on a cumbersome barge. Moving its muscles a string of beads constantly shaken. Every so often they had to wait for him. Cumbersome toad-barge. Especially when they began to go uphill. Barge-barge toad-toad. When they got close to the joining of the hills, Chalena rubbed his eyes. Could what he was seeing be true? No. It couldn't be. Everything was all his imagination. Nothing that lay before him existed. It was all occurring in his own mind. Everything he was looking at was much too absurd. But wasn't it always that way? Maybe ever since he had set foot in Santorontón everything was absurd. He came from the South. Sailing on a sloop of mist. Coming from lands of mist. From where? From the shadows? How had he been born? Out of what mother? A woman like others? When he began to sow his memories, he was rolling on the boards of a deck. Hearing the voice of a drunken skipper. Could it have been his father? He'd never called him son. He never had a word of love or sympathy for him. Worse still. One fine day, in the midst of a bout of drunkenness, he told him that he'd found him on a trash heap. He'd let out a lash of a laugh. "Probably your mother didn't want to carry her sin around with her. And she threw you away like you were so much shit. I picked you up there. Out of pure pity. You were screeching like a demon. I brought you on board. And I gave you my name. Only because I didn't have any other at hand. But I'm tired of having you use it. One of these days I'm going to take it back from you. Do you hear me? I'm going to toss you back into the village. Into the trash. That's your place. The place where

you should always be. The trash. Your place." Which one? Which village was that? Where could the woman be? The one between whose legs his head first appeared! The older sailor explained it all to him. A lie! Everything the skipper said was a lie! The skipper was his real father. One fine day his mother—Crisóstomo's—came on board the sloop. She was carrying him wrapped in rags. She showed him to the skipper. She was weeping with rage: "Here's what belongs to you, you bastard! Rotten husband! Rotten father! I'm going off with someone else. At least he'll give me something to eat. I'm going far away! But I don't want any bother." The skipper was drunk as always. He tried to pounce on her. He couldn't. He held out his hands for a moment. Maybe to grab her. Or to hit her. He fell. He let out a string of words. Which nobody could understand. Which hung—like dry sardines—on a gust of the southeast wind. She didn't move. When he was on the deck, she leaned over. She dropped you on top of him: "Take him, you bastard! Let's see if you can starve him to death!" "Ever since then," the other sailor explained, "he's been drunker than ever. And his drunkenness infected the sloop. That's why they don't call it *The South Wind* any more. They've named it *The Souse Wind*. And the name fits. Haven't you seen the way we stagger along all the time? We zigzag from east to west and north to south. We bump into everything. Even the docks in the city. I don't know why we haven't fallen apart or sunk yet." Why should it? He'd heard him say: "Don't worry, you Dummies. Old Longtail looks after drunks." Who can say who looks after them. What's certain is that *The Souse Wind*—even though it had a hard time staying afloat; even though it went snaking in all directions—always got to port. He had the image of *The Souse Wind* tattooed on his mind. The same as its smell of mango rinds, cane liquor, and rotten clams. On the other hand, he remembered almost nothing of the sailors. And only a few details of the skipper. His voice most of all. That he had engraved in his memory. His whiskey voice, rising, loud, full of orders. "Come on, Birdbrain," that's what he called him by, never by his name, "come on, Birdbrain. Warm up my coffee and fry me some plantains." "What happened to the jib, Birdbrain?" "Birdbrain, why haven't you trimmed the lifts?" "When I get back, with my drinks inside, I want to see the deck swabbed down. I pity you, Birdbrain, if it doesn't gleam!" When the drunkenness affected his brain a little and made him walk as if he were avoiding an eddy, he treated him formally. He adopted an attitude of respectful mockery. His little eyes rolled. He smiled, showing the only teeth he had left. His stammering voice took on the bittersweet taste of moquiñaña honey: "Mr. Birdbrain, would you be so kind as to give me a hand in raising the waterways?" "Mr. Birdbrain, I'm going to get a little shut-eye, would you advise me when the tide changes?" If he neglected to fulfill one of the requests the skipper stood looking at him. He twisted all over. Trying to preserve his balance in that way. He tried to look at him through his alcoholic night. He didn't insult him. On the contrary, his smile became broader, gooier. His look more distant, more stupid. The mocking tone more insulting: "Mr. Birdbrain, why are you such a birdbrain?" No! That man wasn't his father. And even if he was, what difference did it make? He hated him with all his soul. With a circulatory hatred that ran all through his body. He also hated everything around him: the sloop, the river, the sea, the cities, the villages, the people, the animals. It was a fermenting hatred that kept growing and getting stronger, day by day. Cursed be everything that existed! If it were left up to his hand, he'd make the whole world disappear. For the time being, he had to stop being what he was. He had to transform himself into another person. Different. He'd squash the rest like worms. He'd make servants out of them. Without their having any other will but his orders. But how? How? The voice of that faceless skipper kept decorating the landscape. Without a face for him because he'd erased it? Or was it that he'd never really had one? The voice kept on shaking him, impregnating, maddening him: "Mr. Birdbrain, please buy me another bottle of liquor." "Mr. Birdbrain, would you care to have a drink with me?" "Mr. Birdbrain, get me a woman." "Mr. Birdbrain, get a woman for yourself too." "Don't you like women, Mr. Birdbrain? What do you like, then, Mr. Birdbrain? Ah, I know, the only thing you like is money! Money, Mr. Birdbrain!" To get away from there. To leave the damned drunken sloop. More damned than drunken. Abandon it with all inside. Escape in any way he could. And liquidate them once and for all. The project ripened on long wakeful nights. He felt inundated by the nettles growing inside his skin. He began to erase the image of everything around him. Sunk in the sweet dream of future vengeance, he almost didn't hear the orders: "What's the matter with you, Birdbrain? Can't you hear me?" "You're woolgathering, Birdbrain? Are you jerking off? I'll have to give you a few whacks, Birdbrain! To see if you'll wake up!" He planned everything carefully. It was a dark night. High tide. The skipper's drunkenness was total. "Would you awaken me when the tide has risen, Mr. Birdbrain?" Sleeping now, snoring under the masts, at full blast. The sailors too were half-lit. They were sleeping near the boom. Wrapped in the small jib. He checked the general sleep. Then he threw some provisions into the only canoe. Later, armed with an ax, he jumped into the water. He got under the hull of the sloop. Toward the stern, with the blade of the ax, he began to loosen one of the planks nailed to the sternpost. As soon as the board opened up the water entered swiftly. He threw the ax away. He climbed into the canoe. And he paddled at full paddle. Would the skipper and the sailors wake up? Would they have time to jump in and swim? In any case, if they did, they'd be in the middle of the river. Rather, almost in the middle of the Gulf. How could they reach shore? How could they be picked up by anyone? He seemed to hear them shouting in his ear: "Birdbrain, what if he really is your father?" His father? Even if he were. What difference did it make? And even if it did it was already too late! He was far, far away! Besides, *The Souse Wind* had probably already gone to the bottom with the two sailors and the skipper. In spite of all, he heard the voice again. Or this time was it the voice of the skipper himself? "Birdbrain, Birdbrain, Birdbrain! What a bastard you are! Birdbrain! Birdbrain! Birdbrain!"

"Don Chalena! Don Chalena!"

"Sir, look!"

"Where?"

"There! The bog'll be ready soon!"

What he saw was ominous. A kind of collective fever was shaking that vegetable-animal world. Everyone was working. The trees were falling, falling, cut down by the men. They cut off the branches. Trimmed the thickest ones. The ones that could be used as stakes or crosspieces. Immediately the monkeys climbed up onto the logs, trying to clean them. They took off leaves, flowers, fruit, or vines. Sometimes they carried the pieces of wood themselves to where the hills were coming together. On other occasions they didn't. Who knows from where, hundreds of bats had appeared. They were the ones who did that job. They flew heavily in multiples of seven. They clustered underneath the logs. And took flight again. The logs rose up then as if they had wings.

There weren't only monkeys and bats. Other zoological species also lent their services. As at all crucial moments they seemed to forget their everyday differences. In an implicit pact they didn't devour each other. When they bumped into each other by chance they prudently withdrew. Without answering to their natural instincts of aggression. They continued using their own languages. From mammals to reptiles. Nevertheless it might be said that a dynamic synchronism had joined those expressions together in a single, exclusive language, one integrated into the voice of the jungle. Where in the same way the sound of steps flowed together with the flapping of wings, the dragging, the clearing of underbrush, and the cutting of wood. None of the members of the scale of life stopped moving for a single instant. No one hesitated. It might have been said that they were fulfilling precise, defined orders. For their part the men and women continued working on the joining of the hills. Without rest. They gathered the material brought them by the monkeys, the bats, the badgers, the deer, the wild boars, the jaguars, the vipers...Some drove the stakes into the ground. Others wove the framework. Others tied it together. Others placed stones to form the broad mortar made from black earth mixed with muyuyo seeds and other glutinants. The monkeys helped them exclusively on these chores. Their collaboration was magnificent. They seemed to understand the words. And more than the words, the expressions. The gestures. The looks. When they couldn't reach the height required for some piece of work, they would climb up onto one another's shoulders until the exact distance was reached. When they had to cross a gully, or wade an inlet, they formed a chain among themselves by means of their limbs and their coiling tails until they formed a regular bridge. Those who were carrying the many loads passed over it. Overseeing the great work was the Cross of the Burned Christ. Like another stake they had driven it into the side of one of the hills. Cándido, who had thought he would have to encourage the people, soon saw that it wasn't necessary. And he was doing his duty like anyone else, in the work. The others seemed to be possessed by some kind of mechanical gears. The work grew under one's eyes. Uncontainably. As they noticed it, Juvencio and Clotilde exchanged looks of joy and stimulation from time to time.

Chalena, with a cavernous voice, shouted:

"Hey! What are you doing there?"

They didn't hear him. They continued imperturbably at their

tasks. Without stopping for an instant. Without even looking behind. The homunculus raised his voice:

"What are you doing there?"

An identical silence. An identical lack of attention. The Boss, red as a snapper, turned to Salustiano. In his eyes one could read rage and impotence. Understanding it, the Political Chief shouted:

"Didn't you hear? What are you doing there?"

Obviously the millions of noises were very loud. The shouts were of no avail. Chalena, more and more nervous, ran his hands over his face. Then he began to play with his bandanna. What to do? What to do? Salustiano looked at him desolately. The toad—the capon capon toad—no longer spoke to him. Simply with his look he indicated the carbine. Caldera understood. He half-nodded. He rested the weapon on his right shoulder. Fired. The detonation was multiplied by the hundred voices of the echo. The entire jungle seemed to move. It turned its millions of eyes toward the newcomers. Then it stopped, as if under a hypnotic impact. The silence grew in its countless vegetable tongues. The first to move was Cándido. With the frame of silence his voice sketched out a flame of anathema.

"You people! What do you want here?"

"Why are they cutting down the trees?"

"To make a bog."

"By what right?"

"That of defending our lives. Santorontón can't die of thirst."

"No one's died of thirst. I gave everybody all the water they needed!"

"They had to pay for it. And at what a price!"

Toad, Toady, Toadstool he grew when the moment to give orders arrived.

"All right. Enough. Stop your work!"

A smile of bitter mockery folded the lips of the old priest.

"Oh, yes?"

"If not, the village authorities will make you!"

Cándido stopped smiling. His voice became cutting. Hard.

"Look, Don Crisóstomo. It would be best if you people got out of here. This will stop nobody. Did you hear me? Nobody!"

The batrachian sweated rivers. His pitahaya balloon head seemed to swell.

"That's what you think. I own the village. I got it in exchange for a little water. The Santorontonians belong to me. To me!"

He addressed the ones working.

"You tell him! And come! Come with me! From now on you'll have all the water you want. Without paying a cent. Free!"

Cándido couldn't stand anymore. He shouted:

"Get out of here!"

At the same time he took a step toward Chalena. As if it had been a signal, the men and animals, in a synchronized move, also advanced in that direction. The Giant repeated:

"Get out of here!"

The Boss went back to his people.

"They asked for it! Shoot them! Kill them!"

They didn't obey him. No one made the slightest sign of picking up his weapon. Salustiano—in an unusual transformation—expressed himself:

"I'm not getting mixed up in this anymore, Sir. If you want to, it's all yours!"

He went over. Snatched the carbine from him.

"Me, then yes. You'll see!"

One, two, three, four, ten stones rained down on him. The monkeys, of course! A tremendous shouting shook the jungle. A hit on the arm made him drop the weapon. He looked around disconcertedly. It seemed as if the whole jungle were coming down on him.

"You'll pay me for this!"

He realized that he was running. All his people were running. He, a little behind. He looked in the direction of the joining of the hills. Most of the inhabitants of Santorontón and the jungle had already turned their backs on him. As if nothing had happened, they were deep in their task once more.

"They'll pay me for this!"

TWENTY-SEVEN

Atlantic. His eyes were clothed in oceanic charts. He had been born almost in a cradle of crags. Listening to the gabble of frozen seas. Which sometimes wrote fantastic ideograms in snow. Between prayers of wind and caresses of iodine. And now—paradoxically—he was so much someone else and so far away! Oystering himself in the navel of the tropics. Living with a school of beached sharks. What else were Chalena, Carranza, and the rest?

"Hurry, Filemón! If we get there too late the Witch Doctor's family will be asleep already!"

What kind of face would Bulu-Bulu put on when he got the word? His usual Monkey Face? Most likely not. Even though that was his nickname. He would show, rather, a Beelzebub face. Bulu-Bulu Beelzebub on Balumba. He would twist in dislocated facial changes. Or would he appear as a Jaguar? Didn't they say that Bulu-Bulu at critical moments underwent the metamorphosis into The Spotted One? Who knows! What's certain is that he would twist about like a pompano stuck with a harpoon. He twisted around when they announced to him: "You're being sent to the threshold of the Equinox. There where a belt of fire divides the Earth in two. And land and sea burn with green flames." Later on he found out that they were exaggerating. The green flames were in the lowlands. The edge of the ocean. Or already climbing up over the real belt of fire. From the Pacific. The belt of fire—changed into two there—by chains of very high mountains. Drunk with volcanoes. Which lifted *cundurungas*—condors' necks—above the clouds. Later on they delimited him even more: "You're going to Santorontón." He asked, ingenuously: "San Torontón? Some new saint? I've never heard of him. Since there are so many..." "No. It's not a saint. It's a place with that name." "Oh!" "On the seashore. Santorontón. Where the Devil still dances on the tip of his tail. Where the Son of Man has still to win his final battles." From then on he felt more Atlantic. From a northern Atlantic that borders on the Arctic. Atlantic or Atlantis? As if his atlantism had given him stilts on which to see from up high.

"What's wrong, Filemón? Why are you sleeping? Has your paddle turned into a pillow?"

He had to change sextons. He was getting more bony and cuneiform every day. An anticipation of the boneyard, his skin let the periosteal structure show through. He awoke tired. A laziness accumulated over seven decades. "Yes. Soon I'll have to replace him." How curious! He also had the impression that the canoe was sleeping.

"Filemón! Filemón! Wake up!"

Since he didn't answer, he looked back. He was snoring. He had rested on the handle of the paddle. Now it really was a paddle-pillow. The thin piece of something at a slight angle. Stuck in the water. Not sinking. Just as if the sea had become solid. Could it have become solid? In any case it wasn't made of water. It was a sea of glass that imprisoned the canoe. The canoe, in turn, a calaboose. With growing concern and fear, his voice of clay.

"Wake up, Filemón, wake up."

To give himself courage, like one who throws a useless seed into the void, he murmured:

"We'll get there too late. You'll see. We'll get there too late."

A sound in front of the bow made him turn. The water—the glass, rather—was breaking. In a short while a great thick vertical beam appeared. Then some thorns. A Crown of Thorns. Immediately a Face. A bleeding Face. The arms of a Cross. Nailed to its ends two Hands. Two bleeding Hands. A Body. A bleeding Body. Legs nailed by the Feet to the lower part of the Wood. Bleeding legs and feet. Finally, the whole Cross came out of the Glass. It remained suspended in the air. Just barely brushing the halted liquid surface. A light that came from who knows where outlined the Image over the frame of shadows. Was it Christ? Yes. It was Christ. Cándido's Christ. The Burned Christ. He raised his head. His eyes—a net of invisible unknown things—enwrapped the face of the Priest. He asked in a severe, somewhat sad voice:

"*Quo vadis?*"

The cleric, out of control, in a sea of hypnosis, was going to reply mechanically: "To Rome. To be crucified again." He recovered. Got control of himself. Tried to appear normal, tranquil.

"Just rowing around. Taking a spin."

"So far from Santorontón and so close to Balumba?"

He felt more and more in control of himself. He even sketched a smile.

"The current took us. Since Filemón doesn't have much energy anymore."

The Cross gave a leap. It stayed above the canoe. Floating. At an angle. The face of Jesus came to within a few inches of the face of the Priest. The voice emerged even more severe.

"Why do you lie, Gaudencio?"

"I, Crucified Jesus?"

"You! Yes! You!"

"You're mistaken. I..."

A superhuman force threw him onto the bottom of the canoe. He fell to his knees. The Cross, at the same time, straightened up. The Crucified One thundered:

"This is the limit, Gaudencio! Don't you realize what you're doing?"

The priest felt unhinged inside. A microseaquake. His arteries were bubbling. There was pounding in every corner of his body. On his knees he moved toward the Cross. He tried to kiss the feet of The Crucified One. He kissed them. He shuddered. The wounds were open. Blood was flowing from them. His lips were soaked. He moaned:

"Forgive me! Forgive me, Lord!"

"Do you think you deserve forgiveness?"

"No, Lord. But your mercy is infinite."

The Nazarene made a gesture of displeasure.

"That's what you and people like you think. That's why you abuse things."

"Hear me, Lord! Forgive me!"

"Uhm! We'll see about that. For the time being let's have a little talk. Sit down. I'll do the same."

"Are you going to get down off the Cross?"

"I can, can't I? Don't you think I get tired of being nailed up there all the time?"
"Yes, yes. Of course you do."

The Cross floated vertically on the sea. Christ had settled himself on the little seat in the bow. Gaudencio, as before, was still sitting in the middle. Filemón was no longer snoring, although he was still asleep. There was total silence and quietude around the canoe. It was Jesus who first spoke.
"Now, tell me. Why do you want to convince Bulu-Bulu and his family that they should call off the wedding?"
"The women of Santorontón asked me to. You know that."
"Of course I do. But you, why did you accept?"
"It was the right thing, wasn't it?"
"Right for them or for your conscience?"
"For them... and for my conscience!"
"Do you really believe that?"
"Don't you?"
"I'm the one asking the questions. Don't forget that!"
"That's true. Forgive me... Well, yes. I do believe it!"
"Can you tell me why?"
"In the first place, none of the requirements of the Church has been fulfilled."
"Don't come to me with fairy tales!"
"In the second place, that marriage would be a sacrilege!"
"Don't make me laugh, Gaudencio."
"Don't you think so?"
"Not in the least."
"You surprise me, Crucified Jesus."
"Don't be surprised. You've administered the sacraments and help of the Catholic religion to worse people and under worse circumstances. And not just this. You've dared, from here, from Santorontón, to divide up heaven among a group of evil people. Real monsters!"
"*Errare humanum est.*"
"Save your Latinizing for a better occasion. Don't make me lose my patience."
"Thy holy will be done, amen."
"Oh, boy!"
"All right, Lord. But I beg you to be less severe in your judgments. Why only against me? Almost all around the world the

Church today does the same thing. Besides, I've got to tell you what I think. And I think that nobody—hear me well, nobody!—among the inhabitants of Santorontón is anything like Candelario Mariscal."

"I repeat. Don't make me laugh, Gaudencio."

"Jesus, please!"

"Are you fooling me? Do you really think you are?"

"Yes, Holy Christ. Hasn't he killed hundreds—maybe thousands—just for the pleasure of killing? Hasn't he raped every woman he came across, without respect for age or status? Hasn't he even raped little girls? Hasn't he despoiled everything he found in his path? Hasn't he sown destruction and panic over land and sea? Didn't he set fire to your very own church? Don't you yourself show the marks of that fire on your face and body? Lastly, isn't he a son of Beelzebub?"

"I see that you're still the one asking the questions."

"Forgive me again. But..."

"Besides, you ask me a lot of questions at the same time. It doesn't matter. What matters is getting things and positions clear. I'm going to answer you. Here in Santorontón—not to mention other places like this or even worse in the world—there are a lot of men like Candelario Mariscal."

"How can you say that, Lord?"

The Nazarene spoke in a calm voice. As if he were talking to himself. He didn't even look at Gaudencio. His eyes were lost above beings and landscape. In a distant net casting. Distances in space and, above all, in time. The serpent. Could he have been thinking about the Forbidden Fruit that the serpent got Eve to taste in Paradise so that she and Adam would open their eyes and discover that they were naked? Oh, serpent, serpent! Or about the Universal Flood, in which his Father destroyed all the men he had created in his image and likeness when he found them to be sinners? He only saved Noah and his family, in the Ark of the Covenant, with representatives of all the zoomorphic species. The serpent among them. Serpent. Seven times serpents. Or was he thinking about another total destruction, that of Sodom and Gomorrah, also by a Flood—a Flood of Fire, serpent of fire? Meanwhile, within the duality of thought and word, he went on:

"Candelario Mariscal is polyhomicidal. I know. He's committed every crime in the book. That's certain. He set the church on fire. True. Although on that occasion he was the prisoner of alcoholic delirium. Still, that's obvious too. As for the rest, some people have their doubts. That his father is Beelzebub? That his mother is Pancha the Mad Mule? Can they prove it? There are others who say he's Father Cándido's son. All in all, even supposing that all this is also true... Colonel Mariscal has something in his favor!"

"Are you going to defend him, Jesus?"

"No. I'm not going to defend him. I only want us to judge him together. He's evil. There's no doubt about that. Still, his evil turns out to be an explosion. A predestination. The role given him to play. Obeying outside causes. The product of a mind unhinged by illness, vice, or heredity. Besides, when he acts, he does so openly. Without hiding. Without trying to hide his deeds or his motives. Without trying hypocritically to gain heaven by paying a few coins. Nor, for the same quantity does he try to obtain respect and appreciation, fear, or hate of his fellows. A murderer, a thief, a rapist. Of course he is! But do you know what the forces that drive him on are?"

"Lord! What are you saying! You! You, defending the Son of the Devil!"

"On the other hand, have you thought about the others?"

He babbled:

"The others? What others, Crucified Jesus?"

"Don't play the fool. Your people. The ones who run Santorontón. Have you thought about Chalena, for example? You don't know it, but he started out by murdering three people, his own father among them... What you do know is that he tried to make the whole village die of thirst! Did what he did to Timoteo Ruales to put the blame on Dr. Balda! For diversion he wanted a rose to grow in the hand of a child! Ordered his death along with that of his mother! Tried to wipe out all the creatures of the jungle just because! And all of it coldly, just for power or for money!"

Gaudencio made the sign of the Cross.

"In the name of the Father and of the Son and of the Holy Ghost. Amen."

The Son of Mary paid no attention to him. He went on:

"What can you tell me about Espurio Carranza, who has so many dead people under his belt? Who lets sick people die if they don't pay him? Who gives their corpses to the buzzards if they don't pay him?"

He didn't look at him straight on. The Nazarene's eyes seemed to flash. It would be impossible for him to stand that look. Oceanic. More than Atlantic. Cosmic.

"With all due respect, I think you're exaggerating."

Christ's tone swelled. His words, now, were hammering. Shaking.

"What about all the others who run the village? They, in just the same way, are a collection of wicked hypocrites. Day after day they commit hundreds of crimes, sheltered by what they call law and justice. And the worst acts—those that maybe not even you know about—they perform in the shadows. Hidden. Thinking they can hide from the sight of God."

He paused. He looked at Gaudencio. Intensely. Penetrating him. The cleric, although he tried to avoid him, couldn't have. He had to thread his eyes along the impact of that look. The Son of Mary went on:

"You, yourself..."

He stammered:

"I...t-t-t...too...L-L-L...Lord?"

"Yes. You. You too. You've made a pact with them. You're the first of their accomplices. You agree with what they're doing. You've sold them eternal salvation for a few coins. You've allied yourself with them. You've dared, several times, to challenge me. On the other hand, they've turned their backs on your people, the underdogs, the ones who need you most. You're now one of the bosses in the village too."

He lowered his head. He felt trapped in a net of fishhooks. He had evidence that any intent to escape would only make the barbs of those hooks dig deeper. In order to say something, he mumbled:

"I'm confused, Holy Christ."

He seemed to doubt for yet a few moments. Crushed by the weight of the arguments of the Son of Man. He recovered. Raised his head. Looked into the eyes of his Questioner again. An impotent rage boiled in his chest. A kind of intimate rebellion, impossible to contain, was invading him. When he spoke again, his voice was a strange deep bass with an infarction in it.

"Will you let me tell you what I think, Lord?"

"Why not? Speak!"

"I think that...you've become an agitator. A revolutionary."

"You're wrong, Gaudencio."

"What? Aren't you, then?"

"You're wrong when you say I've become one. I always was. That's why they crucified me. That's why they keep on crucifying me now every day. And my own people—or those who say they're mine—sacrifice me, which is even worse!"

Disconcerted, the priest, with a certain desperation, said:

"What you're saying is contrary to everything I ever learned. Contrary, furthermore, to a large part of ecclesiastical tradition, doctrine, and discipline. So, only the disinherited, the humble, the miserable should enter the Kingdom of God? Those on higher social levels are condemned beforehand?"

Christ smiled. With a certain bitterness.

"I see that you're still questioning me. You still don't understand. Or you don't want to understand. And you keep on carrying grist to your mill."

"Well, isn't that what you're trying to tell me?"

"No! I never stated that those who have nothing, the victims of the exploitation of others, are the only ones who can enter my Father's Kingdom. Much less that those of the higher social classes lack hope for salvation. The problem is not one of power and wealth but of conscience and conduct. Although a greater number of times power and material goods harm men, the opportunities belong to all. The doors of Heaven are open to all who deserve it. Not just to those who pay. Hear me well! You—and priests like you—shouldn't ally yourselves only with the bosses either. Sins are venial or mortal according to their nature and not the political, economic, or social position of those who commit them."

Gaudencio began to feel better and better. This level of dialogue seemed more ad hoc to him. It was getting away from the personal level—which touched him so closely—and was passing on to less concrete and more general boundaries. He argued:

"Following that criterion, the Church wouldn't prosper. Those who have nothing, can give nothing. Even if they wanted to. And important churches. Artistic and cultural works. The high seat that the Leaders of the Church must occupy. The manifestations of the external ritual. The great enterprises of different kinds. The catechization and domination of the masses. All. All can only be attained with the help of those in command. Ever since there was the schism between Temporal Power and Eternal Power, it's the only thing we have left. Convince yourself of it, Jesus. So that the Church can be strong and can amply fulfill its functions, it must have in its hands all the possibilities of wealth and power. At least as long as the World continues as it is."

Christ replied, in a lively way:

"And turn against Religion? After all, which is the more important? Religion or Church? Do you think that a strong Church with a weak Religion will turn out better? Or have you come to the paradox of a Church without a Religion to sustain it?"

As if to himself, Gaudencio murmured:

"In all humility, I say to you, Lord, that I'm still confused. As if we were talking different languages. I never thought that the Church of today—as you give me to understand—was so far away and so much against the Religion."

"Truly, don't you think that it's that way?"

"I repeat, Lord, I'm confused. Everything you tell me is so contrary to what I've been taught. To what I've seen in the places I come from. To what I've practiced ever since I began my ministry."

Jesus asserted, benevolently:

"You're right, in that. In your world—in the world from which you come—genocide is daily bread. There are men who with one single word or one single gesture can put an end to millions of human beings. And there are princes of the Church who not only absolve them but sometimes applaud them. But we're not there. We're here. In Santorontón. In a place where things begin to invent themselves. For your part, think on it. Even for the salvation of your own soul!"

He was startled.

"Of my own . . . soul? Is . . . it in danger too?"

"Ask your conscience. For the moment remember that Colonel Candelario Mariscal isn't that much worse than the rest. If he is worse. For the moment he deserves an opportunity for his repentance and contrition."

There was a silence. The Reverend Father was worried. But he knew that it was his only way out. For a moment the figures of Doña Prudencia and her followers surrounded him. With hair and skirts blowing in the wind, their faces aggressive. They threatened him with their fists held high, waving them in front of his eyes.

"All right, Lord. But what shall I tell the women of Santorontón?"

"The truth. That you were unable to get to Bulu-Bulu's."

"Uhm! They won't believe it."

"You don't have to tell them what happened. Simply show them that it's the only thing you can tell them. As imaginative as they are, and knowing the Wizard, they'll think that he vanished into thin air, with family and house. Who knows, maybe with the island of Balumba itself. Or maybe you can tell them that he put a blindfold of smoke over your eyes."

In spite of his self-control, the words came out:

"Thy will be done, Lord. On earth as it is in heaven. Amen!"

A paddle stroke made him look behind. Filemón was paddling. The liquid had ceased to be hardened crystal. Now it was simply water. Salty seawater. He returned his look to the bow, to say something else to Christ. No one was there. He rubbed his eyes. Could he have been dreaming? He noticed that the sexton was turning the boat, changing direction. He was steering, without a doubt, for Santorontón, whose lights were blinking on the horizon. He raised his eyes a little more. In the distance there was a kind of halo that was moving rapidly toward the village. Inside of it the Cross was clearly framed.

At that moment—in a hoarse voice and as if to himself—Filemón spoke:

"You see, Father Gaudencio. We've been rowing for hours on end without finding Balumba. It's probably vanished into thin air, Witch Doctor and all."

TWENTY-EIGHT

Lying there. Wounded there. Suffering there. There. Looking at her. The big eyes. Very big. All eyes. Feverish. Frightened. Following her with lasso looks. Wrapping her. Drawing her. Walls of eyes. Chains of eyes. She could no longer escape. She was tied. Definitely tied. She wouldn't try it ever again. Besides, it would be in vain. She'd proved it. Death had given her back. It seemed to have rejected her. It had made her change course. Return to Father Cándido's house. State that she belonged to the doctor. That doctor who was there. Lying. Wounded. Suffering. Looking at her.

"You came back."

"Yes."

"Couldn't you leave me?"

Did he know? Did he know everything, then?

"No."

"Don't try it again."

"No."

He smiled.

"You see. We're tied together, one to the other, forever."

"Yes. But..."

"Say what you were going to."

"It can't be."

"Why not?"

"Just because."

His strength left him. He began to see her as unreal. Blended into himself. The same as if she were blooming out of his body.

Especially his eyes. Curiously, he saw her naked. Similar to that night when she had got into his bed. Of course, her eyes had been different then. They'd had a strange distant glow. Everything that enveloped her irradiated absence. Not now. She rose up before him. Vital. Beautiful. Attractive. Present. And, especially, all his. His? He lacked strength. More and more. He repeated, his voice diluted by his inner mist now:

"Why not?"

The answer had a fatalistic tone.

"What can't be, can't be."

She was blending in with the other forms. Was she there or had she gone? He, was he stretching out his hands? How could he know? He begged, with anguish:

"Don't leave."

"I'm not leaving."

"Don't try it again..."

His eyes closed on him. Did he have lead on them? Or were they sticking? He repeated, his voice in threads:

"Don't try it again."

"I won't."

He was now almost floating between two waters. On the borderline between awake and asleep. Did he say it or did he only think that he was saying it?

"If you try it again. If you leave me..."

"What?"

"Life won't have any meaning for me."

Had she heard him or not? She couldn't hear. In the city she couldn't hear. Or see. It was as if the shadows had begun to fight inside the cave. Bats wounding each other? Or wounding her? They were beating her. They were making her walk with a stagger. Or they were throwing her against the stone walls. Or ten, twenty of them were coming together. Twenty of them to immobilize her. Was she immobilized? With their sinewy wings they had pinned her to the ground. In a whirlwind of eyes they tried to penetrate beyond her silence. Suddenly those eyes grew. Gasoline lanterns that danced around her, sprinkled with green light. Within that light absurd beings were rising up. Unknown landscapes. The city began to show its luminous teeth to her. Was it the city? She didn't know. It was juxtaposed, mounted in double exposure on the macabre images. Candelario. Killing her Old Folks. Approaching her. Killing them. Touching her.

Three. Four machete blows. Pulling off their clothes. The Old Folks naked. She naked. Giving them the machete. Steel machete. Giving her the machete. Flesh machete. Absurd waves of veins and nerves and broken muscles. Mounting them. Mounting her. Blood of the Old Folks. Her blood. The Old Folks dying. She dying? Had she lived it? Had she agonized it? Was she dreaming? The testicles on a string. He on top of her. No longer he. He-others. Always he—always others. No longer just a man. Also wild beasts. Or men-beasts? The string of testicles. He? Really he? Really others? She cutting off their virile parts. The Old Folks. The men. The jungle. The cave. Dawning. Outside it? Inside it? The tender images, like a gigantic fan, carrying away the homicidal wind. The string of images fleeing. It was as if her farm had been transformed. Her gentle Daura, with flowers, plants, trees. Not dry, sandy land. Gentle land, rather. Gentle with caresses. Old people. Dressed in white. Where was she?

"Where am I?"

"Are you feeling better?"

Who was talking to her? A man. Tall. With dark eyes—behind the glasses—penetrating. With a perennial nervous smile. With a repeated tic in his head, as if he were trembling. With affable manners. With soothing sympathy.

In spite of everything, she looked at him aggressively.

"Who are you?"

He continued smiling.

"Carlos Alaya. Dr. Alaya."

"Oh! What do you want?"

"To cure you. Just to cure you."

He repeated the question:

"Are you feeling better?"

"Better? I'm fine."

As if to convince herself, she repeated:

"I'm fine."

And with sudden confidence.

"Just that I think I've been sleeping. All the time. How long have I been here?"

"A week."

"A week? I don't remember. I don't remember anything... Who brought me?"

"A friend of mine sent you. A classmate, who's in Santorontón now. Dr. Juvencio Balda."

Juvencio Balda. There he was. Lying down. Looking at her. Sucking her in with his eyes. He wasn't sleeping. Couldn't he sleep? Could he be thinking that keeping his eyes open was like holding her prisoner in them? Could he be thinking that only in that way could he stop her from going away? He didn't know that she could never leave him. That she was stuck to him. Glued to him. The rudder on a sloop. If she left him—if she could leave him someday—he would be adrift. Rolling or zigzagging. On the fingers of the sea.

Of the sea. He was coming out of the sea. The water was trimming him with iridescent pearls. A living diadem—Cross and all—he advanced slowly. It could have been said that the Wood weighed more than on other occasions. Was he fatigued? Or was he doing it on purpose in order to slide it along the ground? Cándido, who was by the door, watching him come, went over to him solicitously.

"Can I help you?"

"What a question!"

"I see that you're arriving in a magnificent humor."

"Cándido!"

The Cleric pretended not to have understood. He put his shoulder under the Cross and helped him move forward. He couldn't bear the prolonged silence.

"Wouldn't it be better if you got up on it?"

The Nazarene looked at him reproachfully.

"Do you think I don't get tired of being nailed up there all the time? Do you think my wounds don't hurt? If you want to test what I feel someday, you can take my place for a few minutes. You'll see just how pleasant it all is."

The Priest grunted grouchily:

"I'm not the Son of God. I didn't come to have them crucify me for the salvation of mankind. I'm a poor old Priest. I don't have a church. And I even have to risk my neck looking for my sheep. I do what I can to cooperate with you. And you still get angry!"

They were getting close to the house. Christ stopped. A wave of affection lighted up his countenance. He murmured:

"Forget it, Cándido. It's just that the things I've been seeing put my nerves on edge."

"What things?"

"The ones that are happening in this world."
"My world is Santorontón."
"It's the same everywhere."
As if they'd come to an agreement, they laid the Cross to one side. They sat down on a log. In front of the house. Jesus looked at him. Steadily. Intensely. He asked him:
"Are you still standing firm?"
His accent filled with sorrow.
"Still, Lord."
"Then if you think that your godson is so bad, why did you let others as bad as he enter your church? Those on Gaudencio's golden list, for example."
"It's just that..."
"Do you think, perhaps, that Candelario is...worse than Chalena or Espurio, to name only two?"
"Who knows, Lord!"
"Gaudencio himself, you know what he's like! And yet he goes on saying mass, baptizing, giving communion, using the word of God for his own ends!"
"Yes, but..."
"Do you also think that only the rich, those in command, should be, in a like manner, the masters of religion?"
"You know very well I don't. But..."
"But what?"
"The sinners! It's the sinners who can't enter the House of God!"
"Oh, what will become of you, Cándido! What's the House of God there for, then? What does the Church exist for? Why was religion born? Why are you there? Why did I come into the world, to be crucified? To help sinners! The ones who are saved don't need us. And the ones who have everything. The ones who can do anything out of pride fool themselves or try to fool us! They think they can buy everything they want. You've seen it. Besides their worldly goods down here they're already reserving, on time, their little lots in heaven. I repeat, the good don't need us. If everybody were good, what would we be doing here? The evil-doers, the sinners, the ones who aren't on the straight path...they're the ones who need our help most! Even though, on the other hand..., who is free of blame? Who can cast the first stone? You, yourself..."
"Me, Lord?"

"Why did you enter the Seminary? Wasn't it because lust was devouring you?"

He looked at him with anguish.

"That's true. But I repented."

"Are you the only one who can repent? Are the rest condemned beforehand?"

He pounded his chest, contrite.

"*Mea culpa! Mea . . .*"

"Cut that out. And reflect."

Through the shadows, he tried to read the face of the Nazarene. He murmured hesitantly.

"Frankly, I don't know what to think. Before, I saw everything so clear. So clean. Now I'm walking through a sea of shadows. Sometimes . . ."

"Don't stop."

"I think you've gone crazy."

"Cándido!"

"And you're driving me crazy too."

Out of the sea, in the same way, came Gaudencio. Atlantic. He bore a cocktail of labyrinths in his mind. What to do? What could he do? At the earliest moment of the following day he would be visited by all the ladies of Santorontón. What would he tell them? That he had run into Christ? That the Latter had dissuaded him from his purpose? That he had visited Bulu-Bulu? That he had been unable to convince him? Would they believe him? Wouldn't they believe him? And what if they discovered the truth later on? In any case, it made no difference. What they wanted was for the wedding not to take place. The way in which it was stopped didn't matter a whit to them. For the sake of saying something. So as not to feel so alone, he addressed Filemón.

"Will Doña Prudencia and her companions accept our marrying Colonel Mariscal tomorrow?"

"In no way, Reverend!"

"Will they try to stop it?"

"Of course, Reverend!"

As if to himself, he murmured:

"Of course! They're going to be furious!"

The sexton commented:

"They're capable of destroying the church on us. Or driving

us out of the village. Or beating us until they've done us in. You saw what they were like tonight!"

"That's true."

"But the Colonel . . ."

When he named him he made the Sign of the Cross. He went on:

". . . the Colonel's not going to sit idly by."

"I hadn't thought about him. You're right, Filemón. So, all that's left to us now is to commend ourselves to divine mercy! *Consummatum est!*"

As always, when the Priest came out with some Latinizing, the Sexton murmured:

"Amen!"

Gaudencio didn't seem satisfied. He came out with another. As in his conscience he remembered Pontius Pilate:

"*Quod scripsi, scripsi.*"

"Amen!"

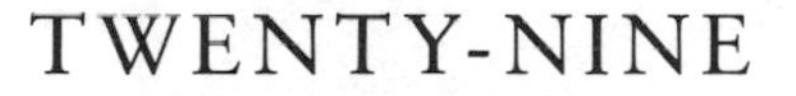

TWENTY-NINE

When Indian summer was over the rains grew stronger. A blue song bit the zinc roofs. The water overflowed the tanks. The tender green of the leaves turned into frothy laughter over the ochre cracks in the earth. It seemed that the coconut palms were greeting with a bow, waving their handkerchiefs woven of jade harpoons. The monkeys shouted, hammocking happily in the high branches. The bats frolicked with their winged acrobat bodies. Men had ears of corn flourishing on their teeth. They felt free again. The invisible liquid links no longer chained their wills. The bog, enormous mirror pregnant with colors, addressed the heavens with its hands of dynamic crystal. Only Crisóstomo Chalena—toad toady toadstool—was sad sadly sadfool. Those bastards, were they going to get their way? Would he, as before, have to kiss the Santorontonians' asses? And then only if they let him. If they didn't boot him out of there with a nice clean kick where the sun doesn't shine on him. Maybe it would be worse! If they locked him up in a prison of mocking laughs and looks. Suddenly he remembered his Papa—could he really have been his Papa? And once more the swinging word—a dislocated bell-clapper—went from the jungle to his ear. From his ear to the jungle. Hurry-Worry. Birdbrain-Herdbrain. Worry-Hurry. Herdbrain-Birdbrain. Could the others be hear-seeing him? Could they know that that was his Papa's baptismal word? If that was so, what would they think? Worry-Hurry. Herdbrain-Birdbrain. Worry-Hurry. Herdbrain-Birdbrain. Herdbrain-Birdbrain. He had to do something! Worry-Hurry. Herdbrain-Birdbrain. Drag himself before Gaudencio like an epileptic snake? Or settle the matter decisively? Walk around Candelario Mariscal's house with lighted candles? At night, of course. Dance on his knees and cry for mercy from the Colonel? So that he would call his father. The One We Know. What if the Colonel wasn't the son of Old Longtail? And if he got heated up and set his ass on fire with a board? Why didn't he call Himself himself? Himself didn't pay any more attention to him. He'd slipped out of his hand. So? Seek help from Bulu-Bulu? Would he give it? Maybe he wouldn't pay any attention. Maybe even he couldn't make contact with The Evil One now. Better to leave the Witch Doctor alone. On the other hand, hadn't he done it on his own before? Wasn't he always alone? He'd talk to him directly. He'd call him later when there was more silence in the night. Besides, you can't beat around the bush with the Other. He didn't like go-betweens. He rocked in the hammock, desperate. The shadows unglued the outline of everything around him. From the neighboring houses came the exhalations of silence now. The shadows were becoming thicker. Like a wood of interwoven ebony trees. Suddenly he felt that he wasn't alone. There was a shape beside his hammock. Who? Who could it be? Could it be the Mute who had returned? Fool. How could she have returned? You know very well that she'll never return. Neither she nor her son Tolón. If only it were Himself. He looked, trying to knife through the shadows. It was Himself. The light of his flaming eyes served as a lantern. He was half bent over. Melancholy. With the tip of his tail he scratched his chin. Chalena shook his head from side to side, resentful. He reproached him:

"So you finally came."

The Other muttered, very sad:

"I was busy. Times are bad. You have to work very hard to get a thousandth of what you got before."

Chalena maintained his tone:

"You knew I needed you, didn't you?"

He sighed.

"Yes."

"Why didn't you give me a sign? I would have been so thankful for a show of confidence. Support."

"You think I don't need that show myself?"

He looked at him with hesitation.

"Are things that bad?"

"Worse than you can imagine. We're double-fucked, Crisóstomo!"

"I don't believe you."

The Evil One's tone became whining.

"It's true. On the one side I keep losing more and more prestige. On the other the competition is getting greater and greater. It seems that the world is waking up. Especially the young people. They want to live without making use of our services. They want things that were sins before not to be sins now. Besides, they're beginning to realize that sinning is always more expensive. And since every day there are fewer richer rich men and more poorer poor men, sins are beginning to be out of reach. What do poor people have left to sin with?"

"You're exaggerating!"

"No. A thousand times no! . . . The first, pride. What have poor people got to be proud about? Their misery, their failure, their lack of everything? It's like a skeleton flaunting his bones. The second, avarice. An avaricious person is one who has wealth left over and stores it away. How can a person who has nothing and lives off long-term loans put anything away? The third, lust. Lust is a sin of people who are full. Those who have time, money, and power to dispose of. People who have a hard time supporting a wife, how are they going to be able to have the extra time and energy just to look for the satisfaction of their carnal desires? The fourth, envy. In order to have envy, you have to feel similar desires. A crocodile can envy a shark. One rules in the River, the other in the Sea. They have similar hungers. The latter can be pained that the former has eaten a hundred Christians while he's only devoured twenty. Or something like that. But a mullet or a chub can't envy a shark. Poor people could be envious of one another. But their needs make them equal. The fifth, gluttony. Hahaha! Can you imagine a poor person sinning because of gluttony? Gluttony is the product of abundance, excess, and when do you find that on the table of the poor? The sixth, wrath. Well, anyone can have wrath. But someone who lives by being beaten down, humiliated, always on the bottom, has to swallow his anger! If he raises his head, it will cost him dearly. Afterward he'll have to sink it down all the deeper! On the other hand, the one who can do everything, the one who thinks that with his money he can open all doors, becomes haughty, insolent. Any obstacle ignites his rage. The seventh, sloth. How can anyone be lazy when he has to work so that he and his can survive? Underdogs are born working and die working. Sometimes they don't even rest on the seventh day. Their destiny is to produce for the consumption of others. Yes, my dear Crisóstomo, in this field of soul-fishing, things are getting more and more difficult."

"It was always the same, wasn't it?"

"No! As I just told you, wealth is being concentrated more and more in fewer hands. In the same way, the number of sinners, practicing or potential, is becoming less. And all this has happened when it looked as if things were going better than ever! Just imagine, I was thinking about enlarging hell! Or setting up a branch here. In this world. Why lose time transporting souls off to my Kingdom? The ideal thing would have been to set myself up among them. Furthermore, a great many of the inhabitants of this planet were candidates for subjects of mine. The most important promotion and publicity are being handled by my partners. Suddenly everything's fallen apart! The world's standing on its head! I don't know what to do. Who would have thought that the Devil's business would be the worst business one day! You can see it here. You, who were my favorite partner, are being defeated. You've had to ask for my help. I wonder if I can give you any."

A sudden growing noise startled them. In the great silence it was growing, minute by minute. Running and voices coming closer. Also a tiny squeak of wheels. Little wheels. Beelzebub muttered, ill-humoredly:

"That's all we needed. Their coming to interrupt us! I'm leaving!"

"Why don't you wait? It'll all be over right away."

"I can't. Now I have to give every matter much more time than before. I'll see you later. Or another day."

"All right. I'll expect you."

The hammock was left without the sulfurous comrade. Chalena tried to think about the strange things he had heard. He was prevented by the string of shouts that hung in the air:

"Chalena, you son of a bitch, I'm going to see what color your blood is!"

His testicles rose up into his eyes. Octopuses of fear clouded them over. Who? Who could it be? He feverishly tried to identify that voice. In vain. He couldn't locate it in his present. Less in his past. The shouts continued soaking the house with their bitterness.

"Where are you, you bastard? Come out if you've still got a little of the man left in you."

A stranger. An absolute stranger. But then why the certainty of the words? Why such direct hatred and insults? Could he really be a stranger? That was the most probable. Some one of the thousand enemies he had made by chance. That was the major product of his pact with The One We Know. Or could it be someone who wanted to attack Santorontón? Evil tongues had spread the alarming news. Some pirates were pillaging the village. Or could it be a single person? That Ogazno in whom many didn't believe? Others, on the contrary, swore that they had seen him, night after night, dancing on the crest of the waves. In the meantime the aggressive shouts continued approaching. The shouts and the noises. Clearer and clearer the squeaking of small wheels could be heard, in addition to the steps. Or weren't they steps but rather the blows of fists against the ground? He tried to scratch the darkness with his eyes. Nothing. In a little while it wasn't necessary. In front of him, at the foot of the hammock, he had Timoteo

Ruales. He tried to say something. Too late. Now he had him on top of his belly. Timoteo Ruales? The Cripple looked at him with twisting eyes. Screwed into his own eyes. He muttered:

"You?"

"Yes. Me. I've come to drink your blood."

Drink his blood. A bat. Could he have turned into a bat? "Why?"

"Don't play the fool. You know very well why."

Worry-Hurry. Herdbrain-Birdbrain. He tried to look innocent. "Really, Timoteo. I don't know."

The Cripple squeezed his stumps against the bland belly of the biped batrachian.

"Oh, no?"

He repeated the blow. Chalena let out a shriek.

"Ahhh! You're killing me!"

"Not yet."

"What is it you want?"

"Where are Carmen and Tolón?"

He grunted:

"How should I know?"

Another blow made him lose his voice.

"You don't know?"

He sighed.

"Well... I know that they went away."

"Where?"

"Who knows!"

He squeezed his throat. He squeezed it long, intensely. The eyes began to bulge. As much as he tried to take away the Cripple's hands he couldn't. Tong hands. Boa hands. His neck was on fire. He was smothering.

"Aren't you going to tell me?"

Was he dying? Was "that" death? The shadows fought with machetes. The glass teeth of the wind seemed to tear his lungs. Bite his throat. Scratch his nose on the inside. Was that what dying was like? And The One We Know, wasn't he going to do anything? The big bastard, was he going to leave him hanging on his anguish? In the whirlwind, darker and darker, he seemed to see the horrible head with sharp horns and flaming eyes. He guessed more than he heard his words: "Don't you see that I can't, Crisóstomo? We're double-fucked." Still inside he grunted: "Yes, Mr. Dummy. Double-fucked. And you're going to lose another soul. Mine!" The face of the Lord of Shadows contracted. He shed a tear. Of displeasure? Of rage? Of impotence. He leaned his head over and broke into a run, on tiptoes. Disappearing. Almost immediately the voices—outside him now—of Salustiano Caldera and Rugel Banchaca were heard.

"What's going on, Sir?"

"Someone told us you needed help."

"We couldn't see his face."

"We only heard his voice."

"Here we are for whatever we can do."

"Just say the word."

Since he didn't answer they came closer. They saw what was happening. They quickly grabbed Timoteo Ruales. Where they could. The Cripple defended himself like a she-shark in heat. In vain. The men held him, one on each side. They lifted him up. In spite of all, Timoteo managed to give Chalena another blow. In the middle of his legs. If he had been able to coil, the Toad would have made himself a viper standing straight. He couldn't. He remained motionless. In silence. Finally he muttered:

"He was trying to kill me."

The Cripple threatened:

"And I am going to kill you. Toady. Tomorrow. The day after. Someday!"

Chalena didn't answer. With his eyes he was looking for something he couldn't find. Finally he saw it. A harpoon. He got up from the hammock. Took two or three steps. Hesitating. He almost couldn't walk. He felt all in pieces. Outside and inside. Mashed potatoes with feet. He made an effort. He bent over. He picked up the harpoon. In the night the metal of the weapon glowed. Timoteo realized what was happening. The others too. The Cripple shook himself. Useless. The other hands of iron still held him. The Toad raised the weapon. The eyes of the other three opened wide. Salustiano suggested:

"Don't do it, Sir."

And Rugel:

"You'll get in trouble, Sir."

The harpoon. Hands on the harpoon. The toad panted. Could he? Would he have the strength to throw it? He looked at the target. The Cripple. The target. He got set. The three pairs of eyes. Salustiano begged:

"Don Crisóstomo. Don't be a damned fool."

And Rugel:
"That's right! Why scratch an X-Bonetail on its fang?"
Did he hear them? Or didn't he? He threw the weapon. A dull sound was heard. At the same time a moan. The Cripple fell. Chalena went closer. With his two hands he pulled out the weapon. He raised it. Struck again. Raised it. Struck. Raised it. Struck. Finally.
"There!"
Salustiano asked:
"What do we do with him now?"
"We'll bury him."
And Rugel:
"What did the Cripple want?"
A laugh that reached to the eyes was encrusted on the oystered face.
"He was looking for his wife and son."
Salustiano suggested:
"Why don't we throw him into the water instead?"
The Batrachian:
"Really. That way they'd find him all the quicker."
The others fell serious. Thoughtful. The memory of the tremendous image danced in them. After Juvencio had cured Tolón, they'd put him and the Mute into a canoe. A dugout canoe. Without oars. They'd towed it out to the sea lanes of the Gulf. There they'd turned it loose. All that at night. A rainy night. Without heeding the four eyes. Four eyes. Horror turned into tears. The shouting hands. Tolón's intelligible shouts. And the unintelligible ones of the Mute.
Chalena changed his mind.
"No. We won't bury him and we won't throw him into the water. We'll leave him near the little doctor's house."
"What for?"
"Yes. What for?"
He didn't answer. He went on:
"We'll lay the harpoon near him. And tomorrow..."
"Oh, yes...!"
"Yes. Yes!"
"It won't be hard to fix the blame."
"Of course. People saw them get in a boat together."
"Dr. Espurio took Timoteo to see him."
"That's right. And the Cripple was furious with the little doctor."

"We can even accuse him of the disappearance of the Mute and Tolón."

"Nobody would believe it."

"What difference does that make? We'll believe it ourselves. We'll swear to Father Gaudencio. And he..."

"That's it. He..."

"He'll help us in everything, right?"

"How could he not help us?"

THIRTY

The first steps with her support. She was so strong and he was so weak. Was he talking to her? Was he transmitting his desires from one mind to another? Were the shadows and the silence raking his ears, his eyes, and his tongue? Take me to the Christ. You'd better rest a moment. The Christ. He's grown, hasn't he? Who? The Christ. He's become a giant. He fills the room with his open eyes. I mean, he lowers his arms. He crosses walls, mountains, and the sea with them. To embrace the world. Can't you see? No, Juvencio. I see him as he always is. You're wrong. He's grown. A strange force is crackling in his eyes. A germinal force. Can he be coming to life again? Did he ever die? His wounds have become luminous. You do see that, don't you, Clotilde? No, Juvencio. He looks just the same to me. The same as every day, ever since I could see. Take a good look, Clotilde. Christ is burning. He's a torch. A living torch. That's how it must be, Juvencio. That's how it must be.

When Christ noticed it, did he raise his head? Did an affectionate smile flutter on his lips? The doctor made an effort to clarify his phantoms. Gain control over himself. He murmured:

"Thank you, Lord."

The Crucified One's smile seemed to grow broader. Inside himself the doctor heard the Voice.

"Thanks be to you, Juvencio."

He shook his head. As if among dancing clouds, in threads of colors and outlines, he could distinguish the Image. Was it the Nazarene? Was he there? Was he living? Was he dying? Was he dreaming? He reached out his hand. He touched the feet of the Christ. There where the Great Nail made the Flesh bloom.

"Why thanks?"

Again the inner Voice:

"For everything you've done for my people."

Your people? Of course. We're all your people. But these are more mine than yours. More mine. Ever since I was born. There. In the city. At the foot of the swinging docks that walk out on mangroves over the River. The custard apples caracoled their green-black eyes—everything eyes—in lovers' hearts. Along the sea drive—seawall seawall oh my seawall—the carts are pulled to the rhythm of the mules. The tongues of gas dying yellow tongues licked the knives of the shadows giving evidence of doorways. Wrapped in the musical net of the ice-cream vendors and the million steamy vertebrae of seagoing ships. Mine. The ones born like me on the threshold of streets streaked with cacao. Men-river. Men-cacao. To live drowning—blind watchmen toasting on an anchor in the sun—without sinking. In delicate balance. Maybe, maybe not. All yes or no. Is it worth living? Is it worth dying? Is worth worth anything? Is it worth living, Clotilde? I need your calm look. Your hammock shoulder. Your pillow smile. For you to throb in me. I want to breathe with my face sunk in your hair. Or probing your breasts. I want to live in you, Clotilde. I want to travel in you, as in a labyrinth with no exit. Mine.

The dialogue *in mente* went on:

"Which ones are yours?"

"The people of Santorontón. And the lesser beings, with other languages—defenseless for the most part—from the jungle. Especially these last. If it hadn't been for you, they would no longer exist."

"Oh, Christ, Christ, Christ . . . !"

Take me to the sea now, Clotilde. What for? I have to get my canoe. Get back to my house. Go back to work. I can't live on gusts of wind. Juvencio, you shouldn't leave. At this moment your life isn't worth a thing. Crisóstomo's harpoon is lying in wait for you. Espurio's anger-envy. Father Gaudencio's poison. The vengeance of the others. But I can't stay, Clotilde. I can't.

"I can't stay."

"Yes, you can, Juvencio. Stay as long as you want."

"Oh, Jesus, Jesus, Jesus . . . !"

As long as you want. Why wait? Tonight you reach out your hands to stroke my face. My patients need me. I need them too. I came to Santorontón to heal them. And to heal myself. Healing them to heal me. Besides, the city has a thousand mouths waiting to devour me. Walking in it is going on my knees over fangs of stone. Hungry fangs. My clothes—a size too small—spread laughter. My arms and legs showing shamefully out of the sleeves and short pants. From the bleachers of a circus I fell in love with the Ecuyère. The hooves of her violet steed pound on my eyes in the midst of the dust. I don't have the courage to save my eyes. To raise them up toward her winged saddle. Much less rub them on the scanty clothing that girds her body. Why? It would be as if a snail wanted to swing between the wings of a bat. My shell, made out of all abstinences, only allows me to drag myself along the sand—oh, snail, snail, gastropod with a limestone snake on its back. I saw the Ecuyère one single time. Even though I kept slipping in surreptitiously under the canvas of the tent. One single time. She was alone. In her dressing room papered with her posters and pictures. She was alone. Naked. The first naked woman I'd seen in my life. She was combing her hair in front of a mirror. Naked. The loose strings of mammee seed hair on her hips. Naked. Sticking my head—my eyes—in under the canvas. Naked. Later in my dreams and waking hours. At school. At home. In the street. Naked. The Ecuyère. Naked. One single time. Even though my eyes stay on the rug waiting for her to pass. Or, rather, for my own encrusted eyes to pass into the amethyst hooves. I don't dare look at her. Hammocks of illusion stretched from my eyes to the gleaming equine skin. Amethyst equine.

Even though you want to leave, Juvencio, you can't leave me. We need you here too. More than anyone could need you. You're wrong, Clotilde. The Moon is calling me. The Moon and the River. Moons. The Moons. The seven Moons wreathed among the emerald coconut palms. Seven Moons silver shields in the eyes. The Moons. The seven Moons. Then he would rent a bicycle to run between the points of the Moon. Or do acrobatics among the seven Moons. Over the roofs of the city, a trampoline of tiles, getting entangled in the clouds. Or sometimes the string of a kite would shake me. The two automatic wheels—wheeling wings of steel—pulled me out of the enormous circus wheel. The Ecuyère. I wanted to cross the canvas roof held up by the poles. The Ecuyère. I dreamed about her in a circus of froth. I mounted on a rainbow horse. Beside her. At other times I used four stilts—with my four extremities—to pick things up on the Hill. To pick cherries or to steal a hair from the Widow of the Tamarind. With one single hair we could get what we wanted: a purse of gold, an invincible wand, or a plate that was always full. I don't want the gold, or the wand, or the plate. I want only the Ecuyère. With her top hat. Her minimal red velvet costume. Or, still better, without hat or clothes. Naked. As I saw her the only time I saw her. To keep her in a coffer under seven keys. When I go to school. Or take her at night to go along the River. The River that engenders two rivers on the banks of the Hill. There where Orellana looks at himself. Preparing for his leap across the Andes. To find the largest of all rivers. Captain Orellana living bridge joining the enormous fluvial currents. The Bearded Patriarch who with a Gulf mouth links the Pacific and the Boa Constrictor with billions and billions of blue scales that sinks its liquid teeth into the very lungs of the Atlantic. The Ecuyère. The Ecuyère who went away with the circus. Who lasted as long as the canvas raised with ropes and poles lasted. She left along with the three proboscids sick with spleen. With sleepwalking lions and tigers. With clowns colonies of amoebas or Koch bacilli, made of plaster, cardboard, and agony. With two trapeze artists hanging from the dream. With a tightrope walker who traveled with two coffins, foreseeing a death that would slice him in two. With three jugglers who had the secret of creating seven agile fingers on each hand. With seven blue and red horses. And one single amethyst horse for the Ecuyère. The Ecuyère who went on. Who went on galloping. Galloping in my eyes. In my eyes during a childhood that was spread out. Spread out like a casting net. Like a casting net in an inlet. In inlets sown by the great mullein. The great mullein of fatal yellow.

"You'd best come back to the deerskin, Juvencio."

"I'd best leave, Clotilde."

"You're weak. Rest."

"I'll rest at home. You'll come see me when you can."

"You couldn't get to the shore. Much less paddle. Even less buck the current. And the men are following you. They don't just want to kill you. They want to ruin you. Make you out a murderer. They accuse you of the death of Ruales. They've already invented witnesses, motives, actions. And if not, they'll invent another death. Or maybe something just the same or worse. No one can tell what they're plotting. Or how they're putting it all together. Or what kind of idea they're working up to get rid of you. And make you see stars with your eyes behind you!"

"That's all in your imagination, Clotilde."

She paid no attention, went on:

"Besides, the whole village is nervous. You don't know because you haven't been aware of anything these past few days. You were in such bad shape! Completely unconscious! But tomorrow Colonel Candelario Mariscal is getting married. He's getting married, legally and properly, to Dominga, the daughter of the witch doctor Bulu-Bulu."

He reacted.

"Tomorrow?"

"Yes. Tomorrow."

"Then all the more reason for me to leave. I have to prevent that wedding."

"You too?"

"Yes. Me. Me too."

"Why, Juvencio?"

"Because... because I have to."

I have to stop that wedding. Candelario Mariscal has to marry you. Why? He was the one who made you a woman, wasn't he? No one's made me a woman, yet. But... Even if he were the only man on earth. Even if I were melting away with the desire to have a man, never would I link up with him! You mean it doesn't bother you for him to marry someone else? Me, why?

Oh. And doesn't it bother you? Not me either. Why should it bother me? But it does. I've got to stop that wedding. I've got to stop it.

When Gaudencio reached Santorontón, he had a surprise. On the shore, like a swarm of furious moquiñañas were the female Santorontonians waiting for him. Ña Prudencia was still their captain. As soon as the canoe approached they surrounded him. They seemed to be questioning him with their whole bodies. With their twisted mouths. Their anxious eyes. With their tense gestures and expressions. The words wrapped him up in hundred-stringed knots that kept tying him up. He tried to talk. He couldn't. He was surrounded by chains of shouts that grew in the thick night.

"What happened, Father?"

"Did you see Bulu-Bulu?"

"Did you convince Crisanta?"

"Did you put fear into Minga?"

"Is the wedding off?"

"How did they react?"

"What did they finally tell you?"

What did they tell me? What could they have told me? Would he tell the truth to those furious women? Would they believe him? Even if they believed him, what difference would it make? He knew that when they discovered the results of his mission the only thing that would send them into convulsions was the fact that he had failed. Knowing that the wedding of the Colonel to the daughter of the Wizard was going to take place in any case. All the women in the village—against their wills—would have to go to church. They would have to put on their best clothes to attend the rites of the sumptuous ecclesiastical ceremony. Because, needless to say, it would have to be sumptuous. I'll put on some of the spectacular vestments I've kept in the bottom of my trunk for great occasions. The Colonel had said nothing to him. He doesn't have to tell me. After all, it's a memorable occasion for me and for the church. I'm not going to let it pass just like that. Even if the Colonel doesn't pay me I'll have to do it in the best form possible. He already knew the temper of the blessed—blessed?—military man. Besides, he'd probably pay something. Pay splendidly. Who knows but that he'd pay better than anyone else. Didn't they say he's robbed so much? Even though a lot of people assert that he hasn't got anything left, that's to be seen. Money is sticky, like the pulp of a star apple. Even if a person doesn't want it, it sticks to his fingers. Don't let them come to me with tales. Money is money. In Santorontón the same as anywhere else. So? The women of Santorontón would have to resign themselves. He, for his part, would resign himself to listening to them. Of course, he would try to calm them down a little. Not with words of consolation. That wouldn't get any results. Rather, with tactics. With a little malice. The least of all evils. Let those women do what they would. Say what they would, that's their lookout! I have to fulfill my holy ministry. *Ubi bene ibi patria*. No. Not that. The Burned Christ might be listening. Nobody knew at what moment he might decide to appear. Better *Sursum corda*. *Sursum corda*. Too bad he couldn't say it to the Santorontonian women. But why not? Why not?

"*Sursum corda!*"

They looked at each other, disconcerted. Was he in his right mind? What could he be trying to tell them with that? Was there something in those words that was an answer for them? Why was he talking to them in a different language? In a chorus:

"What?"

"*Sursum corda!* Lift up your hearts!"

Ña Prudencia made a signal for the others to be quiet.

"We've got them lifted way up, Father Gaudencio."

"How glad I am to hear it, my daughters."

The women showed signs of impatience. This was going on too long. What was the reverend father up to? Was he trying to trick them maybe? Or had the Witch Doctor—with his seventy-seven wiles—wrapped him up and held him dancing in the palm of his hand? They shouted again, mingling their voices:

"Tell us now what happened, Father."

"Don't keep us wondering like this."

"Did you convince the Witch Doctor and his family?"

"Is the wedding off?"

"Please tell us something, Reverend Father!"

Gaudencio raised his arms solemnly. They all fell silent. Then he made the Sign of the Cross. The women imitated him. He knelt. They likewise. Filemón intoned a Hosanna to himself. He thought, he's got them convinced now. That was the way he always did it. When he had them calmed down, he would tell them what he had to tell them. He knew him quite well. In order to manage his sheep, as he called them, and to get money out of his neighbor, there was nobody like him. Otherwise, the man had his merits. For example, he abstained from the sins of the flesh. And sometimes he would assert: "That's what hurts me most, Filemón. I like—forgive me, Lord!—I used to like women very much. And I keep on liking them—forgive me again, Lord, but it's the truth!—I close my eyes so they can pass without my seeing them." The sin of gluttony, yes, he couldn't conquer that. "It's all I've got left, Filemón. Eating. Everything else is forbidden me. Eating." It was the only thing that could be done there. Eating: Crabs—strings of coral. Oysters—blue-black diamonds. Shrimp—curled rose petals. He was also a little proud. "Why shouldn't I be proud, Filemón, in the midst of such humble and backward people? I'm a high-class man. My destiny is to be a prince. A prince of the Church, at least." Filemón—a juggling act of erect bones—looked at him with the greatest attention. He already had them reciting the Rosary. They were accompanying him against their will. With their knees ground into the sand. As if they were a gathering of turtles laying their eggs on the beach. When one Hail Mary was finished, another began immediately.

Ña Prudencia could stand no more. Between one prayer and another, she stood up and roared:

"But, Father Gaudencio..."

They were being bitten by the cold. The rage. The confusion. They began to get a vague idea that the priest was fooling them. But what could they say? What could they do? He was their beloved Father Gaudencio. The Shepherd of their souls. The one who knew—inside the confessional and out—all their secrets. Since he was already starting.

"Hail Mary..."

Before the chorus could follow him, she interrupted, furious:

"Don't you think that's enough already?"

The Priest, imperturbable, signaled her to be silent and went on:

"...full of grace..."

When the last prayer was over, the women of Santorontón were defeated. Deeper and deeper they felt the damp little teeth of the sand on the skin of their knees. The guffawing cold of the sea gave them salty tickles on the back of the neck. From time to time, the Southeaster—with its combs full of needles—scratched their skulls. Or their long hair was threatened as bat wings pulled it out. The great majority prayed in a monotone. From inertia. The same as canoes slip along when the paddle pushes them.

They no longer had the slightest notion of what they were doing. What they yearned for was bed. Rest. The tight heat of their men. Sleep. On the other hand, some, within themselves, began to repent the long hard hours. The attitude assumed. The acts committed. They even began to curse Jovita, Prudencia, and the other leaders. After all, Dominga's backside belonged to her. She could do with it whatever came out from inside her. If she wanted to hand it over proper and legal to Colonel Mariscal, and if he was fighting for the Priest's blessing, what did it matter to them? It was their business. In a certain way they were evenly matched. Why did the women of Santorontón have to tear their veils at that funeral? Besides, if Candelario found out that they'd been against him, he'd never forgive them. They imagined seeing him with his air of fuck-me-fuck-yourself. Dusting off the machete and the carbine that he certainly had sleeping since the time he was up in arms. Who would dare confront him? None of their men, no doubt about it. Maybe some of them, the women, would have the will to do so. But how? The only things they could manipulate a little were pots and pans. A few fishing tools: the harpoon, the gaff, the hook. Was that enough to do battle against Colonel Candelario Mariscal? Just thinking about it was enough to make their guts burst out laughing. Besides, what was the object? They knew that he'd keep his promise. He'd have lunch on all of them and turn Santorontón into a cemetery. Besides, the one who'd got them into that kettle of fish was acting like Captain Spider. She'd sent them off on a badly tied raft to provoke the crocodile with open jaws. And she'd stayed on dry land. Could that be why a lot of people didn't called her Jovita, but Jodita, Madam Fuck-You? Well, why hadn't they thought about that before? Why had they let themselves be sweet-talked by Espurio's wife? That might have been all right before. When the doctor-gravedigger was the only one in his respective trade. Now there was a new doctor: Juvencio. A new undertaker: Father Gaudencio. About the one—from the cures he'd effected in people and animals—they had the certainty that he was superior as a physician. About the other, how could they doubt that his cemetery was sanctified? In any case, it was too late to repent. In the future—if there was to be a future—they would have to tread carefully. Who knows, maybe Jovita and her husband had a deal to get all the families of Santorontón caught in that trap of shadows! In that way they were probably in complete agreement with the

Colonel. He would supply the corpses and pay them for the burials. Wasn't that why he'd sent Ña Crisanta to tell them? In all truth, why hadn't they thought of that before? Why did they let the wife of the doctor-gravedigger fog their eyes? Maybe the best thing would be to leave right away. Not even wait for Father Gaudencio to give them the results of his mission. The less compromised they were the better the chance of saving themselves. Or maybe they could ask him to perform the wedding. Forget what they'd asked him during the late hours of that night. They exaggerated their transformation. They thought that such a wedding would be a great festival for the village. They would have a wonderful time. Who knows, there might even be a dance. Food. Drink. And all the rest...

Gaudencio's voice interrupted their meditations.

"Well, then, my dear children."

The Chorus—with few tones of anxiety or interest and many of boredom or displeasure—inquired:

"What?"

He put on the face of a martyr.

"I wasn't able to do anything with the Witch Doctor and his family."

This time there was synchronization in the Chorus. The interest was common.

"No?"

"No, my dear children. As hard as I tried, I couldn't reach Balumba!"

THIRTY-ONE

Every day at dawn José Isabel Lindajón would look at the sky. Up above, the clouds seemed to be hitting with their cottony fists. They came from the Gulf. They started out golden from the kiss of the young Sun. Then they turned gray. And last they became almost black. They pushed each other, afterward, until they settled over the jungle at whose feet Santorontón lay. It's going to rain today. Today it shall rain. And it's going to screw up the bog. We still have a piece to cover up. The earth in the wells isn't dry. Why did we beat ourselves to death working so hard? Our efforts will be useless. A cloudburst's going to fall at any moment now. And Candanga will carry everything off. But the day would pass. People kept working in a frenzy until late at night. The low storm clouds, almost entangled among the branches of the trees, marched off. Or scattered. Disappearing.

"It didn't rain, did it, doc?"

"That's right, José Isabel. It didn't rain."

"Let's see about tomorrow."

"Let's see."

On the following day, the same thing took place. José Isabel with his anxiety as sentinel got up even earlier. His eyes, accustomed to harpooning the shadows, tried to pierce the unborn dawn. They wanted to discover—guess, rather—the route of the clouds. In view of the failure of his effort, the anxiety took root even deeper in his spirit. As for today, now it's going to rain. And we've still got only a little more to go. It's probably a question of two or three more days. To finish raising the palisade. To make the thick wall. Will the wall hold? It has to hold. We've raised a wall that looks like the base of another mountain. Of course, we were only able to do it because the animals helped us. All of them. Especially the monkeys and the bats.

"When the water fills the bog, won't everything come down?"

"I don't think so, José Isabel. And don't you be thinking so. It would be horrible."

"Why, doc?"

"Can you imagine that mass of water falling on the village? It would be like a mountain coming down on us."

"Oh, goddamn! I hadn't thought of that."

Days and more days passed. The wall was now being finished. It was finished. It was already drying out. It was dried out. Soon the rains returned. Torrential rains that sowed the slopes with gullies. Indian summer was giving out its last mouthfuls. They were all smiling in the jungle. And the great majority in Santorontón. The laugh of the monkeys was easy to observe. The other laughs—those of bats, jaguars, ocelots, badgers, deer, colemba birds, squirrels, snakes, etc.—more difficult. With all that, José Lindajón was sure: the animals were bedecking every leaf on the trees with laughter. Why shouldn't they be happy—dying with laughter—when they saw they wouldn't be lacking water? They won't have to depend on puddles or wells anymore. And even less, much less on stealing water from Don Chalena. Don Chalena! That idiot was going to rot with rage. His guts a handful of raging worms will want to come out of his mouth. What could that son of a bitch have thought? That he was going to get his way?

"Now Don Crisóstomo is going to see how it feels when the rest aren't thirsty."

"Especially since it's no longer in his hands to take thirst away or not."

"Others must be like scorpions on a hot stove too. Sticking their own poison into themselves."

Juvencio looked at him with attention. He seemed to be dancing a peek-a-boo dance. His body was moving to the rhythm of his words.

"Your tongue's running away with you, José Isabel. Better still, your whole body's running away with you."

He didn't make any comment. He went on:

"...like old open-fly-face Dr. Espurio."

"Really, did you eat a parrot's tongue for breakfast?"

This time he looked at him. Affectionately. He smiled.

"No, doc. I'm swimming in my skin. I'm happy. Why shouldn't I be? Now that we don't have to give up anything to be able to use the water we want. Even shame is ours again, doc."

"What do you mean by that?"

"Before, our shame wasn't our own, it belonged to Don Chalena."

He began to peep over the edge of the dam every hour. At first the thirsty teeth of the bottom drank in the water of the initial cloudbursts with long swallows. Goddamn it! Is the bog going to suck up all the water? We should have had more time to lay a lot of stones. Or even banks of palisades. Now what are we going to do? Panic began to get hold of him. He came down a sack of disconnected bones. Will gone. Spirit gone. Almost unaware of anything. Nothing had been worth it. In the end they were going to be fucked up just as much as before. Maybe more. Now Chalena would turn the screws even tighter.

"The bog's not going to work, doc."

"Be patient, José Isabel."

"Look. Several cloudbursts have already fallen. And all the water goes to the bottom. The bog is never going to fill up."

"You'll see that it will."

"How can it fill up! The One Whose Name Isn't Spoken has been helping Toad Face again. We should have expected it. That's the way everything's always been here. The one who holds the frying pan is the one who fries the mullet, doc."

"You're wrong. It's going to be different now. Be patient."

On the following day he went back to the banks of the reservoir. Anxiety made him walk on air. Just as if he were trying to avoid tacks laid point up. He was almost flying. The bog would probably be even drier. Maybe the only thing it was going to be good for was breeding mosquitoes. So there'd be more cracked-land laughter in the summer. Or at best, so an impassable mud swamp would appear. Everything in vain, then! When he looked over the dam he gave a leap of joy. It was already beginning to fill up. It could be seen—a growing mirror—there at the bottom. And the more it rained, the more it grew in size. Soon it reached the highest levels. Soon it began to overflow. The long-haired trees with their imploring arms seemed to be bathing upside down on the enormous surface. The sides of the hills were dressed in dynamic liquid tunics. And the small grasses stood on end so as not to miss the spectacle.

"You were right, doc. We're going to have water until the end of summer."

"Maybe even until next winter, José Isabel."

"Don Chalena's not going to screw us anymore."

"Not Chalena, not anybody."

Chalena had begun to see crosses. Crosses. Crosses, everywhere. Superimposed on all things. And on all beings. Not church Crosses, with the Christ nailed to them. No. Little crosses. The kind that bloom on graves. As if the horizon that his eyes dominated were one enormous cemetery. Goddamn them. They'll pay me back. I've still got ways to screw them, even though my Partner has abandoned me. And what if he hasn't abandoned me? If he's only waiting for a chance to help me? How can he lose a lot of souls—mine and those of the people with me—just to give himself the pleasure of setting me adrift? He has to help me. And if not, I'll take care of things alone. Of course things are looking dark as ants. You might say that everything is turning its back on me. Everything and everybody. Even those ass-kissing bastards who say they're on my side. But I'll get them yet—them too—backward and forward. Always crosses. On the line of his eyes, eyelids, eyesockets. Over his mouth—he was already almost all mouth—always crosses. Was that to be his fate? In the end would he be left with that long perspective of crosses as his path? Sir, we came. Yes, we came to tell you. Sir. The Santorontonians are getting bolder. They don't pay any attention to us, Sir.

"They even refuse to pay their debts."

He sat up. He could still sit up. His belly and his mouth—made into a single thing—looked like a rolled up and erect mattress. Erect?

"Oh! It's you people."

Salustiano Caldera and Rugel Banchaca were disconcerted. All their authority—as Political Lieutenant and Chief of the Rural Guard respectively—hung suspended like fallen hands. Hairy snakes. They didn't dare look at the Toad-toady-toadstool.

"Yes, Don Chalena."

"Us."

"We don't know what to do with the Santorontonians."

"They don't even take us seriously."
"They laugh in our faces."
"We would have arrested them."
"Or punished them."
"But there's a lot of them."
"The whole village."
"Even the rural guards refuse to obey us."
"We're fucked up, Sir."
"Double-fucked."

Fools. They weren't. They were born that way. Double-fucked. If my belly didn't bother me so much. If my mouth didn't weigh as much as my belly. I'd go collect from them myself. They'd have to pay me. In one way or another. You'd see. But I'm more belly and more mouth than myself. I'm a man stuck to a belly. I can hardly get around. Can't you see? And are the Santorontonians really going to stop paying? What then? What's going to happen to my money then? My pretty little money! Am I going to lose my money? My pretty little money! No! Not that! I'll go on my knees and beg them to pay me. I'll do anything for them to give me what's mine. Get a hold of yourself, Crisóstomo! Watch out, you're going to burst into tears here over your money. What'll that get you? Besides, what are they going to pay you for? Why should they pay you if they no longer have the spectre of water tickling their bodies? No longer feel the stabs of sand cracking their throats. Or the sandpaper fire burning their lips. They wouldn't have the fear of drying out like plantains on the beach either. Without doubt the women would stick their tongues out at him now. Or throw urine in his face. If they didn't turn their dogs loose on him. Hit him. Throw a few stones. Or fulfill a threat they made to him a certain day. "We're going to strip you naked, Mister. We're going to daub your whole body with moquiñaña honey. And then we're going to tie you to a stake in the center of the square. So that the dogs can start licking you and the gnats and mosquitoes can finish it off biting you." Toad-toady-toadstool, he began to hear—inside his mouth, inside his belly—the humiliating tolling of the bells. Hurry-Hurry. Hurry-Worry. Herdbrain-Herdbrain. Birdbrain-Birdbrain.

"So, Sir. What do you want us to do?"
"Can we still do something?"

He looked at them. They seemed imprisoned in a jail that had nothing but crosses instead of bars. How funny they looked! Suddenly he no longer saw them standing but lying down. Lying down—six feet under the earth—pale. Motionless. With a cross on top. Were they dead? No? Yes? How funny! He looked a little beyond. And the vision was multiplied. It wasn't only Salustiano and Rugel who were under the ground any longer. It was all the people of Santorontón. Quiet. Stretched out. Always with a cross on top. The laughter made waves on his stomach. It was a minimal laugh. That of a happy rat. Rocked in a cradle by two cats. Heeheehee. Heeheehee!

"We have to do something."

"But what, Sir?"

"But what?"

"Anything."

"What if we can't do anything?"

"They're even capable of beating us up."

He meditated for a few seconds. He underwent a sudden change.

"Then let's wait. A little. Their turn will pass. Soon it will be ours. We'll have the last laugh."

"That's the way it will be, Sir."

"That's the way it will be."

"Of course that's the way it will be."

The others—worried—left. He saw them—through the crosses of the first row—walking among the other crosses. With all the Santorontonians lying there. He felt a weight by his side. Could his belly have hung up on him? No. The familiar smell of sulfur reached him on the hammock. Could it be The One We Know?

Hours later—at Sundown the silver tambourine Moon came out—the Santorontonians held a meeting. In the square. In front of the church. They had—in spite of the growing bog—their souls hanging on a thread. Comments boiled in them like crabs being cooked alive. They rose up in unison. Almost without individual identities. The same as if they all had a single voice. Or the dialogue generated a monologue. A monologue made up of the different vertebrae of different beings, which kept threading together and unthreading. Goddamn it! Did you people see what we saw? Who hadn't seen it in the village? The way Don Crisóstomo was flying! No? He was flying without wings. Like a ball that had just been kicked. In what other way could the Bastard fly? He had to have been kicked in the belly. With a kick or with wings—or, who knows with what!—what's certain is that The Cursed One had lifted him up. I thought he'd left here for good. Me too. And me. And me. And me. We all thought so. Especially because of the bog. Of course. Finishing the bog must have brought on black vomit in him. Or at least drool. That's it, drool! Drool in lots of colors. No, black drool. And yet he came back. But before that he fell into a canoe. Aha! With four oars. The damned thing was waiting for him in midstream. How strange! No? Nobody had seen it before. Or did it pop up from the bottom? Or could it have been something else? What? The canoe. Wasn't the canoe a canoe? Who knows! What was it, then? God only knows! Maybe a huge turtle. As big as a canoe? There are some even bigger. What about the oars? What dumb oars? They were probably the turtle's legs. What's certain is that Toad-Belly... Toad-Belly? You mean Belly-Toad. Or Belly-Belly. That's it. Belly-Belly came back. More trouble! He should have fallen into the water. And not shown his nose around here again. Nose? He hasn't got a nose. He's got a belly. All right, belly. He shouldn't have shown his belly around here again. The strange thing is that he didn't come the way he went. That's certain, isn't it? He was hugging something. True, what could it have been? Who knows! It must be something bad. Of course. How could it be anything good if Chalena was bringing it? Could it be poison to throw into the bog? Or dynamite to blow it up? Could The One We Know have given it to him? Who else? That's it. Who else?

THIRTY-TWO

From the top of the hill he looked down at the village. The lights blinked strings of fire beetles. What could the Santorontonians be doing? He felt like spitting down on them. A barrage of spit. Spit that would bathe them in fear because it came from him. Maybe there wasn't a single one—of those who were still awake—who wasn't thinking about him at that instant. As for the sleeping ones, they were most likely suffering him in their dreams. All, without doubt, thought it couldn't be true that he—Colonel Candelario Mariscal—was going to stretch his legs, from thence forward, with only one female. Especially, blessed by a priest. And in Father Gaudencio's reinforced concrete church no less. His teeth made music with his impulse to laugh. Dummies! They don't want to realize—or do they and that's why there's a full wind on the poop?—that I would have ground them to shit if they'd tried to stop me. I'd take out my snoring machete—I've still got it sleeping under the mattress—and write my name in blood on all their bellies. It would have been good, Colonel. You're probably missing a funny sight. Maybe you'd have a better time debellying them than you're going to have tomorrow with Dominga. Dominga? A good time with Dominga? Don't play the sly fox, Candelario. It's got nothing to do with Dominga. If Chepa—the damned dead woman—hadn't been squeezing you night after night, you never would have seen Bulu-Bulu. And much less take his "medicine." So what more do you want? If his medicine cures you and is good, what more do you want? And it's the honest-to-

God truth that Dominga—Dominga-medicine—would even light the candle of a corpse. With her you won't have the urge to give pleasure to the seven. And with living flesh. Not with one who comes from out of the earth to see you. Give thanks to Heaven—to Heaven, Mr. Dummy?—for having put Bulu-Bulu in the middle of your path. Do you realize what it's like living always tied to a dead woman? To have to stir up her custard apple without any rest? And tonight? Will you have a visit from her tonight? Maybe she knows it all. The dead know everything. Maybe she's already coming on the wind to rub you between the legs. She'll try to concentrate all her urges. To squeeze out the last juice you've got left. So that you won't be able to do it even a single time with Dominga tomorrow. Or will the dead woman be satisfied with that? Won't she want to freeze my balls with her graveyard kisses, like other times? Will she leave my deal like the dry skin of a snake after shedding? Will everything be for pleasure? Will things be what they were before again? If it's like that, I'll ruin the Witch Doctor Bulu-Bulu. I'll blindfold his eyes for good with a pair of shots. I'll knit his hide with the tip of my machete. What if the Wizard turns into a lot of Wizards? If you have to fight with fifty, a hundred, or more at the same time? If before you touch him he divides up into several parts? If each one of those parts—body, arms, legs, and head—attacks you separately? You know, Candelario. Grappling with a Witch Doctor isn't the same as fighting with anybody else. While you hit him on the head—or on one of his multiple heads—he can turn you into a sieve with his teeth, his fingernails, his blows. Besides, what if it's true that he hoards a lot of lives? If you finish off one, won't you have to face a lot of others? Of course, if he turns into a jaguar, you can turn into a jaguar. If he's a bat or a crocodile, you're a bat or a crocodile. And if an X-Bonetail, an X-Bonetail you too. That's what you were born for. And in the end? What would be the end of so much fighting? Would Bulu-Bulu still have his way? I don't think so. You don't think so, Mr. Dummy? No. I don't think so. Not even a Wizard can ever win over me. The only one who can defeat me is my godfather. He and his Burned Christ. I'll never fight with them. The rest of them I'll stick where the sun never shines on me. The Witch Doctor too? Why not? They can't beat me on these things. That's why I am who I am. And really, who are you? They all say you're the son of Old Longtail. Can it be true that my father is Old Longtail? Goddamned Longtail. Goddamned Devil. Because he's a bastard. If he weren't he wouldn't have left me at the door of the church. Where my godfather found me. Besides, he would have come looking for me one day. He wouldn't have allowed what's happening to me with Chepa. Or did he send her himself so she could give me pleasure all the time? He probably thought that in that way I wouldn't have any more problems with females. One alone would go to bed with me, for life. One alone. For life. And dead. When the catfighting was over she'd go off without causing me any harm. To bury herself again. Six feet under, in "The Fireflies." Goddamn it! But the honey has already reached up to my neck. That bottom clogs me all over my body. Just seeing her makes me curl up down to my bones. Why, if my father is the Soul-Swallower, doesn't he realize that I'm tired of getting into her? Why doesn't he take her off to sharpen other harpoons? No! I don't believe that I'm the product of Old Longtail! Old Longtail and a mule, as they say. Or that Father Cándido is my father as other tongues let on. He's only my godfather. Why do they think that way? You think he's incapable of having children. Not that. Father Cándido is very much a man. As much a man as any Santorontonian. It's something else. When he became a priest he tied up his you know what. And even if he wanted to untie it sometimes, he can handle it! That knot is good for him. Otherwise these islands would be populated with Mariscals. Who knows, maybe they'd stand teat to teat all the way to the Gulf. Of course my godfather is very much a man! I've seen his eyes light up when a female approaches. He can handle it! He closes his eyes. Clenches his fists. And he certainly prays. He can handle it! Or maybe he insults himself for having become a priest. Or for having tied such a strong and bitter knot. And that—among other things—is the goodness that my godfather has. He can handle it! Why shouldn't he like bottoms? He can handle it! He's woven himself an invisible net that holds him with its sinkers and cords. No. I don't think my godfather is my father. Even though I love him as if he were. He's the only light I've got inside. Oh! If only he understood me! If he hadn't thrown me out of his house! If he hadn't thought that I burned down his church just for fun! Everything would have been so different! Really, Candelario? Aren't you fooling yourself? Aren't you trying to fool yourself? And your insides a nest of scorpions, wasps, and worms? You did what you did because you were less man than crocodile. Now you've calmed down because Colonel Moncada knocked down your coconuts. Because the years are making you soft, termite-ridden, a rotten log. And especially because the dead woman has been hanging from your balls. If not, even if you went on changing the places that you mark with your footsteps into insane asylums and cemeteries. Here I am, Candelario. Nothing could hold you back. Here I am. Or can it be true that your father—if it's true that your father is the one of the Seven Seven-Thousand Horns—was using you to send more souls to the Seven Seven-Thousand Hells? Then haven't you done everything you've done? Was it the Green-Red-Soul-Swallower—green sulfur, red flame—who did it? Was it the hand of the Fuck-Yourselves-Everybody-Here-I-Am that pushed your hand to burn the church, soak the Quindales in their own blood, spread rapine and death over land and sea? I've come, Candelario. Don't you see me? Then you're not guilty, it's The Other One? Dummy, a thousand times Dummy. What difference does it make if the Soul-Swallower pushed your hand or not? Whether you did it by your own volition or not? It was all the same. He'd done it. Candelario. Candelario. Don't you see me? Was he repenting? Did it hurt him to be the son-of-a-mule that he was? It was all the same. Hurry up, Candelario! It's getting late for us. It was all the same. We can't lose time, Candelario. Hurry up! It was all. You've fallen asleep with your eyes open. All. Candelario. What's wrong, Candelario? All. I'm coming with more desire than ever. Hurry up!

The Dead Woman was before him. In the raw. As always. What a fine female! In spite of his knowing that she was dead, he felt his fly bulging. Only because he was so convinced, he couldn't stop from being convinced. Good and dead, goddamn it. Good and dead, damn her. Six feet—or would it be more or less—under the earth. Maybe nothing but bones now. And really, how could she put flesh on top of them? Firm flesh. Flesh like the best that any woman ever had. Good and dead. There. In "The Fireflies." Mourned by her first husband. Casimiro Caliche. —He, Candelario Mariscal, was he her second husband?— Good and dead. And yet there she was. Standing. Before him. Mammee teats. Festival hips. Before him. Looking at him. The eyes. The eyes the eyes the eyes. Slashing muyuyo seeds. Digging in with return-trip hooks. The same way fish hooks attach themselves. Warm as a brazier brick. Yes. How good the Late Lady was, his late lady! Would it be better if he backed off and stopped this marriage to Dominga? If he went to Gaudencio right off and asked him to cancel it all? Or not say anything to anybody and leave Santorontón? Chepa would look for him wherever he went. Everything is easy for the dead. And pleasure only wants to get more pleasure. On the following day nobody would know anything. Except that he'd vanished like smoke one more time. Even the Witch Doctor would think that he'd gone off with Himself. Caught up in his seven thousand horns. Or his seven thousand tails. It would be the best thing indeed! Why should he look beyond Chepa for what he had there night after night? Yes. It would be the best, but...But what? He was already tired of the same thing. He wanted to try some new clams. Especially a living woman's clam. Oh, what damned fools men can be! They want to look outside for dark conches when they already have one sizzling on the fire! Oh, what damned fools we are, Candelario! What damned fools!

"Hurry up, Candelario!"

"Of course, Chepa."

"The night isn't going to last the rest of our lives."

"That's right, Chepa. That's right."

As if to test, one more time, that she was throbbing, he touched her. The skin stiffened him. A wave of needles danced in his body. His little hammock teeth. His algae froth blood growing inside him. Chepa smiled.

"Am I still good?"

"More than ever."

"So..."

"What?"

"Jump to!"

Jumpy-jumpy-jumpy-jumpy. Jumpy-jumpy-jumpy-jumpy. Jumpy-jumpy-jumpy-jumpy. And to think there were times—so many years ago—when he could have been content just to be near her. Taking off her clothes, one by one, just to satisfy the hunger of his eyes, his nose, his hands. Just having her close by. Now, on the other hand, a hairy sea. A sea of flesh on which he sailed without respite. Crest after crest rocking him. He, all paddle.

Paddle of blinking spasms. Salty eyelashes running over his body. Stretching out along his fingers. In his mouth. In the screw he was screwing in. Blooming with light and shadow. Life and death. Damned Dead Woman. Dead woman damned. Was she dead? Could she be so alive being dead? So alive and so good. So damned good. Jumpy-jumpy-jumpy-jumpy. Jumpy-jumpy-jumpy-jumpy. Once. Again. How many times?

"Jump to."

"Yes."

"More."

"Yes."

Jumpy-jumpy-jumpy-jumpy. Jumpy . . . jumpy . . . jumpy . . . jumpy . . .

"Are you tired?"

"No."

"So?"

"Nothing."

Jumpy-jumpy-jumpy-jumpy.

Jumpy-jumpy-jumpy...

Jumpy-jumpy...

Jumpy...

"Jump to, more!"

"Wait!"

"Why?"

In order to say something, he asked:

"Don't you want... a drink?"

"Me? No. What for?"

"Well, I do. I'm going to have one!"

He got up. Went to get the cane liquor—mule-killer. He raised the bottle. Took a few long swigs.

The Dead Woman sat up. Hot-coal-eyes followed his movements. She snorted:

"Come on, Candelario. Don't give me any of your damned foolishness."

"Huh, what?"

"Do I have the face of a Crab-in-fresh-water?"

"I don't know what you're gabbing about."

Chepa sat down. Sparks. All of her nothing but sparks.

"Do you think you're going to fog my eyes? Don't be so well-uh-now, man. I'm way ahead of you."

Rage continued to light her up. She added:

"You bastard! What you're doing is trying to keep what you've got left for Minga!"

Candelario held back. He admonished her:

"Mullet won't enter a blocked inlet, Chepa."

The Dead Woman stood up. She got off the mattress. She showed her teeth, insulting:

"Hahaha! Hahaha! Back there in 'The Fireflies,' where I'm under the ground, nobody threatens me. Not sharks, not jaguars. Besides, why are you getting so nasty? Not even the fire-shit ants are after you."

"Don't you have the fire-shits under your belly button?"

"Keep on playing the innocent! You know damned well that I know everything!"

He became a little edgy.

"And what is it you know?"

"Everything. So as not to fool around with me anymore you went to see Bulu-Bulu. He told you that to get rid of the dead woman the best thing was a living one. And he wrapped up Dominga for you. You've convinced the whole village—even Gaudencio the priest—that you have to get married. Isn't that how it is?"

He showed his teeth. From rage? From laughter. He showed his teeth. Just in case, he said evasively:

"What the dead don't know, eh?"

The Dead Woman looked at him with disdain. She came closer. Dead Woman. Dead Woman in flames. Was her skin burning? Was she going to burn him? Chirigua torch. Or was it tucuma? Tucuma torch? Torch. Yes. It was tucuma wood. Tucuma torch. Tucuma to make marimba keys. Or wooden harpoons. Tucuma torch. Did he touch her? Did he jump on top of her again in order to calm her? Did he pound her fuzzy crab again? Nothing would calm her. Nothing would cool her off. She was made of a torch. What if she burned. Careful, Candelario! You might turn to carbon! How could you do your duty to Dominga then? How could you present yourself in church? Burned. Black. Crisp. Carbon. They'd all make fun of you. Make fun? Not that. You'd pull out your machete and make them—from Crisóstomo to Gaudencio—dance like a curiquingue hawk. To make them all pay you, you'd order them to take off their pants. And you'd watch them dance clean-assed. Clean-assed. That's all you needed. For the Dead Woman in flames to burn you! The Dead Woman–Candle. Candle-Sea. Candle-Land. Candle-River. Candelario.

"Candelario. You're worse every day."

"Stop bothering me."

"Do you think you're going to mount Dominga?"

He couldn't stand any more.

"Of course I am, goddamn it. Why not?"

"Hahaha. Hahaha. Don't make me laugh, you son of a guava."

"Laugh all you want. It doesn't bother me."

"You'll see tomorrow what kind of laugh comes out of my little place."

"Really and truly?"

She paid no attention. She went on:

"I'll let you go to the church. Be blessed by the Priest. Be married. Have your lively party with everybody in the village there. Come to this house. Let the two of you—Dominga and you—get stripped. Let you hug. Let you do everything you want at the hour of hours. Except..."

"Except... what?"

"You know what."

The Colonel felt himself boiling. He kept himself under control. His voice filled with mockery. He repeated:

"Really and truly?"

Chepa didn't notice—or refused to notice—the tone. She went to the door. There she turned.

"If you want, I'll tear your balls off right now, with my teeth. What for? I'll lend them to you. Until tomorrow. They can keep hanging on you. Until tomorrow night. So Dominga can have fun touching them. Touching them on you. Because that's the only pleasure she'll be able to have."

Candelario couldn't stand it any longer. He advanced toward her. He grabbed her arm. Curious. He felt a hard, rigid arm. Skeleton. He wasn't frightened. He roared:

"Get out of here now and don't fuck me anymore!"

Skeleton. Skeleton at the door. Bony laugh. From polished maxillaries. Skeleton. Light in the hollow sockets. Mortuary light. From taciturn tapers. Skeleton laughing. Bony laugh. At the same time the laugh of a crocodile as it swallows its prey. Bony.

"Only that pleasure. Because the pissy-places—yours and

hers—will never be able to come together. Do you hear? Never. When you try to do it, I'll separate you. With this hand. With this..."

She showed it. Long. Extended. Open. Bony flower. She went on:

"A hand of ice. From the grave. The hand I have there, six feet underground, in 'The Fireflies.'"

THIRTY-THREE

Soon the Sun would sprinkle the nape of the trees with gold. Would night continue encrusted in his soul? Eyes open insomniac he threaded nightmare itineraries together. Long hours. Still, he felt better. Better and better. With the spirit to face the batrachians and vipers of Santorontón who were anxious to liquidate him. The Crisóstomos, Espurios, Vigilianos, Salustianos, and Rugels... To follow the route of a new life. Of affirmation, struggle, and victory. With Clotilde, of course. Clotilde was a tattoo on his senses and his mind. Vertex of his dreams and hopes. He would have to convince her. The two were just one. Tips of the same Moon. Blades of the same shears. If she no longer wanted to—or couldn't—carry on in those parts, he would take her off Daura. They would both go into exile from Santorontón and its environs. They would take Miss Victor. She of the honeyed eyes would help them sweeten life. They would return to his city. His city. His city never turned its back on him. It never withdrew—accordion of asphalt, pilasters of cement—its doorways to deny him shade. Nor lowered its venetian-blind eyelids to ignore him. Nor drew in its shop-window arms to isolate him. Nor had his medical comrades joined together to sink him. Nor its women sutured lips and sexes in order to wound him with abstinence. Nor its whispering docks insulted him by inviting him to leave. It was he. It was he who had wrapped himself up in a diver's suit. An invisible diver's suit. He walked under the tattoo of gold Sun. As if he were skating over mud, within the liquid womb of the sea. It was he. He who had turned his back. His senses stitched up. Robinson Crusoe on the island of his fear and darkness. It was he. He wanted the city to look for him. Stroke him. Conquer him. Kneel before him. Speak words of respect and obedience to him. Give him its myths. Its legends. Its heroism. Its hidden words and treasures. Browser among absurdities embarked on a gyroscope of hair shirts vertebrae diadems of pride myopia swallower. It was he. Microbe-Herostratus. It was he. Undigested piece of pride. Capable of sowing seismic shocks in his own city, just to give himself importance. It was he. From there on he would change. He would return to the beloved Urbs. He, yes, on his knees. Kissing every street. Every patch of asphalt. Every fence of wild bamboo. Every roof of zinc, tile, or bijao reeds. He would return. In search of his roots. His roots were there. In the City-of-the-Two-Rivers. Which became One before it. And it has the sea behind. He would sink into its guts, to find himself. He, too, was made of Paradisiaca Sapientum and Theobroma. By doing it he would feel more himself. I'll rock you, Clotilde, in the green hammocks of my river. I'll take you to the cemetery of palm trees. Where it's a pleasure to live the life that is to come. I'll tell you the stories that hang from the cherry trees on the hill. From the houses that trickle off down to the River. Together we'll see how the City walks. How its vegetable extremities advance day by day in the fever of the swamp. It's a city that walks, Clotilde. That walks inside and outside us. Don't you feel as if it's beginning to grow in your breast and your eyes? It's a city that never stops walking for a single instant. Piercing four horizons at the same time. A city that walks.

"Are you awake, Juvencio?"

"Yes, Clotilde."

"You didn't sleep well, did you?"

"Yes."
"I heard you turning all night long."
"Didn't you sleep either?"
She smiled.
"No."
"You see. We're just alike."
"Are you feeling ill again?"
"On the contrary. I'm better and better."
"So?"
"I was thinking about us. All the time."
"Can I know what?"
He answered her with another question.
"Do you like Daura a lot?"
She became emotional.
"I was born there. I was always there when my parents were alive. Miss Victor's there. Besides, it's the only thing I have. Why do you ask?"
"I'm . . . thinking of leaving Santorontón."
Seven thorns pricked her breast. She controlled herself.
"Maybe . . . Maybe it's the best thing for . . . everybody."
"But . . ."
"What?"
"I'm taking you with me."
A gust of southeast wind seemed to make her lose her balance.
"That can't be! You know quite well. Don't you see that it can't be?"
"Even if it can't be . . . it will be! Even if you're against it. Even if everyone is against it. We're going to the city."
"What about Daura?"
"We'll sell it. We'll give it away. We'll do with it whatever we have to."
"And Miss Victor?"
"We'll take her with us."
"And Santorontón?"
He sat up. Joked.
"We can't take that with us."
She didn't go along with the joke. On the contrary, her face showed a certain anguish.
"What about the patients you have here? And the people you encourage? And your friends in the jungle? They all need you."
"We'll still come to see them. The city's nearby."

"Yes. That it is."

"Besides, I think that Santorontón is going to change. Rather, it is changing."

"Why do you say that?"

"Do you think it's not much that it doesn't depend on Crisóstomo anymore? That it has all the water it wants? That Candelario—Candelario Mariscal himself—is getting married to a woman? One single woman?"

"Last night you thought about stopping the wedding."

"Last night. Now I think the opposite. They have to be allowed to marry. Maybe it will be good for him. And he'll want to make things better in his village. He's the only one here who can bring order. The only one. It just depends on Father Cándido's asking him."

"He'd never ask him."

"Father Cándido will do it if it's for the good of the village."

"Who knows!"

"Besides, that's the Santorontonians' business. You and I have our lives too. Our own lives. That belong to us. Both to each one. We have to struggle for them."

"Juvencio... You'll see... I..."

"So start getting ready!"

Her eyes nests of light. Tenderness was dominating her. Did she have the right to be happy too? Could she ever be happy? Could she succeed in erasing the past images from her memory? It didn't matter. The important thing was that he seemed to need her. Without accepting or refusing, she slowly doled out her words.

"It won't work, Juvencio. It can't work."

Crisóstomo—at that time—bounced on his belly. Strange ball that seemed to have lost extremities and head. Back and forth. Hither and yon. Happy. Happy. Happy. He hadn't slept either. He hadn't slept lately. Rancor, wrath, and vengeance green grinders chopped him up. The masticated mush made furrows in his body and soul. Changed him into an oyster pulled out of its shell. Gelatinous, sad, and adhesive. He got out of bed. He got entangled in a string of curses. He cursed and he cursed. The hour he was born. The hour he chose Santorontón to live in. The hour that Candelario Mariscal came back. The hour that Juvencio Balda appeared there. The hour in which Cándido and his Christ were saved from the fire. Curses. Nothing but curses. In perennial autophagy, feeding only on his bile. That way—from curse to curse—until last night. He hadn't slept then either. Still, there were other reasons. He hadn't slept because he was happy. As if he had an enemy underfoot and was trampling his guts. He was savoring the spectacle beforehand. It would be something unheard of. That would calm his desires for revenge forever. For that alone it was worth having sold his soul. Do you remember, Birdbrain? Birdbrain, no. Herdbrain, better. Was he going to call himself that from this time forward? What difference did it make? What difference did anything make now? The only thing that mattered was getting vengeance. Making those bastards kiss the dust. And there was so little time left. So little! Do you remember, Birdbrain? Do you remember the night when you made the deal with Candanga? The winds were blowing toward the bow. All the winds. That's why instead of advancing you were retreating. Nothing was going forward. Sitting—you could still sit—on a pointed stone on the beach. With an urge to jump into the water. To end your troubles and failures then and there. Suddenly you called him. Without thinking about it. Without knowing why you were doing it. As if you'd sneezed. "Mandinga: Buy my soul. I'll sell it to you for anything you'll give me." You didn't think that He'd answer. You were wrong. He was already there. Answering your call. When you woke up, he was scratching your left ear with his tail. "I accept, Birdbrain!" —For a long time he only called you by that name. Only later on did he call you Don Crisos. And later, Crisóstomo.— He repeated: "I accept, Birdbrain. What do you want for it?" "Money. Lots of it. Lots of money." He smiled the smile of an oven gust of flames. "You'll have the money, Birdbrain. You'll be the most moneyed man in these parts..." And how curious. Everything had changed now. He no longer wanted money. He wanted crosses. Crosses. Crosses. He wanted to sow crosses all over the village. Crosses on the graves of the Santorontonians. Lots of crosses. That would block the way. Until they went out of sight in the distance. Lots of crosses, even if he was left poor again. Poor again? Well. Not so poor. But to put an end, that was for sure, to Juvencio's followers. So as not to have anyone who would stand in his way. Crosses, Mandinga. Lots of crosses. Only crosses. At the prospect of having them, his whole body burst into laughter.

A little while after, Rugel and Salustiano appeared. As always, speaking as a duo.

"Here we are, Sir."
"Here we are."
"What are we going to do?"
"The sooner the better. It's dawning already."
The little ball man irradiated contentment. He didn't know how to express it. Maybe only in the folds of his body. Something unusual, he even invited them to have something.
"Umm... wait a moment. Wouldn't you like a cup of coffee with a green banana cake? Or some smoked mullet?"
"We already ate, Sir."
"Yes, Sir."
They looked at each other—one at the other—with hesitation. They wanted to say something, doubtless. They didn't dare. Finally they got their courage up.
"The only thing is..."
"It's something to do..."
Even though he suspected what the cause of their upset was. Even though he imagined what they wanted to tell him, he didn't want to show it. He asked, indifferently:
"Why don't you come right out with it?"
They dared. They looked into his eyes. Firmly.
"If it's anything against the Colonel..., I'm not getting involved, Sir!"
"Me either..."
He wanted to gain time. Maybe just to enjoy stretching out their anguish.
"Really. Why don't you fry up some corvinas? Or would you rather have some reheated rice with mussels?"
They paid no attention to him. They continued.
"If it's against Him, nobody in the village is going to get involved."
"Naturally, Sir. Who would get involved?"
"It would be tying a rock around our necks. And throwing ourselves into the river."
"Or worse. As if we were digging our own graves. Putting ourselves into them. And burying ourselves with our own hands."
He laughed hard. His round flesh was dancing. Just as if he were made up of hammocks.
"Goddamn it! I can see that you people are fucked up, aren't you?"
The words an eddy spinning around.

"That's the way things are."
"When things are like that, Don Crisos..."
He became serious. Faced them:
"Do I have the look of a jackass caught in quicksand?"
"No, Sir."
"Not that."
He drummed on his belly.
"Then don't worry. Don't worry about anything. I'm holding the harpoon now."
They remained looking at him. Startled. Not understanding.
"The harpoon?"
"What harpoon?"
"No harpoon. What I mean to say is that I'm in charge now! The One We Know made a deal with me."
Salustiano scratched his head. Rugel hitched up his belt. They remained edgy for a moment.
"Won't it be like when we burned the jungle?"
"Or when we were going to stop them from building the bog?"
"You saw how we had to retreat right away."
"With our tails between our legs."
"Without any right to holler."
"To save number one."
He cut them off at once.
"No, goddamn it, no! This time I'll do it differently. Before I wasn't in cahoots with Candanga. Now I am. Candanga had a few words with me. He'll help me with what I want."
"What about the Colonel?"
"Isn't he That One's son?"
"Won't he tell him in time?"
"Won't he defend him?"
"Oh, you people! I always have to chew things up for you. I repeat. This time it will be different! Candanga himself gave me something."
"What you were given yesterday?"
"Is it in the middle of the river?"
"Yes, goddamn it, yes. That's where it lies!"
"Oh, if that's how it is!"
"Of course. If that's it..."

In the meantime Jesus had leaned his head over. He was looking at his comrade a little mockingly. The latter was walking back and forth. Although he wasn't doing anything, he seemed to be absorbed in important business.

"Listen, Old Man."

He didn't look at him. Didn't stop.

"What?"

"Have you got your cassock ready?"

He stopped moving. Raised his eyes.

"What cassock?"

"Oh! Do you have a lot of them?"

"I've got two. The one I'm wearing. And the other one."

"I'm referring to the other one. The one for feast days."

"That one's always clean. You know that very well. Threadbare as it is. But clean. Why do you ask?"

"When are you going to put it on?"

"What for?"

"Aren't we going to the wedding?"

"What wedding?"

"Don't play the innocent. You know quite well. The only wedding there is in Santorontón. Candelario's."

"You go if that's your pleasure. I don't even want to look at that swine."

"He's your godson, isn't he?"

"No godson of mine! He's nothing to me!"

"Besides, you're the only thing he has in Santorontón."

"Get off my back! Leave me alone!"

He paused. Added:

"Besides, why should I go? As a 'butt-in'? He hasn't said a single word to me. Much less invited me."

"Maybe he thought you didn't need an invitation. Or maybe he was afraid you wouldn't even receive him."

"That one isn't afraid of either God or the Devil..."

He faced him with rage.

"...and that's enough! Don't make me rave! Besides, it's best this way. Why should I go through a rough time like that, for the fun of it?"

"If he invited you, would you go?"

He shrugged his shoulders.

"There are days when you get up with your mind all twisted. You only want to tease me. One of these days I'm going to take you out of my house. Plant you on the highest hill. Facing the bog. That way you won't drive me crazy anymore."

Suddenly a voice shook the atmosphere.

"Godfather! Godfather!"

Cándido looked at Christ. Desolate. The Nazarene took his arms off the Cross. He made a gesture of what-did-I-tell-you. Then he winked maliciously.

The voice seemed to grow. Clamorous. Desperate.

"Godfather! Godfather!"

Almost against his will, he shouted in turn:

"I'm coming! I'm coming!"

And to the Nazarene with anguish:

"Now what do I do?"

"Do you still have doubts? You have to go. He's your godson!"

Pained, he reproached him:

"Mine? Only mine? When we found him didn't you convince me that he should stay in the church? Didn't we both enjoy his early smiles? Didn't you have as much fun with his first games and words? Didn't we argue a lot about his future? He's ours—yours and mine. Our godson!"

"All right. Ours! Stop arguing now. And go change your cassock."

"It's just that... he's misbehaved so. He hasn't received any punishment..."

"That's what you think!"

"No! We shouldn't go! I'll go out and wish him happiness. But not to count on us... That's the best thing!"

He took two steps toward the door. The voice of his Comrade held him back.

"Now... he needs us!"

"That one doesn't need anybody!"

"All of Santorontón is against him..."

"Even if it were like that. He's enough for everyone. You know him."

"There are a lot of things that you don't know. And that I can't tell you..."

"You're starting with your mysteries!... Besides, he's stronger than ever. He's got Bulu-Bulu!"

Christ's voice became grave, solemn:

"No one—not even witch doctors have power against certain forces."

The tone of his Friend alarmed him.

"What about us?"
"Who knows!"
"We can try, can't we?"
"Yes. That we can!"
"Well, then . . . I'm going to change my cassock!"